LAST RITES

A low, wet, keening sound came from inside the cell, and Father Freise lifted his lantern as he opened the door. The light fell across something lying on a low cot at the far side of the little room, and Drummond's words died in his throat as the full blast of the stench hit him full in the face.

What remained of the body looked like an overripe banana oozing an iridescent slime. The skin had blackened and split from the swelling within, thick mucus running out of the wounds and pooling on the floor beside the cot.

"Dear God . . ." Drummond whispered in a strangled voice.

Father Freise set down his lantern on a small table near the cot. *"In Nomine Patris, et Filii, et Spiritus Sancti,"* he began, bending down near the dying knight.

An arm shot out and grabbed the priest by the throat, great globs of liquefying flesh dropping from the bone and sinew that held Father Freise in a vise-like grip, pulling him close to the rotting skull-face of the vampire.

Drummond came alive. In a flash, the crossbow was to his shoulder, the bolt loosed. . . .

Don't miss the first novel in the series

KNIGHTS OF THE BLOOD

AT
SWORD'S
POINT

by
Scott MacMillan

**Created by
Katherine Kurtz**

A ROC BOOK

ROC
Published by New American Library, a division of
Penguin Group (USA) Inc., 375 Hudson Street,
New York, New York 10014, USA
Penguin Group (Canada), 90 Eglinton Avenue East, Suite 700, Toronto,
Ontario M4P 2Y3, Canada (a division of Pearson Penguin Canada Inc.)
Penguin Books Ltd., 80 Strand, London WC2R 0RL, England
Penguin Ireland, 25 St. Stephen's Green, Dublin 2,
Ireland (a division of Penguin Books Ltd.)
Penguin Group (Australia), 250 Camberwell Road, Camberwell, Victoria 3124,
Australia (a division of Pearson Australia Group Pty. Ltd.)
Penguin Books India Pvt. Ltd., 11 Community Centre, Panchsheel Park,
New Delhi - 110 017, India
Penguin Group (NZ), 67 Apollo Drive, Rosedale, North Shore 0745,
Auckland, New Zealand (a division of Pearson New Zealand Ltd.)
Penguin Books (South Africa) (Pty.) Ltd., 24 Sturdee Avenue,
Rosebank, Johannesburg 2196, South Africa

Penguin Books Ltd., Registered Offices:
80 Strand, London WC2R 0RL, England

First published by Roc, an imprint of New American Library,
a division of Penguin Group (USA) Inc.

First Printing, August 1994
10 9 8 7 6 5 4 3

ROC REGISTERED TRADEMARK—MARCA REGISTRADA

Printed in the United States of America

PROLOGUE

The hissing camp lantern made the dome-shaped tent in the small clearing glow with an amber incandescence. The young couple inside were locked in the heaving passions of their embrace, unaware of the erotic shadows their entwined bodies cast on the wall of the tent.

Outside, a light mist softened the shadows and stood like beads of perspiration on Wilhelm Kluge's well-muscled shoulders, forming small rivulets as they ran down his back and across his buttocks. The moonlight glinted on a small silver quaich that hung from a golden chain around his neck. Naked, his hands resting on the pommel of his sword, Kluge didn't feel the damp chill of the late summer rain as he waited patiently for his victims to finish their last earthly pleasures.

Finally, the shadows stopped thrusting on the inside of the tent and the sounds of heavy breathing were lost in the hiss of the lantern. Slowly the young man pushed himself away from the girl, rising first to his knees and then to his feet. As he threw back the flap of the tent, a slice of yellow light fell across the clearing.

The rain had stopped, and the mossy ground felt damp through the soles of his thick wool hiking socks as he stepped outside, drawn now by another, more pressing call of nature. Still naked, shivering, he cupped his hands and blew on them to keep them warm as he moved into the pale chill of the moonlight, away from the tent, to relieve himself.

Kluge stepped silently from the shadows and made his way around the tent, avoiding the pale sliver of lantern-light that spilled from the open flap. Stopping just behind the oblivious victim, his sword at the ready, Kluge paused for a single moment. Steam was rising from the moss-covered rocks at the young man's feet; and over the sounds of the spattering urine and hissing camp lantern Kluge could hear the pumping surge of the red tide that rose with each beat of the young man's heart. For a moment Kluge savored the sound, as other men savor a lover's caress.

Then Kluge's sword flashed through the moonlight, the flat arc of its bright blue blade severing the head, sending it bouncing into the darkness. The steaming trickle of urine was lost in a frothing geyser of blood as the headless body crumpled silently forward onto its knees before finally sprawling chest down on the ground.

Turning, Kluge walked slowly over to the tent. He could see her shadow on the tent wall, the lantern showing him where the sacrifice waited. Standing quietly outside, he raised his sword and, with a downward thrust, slit open the thin wall of the tent.

The girl was helpless in Kluge's grasp, paralyzed with fear. Yanking her up by the hair, he dragged her out into the chill moonlit night and, before she could cry out, drew the titanium blade of his sword across the side of her throat.

Her body arched as searing pain exploded through her, but Kluge's viselike grip on her throat prevented any sound escaping into the night. Using his free hand, he drove his sword deep into the soft loam of the clearing.

Then, bending down as if to caress his victim, he pressed his mouth over the wound he had opened in the girl's neck.

He drank deeply, the hot, foaming blood gushing into his mouth as he relaxed his grip slightly on her throat. When he felt the reserves of his powers replenished, he lifted his head and drew a triumphant breath. Then, still holding her by the throat, he pulled his sword from the red-soaked earth and held it high above his head, its sharpened tip pointed toward the North Star.

From the edge of the clearing a hunting horn sounded, followed by others deeper in the woods. As the horns winded their eerie *cour de chasse,* other shadowy figures stepped into the clearing, nearly a dozen of them naked in the moonlight, their swords held before them, blades pointed skyward. As they solemnly made their way to where Kluge stood, he earthed his sword again.

The vampires drew near in a semi-circle before their Master, also plunging their swords into the mossy ground. At his gesture, they approached him one by one, the first of them distinguished by a black eye-patch. As the one-eyed man dropped to his knees at his Master's feet, Kluge took the quaich from around his neck and filled it with the girl's blood, then passed the silver vessel into upraised hands. When the man had drained its contents and returned the quaich, he rose and backed off to be replaced by another suppliant. All drank deeply of the cup, blood running from the corners of their mouths and down their chins, matting in the hair on their bare chests.

Finally, when all had been served and the last notes of the horns died away in the chill air of the forest, Kluge threw the girl's body back into the tent. Pulling his sword from the ground he pointed it once again at the Northern Star and cried, "*Sieg Heil!*"

Together the vampires echoed their Master's salute, raising their blades to the darkened heavens.

"*Sieg Heil!*"

The forest muffled the cry of the vampires, but deep within, the primordial gods listened, and accepted the sacrifice.

CHAPTER 1

The gash on the side of Drummond's head was healing nicely, due as much to the twelve tiny sutures Father Freise had provided as to de Beq's thick poultice. It had been nearly a week since Drummond was wounded, and until today, he had been kept flat on his back. Father Freise and one of the serving brothers kept regular tabs on his condition and, despite his protests, refused to let him get up.

So he had spent his days resting and, in large measure, deciding what to do. There was much to digest; much that, until a few weeks ago, he would have dismissed as utter nonsense. LAPD homicide captains did not go charging off to Austria, simply on the word of a batty old priest, to chase down vampires.

But Drummond had done just that. And however unlikely his own actions might have appeared since then to an outsider, John Drummond was certain of one thing: the so-called "Vampire Slayings" he now knew to have been committed in Los Angeles by Father Francis Freise more than two decades ago would go "unsolved" as far as Drummond was concerned. In the light of what he had experienced in the past week or two, Freise's killings took on the look of justifiable homicide—eliminating a very real evil from modern society.

As to the vampires—both those who now acted as his hosts at Schloss Marbourg and those who had escaped into the woods—Drummond was unsure how to proceed. That first day, after Kluge, his Nazi vampires, and their punker cohorts had stormed Schloss Marbourg, he had been utterly convinced, along with Freise, of the need to hunt down and destroy Kluge. De Beq and his men had been less convinced at first—how could medieval knights, isolated from history for nearly seven hundred years, hope to cope with a world they had long since ceased to know? Yet the knights, indirectly, had been responsible for Kluge becoming a vampire; they were the logical ones to help stop him now. So strongly had Drummond become convinced of that, and of the absolute necessity to see Kluge destroyed, he had even agreed to become one of them—to become a Knight of the Sword.

Even now, Drummond was uncertain just how full a commitment he had made to the knights. It had been six days since Father Freise served him the Communion of the Knights, and yet, unlike the others, he had not yet developed the blood hunger of the vampires.

Perhaps it took longer to develop than de Beq remembered, he thought. De Beq had been vaguely certain that the transformation would take only a day or two at the most. But nearly a week had passed and while Drummond's appetite had returned, it was a tuna-melt and iced tea that he craved the most.

Having had to satisfy tonight's hunger with ill-cooked mutton and potatoes and brown bread, Drummond pushed back his wooden trencher and turned to Father Freise. They were in the great hall of the knights' castle, seated at one end of a long trestle table near the large fireplace. At the other end of the table, several of the knights were clustered around their Master, Henri de

Beq, glancing occasionally in Drummond's direction as they talked in low voices. Drummond had agonized over his decision, but he knew he had no other real choice.

"Frank," he said, "I've been thinking."

"Careful," Freise said lightly. "You've got a head wound."

"No, really. I've given this a lot of thought in the last few days, and I've decided I'm going back to L.A."

Father Freise looked up from his dinner and stared at Drummond for a few seconds before answering. He did not look like a man in his mid-seventies, but his appearance of youthfulness came from an altogether different source than that of the men at the other end of the hall.

"I can't say that I'm surprised, John," he said quietly, "though I did hope you'd stay and help us with the fight against Kluge."

"Oh, I'll help," Drummond said. "It's just that there are a lot of loose ends I have to tie up first." He picked up his mug of ale and took a deep drink before continuing. "Besides, we need a lot more information before we go charging off after Kluge. We already know that his business connections extend to several major cities in the United States and Canada. With his cover blown here in Europe, he may switch his base of operations. In any case, the best way to round up solid information is for me to return to the LAPD and utilize their extensive and very efficient intelligence network."

Freise made a face. "You really think his cover is blown here? That's only true if we can get someone to believe us. I mean, 'Nazi vampires'—really!"

"Yeah, I know," Drummond replied. "I've been telling myself the same thing. Which makes it all the more imperative that we utilize every resource at our disposal to get a plan of action organized and track him down. We can't do that without more sophisticated information than

I can gather sitting here in a medieval castle in Luxembourg."

"I suppose you're right," Freise conceded.

"We'll also need considerable financial backing—some of which I can provide, but I can't set the wheels in motion from here," Drummond went on. "If I'm going to give this operation the support it requires, I have to go back to L.A., catch my breath, and set up the support structure. But I promise I'll be back. After all—" he gave a wry grin and glanced at de Beq and his knights "—I made a promise to him, too."

At his words, the eyes of both men turned toward the other end of the hall, to the white-robed Master of the Order of the Sword and his knights. Henri de Beq looked to be only in his late forties to early fifties, tall and lean, with a short-clipped salt-and-pepper beard and pale eyes that missed little; but he and his men had fought in the Holy Land when Acre fell—in 1291. Drummond still did not understand everything that had caused his path to cross with that of the knights, seven hundred years later, but something deep inside him knew that de Beq and his men were as different from Kluge and his minions as day from night.

Recalling himself with a shake of his head, Drummond glanced back at Father Freise. The old priest looked wistful as he pushed his plate back from the edge of the table.

"Well, I suppose it's necessary," he said quietly. "Have you told him?"

"No. I hoped you'd do that for me," Drummond replied. "I—don't know that I could cope with my pidgin French and his medieval English to make him understand. Would you do it, Frank?"

Freise swallowed uncomfortably, then nodded. "Yeah, I'll tell him."

Standing up, the priest turned his back on Drummond and walked over to the fireplace, staring for a long time at the glowing embers of the dying fire. After a moment, Drummond joined him.

"So, when do you plan to go?" Friese asked.

"If I leave in the morning, I can still make my original flight back to L.A. I don't suppose you'd care to come with me?"

Friese turned to face Drummond. His eyes were red-rimmed and moist, as if he had been leaning too close to the smoke from the smouldering embers on the hearth.

"No, not this time, John. The last time I left this castle, it was to run away from Kluge. The next time I go—well, it'll either be to finish him once and for all, or feet-first in a pine box." The priest smiled. "But you might as well catch your flight. No sense wasting the ticket. Just don't be gone too long. I'm an old man, and I'll miss you. And they—"

He glanced again at the knights at the other end of the room, then shook his head and returned his gaze to the dying embers.

"Why don't you turn in, John? I'll see you in the morning before you leave. And I'll—speak with de Beq."

The next morning, after Father Freise had celebrated Mass for them, de Beq and half a dozen of his men turned out to escort Drummond to the small clearing in the woods where Father Freise had parked Drummond's rented Mercedes after the battle with Kluge. Four of the six were knights, now wearing the formal red surcoats of the Order of the Sword under their white mantles, chain mail showing from under sleeves, swords belted at their waists. The two men-at-arms carried crossbows and kept a wary eye out as they brought up the rear of the little procession. The escort seemed small to Drummond, but in fact it represented about a third of the castle's remaining force. He had thought there were more when he first arrived at the castle, but some had fallen to Kluge and his men, and he assumed that the rest of de Beq's men were too busy with other tasks to see him off.

The walk through the woods to the car was particularly silent, with neither de Beq nor Father Freise really having anything to say. Even William of Etton, whom Drummond had found to be the most talkative of all the knights, was silent as they made their way across the meadow and through the forest. Finally they arrived at the white Mercedes, and as Drummond tossed his bag in the trunk, de Beq stepped forward.

"Sir John," he said without preamble, "I know not if you are truly one of us, but this I do know. You are a knight, made so at your desire and by my hand before this company and before God Almighty."

Drummond felt a chill creep up his spine at de Beq's words.

"Further," de Beq continued, "you are now about to leave us, and we know not if ever you will return." He signaled William of Etton, who came forward with something long and narrow, wrapped in a white cloth.

"So, to protect yourself until you can rejoin your brother knights—" he stared Drummond square in the eye "—I give you this—my sword." From under the cloth, William produced a beautifully wrought sword in a dark red scabbard set with gilded mounts, which de Beq took almost reverently from him and held out across both his palms. "I give you this sword, as one knight to another, and I charge you to return it within a year, or die in the attempt."

He stepped forward and laid the sword across Drummond's hands. Its touch seemed to send an electric shock tingling through Drummond's body, a connection across seven centuries of tradition maintained by the owner of the sword. Never had anything moved Drummond the way de Beq's simple speech moved him. Even more profoundly than at the moment of his knighting, itself so mystical, he now realized that he was bound to the Order of the Sword—that he was one of them, spiritually, if not physically.

Maybe this is how the transformation begins, he thought.

Spontaneously he brought the cross-hilt of the sword to his lips in salute, both to de Beq and to the chivalric tradition that bound them in brotherhood, then solemnly grasped de Beq by the right wrist.

"I promise I'll be back, Henri. With your sword."

Then, without another word, he carefully laid the sword in the trunk of the car next to his bag, closed the lid, and walked around to the front of the car to slide in behind the wheel, not daring to look at de Beq again. He turned the key, and the car started instantly. When he glanced in the rearview mirror, the knights had vanished from sight.

Father Freise opened the passenger door and stuck his head in.

"Going my way?"

"Sure, hop in."

He waited for Freise to get settled in the passenger seat, then eased out the clutch and pointed the stubby snout of the car toward the road. "Where to?"

"Just as far as the village. Oh, and—uh—I hope you can loan me some cash." Father Freise sounded vaguely embarrassed to be asking for money.

"Sure. How much?"

"Not much. Just enough for a bicycle and a few odds and ends, that's all." Father Freise's voice became a little brighter, rather like a kid whose big brother has just given him money to go see a movie. "I've managed to get our knights somewhat organized while you were recovering, but it's still pretty primitive at the castle."

The village was only a few miles down the road. At Freise's direction, Drummond parked in the center of the square, across from what the priest indicated was the local general store.

"I'll be in there, getting a few things," he said, then pointed to another shopfront a few doors down. "By the way, in the last few days I've discovered that's the local infirmary. You might want to have them take a look at that cut of yours before you head out. It's been a while since I did any suturing—about fifty years, in fact—and in those days, I was working with something a bit more sterile than linen sewing thread." Before Drummond could answer, the priest turned and headed into the general store.

Drummond had all but forgotten his head wound, especially in the intensity of getting ready to leave this morning. It had stopped hurting days ago and still hadn't started itching—a good sign that everything was on the mend—but it probably was a good idea to have a proper doctor look at it before he went charging back to America. Glancing at the sign on the door Freise had indicated, Drummond headed into the infirmary.

The waiting room was empty, and Drummond pressed a button on the counter. From somewhere in the back of the building he heard a muffled buzz, followed by an indistinct burst of French. Resigned to waiting, he took a seat next to the door. A few moments later, a young man in steel-rimmed glasses stuck his head around the partition.

"Oui?"

Drummond pointed to the bandage on his head and, in awkward French, started out with, *"Je ne parlez Français . . ."*

"English?" The young man emerged from behind the partition, his hands thrust deep into the pockets of his lab coat.

"No, American."

"Okay, no problem." The young man smiled. "What happened to your head?"

Drummond thought fast. "Fell hiking last week and gashed it open."

"Uh-huh," said the doctor, carefully removing the bandage and peering at Drummond's scalp. "Who stitched you up?"

"Oh, a priest in the base camp. Said he learned how to do it when he was a missionary. Why?"

"Well, because he has done an excellent job—even if he did use linen thread." The doctor stepped back from Drummond and looked him over professionally. "Okay, my friend, come on back and I'll clean you up a bit more."

Drummond got up and followed the doctor back into his surgery. The doctor indicated that Drummond should sit on the examining table, then focused a bright light on the side of his head. The antiseptic he used to start cleaning around the sutures stung a little.

"Yes, indeed, your friend did a very nice job," the doctor said, prodding around the wound. "When did you say this happened?"

"About a week ago. Why?"

"Well, it's just that it seems to have healed very quickly. In fact, I think I'll just go ahead and take out the sutures. It's clear you don't need them anymore."

"You're the doctor," Drummond said as the man picked up scissors and a set of forceps and went to work. A few of the sutures pulled a little, but they mostly came out easily.

"If you don't mind my asking, did the priest put anything on the wound?" the doctor asked as he continued snipping and tugging.

"Yeah, some kind of glop that he said would help it heal," Drummond replied, not feeling it necessary to mention that it had been de Beq who had provided the ointment. "Why do you ask?"

"Because the healing really is remarkable. You've got hardly any scarring. In fact—" He paused. "I'd say that your recovery is nearly supernatural."

"Oh, really? What do you mean, 'supernatural'?" Drummond tried to keep his voice matter-of-fact.

"Just that a wound like this normally takes several weeks to heal, but yours seems to have closed in less than a week." The doctor stood up. "If I were a religious man, I'd almost be inclined to call it miraculous."

"Well, hardly that," Drummond said lightly. "It could be that I'm just from hardy stock. But maybe I should see about getting the recipe, if it works that well. There's no telling what these old folk remedies contain; only that they work."

"Sometimes they work," said the doctor, indicating that he was finished. "Only sometimes do they work."

Drummond hopped off the examining table and pulled out his wallet. "Okay, what do I owe you, Doctor?"

The doctor gave a small shrug of his shoulders. "One hundred francs?" It was more of a question than a statement.

Drummond pulled out two hundred francs and handed them to the doctor. "Thanks. Keep the change."

The doctor smiled and walked Drummond to the door. "Thank you, Mr. . . . ?" The question hung on the air.

"Drummond. John Drummond. From Los Angeles, in case you need to fill out any forms."

When Drummond had gone, the doctor went to his desk, picked up the telephone, and dialed a number written on a small pad next to the black instrument. The line purred a few times before someone answered.

"This is Dr. Maurice LeBlanc. That man you were asking about was just here."

In the general store, Father Freise had neatly stacked his items on one end of the counter and was closely inspecting a red bicycle with the proprietor when Drummond walked in. Looking up, Freise grinned at Drummond and waved him over.

"John, what do you think? Is red a little too flashy?"

Drummond looked at the bike before answering. "Wellll . . . I don't think this is quite the model you need, but the color suits you down to the ground."

Freise looked confused. "Not the model . . . ? I don't get it."

Drummond took him by the arm and pointed him toward a bright red motor scooter near the door.

"That's the model you need, Frank. No pedals. Means you won't get a heart attack pumping that thing up and down the hills."

He half dragged the priest over to the machine. Freise looked it over, then saw the price tag.

"Holy cow, this thing costs nearly a thousand dollars!"

"The best always costs a bit more, Frank. Remember it." Drummond smiled and beckoned the shopkeeper over. Pointing to the red scooter he said, *"Ce—"* He paused for a second. *"Ce—er—motor scooter rouge, s'il vous plaît."*

The shopkeeper smiled broadly. *"Oui, monsieur. La motocyclette rouge, naturellement."*

Drummond followed Freise back to the counter. "Frank, you've got a lot of stuff here. Just what all are you buying?"

Freise picked up a tooth brush. "Twenty of these, for starters. Our friends might live forever, but their breath'd drop a bull moose at fifty yards. Soap, too." He held up a bar of no-nonsense soap. "I've got to civilize them a bit, if we're ever going to get them out into the real world."

Drummond glanced over the other items: toothpaste, two pairs of scissors, a few towels, a scrub brush, rubber bucket, and a bottle of disinfectant. All the items would help, but with no modern sanitary facilities in the castle, true "civilization" was going to be a while in coming to the Knights of the Sword.

Drummond himself was still in the clothes he had worn when he arrived at the castle nearly a week before. He suspected his cords and pullover might stand up by themselves, and he didn't even want to think about his underwear. He had worn one of the knights' long white robes for the days he lay recovering, and had cleaned up as best he could the day before, once they finally let him out of bed, but there was only so much one could do with cold water and no soap.

"It's a start, Frank," he said. And remembering the straw-stuffed mattresses and tallow candles, he added, "I think you'd better get a sleeping bag and camp lantern, while you're at it."

Freise spoke with the shopkeeper, and the extra items were added to the pile. Nodding, the priest indicated that that was all he needed. *"L'addition, s'il vous plait."*

The shopkeeper scurried off to add up the purchases.

"You're going to have to make several trips to get all of this back to the castle," Drummond said.

"Well, then, its a good thing I've got a motorbike to do it." Freise held out his hand. "Thanks, John. I mean it."

"I know you do, Frank." Drummond took the priest's hand. "I know you do."

The shopkeeper returned with the bill, and Drummond counted out a stack of hundred-dollar traveler's checks and began signing them, while the little man set about bundling up Freise's purchases in brown paper wrapped with miles of thick string. When he finished, he counted out Drummond's change and then ducked down below the counter, bobbing up a few seconds later with an old-fashioned white leather crash helmet. He handed it to Freise with a beaming smile.

"Pour vous, mon pere . . . avec mes compliments."

Freise pulled on the helmet and thanked the man, then headed outside with Drummond.

"Well, John, I guess this is good-bye." He held out his hand.

Drummond had cashed the remaining traveler's checks and slapped the money into the priest's outstretched palm.

"Here, take this. You'll need it before I get back." He stepped forward and gave Freise a hug. "And you're wrong. This isn't good-bye, just *au revoir.*"

Without looking at the priest, he turned away and headed briskly toward the car, but before leaving, he lowered the driver's window for a final word with Freise.

"Frank, be careful—you hear? And call me before you do anything rash?"

Putting on at least the semblance of bravery, the priest nodded and smiled back his answer, raising a hand in farewell and, perhaps, blessing, as Drummond pointed the car toward Munich and his flight home.

CHAPTER 2

Drummond reached Munich's Riem Airport with nearly four hours until flight time.

Just time enough, he thought, and turned the white Mercedes into the traffic lane marked "HOTEL."

Pulling up in front of the same hotel where he had stayed when he met Father Freise, Drummond took his suit bag from the trunk and went into the hotel. When he had checked in and had the desk verify that his flight would be on time, and while his bag was being sent to his room, he detoured to the men's shop in the lobby and bought fresh socks, underwear, and a pale yellow cashmere polo shirt. His shopping done, he retreated to his room, and was delighted to see that in addition to a shower there was a large tub in the bathroom.

"Sheer heaven," he muttered, and turned on the taps to let the tub fill while he stripped and tossed his clothes in a heap on the bed.

Five days without a change. Drummond hadn't done that since the army. The tub would be like heaven.

Going back into the bathroom, he shut off the taps and paused to peer closely at his reflection in the steamy mirror. Five days in the same clothes, and a week without a shave. At least his head wound was nearly healed. He ran his fingers over the slight scar, then over the stubble—

actually, the beginning of a real beard. He'd consider shaving after his bath.

Like every other airport hotel in the world, there was a basket full of bath salts and shampoos on the counter next to the sink. Picking up a small plastic bottle of some sort of pine-scented herbal extract, Drummond poured it into the tub and then climbed in. The hot sudsy water felt great as he lowered himself into the deep tub, slowly sinking in up to his chin.

He closed his eyes, laid his head back, and managed to think of nothing for fully ten minutes. The relaxation was complete. He could feel the knots unkinking in his muscles, and the grime gradually lifting from his body. But then, somewhere in the back of his mind, a gnawing worm of consciousness began to bite into the hedonistic pleasures of a hot bath and herbal extracts, and Drummond found himself thinking about his future.

He had no idea what he was going to do. Sitting here in a hot bath in a modern bathroom that would be barely comprehensible to the men he had left behind in the castle in Luxembourg—other than Father Freise, of course—it was tempting to relegate his experiences of the past few weeks to a flight of fancy, to put it out of mind and pretend it never happened, to get on with his life.

But it had been all too real—no mere vacation interlude to be filed away with other memories and only occasionally pulled out for fond reminiscences. Men had died; and Freise, de Beq, and the others expected him to return. In fact, they needed him to help set their world back on its normal axis.

Axis . . . a funny word to use, thought Drummond. *Like the Axis Powers during the Second World War. Like Kluge and his Nazis.*

Kluge. His trail encompassed at least two continents,

and men died where he had passed. The implications of his very existence were almost too terrible to contemplate. And the blood banks, the murders. . . . and vampires. . . .

Drummond shook his head to shake the mood and looked at his Rolex. No wonder the water was getting cold. He'd been in the tub for nearly twenty minutes. Grabbing a washcloth and a bar of oddly perfumed soap, he set about giving himself a brisk scrubbing. Then, pulling the plug with his toe, he stepped out of the tub and into the shower. No matter how relaxing a bath might feel, he never felt really clean unless he showered. Spinning the taps produced a stinging torrent of hot water out of the shower nozzle. Stepping back and adjusting the cold tap to near full power brought the spray to a comfortable temperature, and Drummond quickly shampooed his hair before rinsing off for the last time.

Towelling off, he stared once again at his week-old beard and decided it could stay until he got back to L.A. In the bedroom, he unpacked his ubiquitous gray slacks and navy blazer, along with a pair of black Gucci loafers. His towel ended up over a convenient chair as he pulled on the light blue silk boxer shorts and yellow polo shirt. He had almost forgotten the sybaritic pleasure of being clean. Putting on his socks, he climbed into the slacks and then stepped into his shoes.

For a moment he hesitated about packing the clothes he'd been wearing for the previous week, but in the end decided that an hour in the Maytag would probably rehabilitate them. Folding them into neat little bundles, he stuffed them into the bottom of his suit bag before zipping it closed and folding it in half. Consulting his watch once again, Drummond decided that he just had time for a fast steak before heading over to check-in at the airport.

* * *

The young lady at the check-in counter hardly even batted an eye when Drummond checked in his bag and handed her his sword. Pressing a button next to her computer terminal produced, within seconds, a baggage technician with a plastic rifle case large enough to accommodate the sword. After placing the ancient weapon carefully in the foam-lined container, the lid was closed and the case locked. The baggage technician gave the key to Drummond, along with a separate luggage tag, before he trundled the case away through the crowded airport concourse.

On the other side of the security barrier, Drummond paid a visit to the Duty-Free shop. He marveled at the incredible variety of useless items that embarking passengers were enticed to buy, ostensibly at prices far below those in stores.

"Hello, sir. May I help you?" Drummond was surprised to find the young woman behind the counter was speaking to him.

"Uh, no, I don't think so." He smiled. "I'm just looking."

"Well, then, perhaps you'd like to see one of our Sony CD players. They are on sale."

Drummond was about to decline when he saw the fat woman who had been seated next to him on the flight over, browsing her way through a rack of loden cloth capes. Over her shoulder was a white flight bag that had "Sound of Music Tours" stenciled on the side in bright blue German gothic script.

"Will these things drown out Julie Andrews?" he suddenly asked.

For a moment the girl was speechless; then she recovered her sales composure.

"Sir, if you set the volume high enough, they'll drown out anything."

Embarrassed, Drummond bought the CD player and, making his way over to a rack of CDs, picked out half a dozen disks from the classical music section. Handing the girl his credit card, he scanned the Duty-Free shop, hoping to avoid bumping into his former "traveling companion" while he waited for the transaction to be completed.

With his CD player in his pocket, Drummond headed down to the gate just as they began loading the passengers. Falling in with the rest of the passengers shuffling their way onto the plane, Drummond showed the stewardess his boarding card and then headed toward his aisle seat over the wing.

The aircraft was nearly full, and the middle-aged man reading *Der Stern* by the window looked like he might be the sort who would sleep through most of the flight. With luck, the seat between them would remain unoccupied. Clipping his CD player to his belt, Drummond stored his jacket in the overhead compartment before dropping into his seat. He had fumbled his CDs into the seat pocket in front of him and was finally settling down for take-off, hunting up the ends of his seat belt, when she came bustling up.

Cops are trained to never forget a face, and Drummond could never have forgotten the face or the inflated blond hair of the woman peering expectantly at the seat beside him. Although he had managed to forget her name, Drummond recognized her immediately as his seat mate from the flight over.

"Say, don't I know you from somewhere?" she asked, as he stood up resignedly for her to squeeze past him.

He forced a smile. "Probably not, ma'am."

She plumped into the seat and began stashing her "Sound of Music" carry-on under the seat in front of her, along with a yellow plastic shopping bag that said

"*München Zollfrei*"—Munich Duty-Free. Settling into her seat, she looked as if she was about to ask another question when the stewardess began her in-flight safety monologue. After showing everyone how to inflate their life jackets and how to use a whistle the stewardess sat down, and the aircraft began its long roll down the runway, gathering speed for take off. Teeth clenched and knuckles white with fear as the 747 lifted itself into the sky, for a moment at least the woman next to Drummond was silent.

"Now, you're sure we haven't met?" she asked, once they were airborne looking up at him again as she straightened and wiggled farther into her seat. The question was nearly a challenge.

"I'm sure I'd remember you if we had met before."

Drummond hated lying. Hated it as much as he hated beets, but then sometimes you had to eat beets, just like sometimes you had lie.

"Well, I suppose not. Say, you weren't on the 'Sound of Music' tour, were you?" She sounded as if she was about to remember him.

"No," Drummond said truthfully, "I definitely didn't travel around Austria on the bus with your group."

"How did you know we were on a bus tour?" Her voice rose in amazement.

"I saw the bus at the airport. Now, if you'll excuse me . . ." Drummond plugged the tiny earphones into his head and settled back to enjoy his music.

Pop. The tiny padded speaker jumped out of his ear.

"I'm sorry," she said, rummaging in her bag. "I think I caught your wire with my arm, accidental-like."

"Oh, that's all right," he said, thinking that this woman was perhaps the albatross of cheap air travel.

"Listen," she said.

"That's what I was trying to do."

"Huh? Oh, that's funny. Now, as I was about to say, you look a little pale. Are you all right?" Her concern sounded genuine.

"I'm probably just a little tired. I've been up for several days working with very little sleep." Drummond feigned a yawn. "So, if you'll excuse me?" He smiled his most polite smile.

"Sure. You go right ahead and sleep. Don't let me bother you."

She rummaged under the seat again and pulled a thick paperback book out of her flight bag. The lurid cover showed a vampire who bore more than a passing resemblance to George Hamilton ripping the bodice off a well-endowed woman, his fangs bared, ready to sink into her . . . neck, Drummond supposed, although the cover artist clearly wanted to convey more than that.

With a private shudder, he replaced the earphone and closed his eyes, trying hard to settle into a nap. His rest was interrupted by the attendant bumping into him with a trolley as she came down the aisle with drinks, and again by the woman next to him, just before mealtime.

"Excuse me," she said, shaking Drummond's arm. "Excuse me, but my Bloody Mary wants out."

Half asleep, it took Drummond a second or two to focus on what she had said. "What . . . ?"

"I need to go to the little girl's room. So if you don't mind, could you let me out? Please?"

Drummond stood in the aisle, and the woman wiggled past and headed back to the toilets in the middle of the aircraft. While he was standing, Drummond stretched and absently looked around the cabin of the jumbo jet. For no apparent reason, his attention was drawn to a swarthy man in an ill-fitting suit seated on the aisle three rows behind him, just ahead of the toilets, where Mrs. Albatross now stood impatiently in line.

A hawklike nose jutted out from between two dark brown, intense eyes. Thick, wiry eyebrows almost met above the bridge of the man's nose, every bit as wild as the thatch of hair on top of his head. There was something about the man that caused a little psychic alarm to sound somewhere in Drummond's subconscious.

Turning away from the man with the haunted look, Drummond decided that he was glad airlines took extra precautions with passengers. The man had the look of a fanatic.

She returned. Struggling into her seat, she smiled up at Drummond and stuck out her hand.

"I'm Bea MacDowell. Twenty-first Century Real Estate." Drummond looked at the hand. It held a business card.

"John Drummond. It's a pleasure to meet you." Beets again, this time with carrots. He took the card and slipped it into his pocket.

"Mind if I ask what you do?" Bea sounded like she was about to try to sell him a house.

Drummond settled into his seat before answering. "I'm between jobs."

"Well, once you get settled in L.A. . . ." Bea MacDowell could tell a No Sale right away.

"Look, you'll have to excuse me, but I don't feel very well. Perhaps we could discuss this after we land?" No unpleasant vegetables this time; Drummond was feeling slightly queasy.

Without waiting for Bea's reply, he stuffed the earphones into his ears, turned on the Mozart disk, and closed his eyes. *Die Zauberflöte* filled Drummond's consciousness, conjuring up images of a great snake that for some reason was trying to eat F. Murray Abraham. . . . Drummond drifted off into dreamland.

He was flying high above the forest, his cape spread out like two enormous bat wings. It was midnight, and far below he could make out a castle. Swooping down, he could see a beautiful, dark-haired woman sitting next to the open window. There was something familiar about her, but maddeningly he couldn't see her face. No matter how hard he tried to look at her, his gaze was somehow diverted and he found himself staring fixedly at a golden brooch pinned to the front of her gown.

Frustrated in his attempt to see the face of this woman he seemed to know, Drummond spread his cape wide, rushing headlong over the treetops toward a small clearing where a gentle amber light flickered in the velvet darkness of the forest. The clearing below suddenly exploded in a searing red light, and from above the trees Drummond could see naked men slowly marching toward another figure he knew but couldn't recognize.

The men were well muscled and carried something before them, something almost recognized by Drummond. They stopped in front of the figure the unseen Drummond knew, and one by one they received something from the figure: almost but not quite a cup. Slowly they lifted the vessel to their lips. Blood ran down their chins, and in the distance, mournful horns sounded deep within the forest.

Drummond found himself in line with the men, reaching forward to receive the strange silver cup, bringing it to his lips, the horns growing louder . . . and louder . . . and louder.

He awoke with a start, Mozart's horn concerto filling his head with its glorious baroque sound. He tried desperately to recall the face he had seen in his dream. The man who offered him the cup—he knew him, he had seen him. He was real—not some shadow from his dream.

"Are you all right?" Mrs. MacDowell sounded concerned.

"Oh, I'm fine. Thanks." Drummond felt anything but fine.

"You're sure? I mean, you're not going to be sick or anything, are you? I mean, well, you're very pale."

"No, I'll be all right. Really." Drummond got up and walked back to the toilets in the center of the plane. There was no line of anxious passengers, and he went into the nearest cubical and pulled the folding door shut.

Drummond stared at himself in the mirror, hoping it was the small overhead light that made him look so washed out and pale. Turning on the tap, he filled the stainless steel basin with hot water and splashed it on his face, trying to wash away the memory of the dream and the fear that he was changing. Looking back in the mirror at his pallid reflection, he remembered the pale, almost luminescent complexion of the knights. Perhaps he was becoming one of them, after all. Pulling a paper towel from the dispenser, Drummond dried his face and stepped out of the cubical.

The swarthy man in the ill-fitting suit was blocking the aisle, and Drummond was just about to ask him to step aside when he saw the hand grenade in the man's left hand.

Time was nearly suspended. In extreme slow motion, Drummond saw the terrorist's right hand reach up and pull the pin from the grenade. Launching himself forward, Drummond grabbed the man's left hand in both of his, at the same time driving his knee into the man's kidneys.

The man's legs buckled, and under Drummond's weight they both crashed to the floor of the aircraft. Suddenly time started racing again. People were starting to scream. The swarthy little man struggled fiercely to get out of Drummond's viselike grip, thrashing around in the aisle, trying to open his hand enough to release the grenade's arming spoon.

Drummond held onto the man's hand and tried to knee him in the groin. Finally, getting somewhat on top of the man, he bounced up and down on his back, trying to snap his spine.

In the cabin all around him, panic was increasing as more and more passengers realized that at any moment the grenade could go off, blowing a refrigerator-sized hole in the aircraft. Women screamed and men shouted in panic as people tried to rush away from the menacing struggle on the floor of the plane.

Drummond kept bouncing on the little man, at the same time trying to twist his arm out of its socket. He felt his knees contact the man's head. Jumping up and down even harder, he managed to smash the man's face into the floor, stunning him momentarily. He tried with all his strength to pull the grenade from the man's hand, but with no success.

It seemed as if he had been holding onto the man for hours, when three men pushed their way through the crowd and made their way to Drummond from the first-class cabin of the jumbo jet. The first two men were in airline uniforms, and the larger of the two hauled off and kicked the grenade-wielder in the face, hard enough to fracture his skull. The man was still struggling, though, and the man who had kicked him suddenly dropped to one knee, pulled the man's head back by the hair, and drove his thumb deep into the carotid artery on the side of his neck. Within seconds, the man passed out.

Drummond realized for the first time that a well-dressed man in his middle fifties had moved in to kneel in front of him and was speaking.

" . . . now hold on tight, and for Christ's sake, don't let go."

Drummond was about to tell him he had no intention of letting go, when the other man in uniform leaned forward and slammed a fire hatchet down on the fanatic's wrist. Drummond could hear the soggy thud of bone shattering, and blood was spraying everywhere. The hatchet smashed down several more times before the wrist was finally severed, leaving Drummond holding the bloody hand squeezed around the grenade.

The well-dressed man hardly batted an eye. Reaching down into a small black bag at his side, he pulled out a length of surgical tubing and quickly threw a tourniquet around the stump of the terrorist's wrist. As soon as he had it secured, the two uniformed men dragged the unconscious man forward, vanishing through the curtain that separated the first-class cabin from the Grand Guingol drama of tourist class.

"I'll be right with you," the well-dressed man called after them, before returning his attention to Drummond. He had a faint accent that Drummond could not quite place. "Can you hold on for just a few more seconds? I'll try to find something to tie down the arming lever of the grenade."

Drummond could feel his hands going numb, his grip slowly evaporating. "I'm not sure . . ."

In the seat next to him, Bea MacDowell reached into her purse and produced a wad of keys strung together on a large blanket pin.

"Here," she said. Popping open the pin, her keys scattering all over the floor of the aircraft, she leaned over Drummond's shoulder and deftly stuck the blanket pin through the hole in the arming lever, effectively locking it in place. "You can relax now, Mr. Drummond."

Drummond smiled weakly at Bea MacDowell and resolved to buy a house from her as soon as they landed. Carefully he opened his fingers just enough to allow the severed hand to fall from his grasp. It landed with a moist thud on the soggy carpet. Still cradling the grenade in both hands, Drummond started to stand up.

The blanket pin snapped with a loud, metallic crack, and the arming lever of the grenade flew out of Drummond's grasp and bounced off one of the overhead compartments. With less than five seconds to live, Drummond clutched the grenade to his stomach and threw himself flat on the floor. From somewhere near his belt buckle there was a loud pop, followed by a few wisps of acrid-smelling smoke.

The grenade was a dud.

Slowly raising himself up off the floor, Drummond couldn't decide if he should laugh or swear.

"Son of a bitch," he chuckled softly to himself, rubbing his bruised stomach. In the seat next to him, Bea MacDowell had fainted.

CHAPTER 3

Los Angeles International Airport diverted Drummond's flight to Lockheed Aircraft's test facility near Edwards Air Force Base. As the jumbo jet touched down on the three-mile long runway, a convoy of military vehicles rolled out to meet it. Dark blue Air Police jeeps escorted the Boeing 747 to a special hangar, where federal agents awaited to question the passengers.

"Please remain in your seats until cabin personnel ask you to exit the aircraft." The senior cabin attendant had repeated the request several times, but people were still standing and jostling each other in the aisles.

Drummond felt something bump against the side of the aircraft. Craning his neck to look out the window, he could just see a gangway being secured to the side of the plane. An Air Force ambulance and a black limousine with diplomatic plates pulled up at the foot of the gangway just as the hatch opened and about eight men entered the plane.

"Who do you suppose they are?" Bea MacDowell asked.

Drummond watched the men coming aboard, all of whom were disappearing into the first-class cabin.

"Well, the four in uniforms are Air Police," he said distractedly. "I suppose the others are federal agents."

Drummond undid his seat belt, craning his neck to

watch as the well-dressed man emerged from first class and went out the hatch, escorted by two of the plain-clothesmen. When the man had cleared the gangway, two Air Force medics and two more AP's came up, presumably to deal with the prisoner. The well-dressed man got into the waiting limo and was whisked away.

"Everyone, *sit down!*"

The voice of an AP crackled through his bull horn. Most people obeyed the command, but a few continued to rummage in the overhead bins. Two AP's with rifles came down the aisles and firmly directed the deaf to their seats. When everyone was seated, one of the federal agents picked up the microphone of the plane's PA system.

"Ladies and gentlemen, could I have your attention, please? I'm Agent Jeffers of the Federal Bureau of Investigation. In just a moment, we will be disembarking you from this plane. Outside in the hangar, folding chairs have been set up in the same seat configuration as this aircraft, so that we can reconstruct exactly what happened. You will be asked to leave by row, and we have to insist on your cooperation. When you leave the plane you will leave all personal belongings and carry-on baggage sitting on your assigned seat. The Air Force personnel now on board will assist you if you have any problems. In the meantime, please remain in your seat until instructed to do otherwise. Thank you."

He handed the microphone back to the stewardess, then leaned forward to whisper something in her ear. She nodded, and Drummond could tell by her gestures that she was directing them to his seat. He and another agent headed down the aisle, stopping behind and ahead of Drummond's aisle seat.

"Mr. Drummond?" Agent Jeffers' question was rhetorical. "Would you come with us, please?"

Drummond stood up, the dried blood on his cashmere shirt crackling and snapping as the folds and wrinkles stretched themselves out, and held up the hand grenade.

"Should I bring this, or leave it on the seat?"

The agent grinned. "Guess you'd better bring it."

Outside in the hangar, Drummond was led up a narrow flight of stairs to a small office that overlooked the entire building. On the floor below were three hundred and fifty chairs set up to simulate the interior of the aircraft, with galleys and toilets marked off in tape. From this vantage point, Drummond and the federal agents could watch as the passengers were brought in row by row and seated in the hangar.

"Now, Mr. Drummond, you seem to have made yourself quite the hero of the day," Jeffers said, sitting casually on the corner of a desk as he spoke. "While we're waiting for everyone to settle in down below, would you mind answering a few questions?"

"Ask away," Drummond replied. He set the grenade on the desk and took a seat.

"Let's start with who you are," said the other agent, speaking for the first time.

"John Drummond. Captain, Los Angeles Police Department."

Drummond quickly supplied the basic information and his badge and ID, along with the telephone number of his commanding officer at LAPD headquarters. Jeffers excused himself—Drummond guessed he was going to phone LAPD—leaving his partner alone with Drummond.

"Homicide, eh?" the remaining agent said with a slight smile. "I would've guessed vice, by the beard."

Drummond ran a hand over his stubble.

"I've been on vacation. Thought I'd give my face a rest, too."

"Fair enough. So, what exactly drew your attention to the man with the hand grenade, Captain Drummond?"

"The hand grenade itself, Mr. . . . ?" Drummond let the question hang in the air.

"Durkey. Special Agent Nat Durkey." The agent's voice remained casual. "You say it was the grenade. When did you first notice it?" Agent Jeffers returned to the office.

"I hate to interrupt, but I think we're ready for the reconstruction, Captain Drummond. So if you'll just step over here—" he led Drummond back to the window that overlooked the hangar "—we'd appreciate it if you'd tell us what happened."

From his vantage point, Drummond explained the sequence of events, which Agent Durkey then repeated into a small walkie-talkie. On the floor below, a man in blue coveralls got up from next to Mrs. MacDowell—Drummond wasn't sure, but the man seemed to look relieved when he rose—and went back to the taped area that represented the toilets.

"How long were you in the restroom, Captain Drummond?" Jeffers asked.

"Not long. Two, maybe three minutes."

Agent Durkey spoke into his handset, then looked at his watch. The minutes ticked by. "Now!" he said.

A short, pudgy man in red coveralls stood up, blocking the aisle just as the man in blue stepped out of the imaginary toilet.

Over the next two hours, the agents carefully pieced together a careful reconstruction of the attempted hijacking of the aircraft, with Drummond correcting any errors that he spotted. As they walked through the hijacking for what seemed to be the hundredth time, the AP with the bull horn entered the office.

"Search complete, sir." Drummond could hear Nebraska cornfields in the young man's voice.

"Thank you, Lieutenant. You can put them all back on board and send them to LAX." Jeffers turned to Drummond. "It will take close to an hour to do that, Captain. Would you like to clean up a bit before you leave?"

Drummond glanced at his blood-soaked clothes.

"Yeah, that'd be appreciated."

"No problem. Give Nat your sizes, and we'll get you some clothes at the PX. In the meantime, I'll run you over to the BOQs." Standing, Jeffers picked up the hand grenade that Drummond had set on the desk.

"By the way, you were very lucky, Captain Drummond. Very lucky, indeed. Do you know anything about explosives?"

"Only that they're dangerous. Why?" he asked.

"This grenade isn't a dud. It's designed to go off on impact. When you flopped down on it, it could very easily have exploded." Jeffers smiled. "Like I said, you're a very lucky man."

At the Bachelor Officer Quarters, Drummond took a fast shower while Agent Durkey invested some of the taxpayers' money in new clothes for Drummond. Looking at the clothes Durkey had brought back from the PX, Drummond realized that his luck had run out. The chocolate-brown trousers were an inch too short, and Drummond checked the back of the electric blue-and-black shirt for the name of the local bowling alley before he put it on.

The worst, however, were the white tube socks. Slipping into his black Gucci loafers, Drummond felt like a candidate for Mr. Blackwell's worst-dressed list. He made a mental note to take Special Agent Durkey's name off his party list.

"I have to ask you to sign the receipt for the clothes."

Agent Jeffers sounded almost apologetic. "And if you don't mind, I'll have to keep your old ones."

"Sure thing," Drummond said as he scribbled his signature across the receipt and handed it back to Jeffers. He'd had the cashmere polo shirt for less than twenty-four hours, and it and the slacks were ruined anyway.

On the way back to the jet, Drummond decided to ask about the well-dressed man.

"Incidentally, who was the man—I assume he was a physician—who helped deal with the hijacker? I saw a limo take him away."

Jeffers glanced at him sidelong, his expression betraying nothing.

"You saw nothing, Captain," he said quietly. "I'd advise you to remember that."

Drummond immediately shut up. Putting two and two together, he decided that the well-dressed man must have been the terrorist's target. And if the Feds didn't want to talk about it, that was fine with him.

Out on the tarmac, the jumbo jet sat waiting patiently as the jeep drove Drummond and Jeffers along the runway access road. As it pulled up at the bottom of the gangway, Drummond hopped out and headed up the stairs two at a time. At the door to the aircraft, the stewardess stopped Drummond for just a minute—long enough for the captain to announce his arrival on board over the PA system. Immediately the passengers broke into cheers and applause, and Drummond could feel the back of his neck burning red.

As the commotion died down, the stewardess led Drummond forward into the first-class cabin and put him in one of the thick leather seats.

"Can I get you anything else, Mr. Drummond?" she asked with a Pepsodent smile.

Drummond looked at the empty seat next to him.

"Yes, there is. If you don't mind, would you please ask Mrs. Bea MacDowell to join me?"

Some seven thousand miles to the east, a black BMW jounced over the rough forest track toward a clearing at the edge of the woods. Half a dozen assorted police vehicles were already drawn up in what had become an impromptu parking area, and fluorescent orange pylons supporting festoons of wide yellow tape fenced off a crime scene. Easing the BMW up to the barricade, Vienna Police Inspector Markus Eberle switched off the engine and stared at the cluster of policemen standing near a small tan tent at the far edge of the clearing.

Funny, he thought, how the living huddle together trying to ignore the dead.

Through the streaked windshield of the BMW, he could see the torso of the headless man not far from the tent, chest-down on the muddy, blood-soaked turf. The feet were wearing socks. A few meters away from the body, more pylons and yellow tape corralled what was probably the victim's head.

Shaking his head, Eberle got out of the car. A few heavy drops of rain fell from the graying sky, peppering his Burbury with golden-brown spots as he picked his way across the muddy ground toward the policemen clustered by the tent. Most of them wore extremely grave expressions, and a few looked sick to their stomachs. They stepped back as he approached, and Eberle got his first glimpse of the girl's body draped across the sagging tan canvas.

Despite nearly a decade working homicide, the unexpected sight of the body, its head cocked back at a crazy angle and a jagged purple wound gaping at the throat, momentarily froze Eberle in his tracks. The victim looked no more than seventeen or eighteen, her lifeless green eyes staring up at the dark gray clouds that moved with resolute swiftness across the sky, away from the scene of the crime.

Recovering from his initial surprise, Eberle took a deep breath and slowly surveyed the crime scene. The local police had made a thorough job of it—too thorough, in fact. In setting up the pylons and stringing out endless meters of the bright yellow tape with "POLIZEI" neatly blocked on it in large black letters, they probably had trampled any clues into the mud.

Eberle walked over to where the first corpse lay chest-down. It was hard to estimate how old or how tall the man had been, now that he was separated from his head. A few meters away, the head lay behind its own protective police barricade. Eberle walked over to the yellow tape and crouched down to get a better look at the victim's face.

It was the face of a blondish young man in his mid-twenties. Normally clean shaven, the cheeks were covered with a light five o'clock shadow, and above the bluish-gray lips, a ginger-colored mustache drooped at the corners of the mouth. The blue eyes, like the eyes of the girl, were wide open in stark terror.

Eberle crouched lower, then turned his head to see what the young man might have been watching in his last moments of consciousness.

What was the last thing he saw? Eberle wondered. How long does the brain function, once the head is severed from the body?

Certainly two or three minutes; there was enough oxygen in the brain to allow it to function for at least that long. Eberle remembered reading that, in France, after a criminal had been guillotined, the head was picked up by the executioner and held up to see its body. Sometimes the lips had moved, and the eyes had even blinked. . . .

A green-and-white police van pulled into the clearing and parked next to Eberle's black BMW. Standing up, Eberle tried to banish the thought of what the last few minutes of the dead man's life might have been like. Ignoring the mud, he walked quickly over to the van, signaling the passenger out with a wave of his hand. A man in his early thirties hopped out as Eberle approached, making a face as he landed in mud.

"Well, they picked a good place for it, Markus," he said, moving to firmer ground. "What's it look like to you?"

"Not so good, Bubi. Not so good. A decapitation and a girl with her throat cut." Eberle sighed. "Local cops have walked all over the place. A couple of them have been sick near the bodies, too."

"Nothing like a bit of a challenge." They had moved to the back of the van, and Bubi Steinmazel opened the door of the mobile crime lab. "I'll take a look around and see what I can find."

Leaving Steinmazel to ferret out what clues he could, Eberle headed back through the clearing toward the policemen clustered near the girl's body.

"Who's the investigating officer?" he asked one of them.

The man pointed beyond the clearing, toward the edge of the woods. "Sergeant Richter, over there with the old-timer who found the bodies."

Following the policeman's gesture, Eberle saw two men in plain clothes interviewing a small, gray-haired man in the loden-green uniform and heavy boots of a forester. He tried to pick his way around the worst of the mud as he slogged over to where they stood talking.

"No, I tell you again," the forester was saying. "Camping is not permitted in this part of the woods. I don't know how they came to be here."

One of the officers glanced up as the old man continued trying to shift any responsibility for the location of the murders onto someone else. Eberle held up his ID, and the man nodded and moved back a step.

"Excuse me," Eberle said, interrupting the forester. "When did you discover the bodies?"

"It was about eight-thirty this morning," the old man answered.

Eberle looked at his watch. Almost four hours ago.

"I see," he said. "And when did you contact the police, Herr Forstmeister?"

At the mention of his title, the little man drew himself up into attention. "About half an hour later, sir."

"I see," Eberle said. "And I gather that camping is not usually permitted here."

"No, sir, although many young couples do pitch their tents in the woods for—" The forester cleared his throat. "For privacy, if you like."

"So, what brought you here?" Eberle asked.

"Last night, about midnight, people in the campgrounds farther to the north complained of being awakened by the sound of hunting horns. It lasted about ten minutes, then it stopped. This morning I came up here to see if there had been poachers in the woods last night."

The forester fiddled nervously with the *gamsbart* on the side of his hat. Eberle eyed him for several seconds before speaking.

"Thank you, Herr Forstmeister. Please give these gentlemen your name and address. We will contact you if we need any further assistance."

The forester saluted, and Eberle nodded in return, then

turned and headed over to where Steinmazel knelt a few feet away from the body of the young man.

"Found anything?" he called out as he approached the forensic technician.

"Yeah," Steinmazel replied, carefully pouring quick-setting plaster into a shallow depression on the ground. "I've got a very clear footprint here."

"Not one of our nimble-footed local cops?" Eberle said, dropping down next to Steinmazel.

"Nope. It's a footprint, not a shoe-print—a bare foot, probably a man's, judging by the size of it." Steinmazel carefully finished pouring the plaster. "I'll show it to you in a few more minutes, when it's set up."

The two men stood up.

"Any chance that it's the victim's track?" Eberle asked.

"Not unless he put his socks on after he had his head chopped off." Steinmazel inclined his head toward the torso. The bottoms of the dead man's socks were caked in mud.

"So, Bubi, how do you read it?" Eberle asked.

Steinmazel cast a calculating look toward the body and the tent, then back at Eberle.

"I figure he was standing here, facing the direction he fell," he said, "when someone came up from behind and cut his head off." He crouched back down and carefully lifted the plaster cast clear of the mud. Turning it over, he gave a grunt of satisfaction and held it up for Eberle's inspection.

"Just as I thought. See how the impression is deeper along the outside edge of the foot?" Eberle nodded. "That's because the assailant's weight shifted in that direction as he swung the weapon that took off the kid's head." Steinmazel stood up and handed Eberle the plaster cast.

"Find a barefoot man with a two-handed sword, and you've got your killer," he said.

"Thanks, Bubi—I think." Eberle stared at the plaster impression of a man's foot for several seconds.

"Bubi, look for more footprints around here. I've got a hunch our killer wasn't alone."

CHAPTER 4

Drummond's secretary had very kindly arranged the manila file folders on his desk into three neat piles: pending, ongoing, and closed. The prospect of going through them all was daunting, but it was better than thinking too hard about what had happened where he was during the two weeks he had been away. To ease back into the routine, he decided to start the day with the pile marked "closed." He picked up the topmost folder, opened it, and read through the arresting officer's report while he had a cup of coffee.

The suspect was a black female, age 62. The victim, described in the report as her boyfriend, was a black male, age 68. According to eye-witnesses, the woman, Ola Mae Harrell, had had an argument with Eugene Tubbs, the victim, shortly before he was killed. Following a heated exchange of words, Tubbs had left the second-floor apartment of the motel, gone downstairs, and was walking past the balcony when Ola Mae dropped a large watermelon on his head, killing him instantly.

Drummond chuckled drily to himself, initialed the report, and dropped it in the "out" tray on his desk, ready to send on to the DA's office for action. He had just picked up the next file when Sandy Morwood stuck his head around the door and tapped on the glass, grinning.

"Hey, John. Good to have you back. Mind if I come in and visit?"

"Sure, Sandy, pull up a seat. How are things on FLASH?"

Morwood flopped into a chair opposite Drummond, nearly spilling his coffee. He was the federal liaison agent for FLASH—Federal Legal Assistance in Solving Homicides—and drew his salary from the Department of Justice.

"Oh, just the usual nonsense. We brought a new computer on-line. It ought to make things run even better. Nothing very interesting while you were gone, though." Morwood sipped his coffee. "Anything interesting on your desk?"

Careful to keep a straight face, Drummond retrieved the watermelon murder file and slid it over to the federal agent.

"Just this. Hope it isn't a copy-cat killing."

Drummond opened the next folder in the "closed" pile and pretended to start skimming it, waiting for the explosion. Morwood nearly choked on his coffee when he got to the part of the report that described the late "Mr. Tubbs" as having been driven into the ground like a tent peg by the force of the falling watermelon.

"God, John," Morwood said between hoots of laughter, "this is funny. Do you mind if I send it out over FLASH?"

Drummond's answer was interrupted by the soft buzzing of his intercom.

"Yes, Alicia. What is it?" Drummond lifted his finger from the red bar on the squawk box.

"There are two men here to see you from the Israeli Consulate, *Capitan*." Alicia only used Drummond's rank to impress visitors. "Can you see them now?"

"Sure. Send them in." Drummond gave Morwood an

apologetic shrug as the agent stood up to leave. Morwood nodded good-naturedly as he brushed past the two men just coming in, and as they closed the door behind them, walked over to the pert Chicana who was Drummond's secretary.

"Alicia, are those guys who just went into John's office supposed to be from the Israeli Consulate?" he asked quietly, bending over her desk.

"Sure. They had ID. Why?" She wrinkled her nose slightly as she answered Morwood's question.

"Because they're both packing iron," Morwood said. "You'd better alert security."

The two men opposite Drummond were well tanned and neatly dressed, but their dark suits were not quite well enough cut to totally mask the bulges under their arms. One look at their heavily scarred knuckles told Drummond that these were no ordinary diplomats.

"Gentlemen, please sit down." Drummond gave them his best public relations smile as he indicated two chairs on the other side of his desk.

As the Israelis settled down, the taller of the pair introduced himself.

"I'm Moses Trostler, and this is my assistant, Abe Meier." The thickset man to his right grunted. "We were hoping that you might be able to answer a few 'unofficial' questions for us." Trostler's English was perfect, without a trace of accent.

"My secretary said you were with the Israeli Consulate," Drummond said politely. "Do you mind telling me what you do?"

Meier shifted in his chair, but Trostler remained impassive as he said, "Not at all. Let's just say that we're with special security at the consulate."

"I see." Drummond left his public relations smile turned on. "What can I do for you?"

Meier leaned forward, both hands on Drummond's desk. "You can cut out the crap, for starters. We know all about you and your Nazi pals in Vienna."

His voice rasped with menace. Out of the corner of his eye, Drummond watched Trostler's reaction to his partner's aggressive display. Nothing in the Israeli's body language indicated any surprise at Meier's outburst.

So that's it, Drummond thought. *Good cop, Bad cop. And well-rehearsed, too.*

"Suppose you refresh my memory, Mr. Meier," he said, "and tell me all about it."

Meier's face darkened with rage, and he half stood up before Trostler's even voice cut across the growing tension.

"Captain Drummond. Who your friends are—well, it really doesn't matter. Just so long as it doesn't affect your career. All we want is a little cooperation, that's all." Trostler's threat said it all: play ball, or we'll go to your boss.

"Yeah," Meier said. "Cooperation. Like you gave your friends who killed Hans Stucke."

Drummond decided that it was time to terminate the meeting, but on his terms. Stretching one foot farther under his desk, he pushed a floor button that triggered a silent alarm outside his office. Through the glass wall behind the two Israelis, he could see two uniformed officers with shotguns already making their way toward his office, Morwood behind them, signaling the secretaries to leave the outer office.

"Gentlemen," Drummond said, as he stood up, "you are both under arrest."

Meier jumped to his feet. "Listen here—!"

The first officer through the door jammed his shotgun into the back of Meier's neck and ordered, "Freeze, asshole! Just move and I'll paint the walls with your brains."

Trostler remained impassive as Meier was shoved face-down across Drummond's desk by one of the cops.

"Captain Drummond, we have full diplomatic immun—"

"Hands on your head!" the other cop barked, underlining the command with a shotgun barrel in Trostler's back.

As Trostler obeyed, Drummond leaned across his desk and removed a large automatic pistol from the man's shoulder holster.

"Desert Eagle .357 Magnum." Drummond dropped the piece into his trash can with a metallic clatter. "It's a felony to bring a concealed weapon into a municipal building, Mr. Trostler." Sliding his hand into Meier's jacket, he pulled out another automatic. "Matching pair. Hope for your sake they're registered, Mr. Meier." It followed the other gun into the trash. As the Desert Eagle crashed into the tin wastebasket, Meier pushed himself up off the desk and made a grab for the policeman's shotgun.

"You fuckin' sonofabitch—"

Meier's outburst was cut short by the sound of the butt of a shotgun being cracked against the back of his skull. Knees buckling but hands still grabbing at the weapon's barrel, Meier sagged at the feet of the officer he had tried to attack. A knee in dark blue serge snapped up, catching the Israeli on the point of his chin and splitting his lip as it snapped his head back.

Reeling under the impact, Meier slowly crumpled face-down on the floor of the office. Trostler had not moved, with the second shotgun still jammed against his kidneys. Stepping from behind his desk, Drummond bent down and snapped a set of handcuffs on Meier. As one of the officers handed him a second pair, Drummond turned to Trostler and smiled.

"Assume the position, Mose."

Meier was stirring as Drummond cuffed Trostler. Very quickly, the two uniformed officers had the two prisoners on their feet. As they led the two Israelis out of his office, Drummond followed far enough after them to signal Alicia, who was returning to the outer office with the other secretaries.

"Alicia, get someone from Special Investigations up here right away, would you?" he said as she came wide-eyed back to her desk. "And while you're at it," he added, almost as an afterthought, "I suppose you'd better call Internal Affairs."

Returning to his office, he sat down on the corner of his desk and picked up the phone, feeling his adrenalin rush start to recede as he tapped in the extension of his supervisor.

"DeGrazzio here."

The voice was deceptively youthful. Commander Joey DeGrazzio had done two tours of 'Nam as an MP before joining the LAPD in 1965, and despite his initial lack of a college degree had moved up through the ranks to become one of the best homicide investigators in the LAPD. He was now finishing a master's degree in sociology. An outspoken critic of Los Angeles Mayor Tom Bradley, his appointment to deputy chief seemed to be on permanent hold.

"Joey, this is John," Drummond said. "I've just had some big trouble down here. I'd appreciate it if you could come right down."

"IAD?" DeGrazzio asked.

"Yeah, but I've asked 'em in," Drummond replied. "Special Investigations, too. I think I may just have caused an international incident."

"Okay, John. Be right down."

The line went dead, and Drummond replaced the receiver. The phone was hardly in its cradle when it buzzed softly.

It was Alicia, Drummond's secretary.

"The Special Investigations officer is here, and Internal Affairs will be down in about ten minutes," she said. "Shall I call Commander DeGrazzio?"

"No, thanks. I've already called him."

Drummond replaced the phone just as the Special Investigations officer came in.

"You Drummond?" he asked.

"Yeah. And you . . . ?"

"Oh, I'm Pete Knickerbocker, Special Investigations." He extended his arm and shook hands with Drummond. "You pop the two Israeli 'diplomats'?"

"'Fraid so," Drummond said.

"Well, then, you're gonna be in a world of shit for the next coupla weeks, pal. I've been working the embassies for three years now, and next to Sierra Leone, the Israelis squeak the loudest when you bust one of their people." He grinned at Drummond. "So, whatcha got?"

"This." Drummond reached down and lifted up his trash can, placing it on the desk in front of Knickerbocker. Taking a pencil, he reached in and hooked one of the guns by the trigger guard and lifted it out.

"Well, well, well. Desert Eagle .357 Magnum. You don't get those with your ordinary diplomatic passport," Knickerbocker said. "You bust them for packing in a public building?"

"Yup," Drummond said. "That and a whole cartload of attitude."

Knickerbocker winced. "Nobody got roughed up did they?"

"Sorry, Pete, but one of them got a little out of hand, and security knocked him down with the butt of his shotgun." Drummond smiled apologetically.

"Shit," Knickerbocker said. "I'll head over to the Israeli Consulate and see what I can do. In the meantime—" he pointed to the wastebasket on the desk "—get these over to the lab for a rush job in ballistics. I don't want them crying for their toys when they walk out of here—and they will walk. I give 'em a couple of hours at best."

"You've got to be kidding!"

"I wish I were. See you, Cap."

Knickerbocker turned to leave just as DeGrazzio was entering the small office. There was a slight shuffle at the door as the men stopped to let one another pass and then both stepped forward at the same time.

"Jeeze, this is like the Three Stooges," DeGrazzio said, when he finally got past Knickerbocker. "So, what's up?"

Drummond quickly filled him in as DeGrazzio stood on his tiptoes to peer over the rim of the wastebasket on the desk, looking at the two pistols at the bottom of the can.

"Boy, these are really big," he said. Then, without bothering to look at Drummond, "So, did you have anything to do with the old guy's death in Vienna?"

"No. Like I said, I was just there as a ride-along," Drummond answered.

"Okay, I buy your story." DeGrazzio glanced at his watch. "You go to lunch. I'll run these down to the lab." Picking up the wastebasket, he headed toward the door. "Meanwhile, don't talk to too many people until IAD gets to interview you." Looking into the can one more time, DeGrazzio let out a low whistle.

"Gee, these things are like cannons."

Dropping into the chair behind his desk, Drummond pulled open the top drawer and scooped out his wallet and some loose change. In the back of the drawer was his pistol snug in a soft leather holster. Contrary to his usual routine, Drummond slipped the stainless steel Smith & Wesson into the waistband of his trousers before heading out to lunch.

CHAPTER 5

The tuna-melt sandwich and potato salad had been Drummond's staple lunch fare for almost as long as he could remember. Certainly in the ten years that he'd been working out of Parker Center, Drummond couldn't remember more than half a dozen lunches when he'd eaten anything else. Finishing the last forkful of potato salad, he was eyeing a slice of lemon meringue pie in the cold cabinet when his beeper started chirruping on his belt.

As he instinctively reached down for the paging device, his hand brushed against the neoprene combat grips on the small .38 caliber revolver snug against his hip. Except for the incident in his office earlier, Drummond felt almost embarrassed to be carrying a gun, but the moment passed, and he popped the pager off his belt and held it near his face. Shading the LED readout with his hand, he squinted to read the message in the glaring light of the restaurant.

REPORT TO OFFICE . . . REPORT TO OFFICE . . . REPORT TO . . .

Drummond slapped a five-dollar bill on the counter and stood up to leave.

"Gotta go, Paula. Thanks." Drummond headed toward the door.

"Hold on, Captain." Paula's voice was husky, reminding

Drummond of Marjorie Main, a delightful old character actress who had been his neighbor when he was a small boy.

"I'm in a rush, Paula." Drummond's voice was pleading, but he had stopped and turned back.

"Thanks for the tip. Here's your iced tea." Paula handed him a large cup and a straw. "Have a nice day."

Standing on the corner, waiting for the light to change so he could cross Los Angeles Street, Drummond saw the three men heading down the concrete apron in front of LAPD's Parker Center. The short, pudgy man in the tan suit and loud tie looked like an attorney, and sweated like one, too. Even from across the street, Drummond could see dark perspiration patches under the arms of the man's jacket.

The other two were the Israelis, and Drummond could tell from their body language that they were not a couple of happy campers. Meier was looking a bit worse for wear and had a thick bandage taped across the back of his head where the security officer's shotgun had raised a considerable lump. Trostler was wearing a pair of expensive Varnet sunglasses that weren't doing too good a job of disguising the purple swelling of a world-class black eye. As he sipped idly at his iced tea, Drummond wondered who had hung one on him. Whoever it was, he decided, he'd have to buy him a beer.

The light changed and Drummond started across, just as the three men reached a dark blue Cadillac limousine parked in front of Parker Center. Trostler was bending to enter the back of the car when he saw Drummond and stood up. Smiling slightly, he pointed his index finger at him and, with an up and down motion of his thumb, pretended to shoot Drummond several times.

Still sipping his iced tea, Drummond reached back and

pulled his gun out of its holster, cocking the hammer back
with his thumb as he drew the small pistol even with his
shoulder and aimed it at Trostler's smirking face. Less
than twenty-five feet away, Trostler's smirk froze on his
face as he stared into the barrel of Drummond's Smith &
Wesson.

Changing direction, Drummond walked diagonally toward the car, still pointing his gun at Trostler. Abruptly
Trostler ducked down and climbed into the car, which
pulled away from the red curb and moved off toward the
Harbor Freeway. Drummond holstered his revolver and,
still sipping his iced tea, went into Parker Center.

Pete Knickerbocker was waiting in the lobby.

"Thought I'd wait down here and make sure our Israeli
diplomats left without incident," Knickerbocker said as he
approached Drummond. "What the hell was that all
about, anyway?"

"Psychological warfare, Pete." Drummond tossed the
empty paper cup into a trash can next to the elevator.
"The tall guy—Trostler, right?"

Knickerbocker nodded.

"The tall guy made a threatening gesture. I just upped
the ante, that's all."

The elevator door opened and the two men stepped in.
Knickerbocker reached over and pressed the button
marked "3."

"You're wanted in 316 for some sort of meeting." He
turned to face Drummond. "For what it's worth, Captain,
those boys from the Israeli Consulate are out for your
hide." The elevator stopped and the doors opened onto
the third floor. Knickerbocker pointed down the hall toward the offices of Internal Affairs Division as Drummond stepped out. "I'd be very careful in there, if I were
you."

The elevator doors closed behind Drummond, leaving him momentarily alone in the hall.

The door marked 316 was closed, and Drummond knocked before trying the knob. A voice said, "Come in," and Drummond stepped into the office.

Commander DeGrazzio stood up as Drummond walked into the large paneled conference room, and indicated an empty chair between himself and an overweight blonde who didn't look as if she belonged in an Internal Affairs "preliminary inquiry." Two more men were seated across the table, and as Drummond moved over to the empty chair, one of the men stood up and extended his hand to Drummond.

"I'm Sergeant Hrisko, Internal Affairs." Drummond shook his hand and then sat down. "Before we begin, I'd like to ask Commander DeGrassi—"

"It's DeGrazzio," the commander interrupted.

"Sorry. Commander DeGrazzio to tell you why you've been asked to this meeting."

"Excuse me," Drummond interjected. "But before this goes any further, I'd like to know who these other people are, if you don't mind." Drummond looked around the table.

"Not at all, Captain," Hrisko said. "Officer Willis is here as a representative of the Police Officers Protective Association, and the lady to your left is Ms. Verna Cartright, attorney-at-law. She has been retained by your union to make sure that I," Hrisko did nothing to conceal his contempt, "don't inadvertently violate your rights."

"Excuse me, Sergeant?" Drummond said. "You're coming on as if I've done something wrong. What's the beef?"

"The 'beef,' Captain, is a big one. I've just had a major complaint from the Israeli government over your treatment of two of their diplomats, for starters," Hrisko's voice had a hard edge to it. "And if that wasn't enough to make my day, I've been given this file, which contains evidence that you are some sort of neo-Nazi involved in the coverup of a murder that took place in Vienna three weeks ago." Hrisko reached out and pushed the file across the table toward Drummond. "The Israeli consul general is really pissed off."

"Well, tough tit," DeGrazzio interjected. "Their goons shouldn't go wandering around Parker Center armed to the teeth."

"Come on," Hrisko said. "Two guns is hardly armed to the teeth. Which, by the way, leads me to ask what you did with their weapons. The consul general has asked for their immediate return."

"Well, tough-the-other-tit, Hrisko," DeGrazzio sneered. "Those creeps were packing guns without serial numbers. I had the lab send them to D.C., so the boys in the FBI could run a ballistics check on them."

"Thank you, Commander DeGrazzio. Captain Drummond, do you have anything to say?" Hrisko leaned back in his chair, waiting for the reply.

"I think the Israelis have fed you a load of crap, Sergeant." Drummond's tone was measured, totally under control. He knew the routine: make him angry, catch him off balance, get him to cross himself up. It would work too, if Drummond had anything to hide, which he didn't. The LAPD was one of the best police forces in the world, and guys like Hrisko kept it that way. Still, Drummond was furious at the implication that he had somehow done something wrong, although he understood Hrisko's motivation.

Hrisko opened the file the Israelis' attorney had left behind when he collected Trostler and Meier.

"Crap, huh? Okay, let's see what this crap is all about." Hrisko held up a piece of paper.

"Two weeks ago, you took a sudden vacation and went to Vienna. On your way to that city, you stopped at a castle in the middle of the country where you met a whole bunch of interesting people." Hrisko handed Drummond a list of names. "All of the people at that castle were the children of Nazi bigwigs. That surprise you, Captain Drummond?"

"This is bullshit," DeGrazzio muttered under his breath.

Drummond handed back the list. "Hrisko, you could say the same thing for almost anybody in Germany over the age of forty-five."

"True," Hrisko replied. "But you can't say that about too many Americans, can you?" Hrisko looked down at the file. "For example, Jack MacBain." He looked up at Drummond. "Jack MacBain made his millions helping Hitler rebuild Germany. Did you know that they were quite friendly?"

Drummond just stared at Hrisko and remained silent.

"I suppose, Captain Drummond, it was a coincidence that you paid a call on Jack MacBain's widow a week before you left for Austria? And that once you were there, you went straight to a secluded castle for a meeting with a bunch of Nazis? Or that, two days later, you went to Number Seventeen Dietrich Eckhart Strasse—the former headquarters of the Gestapo? And that same night, you just happened to show up at the apartment of an old Jew who died under the most peculiar circumstances, after he'd reported having seen a wanted war criminal—some Nazi called Kluge—in Vienna."

Drummond cleared his throat. "I went to Number Seventeen Dietrich Eckhart Strasse to meet a man called von Liebenfalz. Later, contacts of mine in the Vienna Police told me that von Liebenfalz had been in Switzerland during the war."

"You have good contacts in the Vienna PD, Drummond?" Hrisko interrupted. "Was that why they took you to see Stucke? So you could tell your Nazi pals that the guy sniffing after Kluge was dead, and the Vienna PD was chalking it up to suicide?"

"Hey, Hrisko, who the fuck you work for? LAPD or the Israelis?" DeGrazzio's voice slammed into Hrisko's diatribe like a blackjack.

Hrisko gave DeGrazzio a quizzical smirk, then lowered his voice. "Your trip to Vienna was rather sudden, wasn't it, Captain?"

"No," Drummond replied. "I bought the ticket about a week before I left."

"That would have been about the time that Hans Stucke died, wouldn't it?" Hrisko asked.

"Yes, I suppose that could have been at about the same time," Drummond admitted.

"Captain Drummond, have you ever been to the Angel of Mercy Sanatarium in Auburn, New Hampshire?" Hrisko asked.

"Yes," was all Drummond said.

"I don't suppose that you know anything about its founder?"

Drummond was puzzled. "No, I don't. Why?"

"Because its founder was Charles Lamont Packard. Have you heard of him?"

Drummond shook his head, no.

"Charles Lamont Packard spent a fortune trying to keep America from going to war against the Nazis." Hrisko closed the file. "His daughter married Jack MacBain." Hrisko leaned across the table, his voice nearly a whisper. "Why did you go to Vienna, Captain Drummond?"

"Research for a paper I'm doing at USC." Drummond's voice was level.

"Oh, really?" Hrisko sounded incredulous. "Doing a research paper on war criminals, or organizing a reunion for millionaire friends of the Nazi party?"

"Sergeant Hrisko." Verna Cartwright's voice sounded like four packs of Camels a day. "Your balls must be bigger than your brains. The information contained in the file—all of which is highly speculative and circumstantial—has undoubtedly been gathered in a manner that violates numerous state and federal laws. Your use of that information violates the rights of Captain Drummond." She leaned closer to the table.

"Now, unless that file is handed over to me right now, I am going to file the biggest goddam lawsuit ever to hit this department. And as far as you are concerned, I'll be in federal court swearing out a complaint against you personally within the hour." Verna looked down the table at Officer Willis. "Further, I would strongly suggest that this whole proceeding is likely to be cause for immediate labor action—and I don't mean the Blue Flu."

Hrisko looked over at Willis, who nodded perceptibly. Angrily he shoved the file across the table toward the dumpty blonde attorney.

"Thank you, Sergeant," she said, picking up the file. "Now, unless you have something constructive to bring to the meeting, I'd suggest that there is nothing further to discuss."

She stood up, pushing her chair well back from the table. Hrisko stared at her for a moment, then turned to Drummond.

"You can go, Captain. We've nothing further to discuss."

Drummond and the others stood and filed out into the

hall. As they walked toward the elevator, Verna handed Drummond the file the Israelis had sent to IAD.

"You'd better hang on to this, just in case any of this crap floats to the surface downstream." The elevator doors opened and Verna bulled her way in. "If you need me, Willis there has my number."

"Thanks," Drummond said.

"Thanks, hell. I love taking the piss out of those IAD assholes." The doors closed, and Drummond and DeGrazzio waited for another elevator.

"Whooee, what a broad," was DeGrazzio's only comment.

"She really is some piece of work, I'll admit that," Drummond said.

The elevator returned, empty, and the two men climbed aboard. "So guess what I found out about the guns?" DeGrazzio said, as he reached over and pushed the button for his floor.

"What?"

"When I called the guys at the Bureau and told 'em what I had, they volunteered that our two 'diplomats' were probably with the Mossad." The elevator stopped, and DeGrazzio pressed the hold button.

"The Mossad?" Drummond asked.

"Yeah. The Israeli goon squad. Sort of a kosher KGB." DeGrazzio chuckled at his joke.

"They aren't suppose to work in the United States," Drummond said.

"Oh, sure. But they do. So let me give you some advice. Be careful. Watch your back. And drink lotsa chicken soup." DeGrazzio released the hold button and stepped out of the elevator. "And one other thing—"

But the elevator doors closed and cut off whatever else

DeGrazzio had been going to say. Shrugging, Drummond made his way back to his office.

Back at his desk, Drummond tossed his revolver into a drawer before settling down to scan the Mossad file. One thing was certain. For whatever reason, the Israelis had gone to a lot of trouble tying together circumstantial evidence involving Drummond in some sort of Nazi intrigue. It looked like conspiracy, but conspiracy to do what? Kill Stucke? No, Drummond decided, that didn't make sense. You don't involve outsiders in murder. There had to be something else.

Drummond's deliberations were interrupted by Sandy Morwood sticking his head into the office with a grin.

"Well, I see you survived the excitement." He flourished a computer printout. "This just came in on FLASH," he said, handing it to Drummond. "Thought it might be of interest."

"Thanks, Sandy."

Drummond took the FLASH report and gave it a quick scan. Two things jumped off the page at him: the name of the investigating officer, Markus Eberle, and the location of the crime, near Schloss Dielstein.

"Notice anything unusual?" Morwood asked.

"Yeah, a friend of mine is the investigating officer," Drummond said.

"Really? No, I meant unusual about the crime." Morwood's voice held a hint of anticipation.

"Not yet," Drummond said as he scanned the report for details.

"Two victims, male and female. The female was totally drained of blood. . . ."

Morwood let it hang on the air, and Drummond looked up at him sharply.

"Thanks, Sandy. I'll add it to my collection," he said.

"Glad to do it. Figure it's a fair trade for the 'Watermelon Killer' you gave me this morning." Morwood smiled and headed back to his office.

Alone at his desk, Drummond reread the FLASH report, then reached for his wallet. Opening it, he pulled out Eberle's card and, looking at his watch, computed the time difference between Los Angeles and Vienna.

Nine hours. That would make it midnight in Vienna. Picking up his phone, he tapped in Morwood's extension.

"Hi, Sandy? Listen, can you do me a favor?"

"Sure," Morwood replied. "What do you need?"

"Can you FLASH Vienna and ask Inspector Markus Eberle to give me a call?" Drummond asked.

"Consider it done," Morwood said. "Anything else?"

"No, just ask Eberle to call my home when he gets in, that's all. Thanks."

After hanging up the phone Drummond picked up the Mossad file and headed out of his office, pausing at Alicia's desk to tell her he was checking out for the day. It was starting to rain as he eased the red BMW 635 out of the underground parking lot beneath Parker Center, and he switched on the windshield wipers as he nosed the car into traffic and headed out toward his home in Malibu. He stopped for a taco on the way, since there was nothing in his refrigerator, and was home in plenty of time to catch the evening news before settling down to read the file.

Drummond was dozing on the sofa, *Die Moldau* on the stereo and his cat Bear meatloafed on his chest, when the phone rang. Glancing at his watch, he saw that it was nearly midnight as he dislodged the cat and reached for the phone. Markus Eberle's voice crackled on the other end.

"John, I got your message on FLASH. Don't tell me you've got my killer locked up in L.A.!" Eberle laughed.

"Nothing so simple, my friend. It's just that there was another murder victim found in the same area about three weeks ago. I wasn't sure if the information had cross-connected." Drummond stretched and sat upright on the couch.

"Another victim?" Eberle said. "How do you know?"

"I met the local police commandant at a dinner at Schloss Dielstein. He thought it was a dump," Drummond replied.

"A dump?" Eberle said.

"Yeah. Killed elsewhere, and the body dumped there in the woods. Figured it as a drug deal that went down heavy." Drummond yawned.

"Who was the commandant you spoke to?"

"Ah, Reidl. Franz Reidl." And as an afterthought, "He drives a Ford."

"What?" Eberle sounded confused.

"Nothing. Guy's name is Reidl. He's a friend of Baroness von Diels."

"Oh, I know him. Old-line aristocratic family. He's a good cop, though. I'll give him a follow-up call. Can't be that many homicides in his jurisdiction," Eberle said.

"Well, I thought it might help," Drummond said.

"Every little bit. So, how is the world treating you?"

"Not so hot. Had the Mossad in my office today."

"The Mossad," Eberle said. "They are not very popular in Austria. What are you doing working with them?"

"I'm not. They came in trying to prove that I was involved in some sort of Nazi cover-up of a murder in Vienna." Drummond strained to pick up some hint of a reaction in Eberle's voice.

"What murder?" Eberle asked.

"That suicide we visited in . . ."

"Oh, that." Eberle snorted. "That dumb shit Sacher's case. Well, if anyone asks, the official police verdict is murder by persons unknown. I did the follow-up myself. Herr Stucke invited a couple of punkers up to his room. My guess is that the old man was a queer and was looking for some sex. What he got was murdered. Not too uncommon an occurrence here in Vienna. If you want an official transcript, I'll send one to your embassy and they can forward it to you."

"Thanks, Markus. I'll let you know if I need it."

"Sure. Anything else I can do for you?" Eberle asked.

"Yeah. I'd like to open a bank account, preferably with a bank that has an office in Luxembourg City," Drummond said.

"No problem. I'll have my kid sister set it up. She's a manager at Vienna Credit Bank." Eberle chuckled. "They launder all the important money in Europe."

"Okay. Have her fax me at the office. The number should be on the FLASH copy."

"Shall do. Is there anything else?" Eberle's voice crackled slightly on the line.

"No," Drummond said. "That's all."

"In that case, thanks for the tip. I'll call if it leads to anything."

"You do that. Talk to you later. Bye, Markus."

Drummond hung up the phone. Standing up, he pulled off his polo shirt and headed into the bathroom for a quick shower before turning in for the night.

Outside, three men were huddled together in the back of a white Chevrolet van. As Drummond's phone line went dead, a pudgy, bald man in a tan suit and loud tie switched off the tape recorder and turned to his two companions.

"Okay, let's bring in the cop," he said.

Nodding, the two Mossad agents slipped out of the van and headed across the road toward Drummond's beachfront condo. Crouching below the wall that surrounded the exclusive community, Trostler and Meier carefully unrolled a large rubberized sheet. Swinging it like a matador's cape, Trostler stood up and tossed it skillfully onto the top of the wall. Then, cupping his hands, he took Meier's foot and hoisted him up onto the rubber pad.

Lying flat on his stomach, Meier reached down, grabbing Trostler by the wrists. With a powerful heave, he lifted Trostler even with the top of the wall. Then, with his partner balanced on his elbows, Meier dropped into the compound.

Trostler paused only long enough to hear the muffled thump of Meier dropping to the other side of the wall. With the grace of a gymnast, Trostler swung his legs up and over the wall, sitting on the edge for a moment to take his bearings before dropping down to join Meier in the shadows near the wall.

Ahead of the two Mossad agents, a private security guard paused to clock in on his rounds. As the guard fumbled to get the security key into his clock, Meier pulled a tubular slingshot from his belt. Reaching into his pocket, he withdrew a leather ball about the size of a walnut and placed it in the slingshot's pouch, then held his arm out rigidly in front of him and drew a bead on the back of the guard's head. Meier took a deep breath, and then let part of it out, steadying his aim as he released the pouch from his grip.

The sand-filled leather ball smacked into the guard's head like a blackjack. Clutching his clock, the guard toppled forward into the shrubbery below Drummond's condominium. The two men rolled the body into the bushes next to the building and, using one of the security lights as an impromptu ladder, climbed up onto Drummond's balcony.

Drummond turned off the taps in the shower and pushed the glass door open, reaching for the towel hanging on the wall. Grabbing Drummond's wrist, Trostler jerked him forward, sending him sprawling on the tile floor. Drummond tried to get up, but a sweep of Trostler's foot caught him across the ankle and he went down again. Dropping down onto one knee, Trostler pinned both of Drummond's arms behind his back as Meier bent down with a syringe.

Drummond felt a sharp jab of pain in his neck, and then a stinging numbness shot through his body. He tried to get up, but a velvet blackness enveloped him, pinning him to the tile floor with a grip far stronger than that of the Mossad agent.

CHAPTER 6

Warm sunlight flooded the courtyard of Wewelsberg Castle where a few young men and women lounged against their backpacks, waiting for the youth hostel to open for the day. Inside, the ancient caretaker carefully inspected the four small dormitories, the shower rooms, and the communal kitchen and dining hall. All was in order, as usual, but it was a far cry from what it had looked like when he first visited it in 1936. The restoration then nearing completion had suffered during the war and in half a century thereafter, though at least the castle had survived—and some of the work.

He sighed as he remembered that day. He had been about five and his father had brought him to the castle to show his young son the heavily carved paneling on which he had labored for the past year: dark German oak, carved with acorns and oak leaves, swastikas and the *sigrunen* of Himmler's SS. Not all of the castle had been graced with Sepp Dornberger's artistry, of course, and much of his work had perished, but some survived.

The old man glanced up at the ceiling, thinking of the room high above this one, never open to public view— the room in which his father had taken special pride. He could see it in his mind's eye as clearly as he had that wonderful day.

The room was circular, with a high-vaulted gothic ceiling. The thick stone walls were pierced at regular intervals by narrow arrow-slit windows, which allowed the sunlight access through blood-red stained glass, filling the room with a warm sanguine glow. In the middle of the room was a round table, its rim inlaid with ivory runes. A gold chalice, finely wrought with runic inscriptions and encrusted with rubies and emeralds, stood in the center of the table, radiant in the red light that bled in through the high-set windows.

Twelve heavily carved chairs, each like the throne of some legendary Teutonic god, were arranged with military precision around the table. Lying on the table in front of each of the high-backed chairs was an SS dagger, its broad Damascus blade alive with red-washed golden runes: Blood and Soil, Honor and Loyalty.

It was the most beautiful room the young Stephen Dornberger had ever seen, and its awesome dignity far surpassed that of the parish church.

"Papa," he had said, when at last he found his voice, "it is so very beautiful. . . ."

"Yes, Stephen, and its beauty will last a thousand years," his father had replied.

Stephen had been going to say more to his father when a handsome young SS officer entered the room.

"So, Sepp, showing the young one your work?"

"Yes, Obersturmführer Kluge. I was telling my boy that it would last a thousand years."

Kluge bent down to young Stephen.

"A thousand years, lad, will only be the beginning. Our race and our Führer are immortal. Remember that." Kluge had tousled the boy's thick blond hair, then stood up and walked out of the room. That had been their first meeting, but not their last. No, by no means had that been their last meeting.

The old man looked around him. That had been more than a half century ago, and yet the memory of that day still sent a tingle of excitement through him. He had been too young to fight in the war, although after the bomb fell on their cottage, killing his mother and father . . .

He looked at the worn face of the watch on his scarred left arm. It was time to open the youth hostel.

Shuffling over to the door, he threw back the bolt and pulled it open on its heavy iron hinges. The hot sunshine of late September spilled into the cool darkness of the castle, and Stephen Dornberger retreated behind a small counter stacked with towels.

The young people, students mostly, lined up in front of the desk and waited patiently while the old man scrutinized their IDs, collected eight marks, and gave them a towel and a key to one of the bedside lockers in the first floor dorms. They were a remarkably common lot of young men and women, and Dornberger dismissed them from his mind as quickly as he handed them their towels.

Finally, with the last of the student herd checked in, Dornberger came from behind his desk and headed out to the courtyard of the castle. He had just taken down the small sign with ZIMMER neatly painted on it when a young man in his early twenties came riding up on an old Zundapp motorcycle. Cutting the engine a hundred yards from the castle, he glided silently into the courtyard, stopping a few feet from Dornberger.

"Good afternoon, sir," he said. Dornberger immediately noticed the young man's use of the very formal address. "Do you think I might have a bed here tonight?"

Dornberger looked him over very carefully before speaking. "Yes, if you don't mind being in a dorm by yourself."

He pointed toward the far wall of the courtyard. "You may park your machine over there." Dornberger turned and headed back to his desk in the castle.

Dismounting, the young man swung one of his long legs over the back of the cream-colored motorcycle and pushed it over to where Dornberger indicated he should park. Opening one of the panniers on the back of the bike, he pulled out a knapsack and headed into the castle.

"This is quite a building," he said, as he handed over his ID card and eight marks to Dornberger.

"Yes, it is very old—" Dornberger read the name off the ID card "—Herr von Tupilow."

Anton von Tupilow flushed slightly at the older man's formal deference, and Dornberger noticed a thin white scar running the width of his cheek. Mentally he made a quick appraisal of von Tupilow. Tall, well-built but not muscular. Aristocratic name and a dueling scar. Things were looking promising.

He handed the young man a towel and key, then turned and took a key ring from a hook behind his desk.

"Come with me and I'll open up another dorm."

Von Tupilow followed Dornberger up an ancient stone stair past the first-floor men's dorm.

"You will be on the next floor, but you will have to use the showers and toilets on this level," Dornberger said as they continued up to the vacant dormitory.

He unlocked the massive oak door and pushed it open. There were two sets of bunk beds in the dorm, with small lockers placed on either side. Walking over to the farthest bunks, Dornberger unrolled the top mattress and pulled it into place.

"There you are," he said, turning back to von Tupilow. "If you need anything, I'll be in my flat on the other side of the courtyard."

Pushing past the young aristocrat, he headed down the stone stairs and back to his apartment. Once inside, he walked straight to his desk and picked up the telephone, pausing only long enough to check an address book for the number before he began dialing.

Thousands of tiny golden dust motes drifted through the bright slashes of sunlight stabbing into the gloom of the indoor riding school. Ankle-deep in the clean, fresh sawdust, ten young men stood at rigid attention while a stocky, middle-aged man with an eye-patch prepared them for their first lesson in the use of the hand-and-a-half broadsword he held before them.

"The sword is the only fit weapon for a knight, and it is the weapon which marks your passage into the blood-brotherhood of our order." Scharführer Baumann pointed his sword at the man on the extreme left of the line. "You, step forward."

The young man came toward Baumann with his sword at the ready. Halting a few paces in front of him, he snapped to attention and, raising his sword to his face, saluted the one-eyed soldier.

Seated on a quiet white stallion at the far end of the arena, Kluge watched with satisfaction as Scharführer Baumann put the younger man through the paces of sword drill. Only the soft purring of the telephone on the wall eventually distracted him from the lesson.

Almost imperceptibly, Kluge shifted his weight in the saddle, then pressed his left leg against the side of his horse, just forward of the girth. The Lipizzan responded at once, turning smoothly on its haunches. Kluge gave a gentle squeeze to the stallion's flanks, and it trotted obediently along the side of the riding school in the direction of the phone. With just the gentlest pressure on the reins,

Kluge halted his mount within arm's reach of the still-purring instrument and took it in a gloved hand.

"Kluge here."

On the other end of the line, Dornberger's mouth went dry, and he had to clear his throat before speaking.

"Herr Sturmbannführer, I think I may have another candidate for you."

Kluge listened intently for a few minutes, and after thanking Dornberger, replaced the telephone receiver on its cradle. Turning his horse toward the center of the riding school, he brought his heels back into its flanks while releasing the pressure on the reins. The horse responded to the rider's command and went immediately into an elegant passage, floating in midair between each extended stride.

Touching the reins, Kluge halted the white horse in front of Baumann. The one-eyed warrior snapped to attention, saluting his master. Kluge returned the salute with a nod.

"We may have a new postulant at Wewelsberg," Kluge said, reaching down to pat his horse on the neck.

"I will see to it at once, *Hochmeister*," Baumann said, a tight smile playing at the corners of his mouth.

Kluge sat back in his saddle and, without another word, trotted out of the riding school and into the warm afternoon sun.

The painting of the sad-eyed clown kept slipping out of focus. Drummond tried to concentrate on the saccharine figure of the circus hobo, but found that his head kept slipping down onto his chest. From what seemed to be a long way off, he heard the sound of men talking, but he couldn't make out what they were saying. Finally, using all the strength he could muster, he managed to rotate his head enough to see the four men sitting by the door of the cheap motel room. Squinting, Drummond recognized three of them.

Trostler and Meier had their backs to the door, drinking coffee, while the third Israeli "diplomat" sat hunched over the table deep in conversation with another, much older, man.

"Hey, Gluckman. I think our boy's coming to," Meier said, as he watched Drummond's head roll back onto his chest.

The short man in the tan suit stood up from the table and walked over to where Drummond was bound to the chair with silvery duct tape. Reaching into his pocket, he pulled out a small black case and, unzipping it, produced a disposable syringe filled with a pale pink fluid.

Drummond vaguely felt the needle jab into the vein in his forearm and in a distracted way watched as Gluckman slowly injected the stimulant into his system.

"How long?" Trostler asked.

"About three minutes. I could have given him more, but I doubt he'd be able to survive the systemic shock of coming out that fast. He'll feel bad enough, as it is." Finished with the injection, Gluckman stood up and put the syringe back in its case.

Drummond could feel the stimulant burning its way up his arm as it worked its way into his circulatory system. There was a loud rushing sound hammering at his brain as the drug dragged him from his torpor and slapped him into consciousness. As Drummond regained his senses, he was aware of a pungent, nearly sweet smell that seemed to cling to him like the cold wet seat of the chair he was taped to. His mind clearing, Drummond realized that he was sitting naked in his own excrement and urine.

Gluckman looked into Drummond's face. "So tell me,

Mr. Drummond, will you be so kind as to answer a few questions?"

Drummond wanted to tell Gluckman to go to hell, but found himself nodding in agreement instead.

"Good," the chubby Mossad agent said. "Then we can take off some of this tape." He nodded at Trostler, who reached over and ripped off the silver tape that covered Drummond's mouth.

"I'm sorry you are in such a humiliating state, but it's one of the side effects of the drug my associates used to subdue you earlier this evening." Gluckman managed an insincere smile. "As soon as you've answered my questions, you can clean up and go home." He smiled again. "Give me a hard time and you're dead."

Drummond looked around the room at Trostler, Meier, and the other man, and decided that giving them a hard time was the last thing he wanted to do.

"Okay," he croaked. "What do you want to know?"

"I want to know everything you know about this man. . . ." Gluckman held up a faded photograph of a man in a Nazi uniform. "SS Sturmbannführer Wilhelm Kluge."

It was late afternoon when the Mercedes 500SLC pulled to the side of the road just a few miles outside the small German town of Paderborn. The door on the passenger side opened, and two young men in hiking boots, short pants, and thick pullovers climbed out and went to the back of the car. From inside, the driver released the trunk latch so the two young men could retrieve a pair of knapsacks. Slinging these on their backs, they set off purposefully in the direction of Wewelsberg Castle, little more than a kilometer away. In the rearview mirror, the driver of the Mercedes watched until the two hikers vanished into the forest. Adjusting his eye-patch, Scharführer

Baumann then shifted the dark blue Mercedes into gear and drove on into town.

Darkness was just settling when the hikers arrived at the castle. As they walked into the courtyard they saw Stephen Dornberger sitting on a stool, smoking a crooked Dutch cigar.

"Hello, Uncle Stephen," the taller one said. "Have you got a room for me and Erik?"

"Yes," Dornberger said. "The same as last time."

"Anyone else in there?" Erik asked.

"Just you and Karl and the young man I phoned about." Dornberger blew a stream of smoke toward the pale slice of moon showing from behind ink black clouds.

"Good. What's he look like?" Erik asked.

"About your height, but not as broad shouldered." Dornberger took a long pull on his cigar, its end glowing red in the darkness. "He has blond hair and a dueling scar."

Karl gave a soft chuckle. "Baumann should like that."

A lopsided grin crossed Erik's face. "Better take us in and let us introduce ourselves, Uncle."

Anton von Tupilow was stretched out on his bunk reading when Erik and Karl came in and tossed down their knapsacks. Walking over to the bunk, Erik stuck out his hand.

"Hi. Erik Klaussen. Hope you don't mind the invasion."

"Not at all." The other took his hand and shook it. "I'm Anton von Tupilow."

"Karl Braun," said the other hiker, as he walked over to where Anton had propped himself up on one elbow. "What brings you to Wewelsberg?"

"Mostly my old motorbike," Anton said. "And a bit of curiosity."

"Curiosity?" asked Karl.

"Well, yes. Old castles are a hobby of mine, and I was interested to see this one, since it was restored before the war."

"Do you know why it was restored?" Erik asked.

"Well, first because it was a ruin," Anton replied with a grin, "but I've also heard that Himmler, the head of the SS, thought that it had magical powers."

Erik had flopped down on the bunk under Anton's. "Magical powers?" he said. "Really? What sort of magical powers?"

"Well, according to the legends, this castle could never fall to invaders from the East. So Himmler decided that it should become the grand commandery of an order of SS knights. He personally selected twelve SS officers as the foundation of his black order of knights, and four times a year they used to gather here at the castle." Anton sat up cross-legged on his bunk. "It must have been something to see."

"It was," Karl said.

"Oh," said Anton, "you've seen photos?"

"Better," Karl replied. "The caretaker is my uncle. He gave me a tour of the place about two years ago."

"Really? God, I'd love to see the rooms upstairs. They're supposed to have been spectacular." Anton's request hung in the air for several long seconds before Karl replied.

"I could ask my uncle for the keys, if I thought I could trust you." He looked levelly at Anton.

"What do you mean, 'trust me'? What's that supposed to mean?" Anton sounded almost offended.

"Just this: Erik and I—"

"Don't tell him, Karl," Erik's voice interrupted, coming up from beneath Anton's bunk, challenging him to be part of their secret. "It could get us in trouble."

"I give my word of honor, as a von Tupilow, that I will not betray any confidences given to me this evening."

Looking at Anton's face as he spoke, Karl knew that it was time to spring the trap.

"You have a scar on your face." Involuntarily, Anton's hand reached up to the thin white line that ran, razor-straight, across his cheek. "Do you belong to a dueling fraternity?"

"I am a member of the Student Corporation Lutzow. Why do you ask?" Anton said cautiously.

"Because I am going to ask you to swear on the honor of Germany never to betray what you may see here." Karl stared deep into Anton's eyes, looking for a flicker of hesitation. He saw none. "Do you swear?"

"I swear it," Anton said.

Karl took a deep breath and looked at Erik sprawled across the bunk below Anton. Erik shot Karl his lopsided grin and gave him a thumbs-up.

"Then I'll go get the keys." Karl turned and vanished down the stone stairs that led to the castle courtyard.

Anton leaned over the edge of his bunk, trying to get a glimpse of Karl's partner. "Hey, Erik, have you ever seen the castle before?" he asked.

"No," Erik lied. "I haven't. It will be a first for both of us tonight."

"What did you mean when you said it might get you and Karl into trouble if I saw the upper floors of the castle?" Anton asked.

"Karl and I are here to help clean up and restore some of the rooms as they were before the war. If word got out that someone was restoring an SS shrine, we could all be in big trouble." Erik could faintly hear Anton's blood pulsing through his veins as he lay on the bunk above him.

"Well, you certainly don't have to worry about me on

that score," Anton said. "My grandfather was in the SS, and after the war the Russians shot him and confiscated our estates. Besides, that was long ago. Now all of this is 'just history,' as they say at the university." Anton dropped down onto the stone floor next to the bunks as Karl came in with a key ring and three flashlights.

"Here," he said, handing each of them a flashlight. "We're going to need these. My uncle turns off the power at ten." As if on cue, the lights in the dorm went out.

"Well," Anton said in the darkness, "let the tour begin."

Flicking on his flashlight, Karl motioned for Anton and Erik to follow.

"After the war, the British tried to destroy the castle, but they weren't totally successful," he said. The beams from the three flashlights bounced off the white tile walls of the shower room as Karl led them through the dorm and into a long passageway. "They smashed up everything they could get hold of, and then they tried to set fire to the castle before they left." At the end of the passage Karl took them up another flight of stone stairs.

"So was everything destroyed by the British?" Anton asked.

"Oh, no. In 1944, the SS crated up a lot of stuff and loaded it onto trucks, then drove up into the hills, where they hid it in some caves. Afterwards, when they came back, they had my Uncle Stephen brick up the doors to all of the rooms on the top two floors. The British managed to break into all of the rooms, except one." Karl shone his flashlight on an oak door studded with iron nails. "They thought they'd found everything, when they broke into the great hall and the crypt beneath, but the true inner sanctum was never violated."

He fitted a large key into the lock, turned it, then

swung the door open. The shining lights revealed a damaged toilet and a couple of old mops and buckets.

"This is the inner sanctum?" Anton asked.

"No," Karl replied. "This is the landing at the bottom of the stair that leads to it. When my uncle bricked up the stair, it made this little room, which he finished off to look like a toilet. When the British came, they didn't think to knock down the walls, so they never found Himmler's secret knights' chamber."

He sat down on the floor and, placing his feet against one corner of the wall, gave a mighty push. The bricks tumbled in, revealing a hole in the wall just big enough to crawl through.

"Okay, follow me."

The three young men scuttled through the opening and found themselves at the base of a wide turnpike stair that spiraled up and to their right. Leading the way, Karl continued his story.

"Once things settled back to normal, my Uncle Stephen became the caretaker of the castle, waiting for the day when the SS knights would return." They had reached another locked door, and it took Karl several tries to find the right key. Unlocking the door, he turned to Anton and Erik before entering the room.

"Erik, give me your lighter. You and Anton wait here, I'll be right back."

Taking Erik's lighter, Karl eased himself past the door and vanished into the knights' chamber. Erik switched off his flashlight and sat down on the stone steps.

"You'd better turn off your torch if you want to be able to see on the way back down."

Obediently Anton turned off his flashlight, and at once they were plunged into darkness.

"Anton." Erik's deep voice was low, barely more than a

softly spoken whisper. "You were talking about the SS knights back in the dorm. What do you know about them?"

In the darkness, Erik could see Anton shake his head as clearly as if they were sitting outside in the moonlight.

"Just what I've already told you," Anton said. "I guess the war ended the order."

"Well, you're wrong." It was Karl's voice coming through the darkness and Anton jumped at the sound of it. "Sure, Himmler and most of the original knights didn't survive the war, but a few did. And they preserved the order. See for yourself." Swinging wide the door to the knights' chamber, Karl revealed an oak paneled room illuminated by the glow of a dozen thick candles.

For a moment, Anton von Tupilow was speechless.

"My God, it's beautiful."

In the middle of the room, surrounded by twelve high-backed chairs, stood the round table of Himmler's order of knighthood, its edge inlaid with runes picked out in ivory. SS daggers lay on the polished wood before each place, the flickering candlelight shimmering off more runes damascened on the blades in gold, the tips pointing toward the gold- and jewel-encrusted chalice from which the knights drank their blood-oath of communion. In the dim shadows beyond the table, Anton could make out the black-and-silver labrium of the SS and the blood-red flag of the Third Reich, with its black swastika on a white roundel. He did not know if it was the original *Blutfahne*, but it should have been, in this holy place.

"This is fantastic," Anton said softly, stepping closer to the table. "I had no idea such a place existed."

"That's why we're here," Karl said. "To see to it that our order lasts for all eternity."

"Are you telling me that the SS still exists?" Anton asked in disbelief.

"Not the SS," Erik said, "but the order it founded. The *Blutorden*."

"That's right, Anton: the Knights of the Blood," Karl added.

"But aren't they one and the same?" Anton asked.

"Not at all. The *Blutorden* was an inner order, like a religion within a religion. Their ties weren't to Hitler, but to the blood and soil of Germany, to the soul of our race." Karl stepped up next to Anton. "Join us, Anton. Honor your grandfather's memory. Become one of us."

Drummond's mouth felt like it was coated with lint. Now feeling the full effect of the stimulant they had given him, he found himself wide awake with a splitting headache.

"Now, Mr. Drummond, for the last time, why did you go to the Weisenthal Center?" Gluckman stared sympathetically at his hostage.

"Because I thought Sacher did a shitty job investigating Stucke's death."

"What made you think that?" Trostler interrupted.

"Because he chalked it up to suicide, but there wasn't any blood on the walls. The body was in the bathtub, but the walls were clean."

"So?" Gluckman said.

Drummond sighed, impatient despite his discomfort.

"When someone's throat gets cut, they spray the walls with their blood. But not in Stucke's place. The walls were as clean as if they'd been washed down the week before. So I figured Stucke had been killed somewhere else and his body brought back to the apartment to make it look like suicide." Drummond's arms ached from being taped to the chair arms. "So I went back the next day and had another look around."

"Wasn't that a little odd, Mr. Drummond?" Gluckman asked.

"Not if you're a cop. And it did confirm my suspicions about the crime." Drummond cleared his throat. "Most of Stucke's things were still in his flat, except his shoes. His watch, yes; his shoes, no. I figure that he was killed elsewhere, stripped, and brought back to the apartment.

"Then, under the bed, I found a box full of girlie magazines and a scrapbook full of clippings about Nazi war criminals. In the scrapbook was a receipt from the Weisenthal Center. Stucke had ordered a copy of the file on this guy Kluge, but it wasn't in his flat. So, I went to the Weisenthal Center to get a copy of the file to see if it might provide a lead in Stucke's murder."

"So you think Kluge did it, Mr. Drummond?" Gluckman asked.

"No, he'd be too old. I figure he must be about seventy, maybe seventy-five years old. Killing Stucke and lugging his body up two flights of stairs would require a lot more strength than an old man is apt to possess.

"No, if Kluge was involved at all, he ordered someone to kill Stucke and then place the body in the shower." Drummond's throat was raw from the drugs they had given him. "Can I have a drink of water?" he asked.

Gluckman turned to Meier. "Bring Mr. Drummond a glass of water."

He closed his eyes briefly while he waited, rousing when Meier held a paper cup to his lips, carefully tilting it back so the cool water could trickle down his throat. As he swallowed the last of the water, the old man at the table stood up and crossed over to Gluckman. Peering at Drummond through owlish spectacles taped together at the bridge of the nose, he said something in Yiddish to Gluckman, who merely grunted in reply.

"Mr. Drummond." The old man's gravelly voice and Eastern European accent made it difficult for Drummond to follow everything he said next. "Do you believe in *wampyrs*?"

"Do you mean like in the movies?" Drummond asked.

"Don't get cute with us, Drummond." Meier's voice had a nasty edge to it.

"Mr. Drummond," Gluckman interjected, "Dr. Rubinsky worked in a very special hospital in the Soviet Union before he moved to Israel. Kluge was a patient at that hospital for a number of years before he escaped. Please, treat his questions with respect."

"No, Dr. Rubinsky, I don't believe in vampires," Drummond said.

"Well, maybe you should," Rubinsky replied. "Let me tell you about my hospital work in Russia. After the war, there were nearly half a million men in our prisoner of war camps. Stalin decided that only about half of those should be sent back. The rest—well, they were to be vanished." Rubinsky pushed his glasses up onto his forehead and rubbed his eyes before continuing.

"One day in 1946, several dozen 'vanished' Germans were brought to my hospital under heavy guard and put in a special isolation wing. A medical commissar arrived with them and told us that we were to use whatever means were medically necessary to discover what made these men 'special.'" Rubinsky rubbed his hands together and leaned closer to Drummond. "Do you know why they were special, Mr. Drummond?"

Drummond looked at the stooped little man with the bald head and broken glasses and wondered how sane he was. "Let me guess, Dr. Rubinsky. They were vampires?"

"That's a good guess, Mr. Drummond. They were *wampyrs*," Rubinsky said. "And for the next nineteen years, I studied them every day, trying to find out all about them. Some we dissected, and some we starved to death. Some we kept fat and hoped to learn their secrets. Finally came the big breakthrough. One of our researchers discovered that their blood was infected with a virus." He paused and leaned close to Drummond. "You don't know anything about virology, do you?"

" 'Fraid not, Doctor."

"Well, one of my colleagues was a veterinarian, and he noticed that the virus was similar to an equine disease found in some Cossack horses. So I postulated that *wampyrs* might have been infected with a mutated form of this equine virus."

"Equine virus," Drummond repeated.

"It makes perfect sense, Mr. Drummond," Rubinsky went on. "Stories about *wampyrs* have been part of European folklore since the time of the crusades. These same stories have been part of the Eastern folklore tradition for far longer. So where did they originate, and how did they propagate?"

Drummond shook his head.

"I'll tell you. When the nomads of Mongolia moved west toward Europe, they were mounted on the ponies that became the Cossack horse. On the march, these Mongol warriors used to drink the blood of their horses to give them extra strength and energy. Not more than a few swallows at a time, because they needed the horses.

"But I maintain that one of these warriors drank the blood of an infected horse, and—it's a million to one occurrence—the virus mutated and took hold in his body. In a society of warriors who regularly drank the blood of their foes, as well as the blood of their horses, a *wampyr* would pass unnoticed. Unnoticed, that is, until he came into contact with Western civilization." Rubinsky smiled like a university professor lecturing to freshmen.

"So, Mr. Drummond, when did these cultures clash? I'll tell you. During the crusades. The Seljuk Turks were the descendants of the Mongol horde, just as the Norman crusaders were descendants of Viking raiders. At some time during the crusades, our Mongol *wampyr* met a crusader whom he infected—don't ask me how—and that man returned as the first European *wampyr*."

"Did Kluge tell you all of this?" Drummond asked.

"Not hardly. Kluge and his men were most uncooperative. In fact, we kept them alive only as a source of infected blood, so we could try to clone the virus for military purposes," Rubinsky replied.

"If it's not a state secret, what possible use could a vampire have been to the Red Army?" Drummond asked.

"Well, the virus has several beneficial side effects," Rubinsky replied. "First, it causes the adrenal gland to enlarge and produce a highly concentrated burst of energy to the *wampyr*. This accounts for their legendary feats of strength. Second, it accelerates the healing process, giving *wampyrs* the appearance of invulnerability. A cut—or a bullet wound—heals in a matter of minutes, sometimes seconds. Certainly these are two great assets for any soldier to possess. Finally, the *wampyr* has greatly improved night vision and superior hearing. These reasons I don't know why. My specialty was the virus, not what it did."

"You said the virus had beneficial side effects," Drummond said. "What was the downside to infection?"

"The virus greatly retards the aging process, so long as the *wampyr* is given a few ounces of blood a week. But if the blood is withheld, the aging process accelerates. Aging can take place at a rate of five or ten years in a week or less. This process is very painful and leads to insanity at the end. Without blood, a *wampyr* dies in not more than a month." Rubinsky pushed his glasses back down on his nose. "That, as you say it, is the downside, Mr. Drummond." Dr. Rubinsky walked back to the table and sat down between Trostler and Meier.

"Now, Mr. Drummond," Gluckman asked again, "do you believe in vampires?"

"I'm afraid I'm still a skeptic." Drummond stared at Gluckman sitting on the edge of the bed.

"Mr. Drummond, when you were attacked in your hotel room at Palais Schwarzenberg in Vienna, were you attacked by a vampire?"

Gluckman saw the flash of surprise race across Drummond's face.

"Come, come, now. Was the man who attacked you a vampire? Could he have been one of Kluge's men?"

Drummond swallowed several times before replying.

"He might have been one of Kluge's men." In his mind's eye, Drummond could see the young man impaled on the wrought iron spikes of the fence below his balcony pushing himself up off the spikes and running away into the night. "But even if he was a vampire, what could I do about it?"

Gluckman stared at Drummond for several seconds before signaling to Meier. The Mossad agent stood up and, reaching into his pocket, brought out a straightedge razor similar to the one found in the tub with Stucke's body. With a snap of his wrist, he flicked the blade open and walked over to where Drummond sat taped to the chair.

"What could you do about the vampire, Mr. Drummond? For starters, you can go in the bathroom and clean up." Gluckman signaled again to Meier, who bent down and cut Drummond free.

CHAPTER 7

Lev Shapiro was looking at the Christie's auction catalog with a magnifying glass when he heard the muffled purr of his fax machine starting up. Setting down the catalog next to a pile of first-day covers, he shuffled across the floor of his small stamp shop in Jerusalem and went into the back room.

The fax machine was wedged between two scuffed leather stamp albums. Shapiro played absently with one of his sidelocks as the message slowly scrolled out from the machine, nodding to himself. The machine buzzed, once the six-line message had been received, and Shapiro picked it up from the basket and carefully folded it into a small packet, placing it in the pocket of the long overcoat he habitually wore.

Putting an advertisement for an upcoming stamp auction in the machine, Shapiro keyed in a fax number used by the Mossad in one of their many drops in Jerusalem. His thin finger pressed the "send" button, and once the machine made contact he put on a wide-brimmed black hat and headed out of the shop to the Wailing Wall.

It was hot, but it was always hot in Jerusalem in late September. Walking up to the Wailing Wall, Shapiro took the folded fax and tucked it into a crack, then began to pray, rocking back and forth on his heels.

After about ten minutes, a nondescript-looking man in his mid-thirties joined Shapiro in his devotions, a blue-and-white crocheted yarmulke bobby-pinned to the back of his head. Like the stamp dealer, he too reached up to the wall as if to place a prayer in one of the cracks. Instead, his heavily scarred hand took away the fax that Shapiro had stuck into the wall.

Seeing the message delivered, Shapiro finished his prayers and left the wall. A few minutes later, the man in the blue-and-white yarmulke also finished praying and headed off deeper into the Old City. Across the square from the Wailing Wall, the transaction had been observed by an Orthodox Christian priest, Father Archimedes Santos, who waited until his quarry had nearly disappeared into the crowds before heaving his bulk off the rickety bench where he had been seated.

The house was in the Christian quarter of the Old City, one of the buildings bought by some nameless front organization with secret Israeli government funds in an ongoing program of displacing the dwindling Christian population. Father Archimedes also knew it to be a Mossad safe house. He snorted in anger as he saw the agent head up the side stairs and enter the house above the abandoned shop on street level. Sitting down at a small table outside a cafe across the street, he ordered a coffee from the Palestinian Christian owner and settled in to wait for the Mossad agent to come out again.

"So, Eli, what have we got from the stamp man?" Golda Sapperstein said, lighting another cigarette from the butt of the one she had just finished.

The messenger handed her the folded fax. "I don't know, Major. I don't read them. I just deliver them."

Major Sapperstein coughed as she blew a lungful of

smoke into the room. "Well," she said, "let's see what our man in Los Angeles has to say for himself." She unfolded the fax and read the message scrawled in Hebrew across the page.

Have interviewed subject and feel he was not aware of intended target of attempted hijack. I do not think subject will connect our visit with assassination attempt, nor do I feel subject will agree to work for us later. Please advise.

Sapperstein leaned back in her chair and rolled her cigarette between nicotine-stained fingers.

"Eli," she said after several minutes, "I want an opinion. We spent several years setting up a PLO hit man to take out a major player." She took a long drag on her cigarette. "Very clean operation. It would have looked like an airline hijacking that went sour. Everything goes according to plan, except that at the last minute, some schmuck cop takes out our man at thirty-five thousand feet.

"Now, that might be coincidence, except that when we check this putz out, we find that he's been fuckin' around Vienna with a lot of Nazi types. So we pick him up, ask him a few questions, and turn him loose—the usual." She lit another cigarette. "I don't like this dick-head wandering around. What do you think?"

"An eye for an eye. He cost us one of ours, so he pays." Eli scratched the back of his scarred hand. "They shoulda killed the goy."

Sapperstein stubbed out her cigarette and pulled a notepad out of her desk, scribbling a brief message in Hebrew.

"Here," she said, handing the message to Eli. "Take this to the stamp man and tell him it's for his customer in Los Angeles."

Outside, Father Archimedes watched as Eli came out of the safe house and headed back down the narrow street. At the bottom of the hill, he turned into the Jewish Quarter of the Old City and made his way through the winding lanes to Shapiro's stamp shop, unaware of his priestly shadow.

Shapiro was carefully lifting stamps out of an old album when Eli entered the shop.

"Hello," he said without bothering to look up. "I'll be right with you." Holding the stamp with a pair of tweezers, he carefully slipped it into a small glassine envelope before looking up at Eli.

"Well?" he said.

"My boss wants to sell some stamps. Said you might have a customer in Los Angeles who'd be interested."

Eli handed over Golda Sapperstein's message, which Shapiro read before answering.

"First-day covers with a double cancellation aren't much, but I'll see what I can do." Shapiro looked at his watch. "I'll send this now, but I wouldn't expect a reply for maybe a day. I'll call you if my client wants your stamps."

Eli left the shop and headed back up the hill toward the Christian quarter. As he passed by the small Orthodox Church of the Blessed Sorrows, two priests were coming out of the door. As Eli brushed past, one of the priests threw his thick silk cincture around the Mossad agent's throat, while the other drove his fist into the man's kidneys.

Eli sank to his knees without so much as a groan, and the two priests dragged him quickly into the church. Hustling him to a small stair behind the altar, they manhandled him down into the undercroft and from there into the crypt.

"Tie him to the chair, Dimitri," the taller of the priests said, his silk cincture still digging into Eli's neck.

The other priest looped half-hitches of rope around the subject's wrists, securing him to the chair arms, then knelt to tie the ankles.

"Don't kill him, Bartholomew," he said, as he tightened the knots binding Eli's feet to the chair legs.

"Just put some tape over his mouth," Bartholomew said. "I don't want him yelling until I'm ready."

Producing a roll of silver duct tape, Father Dimitri tore off a six-inch section and plastered it over Eli's mouth.

"Now what?" he asked, nervous perspiration rolling off his forehead.

"Now, when he comes to, I ask him questions. Just watch," Bartholomew replied.

He loosened the cincture around their captive's neck. Eli's cheeks began to color as the blood rushed to his head, and his dull eyes popped open wide as he regained awareness. Seeing that the Mossad agent was conscious, Bartholomew slapped him across the face hard enough to send a gush of blood rushing from his nose.

"Now listen to me, you goddamsonofabitch," Bartholomew said to Eli in Hebrew. "I'm going to do things to you that'll make the priest over there throw up, if you don't answer my questions. Understand?"

Eli glared contemptuously at Bartholomew, who leaned closer and said, "Don't fuck with me, Jew, or I'll hand you over to the PLO when I'm finished." Bartholomew suddenly hit him again, turning Eli's nose into an unrecognizable pulp.

Behind him, Dimitri gagged.

"Now then. We are going to have a contest. In twenty-five words or less, what did the message say that you picked up at the Wailing Wall?" His fist slammed into

Eli's face again, then he ripped the tape off his lips. "Well?" Bartholomew said. "What did it say?"

"Fuck you . . ."

"Wrong answer, asshole," Bartholomew said, grabbing one of Eli's fingers and dislocating it.

Eli screamed with the pain, and Bartholomew hit him again.

"Oh, for God's sake!" Dimitri began, trying to pull Bartholomew away from Eli.

"Exactly," Bartholomew said, shaking off the smaller man. "It's for God's sake that I'm asking these questions. Now," he said, turning his attention back to Eli. "What was in those messages?"

"Like I said," Eli mumbled, "ff . . . aaaahhh!"

Bartholomew held up Eli's little finger before his eyes. "Do you see this?" He flung the finger on the floor. "Now, I'm going to rip your cock off next, if you don't answer my question. And then, while you're sitting there wondering what life's going to be like without a cock, I'll gouge your eyes out." Bartholomew shoved his hand down inside Eli's trousers and grabbed him, yanking upward. "So, what did the message say?"

"It's about some cop," Eli gasped.

"A cop? Where? Tell me more," Bartholomew said, his grip on Eli tightening.

"In Los Angeles. I don't know his name!" Eli was on the verge of passing out from the pain. "He prevented our hijacking a plane . . ."

Bartholomew twisted Eli until he screamed in terror.

"One of our agents was killed . . . oh, God . . . please stop . . . please . . ." Eli was whimpering, blood and tears washing down his face onto Bartholomew's black sleeve.

"What else?" Bartholomew demanded.

"Sapperstein told our team in Los Angeles to kill

him. . . ." Eli was panting heavily. "That's all. I swear to God, that's all!"

Bartholomew let go of Eli. "That wasn't so bad, was it? I didn't even have to make the priest puke."

Eli's head rolled forward, and Bartholomew could tell that he was on the edge of unconsciousness. Reaching into his cassock, he pulled out a switchblade and flicked open the blade, deftly stabbing it deep behind Eli's ear. The Mossad agent died almost instantly.

In the corner of the crypt, Dimitri retched.

"How could you?" he said, looking up at the other priest through tear-filled eyes. "How could you?"

"Easy. My school was run by the Christian Brothers." Bartholomew wiped the blade of his knife on Eli's chest. "Help me put this scum in one of these coffins, will you, Father? And then, maybe you could show me where the telephone is."

CHAPTER 8

Dragging himself out of bed the next morning was a major effort. Drummond's head pounded like an out-of-balance washing machine, the residual effect of the drugs used by the Mossad agents the night before. He sat with his head in his hands for a few minutes, then picked up his watch from the nightstand next to the bed.

9:45. He was late.

Taking a deep breath, he stood up and headed into the bathroom. Five minutes under a hot shower didn't make him feel like a new man, but at least it reassured him that he was going to pull through. He didn't want to think about the night before. Not yet.

Towelling off and dressing quickly, Drummond was ready to head out the door by ten. The rain lashing against the sliding glass doors sent him back to the closet for his Australian rain slicker and bush hat. The dark brown waxed-linen coat was perfect for a heavy rain in Los Angeles. Lightweight, ankle-length, and with a shoulder cape that reached to the elbows, it kept him comfortable, dry, and stylish even in the worst downpour. Throwing it on over his gray double-breasted suit, Drummond headed down to his BMW parked under his beach-front condominium.

Once he was through the security gates and out onto

Pacific Coast Highway, Drummond picked up his cellular telephone and called his office.

"Hi, Alicia? I'm running late—yeah, stayed up late reading that Mossad garbage and overslept. Be there in about an hour."

Drummond clicked off the phone and pointed the car in the general direction of Santa Monica. Despite the relative lack of traffic, he kept the speed down to a modest fifty miles an hour. Tuning in KFAC, he let the classical music drown out the slapping of his windshield wipers as he decided what to do about the events of the last twenty-four hours. The question looming large in his mind as he sped along the coast toward the Santa Monica Freeway was whether or not to report last night's kidnapping.

Gluckman, Trostler, Meier, and Rubinsky probably had ironclad alibis for last night. Even if they didn't, Drummond reasoned, after yesterday's confrontation in his office, any action on his part could be made to look like an attempt to get even for blowing the whistle on his Nazi connections.

Drummond had just turned down Lincoln Boulevard when it dawned on him: he'd been set up.

The whole thing, from Meier and Trostler's clumsy shakedown in his office to the report handed to IAD. The whole thing was a setup so they could grab him, question him about Kluge, and deny any of it ever took place if he complained to the cops.

Besides, who'd believe it, even if none of them had an alibi? He could just imagine it.

"Okay, Captain Drummond. Now, about this business with the Nazi vampires . . ."

The police psychiatrist would have a field day. The bastards were clever, goddam 'em. Drummond decided he'd have to give them that much. And they weren't after

Kluge just because he was a Nazi. Israeli vampire killers? Naaah.

Pulling off the freeway a few blocks from Parker Center, Drummond slithered his way through the traffic, crawling along in the heavy rain to the underground parking structure beneath his office. He put the red BMW in its usual parking place, then headed up to homicide on the second floor.

Yesterday's mound of paperwork was still waiting for him. Tossing his coat and hat on the chair nearest the door, he settled down unenthusiastically to deal with it, a part of his mind still preoccupied by what had happened the night before. Half an hour later, he had worked his way through half a dozen field reports when Sandy Morwood stuck his head around the door. "Hey, John, you headed out for lunch?" the agent asked.

"No, not today." Drummond looked up from his paperwork. "I didn't get in until after eleven, and I've got to get all of this off to payroll by three-thirty."

"Okay then," Morwood said. "Can I bring you back anything?"

"Sure. A big cup of the white clam chowder and an iced tea." Drummond opened his desk drawer and fished out two dollar bills. "This ought to cover it."

"Got it," Morwood said, taking the bills from Drummond's outstretched hand. "Hey, you haven't got an umbrella, have you?"

Drummond grinned and shook his head. "No, but you can borrow my hat and coat, if you want."

"Thanks," Morwood said, scooping up the slouch hat and waxed-linen rain slicker. "Oh, I almost forgot. This came in for you on FLASH this morning." He reached into his pocket and pulled out a piece of paper that he tossed on Drummond's desk. "It's from some bank in

Austria." Putting on Drummond's hat and slicker, he headed out the door.

Outside it was raining harder than ever, and the few pedestrians on the street were huddled under awnings or slogging resolutely on despite the rain. Looking at the soggy people crowded together waiting for a steamy RTD "people mover," Morwood was glad that Drummond had loaned him his rain gear. He liked Drummond's sense of style. Pulling the slouch hat farther over his eyes, he stayed just under the overhang that sheltered the apron outside Parker Center, waiting until the pedestrian light had changed before dashing out into the downpour to cross Los Angeles Street.

Half a block away, a man in a baggy black raincoat stood under the awning in front of a travel agent's, watching the figure in the brown waxed-linen rain slicker and slouch hat splash along 1st Street and run into a restaurant called the Nightwatch. Turning up the collar of his coat, he stepped out into the rain and walked in that direction.

Morwood stamped his feet as he came in out of the rain, but he didn't take off Drummond's rain gear. Despite the weather, the restaurant was packed with its usual clientele of cops: those going off duty, who stopped in for a coffee and some conversation with pals working the same shift, and the staff from police headquarters across the street, who wanted to stay in touch with the constantly changing L.A. street scene.

Morwood found an empty stool at the counter and sat down, waiting for Paula to find a moment to take his order. Staring at his reflection in the mirror in the back of the cold box, he pulled down the brim of his hat and turned up the collar of the rain slicker. Squinting his eyes, he imagined himself Clint Eastwood in a spaghetti Western.

"Go ahead, punk, make my day," he muttered to himself, as a stocky man in a baggy black raincoat entered the Nightwatch and walked past him, headed toward the telephones in the back of the restaurant.

The stocky man fished in his pocket for some coins, inserted them in the phone, and dialed a number. He waited a few seconds, then spoke briefly into the receiver before replacing the handset. Turning back to the counter, he pulled a small Uzi machine gun out from under his coat and holding it muzzle down, close to his leg, walked toward the door. As he passed by Morwood, he brought the gun up and fired a short burst into his back.

The force of the bullets' impact drove Morwood forward, sending him sprawling over the counter. The last of the empty brass cartridges cascading from the Uzi hadn't hit the floor before all hell broke loose. From a dozen different directions, policemen drew their pistols and opened fire. The man in the black raincoat tried to make it to the door, but he was already badly wounded. Staggering forward, he crashed through the steamy glass door and lurched toward a convertible waiting at the curb, its top down in the heavy rain.

Behind the wheel of the convertible, Trostler watched Meier burst through the glass door of the Nightwatch and stagger toward the getaway car. Bringing his hand up even with his shoulder, he pointed his pistol at his mortally wounded partner and fired two quick rounds into his head. Then he dropped his weapon on the floor of the car, gunned the convertible into traffic, and headed toward Los Angeles Street and Parker Center.

From inside the restaurant, half a dozen officers poured out onto the sidewalk, firing after the speeding car. Using a two-handed combat stance, one of the policemen cocked his gun and, taking careful aim at the back of Trostler's head, squeezed the trigger of his service revolver.

The 130-grain hollow-point bullet smashed into the back of Trostler's skull like a sledge hammer hitting an egg. The car slewed sideways on the rain slick street and jumped the curb, skidding through a rank of newspaper racks before slamming to a halt against a telephone pole, the dead Mossad agent slumped over the steering wheel.

Drummond waited patiently on hold until Nance Hamilton was able to take his call. Drumming his fingers idly, he wondered how much longer it would be before Morwood put in an appearance with his clam chowder. At this point, his headache could be as much from hunger as from aftereffects of the drugs of the night before.

"Hi, John. How was Europe?" Nance Hamilton's voice sounded as if the sun was shining wherever she was, though her office was only down the street.

"Europe was great," he said. "In fact, I'm thinking about buying some property there and wondered how much I've got in the money market account with your office." Drummond stared out the window at the dark gray sky and lashing rain.

"Well, pushing a couple of magic buttons here at my desk . . ." Nance Hamilton paused for just a moment. "A smidgen more than four hundred thousand," she said. "Do you want to convert to another currency?"

"Yes, I think so. I'd like to put two hundred fifty thousand into an Austrian bank. What's the best way to do it?" Nance Hamilton was probably the smartest trader in L.A., and Drummond knew he could rely on her advice.

"Gold is the best, John. We'll buy bullion here and exchange it for bullion there. The transaction will cost you less than traveler's checks." There was just a hint of smugness in Nance's voice. "Best of all, its untraceable—just in case."

"The bank in Vienna will accept a gold deposit?" Drummond asked.

"Best banks in the world are in Austria; they love gold." Nance Hamilton made the word "gold" sound seductive. "Just give me the account number, and the transaction will be complete in two hours."

Drummond read her the numbers provided by Eberle's sister at the Vienna Credit Bank and thanked Nance for taking care of the transfer of funds.

"Don't mention it, John," she laughed. "That's what the point-oh-five percent is for."

Drummond set down the phone just as Commander DeGrazzio walked into his office, looking grim.

"John, Sandy Morwood's been shot." Anxiety tinged DeGrazzio's voice. "Some bastard blasted him in the Nightwatch."

Stunned, it took Drummond several seconds to respond. "Is he all right?"

"Yeah, but he could be a lot better. His bullet-proof vest stopped the slugs, but there's a lot of bruising and possibly some damage to the spine from the impact."

"Then, he was hit more than once?" Drummond asked, relieved that at least Morwood hadn't been killed.

"I'll say. He took a short burst from an Uzi at about six inches."

"Jesus, that sounds like a professional hit." Drummond shook his head. "Any idea who'd want to take out Morwood?"

DeGrazzio put his hand on Drummond's shoulder. "Nobody."

"What do you mean?"

"They were after you, John. The hit man was one of those Mossad agents we had in here yesterday. His partner was waiting for him at the curb, but he never made it to the getaway car."

Drummond sank back in his chair. "But, how could— Jesus. He borrowed my rain gear."

"That's right," DeGrazzio said. "We figure that they spotted Morwood wearing that Australian rain slicker of yours, followed him into the restaurant, and blasted him." DeGrazzio looked at Drummond and breathed a heavy sigh.

"There's something else you should know," he said. "One of our guys popped the driver of the getaway car. When they pulled his body out of the wreck, this fell out of his pocket."

DeGrazzio produced a small black plastic device with a short aerial and a red micro switch.

"What is it?" Drummond said, though he knew in the pit of his stomach what the answer would be.

"It's a detonator. The bomb squad is down in the basement right now, defusing a couple of pounds of Semtex that's stuck to the chassis of your car." DeGrazzio put the detonator back in his pocket. "Just a guess, but they probably planted the bomb last night. You must've pissed them off more than we realized."

"Apparently so. But, why, Joey? What's it all about?" Drummond asked. *And why did they let me go last night, if they were just going to kill me today?* he added to himself.

"That's what Chief Lopez wants to know," DeGrazzio replied. "He's waiting for us in his office now."

Assistant Chief of Police Red Lopez had an FBI agent with him when Drummond and DeGrazzio arrived at his office.

"Special Agent Harris Raymunds," the black man identified himself, as he and Drummond shook hands.

"Have a seat, gentlemen," Lopez said when the formalities had been exchanged. "Agent Raymunds has been filling me in on the background of the two dead bodies we just sent over to the county morgue. I think you might be interested in what he has to say."

Raymunds' expression was almost wistful as he settled back into his chair and glanced at Drummond.

"The two dead men were Moishe Trostler and Abraham Meier, as you probably know from yesterday. What you may not know is that they were members of an elite Israeli death squad that's an unofficial part of the Mossad. Their usual task has been to hunt down and kill suspected Nazi war criminals, and until recently they'd confined their activities to central Europe and South America.

"Today's shooting is the first instance of their operating in the United States—as least as far as we are aware of. It's obvious that their intended victim wasn't Agent Morwood but Captain Drummond. The question is: why?" Agent Raymunds tucked his mahogany-colored hands behind his head and leaned back in his chair. "Can you shed any light on the subject, Captain Drummond?"

"No, Agent Raymunds, I can't," Drummond replied. He was not about to tell a federal agent about Nazi vampires, or last night's kidnapping—and the latter thought made him wonder again why they hadn't simply finished him last night while they had the chance.

"Well, then, for the moment," Raymunds continued, "I think we'd better get you as far out of town as possible, until Washington can sort this out with the Israelis." The burly black man turned to Chief Lopez. "If you've no objections, that is."

"Objections? Hell, no! I don't want any of my men offed by some goon squad hit men," Lopez said.

"Good." Raymunds' smile sliced across his face like a crescent moon on a dark night. "Captain Drummond, I assume you have a passport?"

"Sure. Why?" Drummond asked.

"There's a law enforcement convention in Stockholm next week, and you've just become a delegate." Agent Raymunds stood up. "Now, let's go back to your place and pack."

As the Los Angeles Police Department helicopter settled down on the beach outside of Drummond's apartment, Raymunds let out a low whistle.

"Lopez told me you had money, but he didn't tell me how much." He grinned at Drummond. "It must be fine."

"Only if I live long enough to spend it," Drummond replied as they dropped out of the chopper and, crouching low to avoid the whirling blades, trotted up the beach to his condo.

Inside, Drummond went straight to his bedroom closet and pulled out a pair of Gurka bags, then hastily began packing. Five minutes later, he had a week's worth of expensive clothes inside the pair of leather and canvas bags sitting in the middle of his kitchen floor. As an afterthought, he fetched a golf bag out of the hall closet and took it into the bedroom long enough to stuff de Beq's sword inside. Well wrapped in a couple of towels it just fit. He zipped the cover closed and secured the little padlock, pocketing the key, then took the bag out to join those waiting in the kitchen.

"Hey, is that Victoria what's-her-name from *Emergency Hospital,* sitting on the deck next to yours?" Raymunds asked from the living room.

"Victoria Riddenauer."

"What?" Raymunds asked.

"Her name is Victoria Riddenauer, and yes, she's my neighbor." Drummond rummaged in the refrigerator until he found a jar of mayonnaise. Unscrewing its lid, he pulled out a wad of hundred-dollar traveler's checks.

"You always keep your cold cash in the fridge?" Raymunds asked.

Drummond ignored the joke and replaced the jar in the back of the refrigerator. "No," he said, "I usually keep it in a snow bank." Turning around, he picked up his bags and headed toward the door.

"Say, John," Raymunds said. "If you don't mind my asking, how do you afford a place like this on a cop's salary?"

Drummond set down his bags and walked over to the bookcase. Reaching to the top shelf, he took down a framed photo and handed it to Raymunds.

Raymunds looked at the photo for several seconds. "This is Cathy Blair, isn't it?"

"Yes. She was my wife," Drummond said, taking the photo from Raymunds and returning it to the top shelf.

"You divorced?"

"No, not exactly. Cathy was injured on the set of her last movie. A stunt went wrong, and she's been in a coma ever since." Drummond picked up his bags. "The studio settled out of court for ten million, plus ongoing medical costs. You're right, I can't afford it on a cop's salary. Let's go."

The Pacific Ocean was the color of dirty pewter underneath the helicopter as it followed the coast from Malibu as far south as El Segundo. Swinging inland, the dark blue police chopper circled Los Angeles International Airport, landing at the police helipad behind the international departures terminal. The rain had stopped and the sun had come out with a vengeance, causing steam to rise from the concrete apron surrounding the airport buildings and pushing the humidity to uncomfortably high levels. Two airport security police met the helicopter and escorted Drummond and Raymunds to the air-conditioned comfort of the VIP lounge next to the British Airways departure gate.

Leaving Drummond by himself for a moment, Raymunds took Drummond's larger Gurka bag and the golf bag over to the ticket desk and collected what looked like a battered camera case. He came back to where Drummond had seated himself, opened the case, and took out an airline ticket wallet printed with the British Airways logo.

"Here are your tickets," he said as he handed Drummond the envelope. "You're already checked in. There's your boarding card. You're traveling under the name of John Olsen, just to be on the safe side." He reached back into the case and produced a Polaroid camera. "Sit still and look at the red dot above the lens." The micro flash went off, and Raymunds pulled out the exposed sheet of film.

"Let's hope this turned out okay," he said, looking at his watch. "Your plane leaves in about ten minutes, and I don't want to have to hold the flight while I mess with this. Meanwhile, here's an American Express card in the name of Olsen—you'd better sign it. And don't forget that you'll have to account for expenses when you get back."

As Drummond took out a pen and signed the card, putting it in his wallet, a timer beeped on the camera, and Raymunds peeled off the backing of the film.

"Not bad," he said, showing the picture to Drummond. There were four, actually, each the right size for a passport. "It almost looks like you."

Handing over one of the photos, he had Drummond sign it on the back with his new name while he rummaged further in the case and produced a U.S. passport, a sheet of transparent adhesive film, and an embossing seal. Placing the signed photo on the appropriate page of the passport, he deftly covered it with the transparent film, binding it in place. Then, using the handheld seal, he embossed the cartouche of the U.S. State Department on the edge of the photo.

"Now, if you'll just sign here again, Mr. Olsen," he said, handing Drummond the passport, open to the appropriate page.

Drummond signed his new name again, then pocketed his pen.

"Great," Raymunds said. "That should do you. You've even got five minutes left till takeoff. Have a good time in Stockholm, Mr. Olsen."

"Just one question," Drummond said as he shouldered his suit bag. "How long is this conference?"

"A week. Hopefully, we'll have everything sorted out by then. Check in with our embassy when the conference is over, and they'll give you an update on the situation." Raymunds extended his hand. "Bon voyage."

Drummond shook hands with the federal agent, who ushered him through a door marked RESTRICTED ENTRY that led directly to the gangway of his waiting aircraft, a British Airways 747 that would take him to London on the first leg of his journey to Stockholm.

Drummond slept most of the way to London. He had not really caught up on the jet lag of his flight home from Munich, much less from his bout with the Mossad agents' drugs, and he was a little disoriented as he woke up and had to remind himself that he was now in yet another time zone.

A slight drizzle was falling as the big plane set down at London's Heathrow Airport. He watched as the plane pulled up to the gate and the ground crew began connecting up the jetway. As he pulled his suit bag out of the closet in first class, the stewardess cheerfully asked him if he had brought his raincoat.

"No," Drummond replied, "I loaned it to a friend in L.A."

Inside the terminal building, Drummond claimed his other bags, cleared passport control and customs, and then found himself in the departures lobby, lugging his bags toward the check-in area for KLM Royal Dutch Airline. A Swedish couple and several British businessmen were in line ahead of him, and as Drummond waited for his turn at the check-in desk, he idly scanned the large departures board above the shops on the other side of the lobby, looking for his flight to Stockholm. As he ran his eyes down the list of cities, he spied a flight to Vienna leaving in less than an hour. Without hesitating, he picked up his bags and walked over to the Austrian Airlines ticket desk.

The young man behind the desk looked up from a mound of paperwork as Drummond set his bags down.

"Yes, sir, can I help you?"

"What's the chance of a seat on the next flight to Vienna?" Drummond asked.

The young man tapped away at the keyboard on his desk. "Only first class available, sir," he said.

"Fine. How much?" Drummond asked.

"One way or return, sir?"

"Open return, please."

"That will be six hundred forty pounds, sir."

Instinctively Drummond reached for a credit card, then thought better of using either of his current names. Looking around, he saw a *bureau de change* next to a small shop selling neckties.

"I'll be right back with the cash," he said.

Leaving his bags next to the counter, he walked over to the *bureau de change* and pulled out his traveler's checks. He started signing checks furiously, handing over a dozen in exchange for six hundred eighty-five pounds sterling and change from the girl behind the inch-thick glass.

Returning to the Austrian Airlines ticket desk, Drummond counted out six hundred forty pounds and handed it to the ticket agent.

"Name, please?" the young man asked.

"Markus Eberle," Drummond replied.

The computer on the desk printed out Drummond's ticket, and the young man tore it off the machine and stuffed it into a paper folder with a prancing Lipizzan printed on it.

"You can check in at counter number four, Mr. Eberle," the young man said as he handed over the ticket.

Drummond took the ticket and headed to counter four. Placing his bags on the conveyor belt, he handed the girl his ticket.

"Passport, please, Mr. Eberle," she said as she tore off the flight coupon.

"I beg your pardon?" Drummond said in what he hoped sounded like a German accent.

"I need to see your passport, some ID," the girl said.

"Ach. Okay." Drummond pulled out his wallet, took out Eberle's card, and handed it to the girl.

"Oh," she said. "You're an Austrian policeman. I thought you were an American by the way you were dressed." She handed back the card. "Boarding is at gate nine."

"Danke," Drummond said, taking Eberle's card and putting it in his wallet. *"Danke."*

On his way to gate nine, Drummond stopped at a pay phone and, running one of his credit cards through the channel on the side of the phone, called Eberle in Vienna.

"Hi, Markus?" Drummond said, when he finally got through to the detective's office.

"John, is that you? Must be pretty dull in L.A. for you to call twice in the same week," Eberle joked.

"I'll tell you all about it when I get in. Can you meet me at the airport in three hours?" Drummond asked.

"Three hours? This is kind of sudden isn't it?" Eberle said.

"I suppose it is," Drummond said. "I'll tell you all about it when I arrive."

"Okay. Do you want me to book you back in at the Palais Schwarzenberg?"

"Sure, that'll be fine. Tell them I'm back for a week, possibly two."

Drummond gave Eberle his flight number and then rang off. Looking at his watch, he hurried down to gate nine and his flight to Vienna.

CHAPTER 9

Vienna's Schwechat International Airport was about the same size as Phoenix's Sky Harbor, Drummond decided as he waited for his bags to slide along on the conveyer belt. As he stood in the crowded luggage return area, his suit bag over his shoulder, two smartly uniformed police officers walked up to him and saluted.

"Kapitän Drummond?" The policeman's tone of voice was more of a command than a question.

"Yes," Drummond replied.

"Inspector Eberle is waiting." He gestured toward the exit. "This way, please."

Flanked by the two policemen, one of whom relieved him of his suit bag, Drummond was escorted through customs and passport control and into the main lobby of the airport, where Markus Eberle stood smoking a cigar.

"John, it's good to see you," Eberle said as he grabbed Drummond by the elbow and shook his hand. "What brings you back to Vienna so soon?"

"I'm on my way to a symposium on violent crime being held in Sweden, and I thought I'd take a detour for a few days," Drummond replied.

"Sweden. Ah, those lovely blond ice-maidens. . . ." Eberle flashed Drummond a smile that featured two stainless-steel front teeth. "Give Arndt your tickets so he can collect your bags, and we'll head off to the hotel."

Drummond started to hand one of the policemen his ticket, then remembered that it was in Eberle's name. Quickly he tore off the luggage claim tags that had been stuck to the ticket envelope and handed him those instead.

"Here you are," Drummond said. "There's a golf bag and another one like this, but larger." He indicated the bag the other officer was holding. "Dark green canvas with russet leather trim."

Arndt saluted and moved off toward the baggage claim area with the other police officer in tow. Taking Drummond by the arm, Eberle led him toward the exit, pausing along the way to stub out his cigar in one of the stainless steel ashtrays bolted to the end of the counter at the Aeroflot ticket desk. As Eberle shot the Aeroflot sign an evil glance, Drummond noticed that Eberle seemed to grind out his cigar with an uncharacteristic vengeance.

"Not too happy with the cigar, huh?" he asked.

"It's not the cigar, my friend." Eberle jerked his head in the direction of the Aeroflot desk. "I hate Russians." His voice was loud enough to be heard by the manager behind the Aeroflot desk. "I was ten when the bastards finally left Vienna in 1955. I remember climbing up on the roof of our house and pissing on the troops as they marched out of the city carrying off everything that wasn't embedded in concrete. If I had my way, I wouldn't let them put a stinking foot in Austria for love or money."

"Sounds unpleasant," Drummond said, as they reached the doors leading out to the street.

"Unpleasant? Shit is unpleasant, and the Russians were worse than shit. They raped the women, killed the men, buggered the little boys, and did everything they could to destroy my city and my country. And they have the god-dammed unmitigated gall to accuse Austrians of having been war criminals."

Drummond could tell he had pressed Eberle's button. "I'm sorry I asked, Markus," he said quietly.

"It's okay." Eberle grinned. "I only carry on like that in public. Periodically, I just like to remind some of our left-wing assholes what it would have been like if the Red Army had stayed."

They walked over to a deep red Citroën CX parked in front of the terminal building. Arndt and the other police-man had just emerged by another door, carrying Drummond's cases, and they deposited them in the trunk of the car when Eberle opened it. As Eberle closed and locked the trunk, Arndt saluted and the two police officers vanished back into the airport.

"This is quite some car, Markus," Drummond said as he climbed into the plushly appointed interior. "I don't think I've ever seen one in Los Angeles."

"Well, don't get the wrong impression. My wife is a director of a big department store here in Vienna, and this is her company car." Eberle signaled before pulling out into traffic. "When she's out of town, I get to use it. Otherwise, it's a police car—or, if I've been especially good, I take my Corvette."

"A Corvette? What kind?" Drummond asked.

"Oh, an old Stingray. I bought it from the U.S. military attache at your embassy about ten years ago. It was really on its last legs, but I'd always wanted one, so I bought it." Eberle turned the Citroën onto the motorway that headed north into the city.

"It took me about three years to rebuild it. Fortunately my friend at the embassy was able to get most of the parts shipped over here in a diplomatic pouch, and another friend at the police garage did most of the work."

Eberle eased the dark red Citroën into the traffic on the Rennweg and after a few short blocks cut over to Prinz Eugen Strasse and turned up toward the Palais Schwarzenberg. "I'll show you my car tonight at dinner." He turned into a set of elaborate wrought iron gates and headed up a formal driveway. "In the meantime, let's get you settled in at your hotel."

As they pulled up in the baroque forecourt, two servants in gold-striped vests and black trousers emerged from a set of double doors and came to open the car doors. Eberle popped the trunk release before getting out, which gave the servant who had opened Drummond's door time to reopen the lobby doors. The man bowed as they passed, and the concierge came to attention behind the green marble-topped desk set discreetly in one corner of the lobby. Impeccably correct in cutaway coat and striped trousers, he bowed as Drummond and Eberle approached, the precise clicking of his heels punctuating his greeting.

"Kapitän Drummond, it is an honor to welcome you here once again. Shall I have your luggage sent to your usual suite?"

"Thank you, that would be fine, Herr—Hubmann," Drummond said, reading the man's name from a discreet name badge as he signed the guest register. He had learned, on his last trip to Vienna, that names—and titles—were very important in Austria.

"Perhaps," said Hubmann, "you and your guest would care to take coffee on the terrace?"

Drummond turned to Eberle and arched an eyebrow. "Time for a coffee, Markus?"

"Sure," Eberle said, glancing at his watch. "But it will

have to be a quick one. I've got to get back to the office and terrorize my subordinates."

The two men laughed as they followed Herr Hubmann out onto the terrace of the Palais Schwarzenberg and settled down at a turn-of-the-century cast iron art nouveau table.

"You know," Eberle said, when he had confirmed their order with the concierge, "coffee is an Austrian national institution. The very first coffeehouses in the world were started here in Vienna in 1683. . . ."

His lecture on Vienna's premier social custom was interrupted by the prompt arrival of their coffee, served by a uniformed waiter complete with white gloves.

"Anyway, as I was saying," Eberle went on, when the waiter had poured their coffee and departed. "As the Turks were driven from the gates of the city, an enterprising Viennese named Kolschitzky found hundreds of sacks of coffee that had been abandoned in the rout of the enemy. He, or so the story goes, opened the first coffeehouse outside the gates of the Hofburg Palace and soon became a millionaire."

Eberle lifted the delicate gold-rimmed white cup to his lips and sipped. "Ah . . . such aroma, such taste . . ."

Drummond chuckled. "Markus, I have to hand it to you. You certainly know how to appreciate life."

"And death," Eberle replied in an even tone. "Do you mind if we talk shop for a few minutes?"

"Not at all," Drummond said, surprised at the sudden turn in the conversation. "What's on your mind?"

"Three killings," Eberle said, taking another sip of coffee. "On the surface they don't seem to be related, but down in my guts I think they are." He set down his coffee cup. "Maybe you can provide a link."

"Go on," Drummond said, not sure of the direction Eberle was heading.

"I followed up on your suggestion that I look at the report filed by Franz Reidl concerning the body they found near Schloss Dielstein." Eberle leaned both elbows on the table. "Now, here is connection number one.

"Reidl's body was dumped in the woods about the same time that the coroner estimated that Hans Stucke was murdered in Vienna. Both were totally drained of blood. In fact, Reidl's corpse had several collapsed veins, as if the blood had been sucked out. Both victims had their throats cut."

Drummond nodded, saying nothing.

"Now, connection number two. Remember the double killing you saw the report about? One victim was decapitated, and the other had her throat cut and virtually all of the blood drained from the body." Eberle gave Drummond a conspiratorial grin. "Here is the clincher. The double homicide took place less than five hundred meters from where Reidl reported finding the first body. Interesting, huh?"

Drummond finished his coffee before replying. "So, what do you think?" he said, replacing his cup on its small white saucer.

"I'm not sure," Eberle said, "but I'd like you to give it some thought, since you made the first connection." He looked at his watch. "I've gotta go. Perhaps we can talk about this over dinner tonight?"

"Sure," Drummond replied. "Where would you like to eat? I'll have the hotel make reservations for us."

"No, you are having dinner at my house. Just the two of us. There, we can talk about this case at our leisure." Eberle stood up. "I'll call for you at seven-thirty."

Drummond watched him walk across the terrace and

vanish into the hotel lobby. He picked up his cup, but
found it empty. On reflection, he decided that he didn't
want any more anyway. Leaving the table, he went up to
his suite, already giving careful consideration to how
much he dared tell Eberle when they met for dinner.

As with his previous stay at Palais Schwarzenberg,
Drummond found that the hotel valet had already
whisked away his suit, blazer, and slacks to be pressed
and laid out his shaving kit in the large tiled bathroom
that adjoined his bedroom. His leather trenchcoat was
hanging in the antique wardrobe that stood opposite the
imposing brass bed, and all of his other clothes had been
neatly folded and placed in the nearby chest of drawers.
He decided that he could very easily get used to this kind
of service.

He sighed and walked over to the French doors that led
onto the balcony, glancing down to the terrace below—
and below that, the spiked black wrought iron railing that
surrounded the Palais Schwarzenberg. The railing onto
which an attacker had impaled himself after being pitched
over the terrace—and from which he had levered himself
up and off with the ease of a gymnast, though the fall
alone should have killed any mortal man. And to be impaled like that, with two spikes protruding through his
back . . .

Shaking his head, Drummond closed the balcony doors
and pulled the drapes. Despite having slept on the flight
between Los Angeles and London, and the infusion of
caffeine in the form of strong Viennese coffee, he could
feel the edge of fatigue beginning to creep over him. He
had to be sharp when he dealt with Eberle later tonight.
Stepping into the bathroom, he turned on the taps in the
center of the massive bathtub and emptied the contents
of a small sachet of foaming bath salts under the splash-

ing water. He went back into the bedroom and stripped while the tub filled, leaving his rumpled gray suit tossed casually over the back of a chair. Padding back into the bathroom, he eased himself into the hot bath and wrestled with the problem of what to tell Eberle over dinner.

There was one other problem gnawing away at Drummond's subconscious, however, and as he sat soaking in the deep tub, it managed to displace all other thoughts. It had come to him in mid-flight, and it remained a growing question.

When the Mossad handed over their file on him to LAPD's Internal Affairs Division, they had mentioned his visit to the Angel of Mercy Sanatorium in New Hampshire. That meant it was possible—in fact, it was highly likely—that they knew about his contact with Father Freise. If they had traced Freise to the castle in Luxembourg . . .

He wondered whether they could move that fast, and suspected that they could. It was obvious from his interview the night before they tried to kill him that the Israelis knew about Kluge, and knew that he was a vampire. How much more they knew was a matter of speculation, and Drummond was willing to speculate that even if they didn't know about Freise and the Order of the Sword, it wouldn't take them too long to find out about them, once they were on the right track. Hopefully, he'd be able to come up with a plan of action after dinner with Eberle—if Eberle could be convinced the whole thing was serious. And at this point, Drummond still wasn't certain how much he wanted to tell him.

Sitting in the tub wasn't waking him up, though. If anything, it was putting him to sleep. Drummond pulled the plug, stood up in the tub, turned on the taps, and adjusted the temperature just on the cold side, then switched the water from the faucet to the hand-held "telephone" shower and rinsed off. He was feeling a bit more clear-headed as he turned off the water and towelled off with a thick white towel the size of a small bedspread.

Padding back into his bedroom, he noted that his gray suit was missing from the back of the chair where he had tossed it—and that his pin-striped suit and blazer were back in the wardrobe, looking none the worse for their hours crushed in his suit bag.

"Yes, indeed," he muttered to himself, as he lay down to catch a nap. "I could get used to this kind of service."

At precisely seven-thirty, Drummond was dressed in his dark pin-striped suit and waiting in the lobby when the bright red Corvette pulled to a halt in front of the baroque tower in the center of Palais Schwarzenberg. Picking up his leather trench coat, he stepped outside and strode over to the car before Eberle had a chance to extricate himself from the seat belts. The doorman, running after Drummond, managed to reach the Corvette's door handle a split second before Drummond would have been obliged to open his own door.

Realizing that he had saved the hotel the embarrassment of having one of their guests have to stoop to such a menial task, Drummond muttered a profound, *"Danke,"* to the doorman and slid into Eberle's car.

"Well, John, what do you think?" It was obvious from Eberle's tone of voice that the red '63 Stingray was his absolute pride and joy.

"Markus, I cannot tell a lie. The car looks super."

Drummond looked across at the jukebox-styled dash of the Corvette and realized for the first time just how cohesive a design the Stingray was. It was as aggressively American as a John Wayne movie, and only a perverted sense of Euro-snobbery would cause anyone to suggest that the car wasn't in the same league as one of the so-called European "super cars."

Eberle grinned as he twisted the ignition key and the Chevy V-8 roared into life.

"I have a lot of fun with it," Eberle said, putting in the clutch and shifting into first gear. "I've got nearly three-fifty horsepower under the hood, which makes me quicker than most Ferraris."

As he eased out the clutch, the car pulled docilely away from the baroque splendors of the Palais Schwarzenberg and moved off into the traffic of nighttime Vienna. Eberle gave a casual running commentary as they went, clearly enjoying the opportunity to show off both his car and his city to an appreciative audience. Sliding smoothly through the traffic, he guided the Corvette effortlessly through a maze of picturesque streets, moving away from the neon-lit inner ring and into a suburban neighborhood of high walls and carefully trimmed hedges.

Finally turning into a cul-de-sac, he pulled the car up to the curb and then, with a bit of to-ing and fro-ing, managed to place it exactly between two large granite gate posts. Crunching along a gravel drive, Eberle hugged close to a hedge until at last he turned and brought the car up in front of his house.

"This is home," he said as they got out.

The pale yellow house with green shutters and green slate mansard roof would not have been out of place on one of the fashionable streets of Paris. On either side of the double doors a pair of bronze Turks stood in a position of submission, holding aloft gilded lanterns that softly flickered in imitation of the gaslights of a century ago. As they reached the top step, the doors were opened by a dowdy woman in her mid-fifties in the black dress and white apron of a maid.

"*Guten Abend*, Herr Inspektor," she said, curtsying slightly as Drummond followed Eberle into the house.

Once inside, the maid took both of their coats and then vanished down a dimly lit corridor.

"This way to the bar, gentleman," Eberle said in a comical English accent. Leading Drummond through a sliding double door, they entered a small sitting room.

Gemütlichkeit is the Austrian word for cozy, and at once Drummond understood the subtle nuance of the word. The room was furnished with comfortable chesterfields and well-padded club chairs pulled up close to the hearth of a carved oak fireplace. Thick blue Persian carpets muffled the sound of their footsteps, and the dark, almost plum-colored walls were nearly covered with a veritable mosaic of prints and small paintings, their gilded frames sparkling in the reflected light of an ornate giltwood chandelier.

"Please, make yourself comfortable," Eberle said, pointing Drummond toward one of the club chairs near the hearth. "What would you like to drink?"

"Scotch, if you can manage it," Drummond said from somewhere deep in his chair.

"Blended or malt, neat or with something added?" Eberle asked.

"Malt, please, if it's not too peaty. With just a splash of water," Drummond answered.

Eberle poured The Macallan into a pair of crystal tumblers and then added just the right amount of water. Handing Drummond his drink, he settled into the club chair opposite and raised his glass in a toast.

"Cheers!"

Drummond raised his glass in response. The rich amber liquid danced with pinpoints of light as it reflected the glow of the tiny flame-shaped bulbs perched on the tips of the faux-chandelles on the arms of the chandelier.

"*Slainte,*" he said, savoring the heady aroma of Eberle's rare old Scotch whiskey.

As he sipped at his drink, Drummond's eyes were drawn to a pair of small paintings above a satinwood side table. Against a bright blue sky, horses with sausage-shaped bodies cavorted with their feet off the ground.

"Those are interesting paintings, Markus," Drummond remarked.

"Ah, you have the eye of a connoisseur," Eberle said with mock gravity. "Those are paintings of Lipizzaners done by Georg von Hamilton in the 1720s. They are actually part of a set of eight, six of which are now in England." Eberle sipped his whiskey. "My grandfather was very fond of them, and after the First War had them sent to Switzerland, along with the family silver and a lot of other stuff."

"Why was that?" Drummond asked.

"Well, after the king abdicated in 1919, there were riots in Vienna, and he was afraid that the Bolsheviks might seize power." Eberle grinned at Drummond. "You see, I come from a long line of anti-Communists.

"Anyhow, things settled down, and in 1921 my grandparents bought this house and had everything shipped back from Switzerland, where they originally came from. During the next war, my grandparents went back to Switzerland, and the paintings and the silver went with them.

"When the war was over, they decided to stay in Switzerland but sent the silver and other valuables back to my father. They kept the paintings, though. When my grandparents died, I inherited the paintings and brought them back home."

The maid interrupted Eberle's discourse on his paintings to announce that dinner was served, and the two men finished their drinks and went into the dining room.

Sitting at a small table in the room's bay window, Eberle poured a rich red claret into gold-rimmed crystal goblets etched with a coat of arms. They had started with a Moselle, to go with an appetizer of Brussels paté. The claret accompanied a hearty wienerschnitzel. Drummond looked at the shield on the goblet and could make out an arm holding a ring.

"Is this your coat of arms?" he asked.

"No, not hardly." Eberle laughed, slicing into his wienerschnitzel. "The Eberles are Swiss. Our arms are three blue boars' heads with a red chevron in the center." He sipped at his claret.

"No, at the end of the war, my father—how shall I say it?—'borrowed' those from his commanding officer." Eberle chuckled at the joke. "Those were Hermann Göring's before my father took a fancy to them."

"Your father was on Göring's staff?" Drummond asked, a little shocked.

"No, no. My father was a physician, and when he went into the military he was assigned to the Luftwaffe. He spent the entire war in Wels, in upper Austria. The day before Germany capitulated, a plane loaded with Göring's personal effects landed at my father's airbase to refuel. The only problem was that there wasn't any fuel left at the base.

"The next day the war ended, and everybody just sat around waiting for the Allies to arrive. My father went over to Göring's plane and started poking around for souvenirs. He came away with these glasses, some silver trays, and Göring's *Reichsmarshall*'s dagger.

"But enough of ancient history," Eberle said between mouthfuls. "What do you think of my theory that Stucke's murder is related to the three bodies found in the wood near Schloss Dielstein?"

Drummond set down his knife and fork. "I think you're right. In fact, I know it."

"How so?" Eberle asked.

"I told you on the phone that the Mossad paid a call to my office in Los Angeles. What I haven't told you yet is why I'm *really* here." Drummond smiled almost apologetically at Eberle. "I hope you won't take offense at what I'm about to say. The Mossad agents accused me of being involved with a group of neo-Nazis trying to cover the tracks of a war criminal named Kluge."

"Go on," Eberle said, as he finished his last forkful of wienerschnitzel.

"They contended that Stucke recognized Kluge here in Vienna, and that Kluge had him killed after he went to the police. They implied that Sacher was in on it, and that's why he jumped to the suicide theory."

"Sacher. Well." Eberle shrugged and wiped his fingers on a starched linen napkin. "Let me tell you a bit about Sacher. There are two reasons that Sacher thought he was dealing with a suicide. One," he held up his thick index finger, "Vienna has the highest suicide rate of any city in Western Europe, so cops see a lot of suicides. And two," Eberle made a "V" sign with his right hand, "Sacher is a piss-poor detective. He couldn't find shit in a cesspit, much less handle a homicide. Hell, eight years ago he was assigned a simple murder case out in the twentieth district, and he turned in a report that said the victims may have been killed by a vampire. . . ."

Drummond felt as if an electric shock had passed through his body.

"They were, Markus. You can bet on it."

"Come on, no jokes, okay?" Eberle said.

"No jokes, but I'll tell you pretty much what Sacher found," Drummond said. "A dead body, maybe several, all drained of their blood." Drummond could tell by the look on Eberle's face that he'd come close to a bull's-eye.

"How did you know that?" Eberle demanded.

"I've tracked the same M.O. in four other cities, and they all point to the same man." Drummond stared intently at Eberle.

"Who?" Eberle finally asked.

"A vampire," Drummond said. "A vampire named Wilhelm Kluge."

Eberle stood up and walked over to the sideboard, returning to the table with two cups of coffee. "John," he said as he sat down again, "how come they let you wander around Los Angeles with a badge and a gun?"

"I know it sounds crazy, Markus, but it fits. Nearly twenty years ago in Los Angeles, a man I believe was Kluge ran a blood bank out on the east side, and LAPD was left with half a dozen bloodless corpses and an unsolved file. Eight years ago, Sacher hits the same pattern here in Vienna—dead people drained of their blood."

"Tell me about the blood bank in Los Angeles," Eberle interrupted.

"Not much to tell, really," Drummond said, knitting his brows, "except that it may have been linked to a company called Euro Plasma Technik in Hamburg. Why do you ask?"

"No reason in particular." Eberle had taken a small leather notebook from his pocket and was scribbling the name of the blood bank in it as he spoke. "Is that all you have to go on?" he asked, looking up at Drummond.

"No, there's more," Drummond said. "A couple of weeks ago, the police in Hamburg uncover a pile of bloodless bodies when they knock down a condemned warehouse. About two months ago in Vancouver, British Columbia, the city closes a blood bank where donors are literally being bled to death. When the police look for the owner, they find his body in a trash dumpster, totally drained of blood. Only it turns out that the body, a real John Doe, isn't the owner. He has vanished." Drummond looked at Eberle.

"Go on," Eberle said.

"Two weeks ago, we find Stucke's body in the shower in his flat in the seventeenth district. It's drained of blood. Last week, you have a double homicide, and one of the victims is totally drained of blood." Drummond took a sip of his coffee, but it had lost its taste.

"I've saved the best until last, Markus," he said, pushing the cup away. "The night before last, I was kidnapped and drugged by the Mossad, dragged to a motel and asked what I knew about Wilhelm Kluge, and asked if I believed in vampires." Drummond leaned back in his chair. "You might not believe in vampires, but the Israeli government apparently does. And so do I."

Markus Eberle went to the sideboard and poured Drummond a fresh cup of coffee. He came back, set the cup in front of Drummond, and sat down again before speaking.

"John," he said, "there is only one thing that convinces me that you are not a raving lunatic."

Drummond raised an eyebrow at Eberle, who smiled back.

"The body that Reidl found at Schloss Dielstein had been totally drained of blood. Not only that, the coroner places the time of death at about the same time that Stucke was killed. Now, I don't believe in vampires, and I don't give a damn about these other murders you've told me about, but I do know this: I have three dead bodies without any blood in them. Now, somehow these murders have to be connected, and if the connection is some old fart of a Nazi, then I'm going to put him away. For good."

"I'll give you your connection, Markus," Drummond said around a yawn. "Then I've got to get back to the hotel. My jet lag is catching up with me."

"All right. What's the connection?"

"Stucke had been pestering the police about seeing this fellow Kluge in Vienna," Drummond said. "The police investigate the report, but decide the man Stucke has seen is at least forty years too young to be Kluge. Kluge bides his time, then has someone off Stucke. When the killer goes to collect from Kluge, Kluge kills him and dumps the body in the woods." Drummond yawned again. "Later, Kluge returns to where he dumped the body and kills the two campers."

"Okay for murders one and two," Eberle said as he offered Drummond a cigar. "But where's the motive for killing the campers?"

"I don't know," Drummond admitted, "unless it was some kind of ritual killing—maybe an initiation of some sort. The beheading puts it in a slightly different light from the others."

"You mean that Kluge could be involved with some sort of cult?" Eberle asked.

With a slight shiver, Drummond thought back to the attack launched against the castle of the Order of the Sword by Kluge and his punkers—and the black knights with Kluge, who had been something else entirely.

"Yes," he said. "Something along those lines."

"Then we'll get them all," Eberle said. "Vampires or not, we'll get them all."

"I'm sure we will, Markus," Drummond said, unable to

stifle a yawn. "But for now, I've got to head back to the hotel."

Eberle looked at his watch. "It's just midnight. Shall I call a taxi, or do you want to take the Corvette?"

Drummond grinned. "I'd never get out of the driveway in that car of yours, let alone find my way back to the hotel. I think we'd better call a cab."

A light rain was falling, blurring the shapes and colors of Vienna as the taxi returned Drummond to his hotel. Looking out the window of the cab as it moved through the neon-lit business district, Drummond wondered where Kluge was, and what he was doing.

The darkness of Kluge's sanctum at Wewelsberg Castle was relieved only by the flickering points of light that danced on the candles held by initiates standing along the perimeter of the room. The silent shadows of the steel-helmeted men, their black capes reaching to their ankles, had been impassive witness to the induction of Anton von Tupilow.

Attended by four of the knights now present in the room, he had been bathed, ritually purified of all corrupting influences, then dressed in a black robe, buttoned high at the throat and closed at the wrists much like a Cossack's shirt, but reaching to the ankle and belted loosely around his waist. On his left breast was embroidered a baroque silver shield displaying twin lightning flashes—the *Sigrunen* of the SS.

Von Tupilow was escorted into the room by two knights, their black coal-scuttle helmets gleaming in the candlelight, black full-dress uniforms immaculate beneath their billowing black capes. Escorting their charge around the great, round table that dominated the room, they came to a halt a few paces back from where their leader sat in a great, carved armchair pushed back from the table, elegant and dangerous in the black full-dress uniform of his rank as an SS *Sturmbannführer*. Rather than a helmet like those sported by all the rest, he wore the high, peaked cap of the officer caste, with its SS pattern eagle and swastika cap badge. He tugged languidly at the cuff of a black leather glove as the two escorting knights snapped to attention and gave him the stiff-armed salute of the Third Reich.

"Sieg Heil!" they said, their upraised arms motionless.

Slowly Kluge rose from his carved gothic chair to survey the knights flanking von Tupilow, taking his time before returning their salute. To either side of him, two more cloaked and helmeted knights held the wooden staffs of the silver and black labrium of the SS and the bullet-riddled banner of crimson, white, and black known as the *Blutfahne,* the Blood Flag, perhaps the most sacred relic of the old Third Reich.

"Heil," Kluge said, in a voice that left no doubt as to his absolute authority over the knights. "Bring forward the postulant seeking admission to our order."

In perfect, disciplined unison, the two knights escorted von Tupilow to where Kluge stood, halting to salute again and then taking two steps back as von Tupilow sank to his knees between them, as solemn as if he knelt in some great cathedral.

"What is your loyalty?" Kluge asked from where he stood.

"Meine Ehre heisst Treue," von Tupilow replied. My honor is my loyalty.

"Then, affirm that loyalty by your sacred oath," Kluge commanded. "Before these knights who soon shall be your brothers, swear it upon the *Blutfahne,* sacred relic of our glorious past, drenched in the gore of our martyred brothers of the 1923 Putsch."

Glancing to his left, he signaled for the *Blutfahne* to be brought nearer. Its bearer stepped smartly forward with a stamping of polished boots and dipped the torn and bloodied banner so that von Tupilow could catch a tattered corner and press its between his hands.

"Unto the blood and soil of our race," he said steadily, paralleling another oath taken to another Führer more than half a century before, "I, Anton von Tupilow, swear loyalty and bravery, and I vow to thee obedience unto death. *Sieg Heil!*"

"*Sieg Heil,*" Kluge repeated.

Drawing a thin-bladed sword from the black scabbard at his side, Kluge stepped forward and took the end of the blood-spattered banner from von Tupilow in his left hand. He saluted with the blade, then brought it down to rest lightly on von Tupilow's right shoulder.

"*Blut und Ehre.*" Blood and Honor.

The sword blade flashed over von Tupilow's head and came to rest lightly on his left shoulder.

"*Treue um Treue.*" Loyalty unto Loyalty.

The blade flashed again, and with a flourish Kluge sheathed his SS officer's sword.

"Never forget, Ritter von Tupilow, that it is the *Blut und Boden*—the Blood and Soil—which binds us together as knights."

As Kluge spoke, the *Blutfahne* was withdrawn and Baumann came forward carrying an SS officer's dagger and a heavy golden chalice, the rim of the latter finely wrought with swastikas and Sigrunen, its double handles supported by the wings of eagles, their talons clutching swastikas set with sapphires. Not taking his eyes from von Tupilow, Kluge pushed up the sleeve of his black SS tunic and then reached out to Baumann, who handed him the dagger.

"Prepare now to join in the holy communion of your brother knights," Kluge said.

The blade sliced deeply into Kluge's flesh as he drew it across his forearm, and bright blood welled up in the cut and streamed down his hand to drip from his fingers. In awed silence, the young Ritter von Tupilow watched as Baumann knelt to catch the blood in the golden chalice, like an acolyte serving some ancient pagan priest, clasping the cup between his two hands as if it were a precious relic. It was no trickery of the candlelight; the blood flowed strongly, pulsing with a steady rhythm of Kluge's heartbeat and quickly filling the chalice. As the blood reached the rim of the chalice, to von Tupilow's amazement, Kluge sealed the wound with the merest pressure from his fingers, smiling faintly at von Tupilow's expression as he wiped away the blood on his arm with a handkerchief that Baumann handed him. There was something thrilling in the way that Baumann raised the golden cup for Kluge to take it, and in the utter majesty with which Kluge presented it to the young man kneeling at his feet.

"Drink this, all of it, and join with us forever," Kluge whispered. His voice sounded as if it came from another world.

Trembling, von Tupilow took the chalice from Kluge's hands and raised it toward his lips, unable to take his eyes from Kluge's. He could feel the glowing warmth of the fresh blood radiating through the hammered gold between his hands—Kluge's blood—and its pungent smell filled his nostrils, promising an exquisite destiny. As he set the cup to his lips and boldly drank, he imagined he could already feel the potency of immortality beginning to sing through his veins.

CHAPTER 10

It's amazing, just how much you can resolve with a good night's sleep, Drummond thought as he lathered his face with his shaving brush.

He rinsed his razor in the basin and carefully trimmed his sideburns first, then brought the razor gliding along his cheeks.

When he had left Eberle's the night before, he hadn't been sure of his next move, let alone how he was going to handle Kluge. At least he had the beginning of a game plan now; and he figured he had maybe a day or two of grace before various people interested in his whereabouts figured out he wasn't in Stockholm.

He pointed his chin at the mirror, scraping away with his razor as he mentally reviewed the day's schedule.

First he had to go to the bank and add Eberle's and Freise's names to his gold account. Next, he had to buy a car and have it fitted with a cellular telephone.

And then, he thought, as he scraped the razor along his throat, *I'll need to do a little shopping.*

Finished, he ejected the used blade into the trash can next to the sink and tossed the razor into his shaving kit, drying his face and splashing on after-shave. Then he headed into his bedroom to dress and went down to the dining room for breakfast.

The drizzle of the night before had given way to bright sunshine, allowing Drummond the pleasure of coffee, juice, and croissants on the terrace of the Palais Schwarzenberg. As he started on his second cup of the rich Viennese coffee, he took out his notepad and made a brief list. He read the list over, signed his bill, then rose and strolled into the lobby of the hotel, heading for Herr Hubmann's desk.

The hotel manager was instantly on his feet, greeting Drummond with a polite bow.

"Good morning, Herr Kapitän," he said. "How may we help you?"

"Two things, if you think you can manage." He smiled at Hubmann. "First, I'll need a taxi in about ten minutes."

Herr Hubmann nodded gravely. "Of course, Herr Kapitän. And the second thing?"

"Could you please arrange an appointment for me with the nearest Range Rover dealer here in Vienna? Tell them I will need to speak with someone who knows English, and that I'll be in their showrooms at eleven-thirty."

"Are you returning to your rooms, Herr Kapitän?" Hubmann asked.

"Yes, I am."

"Then I will have the address of the automobile dealer ready for you when your taxi arrives." Herr Hubmann gave Drummond one of his precise bows. "Will there be anything else, sir?"

"Nothing now, thank you," Drummond said, and headed up the stairs to his room.

Pulling his suitcase from his closet, Drummond retrieved the fax he had received from Eberle's sister, Else Schmidt, two days earlier and sat down at the small desk at one end of his bedroom to copy the address and phone number of her bank into his notebook. Then he dialed the number, which answered on the second ring.

"*Frau Schmidt hier,*" said a pleasant, businesslike woman's voice.

"This is John Drummond calling," he replied in English.

"Ah, Kapitän Drummond," came the reply. "My brother told me you were in town. How can I help you?" Her English was good, but heavily accented.

"I would like to stop by this morning and settle a few details of my account, if that's not inconvenient," Drummond said.

"Not at all. I will be delighted to meet you." Paper rustled as she apparently checked her desk diary. "Can you come at ten-thirty?"

"That'll be just fine, Frau Schmidt. *Auf wiedersehen.*" Drummond hung up, gathered up his papers, and returned them to the pocket of the suitcase. Then, folding his notebook, he placed it in the pocket of his double-breasted navy blazer and went back to the lobby of the hotel. As he came down the stone stairs that led to his room, Drummond saw Herr Hubmann waiting by the door, a small envelope in his hand. Outside, a shiny black Mercedes taxi was parked on the gravelled forecourt.

"The Rover agency expects you at eleven-thirty, Herr Kapitän," Hubmann said, as he handed the pale ivory envelope to Drummond. "And your driver's name is Hans."

"Thank you very much."

The driver had the door open for him by the time he got outside, and he settled into the car's leather upholstery as the driver came back around.

"The Vienna Credit Bank, *bitte,*" he said, as the driver got in.

The bank was only a few minutes from Drummond's hotel. Once he was inside the chrome and marble lobby and had identified himself at reception, a smartly dressed secretary escorted him to the second floor office of Else Schmidt.

"Kapitän Drummond," she said, standing and extending her hand as he was ushered into her office. "It is a pleasure to meet you." She had the same infectious smile as her brother, only minus the stainless steel teeth, and a firm handshake. "Please sit down. Can I offer you a coffee?"

"No, thank you," Drummond said. "I've just had breakfast."

"Well then, what can I do for you?" she asked, settling back behind her desk.

"I'd like to add two names to my account, and if possible collect my check book and check guarantee card," Drummond said.

"That should be no problem." She flashed Drummond a smile. "Now, what are the names?"

"Francis Freise." Drummond watched as she jotted down the name. "And Markus Eberle."

Else Schmidt let out a small gasp. *"Mein Bruder?"* she said.

"Yes, unless you know some reason why I shouldn't trust him," Drummond replied.

"Heavens, no. Markus is too honest. Even for a policeman." She laughed. "They will have to come in and sign bank cards. When can Mr. Freise come in?"

"He can't," Drummond said. "He lives in Luxembourg. If you'll give me a card, I'll have him sign it and mail it back."

"All right." She opened a desk drawer and pulled out a signature card, which she filled in with Freise's name and the account information. "He will need to sign here and here." She made X's beside two lines and passed the card across the desk to Drummond, along with an envelope. "Then have him send it back in this. Now, let me see about your check book and bank cards."

She picked up the phone on her desk and spoke rapidly in German to someone on the other end, smiling as she set down the phone.

"Your check book and bank card will be ready in just a few minutes, Kapitän. Your credit cards will be delivered to your hotel by courier this afternoon. I hope that's not inconvenient?"

"No, that's just fine," Drummond replied.

"Excellent. So, what are your plans for the rest of to-day?"

"Well, I'm going to buy a car and then do some shopping. That probably won't leave much time," Drummond said.

"A car? Perhaps the bank could arrange a loan for you," she suggested.

"Well, why not? Could I have the car registered to me here at the bank until I'm settled in?"

"We can take care of everything." She smiled and handed Drummond her card. "Just have the dealer call me when you've decided what you want. I'll see to the for-malities."

There was a gentle knock at the door to the office.

"*Bitte*," she said.

A young bank clerk entered carrying a large manila en-velope and handed it to her.

"Your check book and bank card, Kapitän Drummond," Else said as she signed a receipt for the package. "Now, is there anything else I can do for you this morning?"

Drummond signed the back of the plastic card she handed him and put it in his wallet. He glanced at his watch as he tucked the check book into his jacket pocket.

"Actually, there is," he said. "Do you think you could call Markus and ask him to join me for lunch?"

"Of course," she said. "Where are you lunching?"

"Good question." Drummond laughed. "What do you suggest?"

"Have you been to the Prater?" she asked.

"No," he said. "Is it a nice restaurant?"

It was Else's turn to laugh. "It isn't a restaurant, it's a place. A big park on the west side of town. Any taxi can take you there. I'll tell Markus to meet you by the Ferris wheel at twelve-thirty."

Drummond's original taxi was waiting patiently by the curb as he came out of the bank. Climbing into the back seat, he handed the driver the address of the Rover dealer, just off the Karntnerstrasse. It was nearly twenty past eleven—just ten minutes to make his appointment.

The traffic was heavy, especially crossing the ring road, and Drummond began to worry that he would be late in arriving at the Rover showrooms. His driver must have sensed his growing impatience, for with the sixth sense that all good taxi drivers seem to possess, he suddenly turned into an alley and, with total disregard for the signs, drove the wrong way down a one-way alley. Just before reaching the end of the alley, the Mercedes pulled into an open set of garage doors, and Drummond found himself in the service department of the Rover dealer. Looking at his watch he saw that it was just 11:30.

Climbing out of the cab, Drummond made his way to the showroom, where three Rovers were parked in a veritable jungle of potted palms. The showroom seemed to be deserted, and Drummond hoped that Herr Hubmann had made it clear that he needed to talk to someone who spoke English. After pushing his way through the underbrush, Drummond was inspecting a blue Land Rover with a stuffed toy tiger on its hood when an elderly mustach-ioed man in a tweed suit and regimental tie seemed to appear from nowhere.

"Ha, you must be Drummond." The man spoke with a patrician British accent. "I'm Adrian Hamilton-Bolt, Rover's resident Englishman." He extended a large bony hand. "The man from Schwarzenberg telephoned and said to expect you." He gave Drummond a quizzical stare. "Said you were a captain, but you don't look like a navy man to me."

"You're right there, sir," Drummond said with a slight smile. "I'm a captain with the Los Angeles Police Department."

"Good," said Hamilton-Bolt. "Never really cared for navy types. Now, what sort of motor do you need?"

"Something that'll cope with snow and ice, stick to dirt roads in the rain, and won't look out of place at Palais Schwarzenberg," Drummond said with a chuckle.

"Well, unless you fancy mock tigers," Hamilton-Bolt gave the offending toy a dismissive nod, "I'd suggest you can give this one a pass. What you want is a Range Rover. They're over here." Pushing his way through the potted palms, he led Drummond over to a white two-door. "Best town and country car in the world," he said to Drummond as he opened the door. "What do you think?"

"What I'm after is a Range Rover Vogue SE, with automatic transmission." Drummond enjoyed the look of surprise that passed over Hamilton-Bolt's face.

"Ha. The Rolls-Royce of off-road vehicles." He closed the door of the white Range Rover. "I've got one in the basement. Give me a moment or two to have it brought up."

Hamilton-Bolt walked over to his desk and pressed a button on the intercom. In German punctuated with an

English accent he gave a few sharp orders, then turned back to Drummond.

"If you don't mind, I rather think you had better stand over here by the desk," he said. "That whole side of the room is a giant elevator."

Drummond stepped over to the desk just as the white car began to slowly sink into the floor.

"Always reminds me of the Titanic when I see them go down like that," Hamilton-Bolt mused. "Especially the white one here. Makes me think of an iceberg."

Drummond watched as the "iceberg" sank from sight, only to be replaced a few moments later by a black Range Rover Vogue rising majestically up out of the depths.

"Ha. Tell me if that's what you've had in mind, Captain Drummond," Hamilton-Bolt snorted. "Top of the line. Best damned car we've got." He brushed his snow-white mustache smooth with his thumb and forefinger as he spoke. "The Pride of England, and the Envy of the Krauts."

Walking over to the car, Drummond opened the door and climbed in behind the wheel. The gray leather interior was smartly trimmed in burr walnut, and Drummond noticed that the car was fitted with air-conditioning and a sun roof.

"What's the top speed?" he asked Hamilton-Bolt.

"She'll just clear the ton," he said. "But she'll cruise at eighty all day long."

Drummond hopped out and walked around the car, giving it a careful inspection. The car was dignified if not stylish, and its four-liter V-8 engine would more than cope with anything Drummond would be likely to encounter short of a Ferrari. Satisfied that the Range Rover was what he wanted, he turned back to Hamilton-Bolt.

"I'll take it," he said. Then, as an afterthought, "Can you fit a cellular telephone to it?"

"Ha. I can have it painted in the Drummond tartan, if you want. A cell-phone is no problem."

Drummond reached into his pocket and pulled out Else Schmidt's card.

"Call my bank," he said as he handed Hamilton-Bolt her card. "They'll take care of payment. How soon can you deliver it to my hotel?"

Hamilton-Bolt screwed a monocle into his left eye and examined the card. "Well, it's noon now," he said. "Would first thing in the morning suit?"

Drummond thought for a moment. "Yes, that would be fine. Thank you."

"My pleasure," Hamilton-Bolt said. "Can I drop you anywhere?"

"No, thank you," Drummond replied. "I have a taxi waiting to take me to the Prater."

"The Prater?" The old man frowned. "Why on earth are you going there? There's no racing today."

"I'm meeting a friend at the Ferris wheel for lunch," Drummond said.

"Ha. In that case, tell your driver to take you to the Volksprater." He smoothed his mustache again. "Otherwise, you're apt to be dropped miles from where you want to be."

"Thanks for the tip," Drummond said, extending his hand. "Good-bye."

"Yes," Hamilton-Bolt said as the two men shook hands. "And thank you very much."

The taxi driver was talking to one of the mechanics when Drummond came out of the showroom, but the moment he saw Drummond approach the car, he ended the conversation and rushed over to open Drummond's door.

"Volksprater, bitte," Drummond said, once the driver was behind the wheel.

With a nod, the man started the engine and drove out into the Vienna traffic.

The giant Ferris wheel in the Volksprater belongs as much to the Vienna skyline as the Eiffel Tower does to that of Paris. Looking up at it as the taxi crawled along in the snarl of city traffic, Drummond remembered the first time he had seen the famous Viennese landmark.

It was in the movie, *The Third Man,* and Harry Lime was involved with black-market morphine—something in short supply in postwar Vienna. There was a grittiness to the film, and to Orson Welles' performance as the amoral Mr. Lime. It was amazing, Drummond mused, how much and yet how little Vienna had changed in the forty-odd years since the picture was made.

The grime of postwar Vienna was gone, and in its place was a bright, vibrant city. But somehow, just as the Ferris wheel remained, Drummond knew that there was a part of Vienna that was still the city of Harry Lime. The grittiness was still there, despite a fresh coat of paint.

Drummond's taxi driver delivered him to the very entrance of the Volksprater, ignoring a forest of traffic signs. Amazed at the aplomb of his driver, Drummond decided that if it hadn't been for the thick concrete posts that prevented the car from entering the amusement park, Hans would have driven to the very base of the Ferris wheel. A glance at his watch told him that he was ten minutes early for his meeting with Eberle.

Drummond climbed out of the taxi. *"Danke,"* he said to the driver.

"You're welcome, sir," Hans said. "Would you care for me to wait?"

"Ah, no, thank you," Drummond said, somewhat taken

aback by the driver's command of English. "I'll find my own way back to the hotel."

"Very good, sir. If you would be so kind as to sign this," he handed Drummond a receipt book, "I'll see to it that the charges are put on your hotel bill."

Drummond signed the receipt and handed the book back to the driver. "Thank you."

"You're welcome. Have a nice day, sir." He rolled up the window and pulled out into traffic, leaving Drummond standing in front of the entrance to the Volksprater with a slightly bemused look.

Turning around, Drummond headed into the amusement park and worked his way over toward the giant Ferris wheel. To his surprise, Eberle was already there and waved as Drummond approached.

"John, you're early."

"And you're earlier," Drummond replied. "I hope you haven't been waiting long."

"Not really. Maybe ten minutes. Else rang my office in the nick of time. Another few minutes and I would have been roped into a meeting with some visiting VIP's from Japan." Eberle grinned. "I'll take *lingos* over sushi any day."

"What are *lingos*?" Drummond asked, although he gathered from Eberle's smirk that it was food of some kind.

"It's a Hungarian snack—a piece of pastry with garlic and paprika. Sort of like a pizza, but without the cheese and anchovies." Eberle laughed. "C'mon, we'll split one on our way to lunch."

Although the deep-fried *lingos* looked like a chunk of pizza, all resemblance ended the moment Drummond bit into the puffy, garlic-flavored pastry.

"Hey, this is really good," he said between mouthfuls.

"Yeah," Eberle replied. "I thought you'd like it."

Moving through the sparse crowd, Eberle guided them toward a small outdoor cafe.

"I hope you like venison," he said, as they sat down at a rustic table. "And potatoes. That's all they do here."

Drummond grinned. "I love barbequed Bambi."

"Great," Eberle said, signaling to the waitress for two beers. "In that case, you're in for a treat."

The waitress set down two large gray steins with domed pewter lids.

"*Prost,*" Eberle said, thumbing back the lid of his and raising it in salute.

Drummond clunked his stein against Eberle's and repeated, "*Prost.*"

The beer was dark and thick and had a slightly sweet flavor. Drummond couldn't tell if he liked it or not, and decided, as he licked the foam from the corners of his mouth, that it was probably a subtly acquired taste.

"After you went home last night, I did some thinking," Eberle said, when he had given the waitress their order. "And there was something I didn't tell you about the killings that happened in the forest last week I think you ought to know."

Drummond paused with his stein halfway to his mouth. "What's that?"

"At the crime scene we found several bare footprints." Eberle took another swallow of beer. "None of them matched either victim, so we figured that the killers must have left them."

"Go on," Drummond said, setting down his stein.

"Remember when I asked you if you thought Kluge could be heading up a cult of some kind?" Eberle asked.

"Yes."

"Well, suppose their initiation involved killing these people and—" Eberle looked around to make certain no one was listening"—and drinking their blood? That would fit in with your vampire theory, wouldn't it?"

"I suppose it would, if it was just an initiation," Drummond said. "But suppose for a minute that they really are vampires. What then?" He regarded Eberle over the rim of his stein for just a moment. "In that case, I'd say they were out hunting."

Eberle paled slightly. "What makes you suggest hunting?"

"Because I think they were out looking for a ritual victim and just happened to find the campers," Drummond said. "Was there any sign of a struggle at the scene?"

"No," Eberle said. "None at all."

"So we can suppose that the killers surprised the man and decapitated him before he could make a sound to warn the girl." Drummond took a sip from his stein. "Then, they dragged the girl out of the tent—"

"Through the tent," Eberle interrupted. "They sliced the tent open and pulled her out."

"And before she could resist, they killed her," Drummond said.

"And then," Eberle's voice had become a hoarse whisper, "when they had finished, they blew hunting horns in the night."

"What are you talking about?" Drummond asked.

"At the campground, near the crime scene, people complained about hearing hunting horns sounding in the woods at midnight." A slight glow of perspiration shown on Eberle's forehead. "The forester thought it might have been poachers hunting by night . . ."

"Not poachers. Vampires," Drummond said. "It was Kluge and his vampires who killed the campers."

"Kluge?" Eberle asked.

"Wilhelm Kluge," Drummond replied. "SS Sturmbannführer Kluge. The same man Hans Stucke reported to the police here in Vienna before he was murdered."

Eberle did not answer until the waitress had set down two steaming plates of venison and withdrawn.

"Come on, John. It couldn't be Kluge," Eberle said, picking up his fork. "Kluge would be an old, old man if he were alive today."

"Markus, the killer not only could be Kluge, I'm convinced he is Kluge. And," Drummond said, "Kluge isn't alone. He's building up some sort of Nazi vampire army. I don't know why, but whatever his reason, he has to be stopped."

They ate in silence for several minutes before Eberle spoke.

"John, I wish I could believe you, but frankly I can't. I'm one of those hardheaded pragmatists who only believes what he sees." Eberle avoided looking at Drummond while he spoke. "You show me a vampire, then I'll believe. Until then—well, let's just say that I'm after the leader of the cult that killed those campers, huh? And leave it at that."

Drummond thought for nearly a minute while he finished his venison.

"Suppose I introduce you to some vampires?" he finally asked.

"Sure," Eberle said in an offhanded manner. "Why not?"

"Can you get a few days off work?"

"Are you serious?" Eberle said.

"Deadly serious, Markus. Can you get away for a few days?" Drummond asked again.

"Maybe next week," Eberle said. "Why?"

"Like I said, I want you to meet some vampires." The waitress arrived with the bill, and Drummond paid it with a few notes pulled from a wad of Austrian schillings.

"How long would it take you to get to Luxembourg from here?"

"Flying? About two hours. Driving? About ten." Eberle grinned. "Wouldn't it be faster to go to Transylvania?"

Drummond laughed despite himself. "I'm serious, Markus. When could you meet me in Luxembourg?"

"Let me see," Eberle said, pulling out his diary. "I suppose I could drive up in the Corvette next Wednesday and come back on Saturday." He looked up at Drummond. "How's that sound?"

"Fine. I'll call you on Tuesday and tell you where to meet me." Drummond pushed himself away from the table. "'Scuse me, but I gotta pee."

"Me, too," Eberle said, standing up. "The drains are out back."

The green-and-white tiled men's room was immaculate, and it wasn't until Drummond finished washing his hands that he noticed there were no towels. Seeing Drummond's predicament, Eberle laughed.

"Another lesson in Austrian custom," he said. "When there is no attendant at the door, there aren't any towels to be had."

"Great. No towels," Drummond said. After shaking as much of the water off his hands as possible, he put them in his pockets, hoping that would blot off any remaining moisture. "Remind me to add towels to my shopping list."

Laughing, the two men walked back toward the entrance of the park.

"Tell me," Drummond said, as they neared the gates, "where can I go to do some shopping?"

"That depends on what you need," Eberle said. "Most of the good men's shops are on the Karntnerstrasse, or over in the Kohlmarkt."

"No, what I need are outdoor clothes. Hiking boots, parkas, that sort of thing," Drummond said.

"Well, then," Eberle said. "I know just the place. I'll drop you there on my way back to the office."

CHAPTER 11

Drummond had to admit it. Eduard Kettner's was possibly the most interesting store he had ever been to in his adult life. Everything from Swiss Army knives to elephant guns were on sale, along with more outdoor clothing and camping gear than L.L. Bean could sell in a century. All thoughts of "minimalist" survival tools went out the window as he wandered through the massive hunter's emporium.

So far, Drummond's escape from the Mossad had gone smoothly. He still didn't know what had changed their minds about him, between letting him go and trying to kill him, but it was only a matter of time until they learned that they had shot the wrong man back in Los Angeles and sent another team out after him. He was reasonably safe as long as he kept moving, but he had already taken a bit of a chance by returning to the Palais Schwarzenberg, where they knew he had stayed before. There was only one place where he knew for certain that he'd be safe until Agent Raymunds could call off the Israelis, and that was back in Luxembourg with Father Freise and the knights of the Order of the Sword.

The knights' castle presented other problems. Living in a medieval castle had always sounded romantic to Drummond, but having spent the better part of ten days at

Schloss Marbourg, he knew that it was lacking in certain basic amenities. He also knew that his stay could last for several weeks, perhaps even months, and that if it did, the clothes he had brought from sunny California would be woefully inadequate in the cold of a European winter.

Carefully Drummond browsed through the store, mentally ticking off all of the things he was going to need for a prolonged stay at the castle. Finally, after mentally considering and discarding several hundred different items, he approached two clerks at the cash desk.

"Excuse me," he said in his most American accent. "Is there anyone here who speaks English?"

The clerks answered with blank stares. *"Nein,"* one of them finally answered. *"Aber, stehen Sie hier, bitte."*

Drummond got the gist of what was said, and the clerk's gesture made it clear that he was to wait.

The clerk spoke again to his companion, then with a slight bow to Drummond left the cash desk. A few minutes later he was back, accompanied by a middle-aged man in velour knickerbockers and shocking blue socks, who was followed at a respectful distance by a pale youth with a sunken chest.

A rapid exchange took place between the clerk and the man in the knickerbockers, and when they had finished talking, the pale young man with the sunken chest bowed to Drummond.

"Exzellenz," he began, "you I am to help, my director says." The young man's expression was as serious as a tax inspector's. "Please to show me, uh, what you want to buy."

Drummond shot a curt bow to the man in the knickerbockers. *"Danke schön, Herr Director,"* he said.

"Bitte schön, Exzellenz," the director replied, returning Drummond's bow.

As they headed down the aisle, Drummond turned to his interpreter. "So, what is your name?" he asked.

"Paul, *Exzellenz*," he replied.

"Well, Paul, my friend, let's start with a knapsack." Drummond stopped in front of a display of every conceivable kind of backpack, and after a brief inspection of the available selection, picked out a knapsack made of black kevlar.

"Put this on," he said, handing the knapsack to Paul.

Nodding gravely, Paul slipped into the straps on the lightweight backpack and settled it on his back.

"Good," Drummond said. "Now for some socks."

Stopping in front of a rack of thick wool hiking socks, Drummond stuffed a dozen pairs into the backpack, then led Paul over to a long rack of shirts. The German hunting shirts were a uniform gray-green color, and all of them abounded with pockets in various configurations. Drummond found a shirt that had pockets on both arms, patch pockets on the chest, and an additional pair of zippered pockets above the patches. With typical Teutonic efficiency, the size was given in both metric and standard European measurement. Drummond quickly pulled six of them from the rack and handed then over to Paul.

"These ought to be fine," he said. "Now, how about some trousers?"

Dutifully following in Drummond's wake, Paul managed to balance an ever-increasing mountain of clothing as Drummond gathered everything he thought he would need for a prolonged siege at the castle. Finally, having stuffed a pair of fleece-lined boots into the knapsack along with a pair of sturdy field shoes, Drummond asked Paul to leave the clothing items at the cash desk and show him the gun department.

It was on the second floor. It was very complete, with

a variety of weapons besides firearms. Drummond looked longingly at the Savage Model 69 pump-action shotgun, but careful inquiry of the helpful Paul confirmed that local laws would probably prohibit its purchase by a nonresident.

The crossbow was another matter.

Drummond shouldered the space-age version of the medieval weapon and, staring through the telescopic sight, drew a bead on a large toy tiger perched on top of a mound of pith helmets. It wasn't a Winchester, but in his position, Drummond considered it the next best thing. Setting the crossbow aside, he picked up one of the short bolts and examined its broad head.

"This is the kind for boar, *Exzellenz*," Paul said.

"And this one?" Drummond asked, holding up a bolt whose head was covered with a series of vicious looking barbs.

"For fish," Paul began. "The line you tie to here." He showed Drummond a small loop on one side of the bolt head. "The shaft of the bolt comes out of the head when the fish begins to struggle, and you then reel it in."

"This seems a little large for fish," Drummond said, closely examining the inch-long head.

"Depends on how big is the fish," Paul replied, with the first flash of humor he had yet displayed. "We have bigger, too." He reached behind the counter and brought up a bolt with a two-inch head, each of its three razor-sharp vanes barbed on the end, and handed it to Drummond. "This is for shark."

Drummond inspected the shark bolt. "How many of these do you have?" he asked.

Paul bobbed down behind the counter. "Only four, *Exzellenz*," he replied.

"Okay, I'll take them. And give me four spools of five-hundred-pound shark-line to go with them." Drummond handed the shark bolt back to Paul. "I'll also want fifty of the boar-hunting bolts."

"Most certainly, *Exzellenz*." Paul vanished into the back room to get Drummond's bolts, leaving him to examine a display case full of knives.

Drummond's father had taught him that the handiest tool a man could have in the wilderness was a good pocket knife. "The only time you'll need it," he had advised his young son, "is when you don't have it."

A Gerber survival knife in the display case attracted Drummond's attention, and he made a mental note to add that and a Swiss Army knife to his growing pile of supplies.

Paul returned with the crossbow bolts neatly packaged and set them on the counter beside the crossbow.

"Will there be anything else, *Exzellenz*?" he asked.

"I want a couple of knives." Drummond pointed through the glass top of the counter, underneath the crossbow. "The survival knife, and that six-bladed Swiss Army knife."

Paul retrieved them from the display case, setting them carefully next to the crossbow bolts.

"And," Drummond continued, "I need a special knife as a gift. Perhaps you could suggest something?"

"Certainly," Paul said. "They are down here, at the other end of the display case."

Drummond followed Paul to the far end of the glass-topped counter, where more than a dozen knives were displayed in two oak trays, richly lined with dark green velvet.

"These knifes are hand made," Paul said, as he lifted the two trays out of the case so Drummond could inspect the knives. "They are simply *die beste*."

"Which one would you recommend?" Drummond asked.

"A skinning knife is the most useful," Paul said, warming to his subject as he picked up a small knife with gold mounts and a stag horn handle. "This has a Damascus blade." He drew the knife from its sheath so Drummond could see the swirls and ridges forged into the blade by a master smith. "Any huntsman would be proud to own such a knife."

It was obvious that Paul would have been delighted to own the knife himself. A glance at the price tag, however, told Drummond that it was far beyond the financial realities of a stock clerk at Kettner's, even one who spoke English. "All right, I'll take it," Drummond said. "Now, how about that large knife with the ivory handle?"

"This is probably the finest knife in Europe," Paul said as he carefully lifted the dagger from the display tray. "It is a copy of a fifteenth-century Swiss dagger that was made by Paul Muller just before he died." He handed the weapon to Drummond. "See how exactly the curve of the pommel and the cross guard match? Can you feel how the swell in the grip fills your hand when you hold the knife?"

Drummond nodded.

"Now, take the dagger out of its scabbard and look at its blade," Paul said.

The finely wrought gold filigree covering the dark blue Moroccan leather scabbard depicted Parzival reaching for the Holy Grail. As Drummond slowly withdrew the broad, spear-pointed blade from the scabbard, rich gold letters danced above the soft silver-gray Damascus waves that Paul Muller had hammered into soft iron years before.

"The blade is made from the iron of a meteorite," Paul said. "In the Middle Ages, such blades were thought to come from heaven."

"What does the inscription say?" Drummond asked.

"It is old German," Paul said. "It means 'A True Knight.'"

Drummond returned the dagger to its sheath. "I'll take them both," he said. "You can prepare my bill."

They carried the crossbow and bolts and knives back downstairs to the cash desk, where Paul had left the clothing, camping gear, and other paraphernalia Drummond had selected. Paul ran the light pen across the barcoded tags attached to the merchandise, his eyebrows going up a notch when he saw the total.

"That will be seventy-three thousand schillings, *Exzellenz*," Paul said, watching as Drummond wrote out the check without batting an eye and handed it to him with his check guarantee card. "Thank you very much, *Exzellenz*."

As Paul dutifully copied the numbers from the card onto the back of the check, Drummond asked, "Do you think you could have these things delivered to my hotel?"

"Certainly, *Exzellenz*," the young man said with a stiff little bow. "You are staying at the Imperial, perhaps?"

"No. Palais Schwarzenberg."

The young man's eyebrows went up another notch, and even greater deference crept into his shaky English.

"I shall myself bring your items to the Palais, *Exzellenz*," he said, giving Drummond another bow, this one bringing his head perilously close to the corner of an ornate brass cash register.

Drummond thanked him, then left the store before the young man could seriously injure himself with another bow. Outside, he hailed a taxi and with a minimum of difficulty made the scruffy-looking driver understand that he wanted to go back to the Palais Schwarzenberg.

The taxi reeked of garlic and stale tobacco, and from

the pitching back seat Drummond watched in some amazement as his chauffeur hauled away at the wheel, pushing the arthritic Audi through the afternoon traffic. Finally, to a never-ending chorus of muttered curses, they hove to in front of Drummond's hotel.

It was obvious by the pained expression on the doorman's face that the "boulevard express" delivering Drummond back to his lodgings was not a welcome sight on the hotel forecourt. Discreetly removing one of his white gloves, the doorman approached the taxi and, with a fair amount of effort, managed to pry open Drummond's door.

"Fuerhunnert schilling," the driver demanded, as Drummond stepped from the taxi. Before he could reach for his wallet, the doorman intervened.

"Has the *Kapitän* come from the airport?" he asked Drummond.

"No," Drummond replied. "I've just come from Kettner's on the Sielergasse. Why?"

Without answering, the doorman turned to the taxi and, bending down, spoke softly to the driver in German, none of which Drummond caught except the tone and the word *Polizei* at the end. The driver stared back in tight-lipped silence.

"There was some confusion over the fare, Herr Kapitän," the doorman said apologetically. "I have explained what will happen if he ever tries to rob one of our guests again. The cost of the ride is forty schillings."

Restraining a smile, Drummond paid the driver, who drove off in a spray of gravel.

"Thank you," Drummond said to the doorman, handing him a one-hundred schilling note. "Four dollars a minute is a little high, even for taxis in Los Angeles."

The doorman bowed as Drummond entered the hotel.

"Thank you, Herr Kapitän."

Drummond headed for the desk and asked if there were any messages for him.

"No messages, Kapitän, but this package arrived by bank messenger at about two o'clock." The desk clerk handed Drummond a sealed envelope.

"Thank you," Drummond said. "I'm expecting the delivery of some more packages later this afternoon. Could you see that they're put in my suite when they arrive?"

"Certainly, Kapitän. Will there be anything else?"

"No, just the key, thank you." As the clerk handed him his key, he turned and went up the stone stairs to his room.

He looked at his watch as he went inside and realized that it was nearly four o'clock, and he still had two important calls to make. Settling down at the desk in his sitting room, he pulled out his notepad and turned to the back page, where he had earlier written down several important phone numbers.

The first number rang repeatedly, and just as he was about to hang up, a woman's voice answered on the other end of the line.

"Hotel im Schloss Dielstein." The voice sounded somewhat hollow, and Drummond hoped that she spoke English.

"This is Captain John Drummond calling," he said. "I should like to book a room for tomorrow."

"One moment please." The voice set down the telephone, and Drummond could hear some kind of commotion on the desk, close to the receiver, and then the click of the line going on hold.

"So sorry, Kapitän." The voice returned after a moment. "Are you still there?"

"Yes, I'm still here," Drummond replied, trying to imagine what the owner of the voice looked like.

"How many in your party, please?" the voice asked.

"Just me."

"Ach, excellent. Then for tomorrow I can give you a room for three days. Or do you need to stay longer?" the receptionist asked.

"Three days will be fine." Drummond had planned to stay only the one night, but an extra day or two might give him an opportunity to become better acquainted with the baroness.

"Very good, Kapitän. We shall expect you tomorrow afternoon. *Wiedersehen.*"

"Wiedersehen," Drummond replied.

Having booked in at the castle, Drummond placed his second call. After the second ring, a gentlemanly voice came on the line.

"Bitte?"

Drummond immediately recognized von Liebenfalz' voice.

"Baron von Liebenfalz, this is John Drummond," he said.

"Captain Drummond, this is a surprise. Don't tell me you have already received my letter there in Los Angeles?" von Liebenfalz said.

"No, I'm afraid I haven't received your letter. I'm here in Vienna. I was calling to ask you to join me for dinner."

"I am sorry, Captain, but I have an engagement this evening, and I will be away this weekend," he said. "Perhaps some other time?"

Drummond could tell by von Liebenfalz' tone of voice that there were no other engagements that evening; only a sense of propriety prevented his accepting the invitation.

"I leave Vienna tomorrow, sir. Perhaps you could join me for a cocktail on your way to your other engagement?"

"Certainly," von Liebenfalz said, the social compromise having been agreed. "Where shall we meet?"

"The Palais Schwarzenberg, if that's not inconvenient," Drummond suggested.

"Splendid," von Liebenfalz replied. "Shall we say, drinks at seven o'clock?"

Drummond said good-bye to von Liebenfalz and had just put the phone down when it immediately began to ring.

"Kapitän Drummond?" It was the desk clerk. "There is a gentleman here to see you. His name is Hamilton-Bolt."

"I'll be right down," Drummond said. Replacing the handset on the cradle, he put on his jacket and headed down to the lobby.

"Ha. There you are," Hamilton-Bolt said, before Drummond had even emerged from behind the large potted palms that flanked the staircase leading to his suite.

"Don't tell me that my car is ready now," Drummond said, as he shook the older man's hand.

"Nope. Bit of a problem on that score, I'm afraid." Hamilton-Bolt screwed his face into a mock-serious frown.

"Problem?" Drummond asked.

"Yes. The car phone chappie won't have you hooked up until tomorrow. I'm afraid that we won't be able to deliver your car until sometime around noon." Hamilton-Bolt looked as if his failure to deliver the car ahead of schedule was somehow an ineradicable blot on Britannia's escutcheon. "Damn bad show."

"Well, I shouldn't worry about it too much," Drummond said. "Do you think it will be ready by noon?"

"Oh, absolutely, even if they have to keep working all night," the older man said. "Now, if we could just take care of one or two formalities?" He reached into an inside pocket and produced a sheaf of papers. "Need you to sign some things—lease papers and insurance and tax documents. A lease is all right, I hope? The bank said it would be most cash efficient."

"Yes, that's fine," Drummond said.

He and Hamilton-Bolt sat down at a small table in the corner of the lobby, and while Drummond signed in triplicate, the Englishman ordered tea. A waiter in white gloves and striped vest brought a silver tea service to the table just as Drummond handed the last of the papers back to Hamilton-Bolt.

"So tell me," Drummond said, "how long have you been in Vienna?"

"Ha. That's an easy one," Hamilton-Bolt replied, giving his tea a stir. "Arrived Christmas Day, 1944."

"Oh, were you a prisoner?" Drummond asked.

"Not on your life—at least not until the Russians arrived. No, I was sent in by His Majesty's Government to negotiate a German surrender with Himmler. Of course, the politicians got it all bollocked up." He sipped his tea from the dark blue and gilt cup. "They should have been dealing with Göring. He grew up in Austria. Anyway, when the war ended, I stayed. Made myself useful to the Allies and a damned nuisance to the Russians." He glanced at his watch.

"Ha. Time to go." Hamilton-Bolt set down his cup. "Sorry for the delay in getting your car to you," he said as they stood up. "Awfully sorry, but not to worry. I'll have it here by noon tomorrow."

"That will be just fine, sir," Drummond said as they shook hands. "I'll see you tomorrow."

Hamilton-Bolt's exit from the hotel lobby was delayed by the arrival of Drummond's packages from Eduard Kettner's. Carefully avoiding a collision with the elderly British gentleman, Paul maneuvered the last of the packages through the door and placed them with the others already stacked neatly next to the desk. When Hamilton-Bolt had gone, Drummond walked over to where Paul was checking items off his list a final time and counting packages.

"Well," Drummond said, "I sure hope it all fits in the car."

"*Exzellenz?*" Paul asked.

Drummond gave him a half smile in reply. "Where are the knives?" he asked.

"Here," Paul said, producing two gift-wrapped packages from somewhere near the top of the pile.

Drummond took the two packages and weighed them in his hands for a few seconds, then handed the smaller one back to Paul.

"Thank you for all of your help at the store," he said. "I hope you will find this a useful gift when you are out hunting."

Paul stared at Drummond in wide-eyed disbelief for several seconds before he found his voice.

"For me, *Exzellenz?*" he asked.

"Yes," Drummond said. "For you. *Danke schön.*"

Turning, he walked across the lobby and into the bar of the hotel. He peered out one of the front windows a few minutes later just in time to see Paul walking out to the Kettner's van, shaking his head and still staring at the package in his hands in disbelief.

Smiling, Drummond headed back up to his room to shower and change before drinks with von Liebenfalz.

He was back in the bar just before seven, sitting where he could see the driveway out to the main street. Just on seven, von Liebenfalz' blue-and-black Bentley pulled up the drive and glided majestically to a halt in front of the main entrance. The door swung open on large chromed hinges, providing just a glimpse of the gray leather interior and polished walnut dash as a well-dressed gentleman in a dark blue suit, homburg, and matching gloves and spats stepped out of the car.

Drummond tried to guess von Liebenfalz' age as he watched him return the doorman's deep bow with an almost imperceptible nod of his head. Seventy-plus seemed to be a reasonable guess. The car had to be somewhere between fifty and sixty years old, and von Liebenfalz had the look of someone who had probably bought it new.

As the baron entered the lobby, one of the bellmen met him at the door and escorted him back to where Drummond was seated in the bar. At the approach of von Liebenfalz, Drummond stood.

"Baron," he said, nodding toward the older gentlemen. "How kind of you to join me for a drink."

"My pleasure, Kapitän Drummond," von Liebenfalz said, pulling off his gray gloves and handing them to the bellman along with his hat and gold-headed walking stick. Settling into a gilded chair, von Liebenfalz carefully adjusted the crease in his trousers before casually crossing his legs. "So, what delightful pleasure brings you back to Vienna?"

The question took Drummond slightly off-guard.

"Sightseeing," he said, hoping that the answer didn't sound too lame.

"Ah, *gut*. And what did you see today?" von Liebenfalz asked. "The Schönbrunn, perhaps?"

"No." Drummond smiled. "Nothing so intellectual. I was out at the Volksprater."

The waiter's arrival allowed Drummond to gracefully change the subject. "What would you like to drink?" he asked.

"Kir, please," von Liebenfalz said.

"And a whisky with water," Drummond added.

Bowing, the waiter retired to the far end of the room, returning only a few minutes later with their drinks on a small silver tray. Von Liebenfalz raised his glass to Drummond.

"Am blanken Schwert, Am Falkenflug, Am stolzen Pferd, Am schoenen Weib. Prost!"

"Prost," Drummond replied, raising his glass in return as he joined von Liebenfalz in his toast. "I'm afraid that since I don't speak German, I'll have to ask you to translate what you've just said," he said as he set down his drink.

"It is the traditional toast of the questing knight," von Liebenfalz said. "A drawn sword, a falcon's flight, a stalwart horse, a lovely wife." He gave Drummond a conspiratorial smile. "Any man who finds no pleasure in these things does not have the spirit of chivalry."

"Speaking of which, you said you had sent me a letter?" Drummond asked.

"Ah, yes. My letter." Von Liebenfalz took a sip of his kir. "I made some discreet inquiries about the Order of the Sword after our last meeting, and through a contact of mine in Switzerland I was able to acquire the insignia of the order from an antique dealer in Paris. Given your— shall we say—'interest' in the order, I thought you might be interested in owning the insignia yourself."

"Do you mind if I ask how your contact obtained the insignia?" Drummond found himself using the same casual tone he might have employed in speaking to someone fencing stolen watches, just before making the arrest.

"Well," von Liebenfalz replied, "that is the same question I asked. After all, the Order of the Sword is shrouded in mystery. The Vatican still recognizes it as an extant order, even though it seems to have vanished nearly seven hundred years ago. As a matter of fact, they still appoint a Cardinal Protector of the Order who is resident in Jerusalem, and who maintains a choir to pray for the order three times a day.

"Even so—" Von Liebenfalz interrupted himself to sip his kir. "If you request any information on the order from the usual channels, your letter is returned, unopened."

"So where did the insignia come from?" Drummond asked.

"Well, one day a very well-bred gentleman entered my friend's shop and sold him the insignia." Von Liebenfalz signaled to the waiter for another drink. "My friend contacted the maker of the insignia in Paris, and they checked their records. The insignia had been manufactured in 1886 for Cardinal Bernardo Bonaparte, a distant cousin of Napoleon III. Cardinal Bonaparte was a nephew of Cardinal Fesch, a half uncle of Napoleon I. Interestingly, both Cardinal Fesch and Cardinal Bonaparte were Protectors of the Order of the Sword."

The waiter arrived with another round of drinks, and von Liebenfalz waited until he had left before continuing his story.

"As far as who the man was who sold the insignia to my friend—well, I really don't know. The transaction was conducted in cash, and all my friend could tell me was that he thought the man might have been Romanian, by his accent. Who he was, or where he came from, no one knows."

"I see," Drummond said. "I don't suppose you would have brought the insignia with you this evening?"

"No, I didn't think to bring it," von Liebenfalz said. "Perhaps I could send it to you on Monday?"

"I'm afraid that won't be possible. I'm leaving tomorrow, and I may not be back for quite some time."

"Might I ask where you are going? Perhaps I could send the insignia to your hotel," von Liebenfalz said.

"I'll be at Schloss Dielstein for a few days, then I'll be touring Germany. I'm afraid I haven't any solid plans," Drummond replied.

"Ah, Schloss Dielstein." A hint of nostalgia crept into von Liebenfalz' voice. "I knew it well, before the war. The old baron was one of the last truly great aristocrats. Please convey my warmest good wishes to his granddaughter."

"I certainly shall, sir," Drummond said.

Von Liebenfalz set down his glass and pulled a gold pocket watch from the breast pocket of his suit. When he pressed the stem with his thumb, the case popped open. Von Liebenfalz gave the watch a studied glance, then snapped the case shut.

"I must be going, Kapitän Drummond," he said, standing up. "Thank you for the drink."

"You are more than welcome, sir," Drummond said. "Perhaps next time you'll join me for dinner."

"Perhaps," von Liebenfalz said. "I'm sure we shall meet again."

The bellman appeared at von Liebenfalz' elbow and handed him his hat, gloves, and walking stick.

"And please," the baron said to Drummond, as he pulled on the gray kid gloves, "do remember to give my regards to Baroness von Diels."

Drummond watched as von Liebenfalz crossed the lobby and vanished, almost wraithlike, through the doors of the hotel.

A drawn sword, a falcon's flight, a steadfast horse, a beautiful wife, he mused. Yes, he'd give von Liebenfalz' kindest regards to the baroness.

CHAPTER 12

Drummond stood looking at the bullet holes in the body of the ancient motorcar: neat, slightly oblong holes where the .32 caliber slugs had struck the side of the car and, passing through the thin metal skin of the vehicle, had deformed before tearing through the upholstery in an explosion of leather and horsehair.

The royal occupants in the back seat had been killed, though not instantly. The Archduke Franz Ferdinand and his wife, the Archduchess Sophia, had been carried into the post office, where local doctors tried frantically to stop Sophia's bleeding. Franz Ferdinand, heir-apparent to the Austro-Hungarian Empire, had refused all medical attention as he sat in a rickety wooden chair in the far corner of the room, in shock and concerned for the quickly ebbing life of his wife. No one, probably not even the archduke, realized that he had been badly wounded in the chest.

At the first sound of gunfire, he had thrown himself across his wife's body to shield her. One of the last shots fired by Gavarillo Princips had struck the archduke in the chest, entering his body behind the row of medals pinned to the front of his uniform. The medals had covered the bullet hole—and with the archduke insisting that he was uninjured, it was assumed that the blood on his snow white tunic was that of his wife.

After trying for twenty minutes to save the life of the archduchess, the doctors had turned to the ashen-faced man in the stained white uniform to tell him that his wife had died. As the doctors approached Franz Ferdinand, he had slid to the floor, dead.

That had been nearly a century before. Drummond found it amazing, in an eerie, surreal sort of way, to be standing in a room where time stood frozen. Next to the bloodstained motorcar that had carried the pair was a glass sarcophagus, and laid out in it was the uniform Franz Ferdinand had worn on the day he was murdered. In this one small room in Austria's Military History Museum, tucked away in a complex called the Arsenal, was preserved the exact moment when a thousand-year dynasty had ended, plunging the world into the most horrible war it was ever to know.

Vienna itself, Drummond mused, was also in a partial state of suspended animation. Von Liebenfalz' apartment, Eberle's home, the hotel where he was staying—all were very much part of a past that had ended on a hot, dusty day in Sarajevo in 1914. Very little had moved. He glanced at his watch and was almost startled to see the sweep second hand moving across its black face, the luminous hands signaling the approach of noon.

Walking quietly away from the wounded motorcar and embalmed uniform, he headed out of the museum and caught a taxi back to his hotel. As it pulled into the forecourt of the Palais Schwarzenberg, he was surprised to see several hotel employees crowded around his Range Rover. It soon became apparent, from the commotion, that a great deal of effort was going into packing Drummond's luggage and all of his outdoor gear into the back of the car, with bags and boxes being inserted and removed like pieces of a giant jigsaw puzzle. Inside, Herr Hubmann greeted him with a polite bow as he approached the desk.

"Kapitän Drummond," Hubmann said. "How was your visit to the army museum?"

"Interesting, very interesting," Drummond replied. "I see my car is here. I hope you haven't had any difficulty in loading it."

"None at all, Kapitän," Hubmann replied. "The car was delivered about fifteen minutes ago." He handed Drummond a thick manila envelope. "These are the insurance and registration documents and," he handed him a leather key case, "these are your extra keys."

"Thank you," Drummond said. "It's been a pleasure staying here again. Is my bill tallied up?"

"It is, Kapitän," Hubmann said, handing him another envelope. "I trust you will find everything in order."

"I'm sure I will," Drummond said, slipping the envelope and the car documents into the inside pocket of his navy blazer. *"Auf wiedersehen, Herr Hubmann."*

"Kapitän." Hubmann bowed and clicked his heels.

"Oh, Kapitän Drummond," Hubmann said, as Drummond turned to leave. "There was a young man here earlier this morning. He left this for you." He handed Drummond a small envelope with "S.E. Herr Drummond" printed neatly across its front.

"S.E.?" Drummond asked, glancing at Hubmann.

"Sein Exzellenz," Hubmann supplied.

"Ah. Thank you." Turning aside, Drummond opened the envelope and took out the folded note inside.

Exzellenz,
I am most sincerely flattered by the generosity of your most excellent gift. There is an old tradition in my coun-

try, and perhaps in yours as well, that when a huntsman is given a knife he must in some way pay for it, lest it cut the bonds of brotherhood that unite all hunters. I hope then that you will accept this payment as a token of my respect and continuing friendship, should you ever return to my country.

Yours truly,

Paul Gemmer

Taped to the bottom of the page was a small Austrian coin.

Smiling, Drummond carefully folded the note and put it in an outside pocket of his blazer as he walked out of the hotel and climbed into his Range Rover. His bags were on the seats behind him, his other purchases stowed behind the back seats. Hamilton-Bolt had thoughtfully left the owner's manual on the passenger seat, and Drummond spent several minutes familiarizing himself with the car before starting up and easing out into the Vienna traffic.

At a service plaza just before the entrance to the autobahn, he bought a large European road atlas and half a dozen classical music tapes, one of which he immediately popped into the Range Rover's tape deck. After a brief consultation with the map, he headed west toward Schloss Dielstein, with Hayden's Trumpet Concerto in E flat providing the background music to the changing panorama of the Austrian countryside.

The Range Rover owner's manual had advised against sustained high-speed cruising for the first five hundred miles, so Drummond used the admonition as an excuse to leave the autobahn and meander along the narrow roads that ran through the small villages to the west of Vienna. As he drove along, Drummond found himself thinking of the Baroness von Diels, idly speculating whether or not Franz Reidl would be at dinner that evening. It had been more than five years since Drummond's wife had been injured, and during that time he had only casually dated other women.

He supposed that it was the remoteness of the baroness that made him wonder what sort of woman she really was. One thing was for certain, he decided. It was unlikely that she would have any interest in him. It was his experience that beautiful women had no shortage of admirers, and the baroness was beautiful. No, some lucky local, like Reidl, would have the inside track on the attentions of the baroness.

It was late in the afternoon when Drummond finally turned off the road from Reid and headed down the dusty, tree-lined avenue of Schloss Dielstein. Unlike the occasion of his previous visit, there were a number of cars parked in front of the castle, including a scarlet Bugatti convertible casually drawn up next to the Teutonic bulk of an older Mercedes-Benz.

Having found a shady spot to park, Drummond got out and headed toward the main entrance to the castle. As he reached the door, he was greeted by Joachim the butler, who bowed formally as he came through the door.

"*Guten Abend, Kapitän Drummond,*" he said. "May I bring in your luggage?"

"Just the bags on the back seat, thank you," Drummond replied.

"Certainly, sir. If you will follow me, the baroness is waiting on the terrace with some of her guests."

Joachim turned and led Drummond across the great hall and into a small sitting room that opened onto the marbled terrace, where an assortment of mostly elderly men and women were having drinks. Stopping at the open

French doors, the butler signaled discreetly for Drummond to wait until he was announced.

"*Sein Exzellenz, Kapitän Drummond.*" Stepping to the side, Joachim bowed as Drummond moved past him and out onto the terrace.

The baroness was chatting with a handful of proper-looking dowagers, but immediately excused herself and crossed over to where Drummond was standing.

"Captain Drummond," she said, extending her hand. "I am delighted to see you."

Drummond took the outstretched hand and kissed it. "It's a pleasure to be here once again, Baroness," he said, savoring for just a moment the subtle aroma of her perfume. "I hope my visit won't interfere with your party."

"Not at all," she said. Then in a somewhat lowered voice, she added, "It will be pleasant to have someone to talk to who is younger than my butler."

She took Drummond by the arm and introduced him to several of the people on the terrace, but always steered him away from them before he could be trapped in a conversation. A servant carrying a tray of drinks came up to them and, with a slight bow, presented the tray.

"Can I offer you a drink?" the baroness asked.

"Certainly," Drummond replied. "Some white wine, please."

"Ah, that is typically Californian, Captain," she said as she handed him the delicately stemmed glass. "I hope our local wines won't disappoint you."

Drummond sipped the wine. Its sparkling effervescence was like biting into a crisp, cold apple.

"There is nothing in California to compare with the charms of Austria, Baroness," he said, lifting the glass in salute.

"Please," she said, blushing slightly at Drummond's compliment. "Call me Maria."

"Only if you agree to call me John," Drummond replied good-naturedly.

Maria's smile betrayed a hint of smug satisfaction as she flicked her gaze out over the terrace and her other guests. "I was afraid you would never ask."

Drummond was about to comment when they were interrupted by Joachim's announcement of another arrival.

"*Sein Exzellenz, der Freiherr von Liebenfalz,*" he said, bowing as von Liebenfalz stepped onto the terrace, impeccably dressed in a light blue suit with snow-white spats and matching Borsalino hat.

Maria let out a little sigh. "Dear old Anton so loves to make an entrance. Please excuse me, John."

She made her way through the other guests and let von Liebenfalz kiss her hand before taking his arm to steer him deftly back to where Drummond stood quietly sipping his wine.

"Baron von Liebenfalz," Maria began, "allow me to present—"

"Chevalier Drummond," von Liebenfalz interrupted smoothly. "What an unexpected pleasure to see you here this afternoon."

"The afternoon is full of pleasant surprises, sir," Drummond said, nodding slightly toward Maria. "I had no idea, when we had drinks last night, that we'd be seeing each other again so soon."

"The world is full of such happy surprises," von Liebenfalz said.

"Yes, it certainly is," Maria said. "Now, if you and 'Chevalier' Drummond," she arched an eyebrow at the use of Drummond's title, "will excuse me, I have to see to the Gräfin von Forschtenstein." Turning abruptly, she left the two men and walked across the terrace to a grouping of elderly dowagers.

"So, did you drive up from Vienna?" von Liebenfalz asked.

"Yes, I did," Drummond replied, still gazing after Maria.

"You have hired a car, then?"

"No. Actually I bought a car a few days ago, and it was only delivered to my hotel this morning." Drummond returned his attention to the baron. "Why do you ask?"

"Oh, I am car mad, that's why." The baron smiled. "What sort of car did you buy?"

"A Range Rover."

"The black one out front?"

"That's it, unless there's more than one out front," Drummond replied, wondering at the interest.

Von Liebenfalz set down his glass. "No, I saw only one. You know, I have always admired Range Rovers, but I have never taken the opportunity to examine one at close range. Would you be so kind as to show me yours? If it isn't too much trouble."

Drummond could see that the baroness wasn't in a hurry to return, so he agreed. At least he knew von Liebenfalz; he didn't know any of the rest of these people.

"Sure," he said, setting his glass next to von Liebenfalz'. "Let's go take a look."

Out in front of the castle, von Liebenfalz carefully inspected Drummond's Rover the way a veterinarian pokes and prods a horse for soundness. Finally, wrinkling his nose, the old man sniffed loudly and pronounced the vehicle fit.

"I suppose I'm too old to appreciate it," the baron said, "but I just can't imagine giving up one of my old cars for something so—so modern and, if I may say it, so soulless."

"There is a lot to be said for the modern car," Drummond replied.

"Have you ever driven a thoroughbred motorcar, Chevalier?"

"No, I don't suppose I have," Drummond replied. "And if you don't mind my asking, what's with this 'Chevalier' stuff?"

"You are too modest, Captain Drummond. Let me take you for a ride in the Bugatti and I shall explain." Von Liebenfalz walked over to the open car and opened the passenger door. "Hop in. We'll go for a little drive."

Drummond climbed in on the left side as the baron came around to the other and got in.

"This is a Type 57C, Captain Drummond," von Liebenfalz said, as the supercharged eight-cylinder engine rumbled to life. "Most people consider it Bugatti's finest road car. I have to say that they are right, although I find it a trifle less substantial than my Bentley." He grasped the long gear lever gracefully arching up from the center of the floor and slotted it into reverse. "I'd say that it lacks the stamina of the British car, although it makes up for it with a sort of nervous energy of its own."

He engaged first gear, and the car accelerated up the drive at a speed that Drummond wouldn't have expected from a car over fifty years old. Turning at the gates, von Liebenfalz soon had the Bugatti cruising at 130 kph on the narrow road that leads towards Salzburg, the wind whipping in their hair.

"Remarkable, isn't it?" von Liebenfalz shouted above the whine of the supercharger, as he put his foot down and the car shot up to 160 kph. "That's one hundred miles per hour. Not bad for a machine that's over half a century old."

As the car sped down the narrow road, Drummond remembered what it was like in a police car in hot pursuit. Driving really fast after a fleeing suspect was the most exciting thing you could do as a cop. Riding shotgun under the same circumstances was the most frightening. Drummond could recall the first time he was passenger in a speeding police car and wishing that he could hide in the glove box until the ride was over.

The Bugatti didn't have a glove box.

Von Liebenfalz finally pulled over to the side of the road and parked in the shade of an immense oak tree.

"Now, you drive back," he said. Stepping out of the car, he walked around the rear of the Bugatti and opened Drummond's door. "Come on, slide over behind the wheel."

"Oh, no. I really don't think . . ."

Drummond's protest died on his lips as von Liebenfalz pointed a small gold-plated Browning automatic at his head.

"Move over, and keep both hands on the wheel."

Drummond did as he was told, wondering if von Liebenfalz intended to shoot him here or back at the castle.

"Now, Chevalier Drummond, before we go any farther, I have a few questions that need answering." Von Liebenfalz kept the little pistol trained on Drummond's head as he slid into the passenger seat and closed the door.

"Shoot," Drummond said, instantly regretting his choice of words.

"I will, if I don't like your answers," von Liebenfalz replied. "Now, what is a knight of the Order of the Sword doing talking to the Mossad?"

For a moment Drummond was stunned by the question and groped for an answer he hoped von Liebenfalz would believe.

"Well?" The gold-plated automatic didn't waver from its intended target.

"To begin with, I don't know what you mean about being a knight of the Order of the Sword . . ."

"Don't lie, Chevalier. It is unbecoming of a knight," von Liebenfalz snapped.

"All right. As far as my meeting with the Mossad is concerned, they wanted to know what I was doing with a bunch of ex-Nazis, such as yourself." Drummond turned his head to look at the baron.

"Did they tell you what we are doing?" Von Liebenfalz' voice betrayed no emotion.

"No, they didn't. And frankly, Baron, I don't give a damn what you're up to, except that because of our meeting, the Mossad tried to kill me," Drummond stared into von Liebenfalz' eyes. "And now it seems that you intend to finish off the job they flubbed in Los Angeles."

Von Liebenfalz slowly lowered his pistol. "Drive back to the castle," he said.

A dark blue Mercedes-Benz limousine was parked out front of the castle, the back quarter of its roof neatly folded down like a convertible. The doors displayed a discreet coat of arms beneath a golden crown, and in place of the usual Mercedes emblem on the radiator cap was a special mascot: two arms brandishing a broadsword issuing out of a princely coronet.

Drummond parked the Bugatti near the Mercedes limousine and then, at von Liebenfalz' command, switched off the engine. His pistol trained on Drummond, von Liebenfalz slowly backed out of the car and then motioned for Drummond to climb out the same side. Only when Drummond was out of the car did von Liebenfalz speak.

"You will walk just ahead of me and do exactly what I say. Do you understand?"

"Do I put my hands up?" Drummond asked.

"If you do, I'll shoot off the little finger of your right hand," von Liebenfalz said. "Now, into the castle."

Joachim met them at the door, and seemed oblivious to von Liebenfalz' pistol and to Drummond's presence.

"Take me to the prince." Von Liebenfalz sounded as casual as a man asking his chauffeur to take him to the airport.

Joachim bowed and led them down the corridor and into the library of the castle.

Sunlight flooded into the room through a stone-mullioned window, splashing small pools of colored light onto the floor where it passed through stained glass coats of arms. Seated at an antique military desk in the center of the room was a distinguished looking man in his mid-fifties who seemed to be deeply engrossed in the report in front of him.

"You can put away your pistol, Anton," he said without looking up from the papers in front of him. "If Chevalier Drummond had wanted to kill me, he could have let the assassin on the plane do it weeks ago." He turned and looked at Drummond. "Hello, Captain. I never did thank you for saving my life."

Drummond instantly recognized the man.

"On the plane. You were the intended victim," he said.

"Yes, and I'm sorry if your clothes were ruined when they hacked off the assassin's hand." The man smiled. "Anton, we've met before, but perhaps you'd be kind enough to formally introduce us."

"Certainly, Your Highness. Allow me to present Captain John Drummond, a knight of the Order of the Sword." Von Liebenfalz turned to Drummond. "Chevalier Drummond, His Most Serene Highness, the Prince of Antioch."

CHAPTER 13

The prince extended his hand and Drummond shook it, bowing awkwardly as he did.

"Your Highness," he said, and then straightened up to look him full in the face. "Just what the hell's going on here?"

"I suppose there are a hundred answers I could give you, Chevalier Drummond, but I hope you'll settle for just one: the truth." The prince closed the file folder in front of him and gestured for Drummond to sit. "All of the guests here at the castle are representatives of the various orders of chivalry that have pledged to restore the Kingdom of Jerusalem."

"The Kingdom of Jerusalem?" Drummond asked, easing into a chair that von Liebenfalz moved closer for him. "I'm sorry, Your Highness, but I don't quite follow."

"The Kingdom of Jerusalem was founded at the time of the First Crusade and existed until 1244, when Jerusalem fell to the Moslems. As Prince of Antioch, I represent the royal family of that kingdom—a kingdom we have tried to win back for the Christian world since the Moslems first desecrated our holy shrines in the thirteenth century.

"We would have recovered our rightful lands and throne six hundred and fifty years ago, if the king of France hadn't succeeded in destroying the Knights Templar," he went on. "The Templars had built an enormous fleet and had raised enough money to finance a century-long crusade. When the French king heard of our plans, he met with us in secret and demanded to be named King of Jerusalem and Emperor of the East. The council of knights turned him down, and in turn he set about ruining our plans by destroying the power and wealth of the Templars. You do know about the Templars?"

"I was in DeMolay in high school," Drummond said uncertainly.

"Ah, then you know at least a little of what I'm about to tell you. The Templars were suppressed and destroyed. During the next four hundred years, our fortunes rose and fell with the politics of Europe. After the expulsion of the Moslems from Spain at the end of the fifteenth century, we had looked to that country to help us regain the Holy Land. Instead, the greatest power in the world went into decadent decline, living off the wealth of its colonies in the New World.

"In the eighteenth century, we had hoped to prosper by supporting the house of Stuart in its bid to regain the throne of Scotland and England. Even the defeat of Prince Charles didn't dim our hopes; but when he turned down the crown of America offered to him by Benjamin Franklin in 1781, we knew those hopes were gone for good."

Drummond frowned at that, for he had never heard anything about an American crown, but he decided this was not the time to interrupt the prince.

"We have been meeting and planning—or, if you prefer, conspiring—since the time of the French Revolution," the prince continued. "We helped bring Napoleon to power in exchange for his promise to mount a crusade to regain the Holy Land. We would have done it, too, if the English hadn't feared what it would have meant to their trade monopoly in India.

"By the beginning of this century, it was obvious that to regain our lands there would have to be certain realignments in Europe. We entered into secret negotiations with the Kaiser, and if Germany had won the war—well, history is full of ifs, isn't it?"

He sat back a little from the desk and toyed with a pen beside the folder lying there.

"With the rise of Zionism we once again saw an opportunity, and again we entered into secret negotiations, this time with a member of the British royal family. It was agreed that after the war Palestine would be partitioned into three countries: Israel, Palestine, and the Kingdom of Jerusalem. Not as large as it once had been, but large enough to hold the balance of power in the Middle East."

The prince paused to glance out the window, and Drummond stirred a little uneasily, reeling with the sheer volume of the information the prince was imparting.

"So, what happened to your plans?" he asked.

A little wistful, the prince returned his attention to Drummond.

"The KGB uncovered our intentions, Chevalier, and decided that our kingdom would effectively prevent their postwar domination of the Middle East. In 1942, they succeeded in planting a bomb on the plane that was carrying the Duke of Kent to a strategic meeting with U.S. General Carl Spaatz. He was killed in the crash that resulted, and once again our plans came to naught."

"And you think you might have a chance today of regaining your kingdom?" Drummond couldn't tell if the prince was serious or mentally unbalanced.

"Certainly," the prince replied. "The timing couldn't be better. Look at the situation the Middle East is in right now. Why, think of how different it would be if the Israelis withdrew to the boundaries of 1947, and Palestine was given most of the occupied lands."

"You said 'most' of the occupied lands," Drummond said. "What happens to the rest?"

"Well, Jerusalem becomes an international city under my control as king," the prince replied. "And a small buffer state is created to protect the interests of both the Palestinians and the Israelis."

"I see," Drummond said, now nearly convinced that the prince was not well grounded in reality. "And just how do I fit in?"

"It's very simple, Chevalier. I would like you to convince the members of the Order of the Sword to support me in recovering my throne." The prince smiled at Drummond the same way an indulgent adult smiles at a less than bright child.

"And what makes you so certain that the Order of the Sword will want to support you?" Drummond asked, slightly annoyed at the patronizing attitude of the prince.

"The Order of the Sword was created by one of my ancestors as the bodyguards of the princes of Antioch. The order must join with me, or it will have violated its oath to serve and protect its prince." The prince stood up, indicating that the interview was at an end. "You'll see, Chevalier Drummond. Once you have told your Grand Master of my desire to have the Order of the Sword support me, they'll come."

Drummond had also gotten to his feet when the prince rose, and just then a gentle rapping sounded on the library door. Before von Liebenfalz could move to see who it was, the door opened and Baroness von Diels entered the room.

"I do apologize for the interruption, Your Highness, but

I really think you need to consider the time. You have important guests this evening, and dinner is in an hour. You will all want to change, I'm sure." She gave Drummond a smile. "Isn't that right, Captain Drummond?"

"Far be it from me to delay anyone's dinner plans," Drummond replied, grateful for Maria's intervention.

"Well then, Chevalier Drummond, perhaps we shall continue our conversation after dinner." The prince turned to von Liebenfalz. "If I could have a word with you in private, Anton?"

Drummond and the baroness excused themselves from the library, closing the thick oak doors behind them.

"Thanks for the rescue," Drummond said, once they were out of earshot of the two men in the library.

"I was glad to do it, believe me," Maria said. "As soon as Joachim told me that Anton had marched you in at gunpoint, I decided that it was highly unlikely that you were part of the prince's little cabal."

"I'm still not sure I understand what he's up to," Drummond said, "and I've just spent the better part of an hour with him."

"Well, it really all seems very silly, except when Anton starts waving a gun about," Maria said. "Every year, for as long as I can remember, my grandfather used to invite the old prince and his friends—"

"The old prince?"

"The uncle of the present prince," she explained. "Anyhow, for years they met here every autumn and discussed ways of recovering the throne of the prince of Antioch. I always thought it was harmless. You know—old men yearning for the days of their youth.

"Five years ago my grandfather died, but in his will he said that as long as the prince wanted to hold his annual meeting here, the castle was to be made available to him.

Then, three years ago, the old prince died, and his nephew inherited the title."

They stopped outside of Drummond's room, and Maria placed her hand on his arm before he could reach for the doorknob.

"John, the prince is a dangerous man. I think he is involved with some sort of plot to recapture Jerusalem by force."

"Well, if he is, he'll have to do it without me. I'm not getting involved with him, that's for sure." Drummond gave her a smile as he spoke, hoping she'd believe him.

"That's a relief," she said, then glanced at her watch. "You had better hurry into your dinner clothes . . ."

"If you mean a tuxedo, I'm afraid I didn't bring one," Drummond said. "Maybe I'd better miss dinner."

"Don't you dare," she scolded. "I'll have Joachim see what he can find up in the attic. You might smell a bit like mothballs, but at least you'll be properly dressed. Now, get ready or my dinner party will be ruined." She gave Drummond a dazzling smile, then headed down the hall to find Joachim.

Drummond undressed and shaved while the huge tub in his bathroom filled with hot water. Sliding into the deep bath, he relaxed for a few minutes, idly wondering what sort of shot von Liebenfalz was with his tiny gold-plated automatic. Many of the so-called "experts" would scoff at that small a gun, but a well-placed shot from a .25 would kill you just as dead as a .44 magnum. And with a lot less noise. Drummond looked at the thin white scar on his left arm and decided that, having been shot once, he was glad he hadn't put the baron's marksmanship to the test.

What bothered Drummond even more than von Liebenfalz' well-armed drive into the country was the prince's knowledge of his involvement with the Order of the Sword. Either he was bluffing about Drummond's involvement with the order, based on Drummond's earlier inquiries of von Liebenfalz, or he had somehow found out about the events at the castle. And, as far as Drummond was concerned, if he knew about the castle he could have only learned about it from one of two people: Father Freise or Wilhelm Kluge.

A discreet tap at the door interrupted Drummond's thoughts.

"I've laid out your clothes, Kapitän." Drummond recognized Joachim's voice through the door. "The guests gather for drinks in twenty minutes."

Drummond pulled the plug and stood up to grab a thick white towel from the heated rack. After briskly drying off, he pulled on a pair of light blue boxer shorts and tossed the towel over the edge of the tub before going back into his bedroom.

Neatly laid out on his bed were several pairs of military trousers in varying lengths, along with a selection of high-collared uniform tunics, all of them black. Lined up in front of his wardrobe were three pairs of black boots, each with small gilt spurs set into the heels. Several collarless shirts were folded and stacked on the dresser, and next to them half a dozen collars lay coiled in a small leather case.

Drummond was trying to figure out what to wear when someone knocked at his door again.

"Come in," he said, picking up one of the shirts.

The door opened and von Liebenfalz started to enter the room.

"Oh, I do beg your pardon," he said, slightly embarrassed that Drummond wasn't dressed. "I'll come back later."

"It's all right," Drummond said. "What do you want?"

"Well," von Liebenfalz began, "I want to apologize for my behavior this afternoon in the car. I am afraid that in my desire to protect the prince I made a total ass of myself. I hope you're not upset?"

"Certainly. No hard feelings. I mean, you didn't shoot me, so how could I possibly be upset?" Drummond gave von Liebenfalz a hard look. "Is there anything else?"

The baron summoned a weak smile. "I'd like you to have this," he said, reaching into his pocket and pulling out a dark red leather case, which he handed to Drummond. "Open it. It's the insignia of the Order of the Sword that I got from Switzerland. I hope you'll accept it as a token of respect and friendship."

Drummond opened the case and carefully inspected the elegantly enamelled blue cross with golden sun wheels set between each of its arms. The cross was suspended from an ultramarine watered-silk ribbon with bright red edges, apparently intended to be worn around the neck.

"It's beautiful," Drummond said. "But I'm not sure . . ."

"Please," von Liebenfalz said. "You could wear it this evening with your uniform."

"All right. Thank you," Drummond said. "Just one thing. How does this attach to the uniform?"

"Oh, that's easy. See these two little loops, here on the ribbon?" he said, pointing them out. "They attach to two tiny hooks inside the collar. The cross and just a bit of the ribbon hang over the top button of the tunic, at the throat."

Drummond inspected the ribbon and one of the tunics. "Okay, I think I've got that figured out. Thanks. I haven't worn any of these before."

"I thought not," von Liebenfalz said, surveying the rest of what was laid out. "Ah—may I make a suggestion?"

"Sure, go ahead."

"Well, if you take a look at the overalls—" Von Liebenfalz noticed Drummond's slightly confused look. "The overalls are the uniform trousers. Anyhow, if you look at them, you will see that they are lined with chamois." He cleared his throat, slightly embarrassed. "The, uh, line of the overalls will be much more flattering if you don't wear—uh—that is to say, they are meant to be worn next to the skin, if you understand?"

Von Liebenfalz was blushing slightly.

"I understand, thank you," Drummond said.

"Ah, well," von Liebenfalz said, visibly relieved. "In that case, I shall excuse myself so you can finish dressing." With a slight bow he turned and retreated, closing the door behind him.

Drummond looked over the overalls before trying them on. There was a strap on the bottom of each leg that was obviously meant to button under the instep of the boot. They were cut very high in the waist, and the actual size was adjusted by a small half belt across the back. All three pairs seemed to be about the same size, with the only difference being the length of the legs.

"Looks simple enough," he said to himself.

After pulling off his underwear, he sat long enough to put on a pair of socks, then eased himself into the longest pair of overalls that Joachim had laid out for him. The fit seemed reasonably good.

Sitting on the edge of his bed, Drummond next tried the boots that were neatly lined up in front of the wardrobe. The boots came in three sizes: too small, way too small and about a half size too big. He opted for a second pair of socks and comfort, and buttoned the stirrup strap under the instep of each boot before standing up. It took a few minutes to get used to the small spurs attached to the heels of the boots, and he twice caught them on the carpet as he walked over to the shirts on the dresser.

Wrapping one of the stiff military collars around his neck, Drummond found that it was exactly a quarter-inch larger than his normal shirt size—which meant that he might not choke to death. Joachim had thoughtfully placed a stud in the back of the shirt's collar band, and Drummond carefully buttoned this through the center of the starched collar. Pulling on the shirt, he did up the front buttons and then fixed both ends of the collar over another small golden stud.

It was actually comfortable. Encouraged, he tucked the shirt tails into the tops of the overalls and buttoned up the fly, then began adjusting the small waist belt at the back. Stepping back to consult the full-length mirror, he caught his spurs again and toppled back onto the bed. "Damn," he muttered to himself, as he stood up again to survey himself. "These things could be lethal."

But he was already looking like some dashing extra from a period film—though the bulge revealed by the nearly skin-tight fit of the overalls made him somewhat self-conscious. Eyeing the tunic, however, he decided that it was probably long enough to provide a decent amount of cover. After trying several tunics for size and sleeve length, he fixed the insignia of the Order of the Sword to the one he had chosen, then eased it on and fiddled with the hooks that closed the standing collar before buttoning up the front. The rakish figure who looked back at him from the mirror was an elegant fellow, indeed. In the black uniform, with the blue and gold cross of the Order of the Sword at his throat, Drummond cut quite a dash.

"Well," he said to his reflection, "let's hope the baroness thinks you're as handsome."

The great hall of the castle reminded Drummond of one of the ballroom scenes from *The Prisoner of Zenda*, and any doubts he had about being overdressed were instantly banished. The room was awash with women in ball gowns and glittering tiaras, their escorts dressed in uniforms or tailcoats covered with medals. There was even a cardinal, unmistakable in his crimson robes, attended by several self-effacing younger clerics in suitably ambiguous black.

As Drummond surveyed the room, trying to identify some of the decorations being worn by the men, Joachim approached with a silver tray laden with champagne flutes. He wore formal livery of dark green, with a row of military decorations on his chest and the ribbon of the Iron Cross folded neatly through a buttonhole of his jacket.

"The *Ritter* would care for champagne?" Joachim punctuated the request with a slight bow.

"*Ja, danke,*" Drummond replied as he took one of the tall crystal glasses from the tray.

"*Bitte schön, mein Herr.* The baroness has asked me to tell you that she is sorry her attentions this evening will be occupied with the other guests. She hopes you will understand."

Bowing slightly, Joachim retreated back into the ballroom, his silver tray at the ready.

So much for being a handsome devil in uniform, Drummond thought.

Sipping his champagne, he moved slowly along the edge of the room, bowing to the ladies who smiled at him and returning the bows of other gentlemen who nodded in his direction. He was standing next to a suit of armor, listening to the sextet in the gallery, when he sensed the presence of someone standing beside him.

"A pleasant change from Mozart, isn't it?" The voice was as soft as the rustle of the crimson silk cassock its owner was wearing, but the accent was pure American.

"Your Eminence," Drummond said, bowing formally to the cardinal.

"Tell me," the cardinal said, "do you enjoy baroque music?"

"Like champagne, Your Eminence, it is delightful, but too much—well, too much of anything delightful can lead to unfortunate consequences," Drummond replied.

"I see," said the cardinal. "Do you suppose that our friends here are too delightful?"

"I would say they're interesting, perhaps even provocative." Drummond nodded to von Liebenfalz across the room. "But delightful is an adjective I would reserve only for our hostess."

"Well, Chevalier Drummond, you surprise me. Diplomacy is an art form that I would not expect to find in a policeman." The cardinal crinkled his face into what would pass for an innocent smile. "We must talk again. Now, if you will excuse me?"

"Certainly, Your Eminence." Drummond bowed as the rustle of scarlet silk receded across the room.

Jesus, he thought, *how does everybody manage to know all about me?*

"Your after-shave is quite alluring," said a softly teasing female voice from behind him. "What is it?"

Smiling, Drummond turned to greet Maria, delighted that she had finally taken notice of him. She was wearing something bottle-green and clingy that, though modestly cut, made her quite the most alluring woman in the room. Diamonds glittered in her upswept hair and at her throat.

"It's called 'Old Wool and Mothballs,' " he said lightly. "You ought to get some for the man in your life."

"I would," she laughed, "if there was one."

Joachim approached with more champagne.

"Another drink?" Drummond asked.

"No, thank you, we are about to go in to dinner. I wanted to apologize for having not been able to speak to you sooner—and to ask you if you would like to go riding in the morning."

"Sure, if you can scare up some britches and boots— that fit," Drummond said.

"Well," Maria teased, "those britches you're wearing look just fine to me."

Drummond could feel his ears turn red. "I—ah—meant the boots," he stammered. "These are a trifle large."

"I'll have Joachim see what he can find." She gave Drummond a dazzling smile. "In the meantime, I must ask you to excuse me. I have to see to my other guests."

My, but she is lovely, Drummond thought, as he watched her cross over to where the cardinal and the prince of Antioch stood talking.

As the baroness reached the prince and the cardinal, a gong sounded at one end of the room and the guests formed into two long lines. Setting down his glass, Drummond eased into one of the lines with the others and watched as the baroness and her two guests walked between the lines, arm in arm. As the entourage passed, formal bows and curtsies marked the passage of the threesome.

Bending from the waist in a deep bow, Drummond watched them pass from the corner of his eye, and unless it was the light playing tricks on him, he thought he saw Maria smiling at him.

In the dining room with the rest of the guests, Drummond found himself seated next to an agitated little man with bushy eyebrows from Finland and an elderly dowager weighed down with several enormous ropes of pearls.

"Look," the little man hissed between yellow teeth. "The prince is wearing his Garter."

Drummond was unable to resist the opening. "Probably holds his socks up," he said.

"No," the little man hissed again. "The wide blue ribbon across his chest. The Order of the Garter. It was given to him last year by the Stuart pretender to the throne of England."

"Really?" Drummond said, beginning to develop an appreciation for the deaf-mute qualities of the dowager to his left.

"Oh, yes," the little man said, squirming in his seat. "This means that the prince has broken off negotiations with the English queen."

"Indeed?" Drummond pretended to study the pattern on the rim of his plate.

"Oh, yes." The little man tugged at one eyebrow and squirmed deeper into his seat. "Of course you know what that means?"

"Certainly," Drummond replied. "With the Prince of Antioch allied to the House of Stuart, it means that we can expect to see kilted soldiers marching in Jerusalem in the not-too-distant-future."

"Do you believe that's true?" the fidgeting midget gasped.

"Oh, yes, I do. I could tell you more, but honor demands silence." Drummond gave the bushy-browed Finn a knowing look. "Don't you agree?"

"But, of course, Chevalier," he said, wringing knots into his napkin. "We must never betray our cause."

The rest of the dinner passed uneventfully, with Drummond counting the tines in his forks and the number of medals worn by the men on the opposite side of the table and casting occasional longing looks down the table at the baroness. Throughout the meal, a string quartet provided a delicate blend of Mozart and Andrew Lloyd Webber to aid the digestion, and Drummond noticed with some interest that the little man with the bushy eyebrows bobbed up and down in time to the music.

At last the meal was over, and Drummond and the other guests stood up as the prince and the cardinal left the dining room in the company of the baroness. Following along with the others, Drummond moved into the ballroom of the castle where the small ensemble struck up a waltz. The prince and the baroness led off on the first dance, soon to be joined by others moving in syncopated lock-step to the classic strains of Strauss. As Drummond watched the elegant couples swirl past in a blur of color, he was joined by von Liebenfalz.

"I am honored, Chevalier, that you have chosen to wear my gift," von Liebenfalz said, tilting his champagne glass toward the decoration at Drummond's throat.

"It seemed appropriate," Drummond replied.

"Then perhaps it would seem appropriate to speak to the Order of the Sword on our behalf?" von Liebenfalz asked.

"Not until I knew exactly what was expected of us," Drummond answered.

"Were the prince to take you into his confidence, would you speak to your fellow knights?" Von Liebenfalz sipped his champagne.

"It depends on what the prince's plans are. Anyway, I'll cross that bridge when I come to it," Drummond said.

"I think, Chevalier Drummond, that you would find it impossible to cross a bridge at any other time." Von

Liebenfalz drew himself up slightly. "Shall I tell the prince that you wish to speak to him?"

"Sure, Baron. But not tonight. I need some time to think." Drummond gave von Liebenfalz a slight nod. "If you'll excuse me, I think I'll be sociable for a little while before I turn in. It seems a shame to waste the uniform."

The first waltz had just ended, and another was beginning. Maria was already whirling onto the floor with another partner, and Drummond was not sure of local protocol on cutting in, so he crossed purposefully to the dowager who had been his silent companion at dinner. He had learned to waltz when his wife was making a period film, and he knew he would be safe from further questions on the ballroom floor.

"Madame," he said, clicking his heels and making her a bow. To overcome either language or hearing problems, he gestured toward the floor and gave her an inquiring look and a smile. Apparently the uniform did the trick, for she raised a silver lorgnette and eyed him up and down, then inclined her head and gave him her hand. As he led her onto the floor, she moved with unexpected grace, and when he took her in his arms, she was as light on her feet as a young girl. He enjoyed watching her enjoyment as they whirled around the floor, wondering how long it had been since anyone had waltzed with her, and was almost sorry when the dance ended. When he had been moving to the strains of Strauss, it had been difficult to stay too worried about the danger he was in.

He danced with several more of the ladies in the next hour, aware of many eyes upon him, apparently causing much speculation among the ladies about the handsome American chevalier who waltzed like a hussar. Eventually, he even got a dance with Maria, though it was impossible to really talk to her on the dance floor. He liked the feel of her in his arms, but the dance was over all too soon, and the prince claimed her for the next one.

He decided to go up to bed after that, for any other partner after her would have been anticlimactic. Besides, no telling how long the party would go on. He had just reached the door of his room when Joachim came down the hallway carrying a silver candelabrum ablaze with the light of five white candles.

"I am sorry, *Herr Ritter,* but the electricity has gone out in your room." He stepped past Drummond and opened the door.

"Permit me," he said, and then stepped aside so that Drummond could enter the room.

"It's a bit chilly in here," Drummond remarked as Joachim placed the candles on a small table near the massive carved oak bed.

"I will close the windows and light a fire," Joachim said, drawing the heavy drapes and then walking across the room to the fireplace. After a few seconds a small flame was flickering on the hearth, and Joachim carefully placed a log across the grate. Drummond was undoing the buttons on his tunic as Joachim placed a screen in front of the fireplace.

"If the *Ritter* will permit me," Joachim said, as he helped Drummond out of his jacket. "I have put your riding clothes in the wardrobe for tomorrow." He carefully placed the black tunic on a hanger and hung it on the back of the bedroom door.

"Good evening, *Herr Ritter.*"

He bowed slightly to Drummond, then stepped out into the hall, quietly closing the door behind him.

Drummond was still staring into the fire, thinking about princes and cardinals and elegant dowagers with silver lorgnettes, not to mention beautiful baronesses, when he heard the soft tapping at his door.

"Yes?" he said.

The door opened, and the baroness entered carrying two champagne flutes and a bottle of vintage Tattinger. She was wearing a dark burgundy satin robe with quilted white lapels and cuffs, and her hair fell loosely around her shoulders. For just a moment, Drummond was speechless.

"Mmmm, a fire," she said. "Joachim must approve of you."

"What are you doing here?" Drummond asked awkwardly.

"I've come," she said, putting out the candles next to the bed, "to help you out of those tight trousers."

CHAPTER 14

Drummond lay facedown on the bed, just drifting between sleep and awareness. Next to him, he could feel the soft warmth of Maria, one of her long legs thrown across his as she snuggled close in the early morning chill. Maria moved, her leg slowly sliding up his thigh, her hand moving along his well-muscled arm and her cheek resting on his shoulder. Drummond could feel her stretch out next to him, her firm body tense against his own.

Relaxing again, she rolled over onto Drummond and, bringing her legs up along either side of his body, straddled his buttocks and began to slowly massage his back. Drummond could feel himself growing heavy with arousal and shifted slightly into a more comfortable position as Maria caressed his back and shoulders.

"I thought you wanted to go riding this morning," he said, as she slipped her hand around his waist and began to tease him.

"I do," Maria said. "Then we can take the horses out before breakfast." She giggled softly as Drummond rolled over beneath her, his hands coming up to cup her breasts.

"Okay, cowgirl," he said, pulling her face close to his. He kissed her tenderly on the lips, his arms wrapping around her in a fulsome embrace. Slowly they rolled to the side, Maria's legs locking around Drummond's hips.

Pulling away from her, he felt her hand guiding him gently toward her.

As he sank back down on her, Maria cooed to herself and hugged Drummond as hard as she could. Together the two of them made love as the sun slowly made its way above the horizon.

When they had finished, Maria stretched across Drummond and pulled the bell cord next to the bed.

"What's that for?" he asked, as he ran the palms of his hands across her nipples.

"Coffee . . . umm, that feels nice." She gave Drummond a quick kiss. "I thought we'd have coffee before we got up."

"What will Joachim say when he finds you in my bed?" he asked, as Maria laid her head on his chest.

"Nothing," she replied. "Servants only talk if you try to hide what you are doing."

Just then there was a discreet knock at the door, followed a moment later by Joachim carrying a silver coffee service. Without a word, he carried the coffee over to Maria's side of the bed and set it down on a small table. Turning, he pulled back the drapes to let in the early morning sun and then, as silent as ever, left the room.

"Does Joachim approve of this sort of thing?" Drummond asked, as Maria poured him a cup of strong Austrian coffee.

"He must. He brought out the good coffee service and the best cups." She handed Drummond a pale ivory cup and saucer with gold rims and a tiny von Diels coat of arms on them. "If he didn't approve, he wouldn't have gone to so much extra work."

"I see," said Drummond, sipping his coffee. "And just how would he have shown his disapproval?"

"Paper cups and instant coffee, I suppose." Maria giggled. "Now, finish your coffee so we can take a bath and then go riding."

After a playful bath, Maria went back to her room to put on her riding clothes, leaving Drummond alone to dress. Walking over to the wardrobe mirror, he saw the welts on his back raised by Maria's fingernails the night before. If last night and this morning had been her way of making up for having ignored him at the dinner, Drummond decided that he wouldn't mind being ignored three or four times a week for the rest of his life.

The rest of his life. . . . While he shaved, he wondered just how long that might be. It had been five days since the Mossad had tried to kill him, and by now his nonappearance at Stockholm would have alerted the Feds and the LAPD that something wasn't right. His original plan to return to the castle of the Order of the Sword now looked less secure, with von Liebenfalz, the Prince of Antioch, and some American cardinal aware, at least on some level, of his involvement with the order.

Still, he couldn't sit around waiting for the Mossad to find him. And there was Kluge to contend with as well. Drummond had hardly thought of the vampire since his lunch with Eberle. How long ago was that? he wondered. Two, maybe three days ago? Just one night with Maria, and he had lost track of the time. He shook his head, as if to clear it.

Keep moving. The first rule of escape and evasion. He had to keep moving.

As he pulled on his underwear, Drummond decided that he'd leave after breakfast. But first, another few hours with Maria.

He went back into the bedroom. Looking at the riding kit that Joachim had turned out for him convinced Drummond that the aristocracy never threw anything away. The

old-fashioned tan britches fit snug over the knee and then
flared out over the thigh. The inside of the leg and the
seat were faced with a soft, almost suede-like leather,
while the fly was cut like a pair of sailor's bell-bottoms,
with a flap front closed with a double row of buttons.

Joachim had also provided a soft golden-brown hacking
jacket and a rust-colored cashmere turtleneck, the latter
of which Drummond pulled on. Standing in the corner of
the room were a pair of well-polished brown riding boots,
and in a small wooden box next to them were ivory-
handled boot hooks, spurs, and a can of talcum powder.

Drummond dusted the inside of the boots with talc and
then slipped the hooks into the flat canvas tabs inside the
boot tops to pull them on. Unlike the night before, the
boots fit remarkably well, and after stamping his feet a
few times to loosen the stiff leather, Drummond was
ready to ride. Pulling on the jacket and pocketing his
spurs, he headed out to the stable yard.

Maria was already there and waiting for him, looking,
Drummond decided, as desirable in her riding clothes as
she had in the bath, with the suds clinging to her firm,
up-turned breasts.

"I hope you are a good rider," she said, as a groom led
over their mounts. "Both of these horses seem to be full
of themselves today."

Drummond bent down and buckled on his spurs, then
took the reins of his horse from the groom and looped
them over his arm. Lifting the flap under the stirrup
leathers, he checked the girth before adjusting the stirrups to their correct length. Finally he looped the reins
back over the horse's head and adjusted the curb chain
under the horse's chin. Satisfied that everything was as it
should be, he grinned at Maria, then vaulted into the saddle without the aid of the stirrups.

"John, that's like in the cowboy movies," Maria laughed. "You must be a marvellous rider."

"There isn't a horse I can't ride," Drummond said in a mock-serious voice. "It's just that I can ride some of them a lot longer than others."

They both laughed at his joke, and then Maria turned her horse and led them out of the stable yard.

A dirt road led from the castle to the fields and vineyards beyond. Touching his horse in the flank with his spurs, Drummond trotted up alongside Maria's horse so they could talk.

"So, where are we headed?" he asked, as he drew even with Maria.

"The vineyards at the far end of the estate. I have to see that the vines have been pruned for next season." She gave Drummond a mischievous smile. "Let's race," she shouted, and was off in a cloud of dust.

Touching his spurs to his horse, Drummond galloped after her.

The man strapped to the chair in the sand-strewn arena watched with terror and uncomprehending fascination as the horse thundered toward him, its hooves churning up dust as it lengthened its stride in an all-out gallop. The rider, like the other riders drawn up in a row at the far end of the yard, was dressed all in black, from cap to boot—a uniform that conjured up unpleasant associations, though the man in the chair could not quite remember what they were. His name was Martin Kelber, and he had no idea how he had gotten here.

Something flashed in the rider's hand as he leaned low out of the saddle, and in the split second before he galloped past, the man in the chair realised that it was a sword, its blade arching down towards his skull. He screamed and tried to throw himself to one side, but only succeeded in spooking the horse and deflecting the rider's aim. The steel bit into his flesh and lifted his scalp, carrying away only a bit of his skull and exposing a small part of his brain to the sky.

"No, goddammit! No!" Baumann shouted at the young postulant reining in his horse at the far end of the tilting yard. "That man is still alive! A live man can kill you—even you, who think you are beyond death!"

"But the horse shied," the rider began lamely.

"Bullshit!" Baumann roared. "That horse didn't shy; you failed! Fail again, and you fail forever." He trotted his horse over to where the postulant sat on his blowing mount. "Now, watch how I do it. And when we have another target ready, I want you to do the same. Or else!"

Baumann kneed his horse around to face the wounded man, strapped to a chair lying on its side in the dusty arena. The victim lay sobbing in the dirt, blood pouring down his face and into his eyes from the saber wound he had just received, soaking into the sand.

"Set that man back up!" Baumann bellowed.

Two postulants dismounted with alacrity and ran over to right the chair, deaf to the sobs of the victim.

"Good," yelled Baumann, drawing a Cossack saber from the scabbard strapped to his saddle. "Now, get out of the way!"

With a shout, Baumann dug his spurs into his horse, causing the animal to rear before plunging to earth in a flat-out gallop. Baumann sat bolt upright in the saddle, the perfect picture of a cavalry soldier at the charge. As he thundered down on his target, he leaned forward slightly in the saddle and swung his saber in a perfect arc aimed at the victim's neck.

Martin Kelber screamed in terror, but to no avail. The

timing was perfect, and Baumann's blade sliced through Kelber's open mouth, the momentum of the horse carrying the blade through his jaw bones and severing his head. A fountain of blood gushed skyward, and Kelber's body jerked spasmodically against the leather restraints that held it upright in the chair. A few yards away, the head bounced along behind Baumann's horse.

Wheeling his charger at the far end of the tilting yard, Baumann galloped back, this time laid low over the neck of his horse, his saber held in front of him on point. As he drew even with the still-rolling head, he leaned out of the saddle and drove the point of his sword into the head, with a sweep of his arm bringing it up above him with a flourish.

Reining in hard in a cloud of boiling dust, Baumann slid his horse to a stop in front of the awe-struck postulant.

"Now, you miserable piece of pig shit, until you can do that, your horse does not shy! *Verstehen?*" Baumann shook the grisly trophy off his saber. "Set up the next target! Next man, get ready!" he shouted to the postulants at the far end of the field.

From an upper floor of the hunting lodge, Kluge watched Baumann's demonstration with pride. Baumann was the best horseman he had ever known, and it gave Kluge deep satisfaction to watch him train their young knights in the ancient skills of the mounted warrior. In this place that the world had become, they were not the specific skills that would be needed in the war Kluge proposed to renew, but the skills taught discipline. That was essential. Kluge watched with approval as Baumann trotted in and out among the young knights, bullying them into becoming cavalry soldiers who could perform any feat on horseback and would obey every command.

Turning from the window, Kluge closed his eyes and conjured up a memory of the first time he had seen Baumann on a horse, galloping through the trees—and later, scattering a Soviet patrol in the forests above Telavi.

It had been late April, and a light snow was falling as Kluge and the other prisoners were herded toward the kitchen by their guards. Out in the woods, far beyond the barbed wire fence, Kluge thought he saw movement somewhere in the trees. Trying not to look as if he cared, he caught a glimpse of horsemen galloping along the perimeter of the forest. As he watched, the horsemen moved back into the woods, out of sight of the prison.

One of the guards hit Kluge in the back.

"Get moving, Nazi swine," he said, shoving Kluge in the direction of the kitchen.

Stumbling forward, his chains dragging at his ankles, Kluge wondered if the riders were Cossacks or merely a band of nomads moving from Turkey to Astrakhan on the Caspian Sea. It was not until much later that he learned that Baumann was among them, and had tracked him down at last. . . .

Sitting motionless on one of the tough, wiry horses that the Cossacks favored, Baumann surveyed the hospital camp with a pair of binoculars, watching men move from one building to another. Some of them were camp personnel, others prisoners. He still had not yet determined if Kluge was among them, or if he was even still alive, but this was the best lead he had yet uncovered.

"So," he said to the man beside him, still watching the prisoners. "These men are Germans?"

"*Da.* Prisoners." The Cossack sat easily on his mount, absently flicking the lash of his knoud against his soft leather boots.

"And this is where your man said the *wampyr* is?" Baumann looked directly at the hetman.

"*Da. Hier. Wampyr. Hier.*" The Cossack chief nodded vigorously up and down, punctuating the word *hier* with a downward jab of his knoud.

Baumann swung his leg over the neck of his horse and dropped onto the thick loam of the woodland floor. Walking away from the small group of Cossacks, he partially sheltered behind a tree and gazed out across the long expanse of snow-silent meadow to the prison hospital in the valley. If Kluge was here, and Baumann could free him . . .

It was good to be free. Baumann himself had escaped from a Soviet prison hospital in the Crimea nearly four years earlier, when the camp was being closed down and the prisoners were being transferred. It had been snowing then, too, and Baumann had used the confusion created by the loading of the prisoners on trucks to make his escape.

Like most successful plans, it was simplicity in itself. For one brief moment Baumann had found himself alone and, almost without thinking about it, had stepped behind a huge oak tree. Incredibly, no one missed him. After eight years, the Russian guards no longer bothered to count their prisoners, figuring that all initiative to escape had long since been beaten out of them.

Baumann waited behind the tree until long after the sound of the last truckload of prisoners had faded into the distance, biding his time, considering the growing number of options open to him, as more time passed and no one came back to look for him. One task that was not optional remained paramount, as night finally fell and he cautiously made his way back to the camp.

Very little had been left behind, but Baumann wasn't

interested in the discards of his fellow prisoners or the guards who had climbed on the last truck and headed east. What he was interested in were the two guards left behind to secure the buildings. Slipping back into his old dormitory, Baumann quietly lay down on his old bunk to wait.

It was nearly midnight when Baumann heard the door of the guards' barracks slam shut and the sound of unsteady footsteps clumping along the wooden porch toward the privy. Rising quickly from his bunk, Baumann crossed soundlessly to the door and stepped out into the snow. Moving across the blackened parade ground like a shadow, he came up behind the guards' privy and circled around to the door in front.

Baumann knew what the interior of the privy was like from countless work details spent in the small cement-block building. There was a concrete gutter against one of the walls that was used as a urinal by the guards. Against the opposite wall was a wide plank with four holes cut into it, set above a six-foot deep cess pit. Between the urinal and the cess pit was a large oil drum that had been converted into a stove to heat the privy in the winter, so that the guards and prison staff wouldn't get frostbite while going to the toilet.

The latrine had been the only toilet for forty-two guards, six doctors, and a hospital staff of fourteen. Once a month a prisoner was ordered to clean out the pit. Baumann remembered when he first arrived at the camp and one of the prisoners, an old man who had been a general in the Czech Army before the war, had refused to climb into the cess pit to clean it out. Two of the guards had beaten him nearly unconscious and then thrown him in. Slowly sinking into the excrement, the old man had drowned.

Standing in the doorway, Baumann could smell the Russian. Easing himself into the latrine, he saw the Russian sitting next to the wall, his trousers down around his boot tops. It was obvious from the way he was hunched forward, his head in his hands, that he had been drinking, and drinking heavily. Baumann stepped up next to the soldier, who slurred something in unintelligible Russian.

Baumann smiled to himself in the dark. *"Nyet, Kamerad,"* he said.

"Huh?" The bleary-eyed soldier looked up at Baumann, trying to focus on him in the pitch-black of the privy. "Who—"

Baumann grabbed a handful of the man's hair and smashed his head against the concrete wall, cracking the skull with a sound like an egg being dropped on the floor. The soldier went limp, and Baumann held him from falling to the floor.

Reaching down to the unconscious Russian's trousers, Baumann pulled his bayonet from its sheath. Leaning his victim against the wall, he used his free hand to pull the head back, exposing the throat, then drove the tip of the bayonet nearly an inch into the side of the Russian's neck, expertly severing the jugular. As he pulled out the blade, hot blood sprayed from the wound, frothy and steaming in the cold, almost luminous in its potency, beckoning . . .

Pressing his mouth over the wound, Baumann began to drink, feeling his strength return with each swallow. He drank until the Russian's heart stopped beating, sucking as hard as he could, coaxing the last mouthfuls, until no more blood could be had from the man's emptied veins.

The privy now seemed to Baumann to be no darker than a room with its shades drawn at midday. Looking toward the narrow doorway, the outdoors seemed as bright as a summer's day. By straining slightly, Baumann could hear the movements of the other Russian inside the guards' barracks. For the first time since his capture by the Soviets in 1945, Baumann felt alive. Picking up the bayonet, he moved cautiously toward the barracks and freedom.

Baumann didn't kill the other guard right away. It had been easy to overpower him, and once he was tied to his bed, Baumann allowed himself the luxury of a shower. There was no hot water, but he did manage to find a discarded sliver of soap, and for the first time in almost eight years he felt clean. He dried himself on one of the soldiers' blankets, then stripped the pants and boots off the terrified soldier he had tied to the bed and put them on. Going back to the privy, he came back with the dead man's clothes and piled them on the table in the center of the room.

The guards had two ancient Moisin Nagant rifles and a total of thirty-six rounds of ammunition between them. Dumping out the contents of their knapsacks, Baumann found two sausages, a can of lard, and half a loaf of thick black bread.

"Are you going to kill me?" the half-naked Russian on the bed asked.

"Yes," Baumann replied. "But not right now."

"Why?" the Russian asked.

"Because I need to escape, that's why." Baumann busied himself with inspecting the two rifles.

"You could leave me tied to the bed. No one will come for two days, and by that time you would be gone. We would never find you." The Russian sounded resigned to his fate despite his pleadings.

"Shut up," Baumann said, peering down the barrel of one of the rifles. "Shit, you Ivans are poor soldiers. Don't you ever clean your guns? Both these barrels are rusted and pitted."

"Ilya and me are clerks," the Russian began.

"I said shut up," Baumann interrupted. "Where is your motorcycle?"

"In the barn," the Russian replied.

"Keys?"

"It doesn't have any. You just switch it on and kick-start it." The Russian tried to shift to a more comfortable position, but found it impossible to move. "Could you . . ."

"No," Baumann said, putting out the lights. "Go to sleep."

"But I have to pee," the Russian said plaintively.

"So, pee."

Baumann settled back on one of the bunks and closed his eyes.

The Russian woke in the pre-dawn twilight to the sound of his motorcycle coughing to life. A few minutes later, Baumann returned, dressed in the baggy uniform of a private in the Soviet Army. Walking over to the bunk where the guard was tied, he pulled his bayonet out of its sheath and cut the Russian loose.

"Get up," Baumann said, dragging him off the bunk by his shirt front. "Outside." He shoved the Russian toward the door.

Legs aching and numb from the cold of the night, the half-naked guard stumbled out of the barracks and fell onto the hard-packed ground. Baumann was right behind him, and when he had dragged him back onto his feet, slid the long blade of the bayonet between his legs.

"This isn't very sharp, so if you stumble it will tear more than it will cut." He pulled the blade slightly upward into the Russian's crotch. "Now, walk."

The guard tensed as he felt the cold blade press into

the flesh between his legs. With Baumann gripping his neck from behind, he allowed himself to be steered to the privy beside the barracks.

"Inside," Baumann said, giving the Russian a shove. "You have latrine duty, Ivan."

The thick plank that covered the cess pit had been removed and placed on the floor next to the body of the other guard.

"Strip, Ivan," Baumann ordered. Numbly the guard did as he was ordered, pulling off his shirt and vest over his head. Naked, he shivered as much from fear as the biting cold of early morning.

"Hands against the wall, feet spread," Baumann commanded. "You know the routine. Just like you made us do in the camp."

"I swear I am only a clerk," the Russian blubbered.

"Not with this," Baumann said, placing the blade of the bayonet against the Russian's throat. "This is a German army bayonet, the kind you bastards use to carve up 'vanished' Germans." He punched the Russian in the small of the back. "Now, spread your legs and step away from the wall."

Biting back a sob, the Russian did as he was told. Satisfied that his prisoner wasn't going to try anything, Baumann bent down and stabbed the dead man half a dozen times in the abdomen, ventilating the corpse so that expanding gases could escape. He was taking no chances that the body, bloated from decomposition, would float to the surface of the cess pit. Whenever the relief troops arrived, he wanted them to think that the two Ivans had deserted.

"All right," Baumann said when he had finished. "Turn around."

The Russian slowly turned toward Baumann, then

launched himself forward and tried to grab the bayonet. The movement took Baumann by surprise, but only for an instant. Balling his hand into a fist, he smashed the Russian's jaw with one blow.

Pain momentarily stunned the Russian. As he staggered backward, Baumann hit him again, this time in the solar plexus, doubling him up against the edge of the concrete cess pit. For good measure, Baumann kicked him in the ribs.

"Get up, Ivan. You've got work to do."

Slowly the Russian struggled to his feet, his jaw hanging from his face at a crazy angle, a large purple bruise forming where Baumann's boot had caved in several of his ribs.

"Pick up your comrade and lower him into the pit," Baumann ordered.

The Russian moved like a wounded animal, half dragging, half lifting the dead man to the edge of the cess pit. Before the corpse could topple in, Baumann reached over and caught it by one arm.

"You first, Ivan," he said nodding toward the pit. "Get in."

Whimpering now, the Russian sat on the rough edge of the pit and eased himself over the concrete blocks that had supported the front edge of the planks. Frost had hardened the top layer of the filth, and it cracked as he lowered himself into the mire.

Standing waist deep in the pit, the Russian pulled the body of the dead guard into the excrement and then, at Baumann's command, stood on it, gradually forcing it to sink to the bottom of the pit. From his stamping up and down on it, the body finally sank from sight. When the Russian got off, the body did not reappear. At Baumann's gesture, the Russian came back to the edge of the pit and started to climb out.

But as the man threw one arm over the side of the pit to hoist himself out, Baumann pinned him to the edge with his foot. Leaning down with the bayonet, he drew its rough edge across the guard's throat.

With a scream that was a gurgle, the Russian brought his hand up to his neck, eyes bulging. As he did, Baumann drove the point of the weapon deep into the guard's chest, puncturing his heart. Several more quick stabs with the bayonet, and Baumann was confident that the Russian would stay at the bottom of the cess pit with his comrade.

Baumann felt the man go limp under his foot, and carefully let him slide back down into the excrement. Returning to the barracks for a moment, he came back with one of the Russian rifles and, holding it by the barrel, used it to push the body down to the bottom of the pit. When he was satisfied that the body couldn't be seen, he threw the rifle in after and watched it sink slowly from sight. Then, picking up the thick plank with the four holes cut in it, he replaced it over the cess pit and left.

The motorcycle had taken him as far as the mountains, and there Baumann pushed the machine into a ravine and continued on foot. The villages of Azerbaidzhan were filled with dark-eyed, furtive people, and Baumann moved among them like a ghost. It took him four months to reach the frontier and cross over into Turkey.

Istanbul, with its bazaars, crowded narrow streets, and opium racketeers, became Baumann's hunting ground. In less than a year, he was back on the Russian border, talking to the nomadic traders and renegade cossacks. He bought information with gold or American dollars and repaid lies with death. When the nomads would head to

Baku and Astrakhan, Baumann would see them off; and when they returned he would be waiting—waiting to hear of German prisoners. And while the nomads searched for his comrades, and Kluge in particular, Baumann stalked the streets of Istanbul.

CHAPTER 15

Da. Wampyr. Hier.

As Baumann looked out across the expanse of snow, watching the Soviet guards make their rounds at the prison hospital where the Cossacks had led him, his escape from the Russians seemed as if it had happened a thousand years ago. He had learned a great deal since then. He watched the camp's inmates for the better part of a day, counting them as they moved about, and decided that there were no more than a dozen guards and perhaps as many as thirty prisoners.

None of the men he had seen looked like Kluge, but that didn't mean he wasn't there. If, as the Cossacks insisted, the Russians did have a *wampyr* in there, it almost had to be Kluge. To find out for certain, he would have to go in. In addition to the guards, there would be hospital staff. He couldn't tell how many there were of those, but it didn't really matter anyway. Civilians were not likely to give him any trouble, and he had already spotted a means of wreaking havoc when he was ready.

His Cossacks moved on, with a promise to rejoin him the following afternoon at the place where they had camped the night before. When it had been dark for several hours—for them—Baumann moved out across the moonless meadow to inspect the perimeter wire, which was supposed to protect the prison hospital beyond. It was obvious that the Ivans didn't expect the prisoners to try to leave, and they certainly weren't worried about anyone trying to get in.

Smiling to himself, Baumann slid easily under the wire without detection and made his way into the camp. Finding Kluge doubtless would be much harder.

He spent the next hour making a closer recce of the camp. Then he hid in the woodshed and waited. Early the next morning, when one of the prisoners came into the shed for wood, Baumann killed him with a single blow from one of the logs. The desire to take his blood was strong, but Baumann knew he would have to wait, if he planned to take the man's place.

Stripping the corpse, he changed clothes with the dead man, then picked up an armload of wood and went out into the prison yard, heading toward the guards' barracks. Inside the barracks, he carried the wood over to the stove and stacked it neatly on the floor.

Yes, he thought as he looked around, *only a dozen Ivans.*

"Hey, you." Baumann jumped at the sound of the voice. "Where's Dieter?"

Turning around, he found himself face-to-face with a stocky Russian clad only in heavily stained long underwear. The man stepped menacingly toward Baumann.

"I said, where's Dieter?" It was obvious that the Russian was used to cowing the prisoners, so Baumann took a step back before answering, keeping his head down.

"The doctors wanted him. I came instead." Baumann restrained an urge to rip out the Russian's throat.

"Yeah? Well, tell that little grass weasel that when Rubinsky has finished playing with him, my boots need to be mended. *Verstehen?*" The Russian scratched himself. "*Verstehen!*"

Baumann nodded. "*Da. Da.*"

"Well, you'd better *verstehen,* or you'll end up in the *Schlachthaus* like that pig of an SS officer." The Russian farted. "Now, get out of here."

The *Schlachthaus.* It was prisoner slang for the special wing of the hospital where the Russian doctors experimented on their German detainees. "Slaughterhouse" was hardly too strong a term. Baumann had learned more than he cared to know about it in the Crimea. As he went back to the shed for another load of wood, he decided that an SS officer who was also a *wampyr* was quite likely to be in the *Schlachthaus.*

Dieter's body was turning a pale bluish-gray color by the time Baumann got back to the woodshed, too long dead now for the blood to be really palatable, and he dragged it into the corner and covered it with logs, just in case some impatient Russian came in looking for more firewood. Satisfied that the hiding place would pass at least casual scrutiny, Baumann picked up another armload of wood and headed toward the hospital.

He had established the general layout the night before from looking in several windows of the sprawling single-story building. As he stacked the wood next to the stove in the center of what appeared to be a doctors' wardroom, possibly adjacent to a treatment area, he heard the voice of one of the Russian doctors speaking to a prisoner.

"So tell me again, Mr. Nazi bigshot. If Jews are inferior and Russians are sub-humans, why is it that I'm here and you are my prisoner?"

"You have it wrong, Dr. Rubinsky. You are my prisoner. You are here because of me." Baumann was astonished and relieved to recognize Kluge's patent-leather voice, though it sounded a little weak. "I know what makes a Jew, but you don't know what makes me. You are like a rat drawn to a cobra, mesmerized by its fatal power over death. If you want to know my secret, just ask. I'll share it with you. But watch out, it could kill you."

Picking up some wood, Baumann kept his head down and went into the room where Rubinsky was interviewing Kluge. As he came through the door, he deliberately stumbled and dropped the wood, causing Rubinsky to turn away from Kluge, whose look of surprised recognition otherwise would have betrayed him.

"What do you want, oaf?" Rubinsky barked at Baumann. "You know that this man isn't allotted any firewood. Now, get it out."

Baumann nodded, pretending to be cowed, and did not look at the prisoner as he picked up the scattered wood. But he had noted the chain around Kluge's ankle that was padlocked to the wall. He wondered whether Kluge was always kept in this room or if they moved him around. In any case, the chain would have to be dealt with once Baumann got back to him.

Closing the door behind him, Baumann dumped the wood into the box next to the stove, then went back outside, heading back around behind the woodshed. From his vantage point in the woods, Baumann had seen the prison generator located on the far side of the camp. The Russians relied on the German prisoners to maintain the camp, and the sight of a prisoner shuffling across the prison yard in the direction of the diesel generator aroused no curiosity. No one noticed when the prisoner went into the generator shed and did not come out.

The generator, like the prisoners, had been captured at the end of the war. Chugging along at a leisurely beat, it produced a steady charge for the banks of batteries that provided the camp's electricity. The voltage regulator on the generator was set to low output, keeping the needle in the VU-meter well into the green. Any increase in charge would cause the batteries to "boil," releasing a deadly cloud of hydrochloric gas, as poisonous to breathe as it was explosive if exposed to an electrical spark. To prevent any sort of accident, there was a vent in the roof above the batteries, and all of the generator cables were sheathed in thick rubber insulation.

Closing the door behind him, Baumann climbed up onto the top of one of the two diesel fuel tanks that fed the generator and removed his outer shirt, stuffing it into the vent. Then, looking at his watch, he stretched out on the tank top to see how long it would take the fumes from the battery acid to reach him. It was dark up here. No one would even notice him if they looked in.

The sharp tang of acid bit into Baumann's nostrils, and he checked his watch.

Twenty-five minutes.

Holding his breath, Baumann stood up and pulled his shirt from the vent. Twenty-five minutes to fill about a quarter of the room with fumes. At low power, it would take at least two hours to fill the room. Baumann guessed that by setting the voltage regulator to maximum output, he could boil the batteries and create an explosive cloud in about half an hour.

All that was needed now was the spark.

Using a small pocket knife, Baumann carefully cut into the main power cable of the generator. Gently scraping away at the rubber insulation, he exposed a few millimetres of the copper wire underneath. Reaching around his neck, he untied the string on his German army ID tag and, swinging it like a pendulum, tapped it against the exposed wire. The shower of sparks produced an uncharacteristic smile on Baumann's leathery face.

Balling his shirt into a pillow, Baumann lay down atop the diesel tanks and waited for nightfall.

It wasn't until evening roll call that the Russians discovered one of their prisoners was missing. At first there was general confusion on the part of the guards, and it wasn't until an individual count was completed that they instigated a search of the compound for the missing German. It took them less than an hour to find Dieter's body in the woodshed, stiff and naked under a pile of logs. Baumann listened to the confused shouts of the Russians over the steady chugging of the generator and waited for the night to deepen.

Shortly after two A.M., Baumann stood up on the diesel fuel tank and stuffed his shirt into the vent in the roof. Lowering himself to the ground, he went over to the generator and turned off the voltage regulator. He took his ID disk out of his pocket and tied one end of the neck string above the bare patch he had scraped in the cable. Pulling the string taut, he tied the other end well below the exposed wires, leaving the metal disk just a few millimeters above the bright copper wires.

Dropping back to the ground, he reset the voltage regulator, then slowly moved the control needle to full power. In the darkness of the generator shed, Baumann could see the bright blue spark that arced occasionally between the cable and the metal ID disk. With a satisfied grunt, he turned and went out into the night.

Moving through the shadows, Baumann quickly covered the thirty meters that separated the generator shed from the hospital and slipped quietly onto the porch of the Schlachthaus. He moved around to the far side of the building and tried one of the windows. Despite initial resistance the window slid open, and Baumann was inside in a matter of seconds.

Voices drifted in from one end of the building, and Baumann could tell from the light fanning out from under the door that this was the doctors' residence. Moving around the stove in the center of the wardroom, he made his way to the room where he had seen Kluge. Gently, very gently, he tried the door.

It was locked, which meant that Kluge probably was still in there.

As Baumann looked at his watch, thick gray-white clouds of acid vapor were boiling off the batteries in the generator shed, rising to the roof and slowly filling the room with their corrosive volatility.

How much longer? Baumann wondered, as the minutes ticked by.

The lights finally went out in the doctors' residence, and Baumann looked at his watch again, just as another tiny blue spark arced between the cable and his ID tag.

Two-thirty-five.

The explosion tore through the camp with the force of a five-thousand-pound bomb, slamming Baumann back against the wall. The guard barracks was flattened by the concussion of the blast, and one of the guards on perimeter patrol was blown through the fence surrounding the prison with such violence that the wires sliced through his body as if it were so much cheese. A huge fireball rose into the ink-black sky, and for a few minutes the shattered prison hospital was bathed in an eerie, incandescent glow.

Then, as the fireball burned itself out, the camp faded into the confusion of darkness, lit only by the flames that boiled out of the destroyed generator shed.

Baumann stood up, shaking his head to clear it. Stumbling forward over the furniture scattered across the floor, he went to Kluge's cell. Bracing himself against an up-turned desk, he kicked open the door only to find the room shattered, open to the sky.

"*Sturmbannführer?*" he called softly.

From under a pile of rubble Baumann heard an answering moan. Throwing aside the remains of part of the roof, he gradually uncovered Kluge, only just conscious. Alarmed, Baumann pulled a folding knife from an inside pocket and made a small incision in his arm, then pressed it against Kluge's lips.

"Drink, drink," he urged.

The warm trickle ran into Kluge's mouth and sent an electric quiver through his body. Like a new-born wolf feeding for the first time, he sucked hungrily at Baumann's arm, feeling a revitalizing power begin to surge into every corner of his being. Not just blood, but vampiric blood. He was still weak and knew it would take time to recover fully, but he could feel himself growing stronger already. His eyes opened and focused on Baumann.

"*Herr Scharführer. Danke,*" he said, as a small trickle of blood ran from the corner of his mouth.

"Come," Baumann replied, pulling Kluge to his feet. "We have to get out of here. I'll give you more later."

"Wait," Kluge rasped. "The chain . . . my leg . . ."

Looking down, Baumann saw that the leg chain still secured Kluge to the wall. He fingered the padlock briefly, then steadied his commander against some fallen timbers, grabbed a double handful of chain, and pulled with all his might. The steel staple set into the wall snapped out with an almost musical ping and Baumann tumbled backwards.

Getting back on his feet, he gathered up the length of chain still attached to Kluge's ankle and put the *Sturmbannführer's* arm over his shoulder. It was an easy matter to pick their way through the rubble and out into the prison yard. The blast had knocked down several hundred feet of fencing, and Baumann and Kluge were able to stumble over the downed wires and head for the safety of the forest beyond.

One of the doctors saw them go. Crawling out from under the collapsed remains of the doctors' residence, Jacob Rubinsky watched as Kluge and another man vanished into the shadows of the night. He tried to follow them, to call out for the guards to stop them, but his own injuries sent him spinning into a pit of unconsciousness from which he did not emerge for several hours.

But Baumann did not take Kluge far just then. Confident that they would not be followed while the Ivans dealt with the fires still burning in the camp, and aware of Kluge's need for rest, Baumann hid them just inside the edge of the forest, where they could watch while they waited for nightfall and the planned rendezvous with the Cossacks. Across the snowy meadow, amid the shattered remains of the prison hospital, they watched the surviving German prisoners forced to dig graves for the dead Ivans, carrying their bodies from the wreckage and lowering them into the graves. Baumann counted nine bodies, only three of whom were presumably guards; the rest he assumed had to have been the medical staff. As the Germans filled in the graves, Baumann could see what appeared to be an argument taking place between the leader of the guards and one of the medical staff.

Suddenly the heavyset guard struck the doctor with his rifle butt, knocking him to the ground. Two other doctors came forward and dragged their companion away from the guards, who were now drawn up uneasily next to the graves, rifles at the ready. The incident puzzled Baumann, for his own experience in the prison hospital in the

Crimea had taught him that the medical team was in absolute control of the camp.

Suddenly a shot rang out, and one of the German prisoners crumpled to the ground. More shots were fired, and the other prisoners started dropping, a few staggering away from the guards. To Baumann's outrage and disgust, the heavyset guard commander approached each body and carefully put a bullet in its head.

Over the next hour, as Baumann observed in horror, the sounds of more shots drifted up from the camp. After what seemed an eternity came silence. Later, the Ivans dragged all of the bodies to the center of the prison yard, doused them with benzine, and set them ablaze. The acrid black cloud eventually drifted into the woods, and the two watchers retreated from its smell. Early in the afternoon, when Kluge seemed to have regained some of his strength, Baumann helped his commander to his feet.

"We will head to the rendezvous now," Baumann said, throwing Kluge's arm across his shoulder. "The sooner we get there, the better our chances of escape."

Kluge nodded weakly, and the two men set off through the forest. They stopped often, for Kluge was very weak. Baumann gave him to drink again, but only a little, lest his own strength be depleted. Finally, late in the afternoon, they approached the clearing where they were to meet the Cossacks.

Baumann stopped dead in his tracks, sensing that something was wrong. At first he was unable to identify what had caused him to stop; then he smelled it.

Cigarette smoke. The thick, pungent aroma of Russian cigarettes. Leaving Kluge resting against a tree, Baumann carefully made his way around the clearing, sticking close to the ground. On the far side of the woods, he spied the olive-drab uniforms of a Russian patrol intermingled with the long black coats of the Cossacks. It was obvious at a glance, from the casual way that the Ivans stood around, that the Cossacks had led them to the rendezvous.

Baumann melted back into the woods. Circling the Cossacks and the Russians, he worked his way around them until he was behind the string of Cossack horses casually picketed between two pine trees. Crouching in the bushes, he watched as a Cossack not more than sixteen years old left a group of Russian soldiers and walked over to the picket line to check the horses. Satisfied that their lead lines were secured to the picket rope, the boy stepped up to a tree to relieve himself.

Moving quickly from behind, Baumann grabbed him in a head lock and snapped his neck before he could scream out. Dragging the boy's body behind some scrub, Baumann took out his folding knife and slit his throat. Blood welled up on the boy's grimy neck, and Baumann covered the wound with his mouth, sucking hard to draw the precious fluid as quickly as he could.

He dared not take the time to drink his fill, but he got half a dozen good mouthfuls. When he had drunk enough to make up for what he had given Kluge, he let the body fold onto the ground and looked back toward the horses. No one seemed to have noticed that the boy was missing. Reaching down, Baumann pulled the handsome silver-hilted *kama* from its scabbard on the dead boy's waist. Creeping forward, he was going to cut one of the horses loose when he heard the man's voice.

"Vladimir?" the voice said, looking for the dead boy.

"*Nyet,*" Baumann replied as he stood up and buried the long blade of the Cossack dagger deep in the man's chest. "*Vladimir ist todt,*" he hissed as he pulled him into the bushes, his hand clamped over the Cossack's mouth.

The man died quickly. When Baumann was certain he

couldn't call for help, he pulled the *kama* out of the cossack's chest and lowered him to the ground. The horses were beginning to smell the blood and started to pull at their ropes, stamping their hooves in the dust and whinnying in panic.

Baumann pulled the Cossack's *shashka* from its long black scabbard and ran to the picket line. He was not going to get another chance like this. Grabbing the lead rope of the nearest horse, he cut it with the saber and threw himself into the saddle. Digging in his heels, he urged the tough Cossack pony into a flat-out gallop, thundering into the clearing, slashing at the Russian soldiers as he raced toward where Kluge was hiding. At the far side of the clearing, the Cossack hetman drew his pistol and fired at Baumann.

Baumann felt the slug bite into his shoulder, but instead of an explosion of pain, he felt rage surge through his body. Rage that the Cossack had betrayed him to the Ivans. He jinked the horse to the right and, swinging his wounded arm in a full circle, bore down on the Cossack.

From his hiding place in the woods, Kluge watched as Baumann leaned forward in the saddle a split second before he brought his arm down, the blade of the saber flashing in the late afternoon sun. The silver arc flashed past the Cossack, and for a moment Kluge thought that Baumann had missed. Then slowly the Cossack's knees began to buckle, and as he swayed forward his head fell from his shoulders as a geyser of blood sprayed skyward.

Thundering hooves approached Kluge, and almost before he knew it, Baumann had grabbed him roughly by the shirt-front and swung him back behind him, onto the rump of his still-galloping horse.

* * *

Kluge opened his eyes. Outside his window, Baumann barked orders and bullied the young knights, demanding that they equal his skill at arms. Watching, Kluge smiled to himself.

Yes, he thought. *Oh, yes. We shall be invincible.*

"You ride very well," Maria said, as they trotted back into the stable yard at Schloss Dielstein. "Did they teach you in the police?"

"No," Drummond said. "My father played polo, and when I was a kid I used to exercise his ponies between chukkers.

"Polo is supposed to be the sport of kings," Maria teased.

"Not the sport of kings," Drummond corrected her. "The king of sports."

"Well, nonetheless, I am impressed with your riding." She smiled at Drummond. "You can ride my horses anytime."

"Speaking of time," Drummond looked at his watch, "I have to be leaving soon."

"Leaving?" Maria said. "I thought you were staying for another two days."

"I had planned to," Drummond said awkwardly. "But since my meeting with the prince—well, I think it would be a good idea if I moved out a little ahead of schedule."

They were in the stable yard, and Maria slid off her horse and loosened its girth before handing the reins to the groom.

"You sound like a man who might be running from something," she said, as the groom led her horse away.

"In a way you're right," Drummond said, wondering how much to tell her. "A couple of men tried to kill me in Los Angeles, the day before I arrived in Austria. And you know about Baron von Liebenfalz taking me to the prince at gunpoint. Last night, at the dinner party, it seemed as if half the people I met were aware of who I was, and why I was here—or at least, why they thought I was here." Drummond handed the reins of his horse to the groom and turned to Maria. "That's why I'm leaving."

"And will you come back?" Maria asked, avoiding looking at Drummond as she spoke.

"Yes," he said, surprised at his own conviction in his answer. "I'll be back just as soon as it's safe."

"In that case," Maria said with a bright voice, "I will have Joachim pack your things while we have breakfast." She gave Drummond a dazzling smile and slid her arm around his waist.

"Now," she said, "would you prefer breakfast on the terrace, or shall we have breakfast in bed?"

CHAPTER 16

With Joachim's connivance, Drummond managed to avoid meeting the prince, von Liebenfalz, or the cardinal when he left the castle later that morning. After settling his account, he pulled out of the gates of the castle and drove back in the direction of Reid. As he headed toward the autobahn that would take him into Germany, one of his classical music tapes blaring, he reflected on the twenty-four hours that had passed since his leaving Vienna.

He wished he understood what was going on. The equation was getting very complicated. It was becoming obvious that, on some level, the Prince of Antioch and an American cardinal were mixed up with the Order of the Sword, and possibly with Kluge as well. There had been something in the cardinal's unctuous manner that had put Drummond on guard—against what, he wasn't quite sure. He also wasn't quite sure about Maria.

She was another complication. He certainly hadn't started out to get involved with her, though he supposed he had returned to Schloss Dielstein partially to test the waters. When they had first met, Drummond had admired her as any man would, but had pretty much figured that she was Franz Reidl's woman. Reidl hadn't been at the party last night—but then, in Reidl's place, Drummond would have avoided it himself.

But that didn't explain her behavior toward him. Not that he was complaining.

Far from it.

After his wife's accident, it had taken Drummond two years to realize that even though the machines kept her alive, their life together was over. Only a strong sense of loyalty had prevented him seeking a divorce. It was that same sense of loyalty that had turned him into a near hermit, but it was a female detective from Auto Theft who had dragged him out of his cave.

They had met at a retirement luncheon for one of the old-timers from Hollenbeck Division, and after drinks and dinner, Drummond found himself having breakfast the next morning with one of L.A.'s finest. They spent the weekend at Drummond's beach house, and Drummond learned the difference between love and loyalty.

Drummond slowed the Range Rover as he approached the junction that led to the autobahn. Reflecting on past romances, he paid no attention to the gray Audi parked on the side of the road that tucked in behind as he headed toward the German frontier.

It had been a whirlwind affair, and after three weeks of athletic sex they stopped seeing each other. There had been three or four other women since then, but Drummond had stayed distant from all of them.

All of them, that is, except Maria. Somehow she was different.

More, he supposed, *like my wife.*

Drummond slowed the Range Rover again, getting ready to turn onto the on ramp of the autobahn. Behind him, in the gray Audi, von Liebenfalz also slowed down.

* * *

The Alitalia 747 from Los Angeles was just touching down at Rome's Leonardo da Vinci Airport as Drummond's Range Rover, followed by von Liebenfalz' Audi, joined the fast-moving traffic on the autobahn. The big plane rolled to a stop next to the terminal, and among the passengers disembarking was a young priest who had been flying in the first-class cabin. Shuffling along with the rest of the passengers, he moved slowly toward the Italian passport control point.

"Passport, please," a small man in a natty uniform said, as the priest finally reached his desk.

"Sure thing."

The priest handed him a Vatican diplomatic passport, which the man opened and inspected, comparing its photo with the suntanned young man before him.

"Your name, please, Father?"

"Reverend Thomas Berringer, Office of the Cardinal Secretary of State for the Holy See," he said, smiling as the man looked up.

The man handed back the passport. "*Si. Grazie.*" He saluted. "Follow the blue line, please, Father."

Father Berringer followed the blue line into customs and walked up to one of the blue-clad customs officers. Presenting his diplomatic passport, he spoke rapidly in Italian and then, nodding at the customs official's salute, left the customs hall without opening his one carry-on bag.

Outside in the arrivals concourse, a chauffeur in a black uniform was waiting for him, holding a sign with his name on it.

"I'm Berringer," the priest said.

Without a word, the man took Berringer's flight bag and led him out to a dark blue Cadillac waiting at the curb, briskly installing bag and priest in the limousine's spacious back seat. With an efficiency that surprised Berringer, the man very quickly worked the big Caddy clear of the traffic snarl that perpetually engulfed da Vinci Airport, and soon had them heading north along the Mediterranean coast.

"How long?" Father Berringer asked in Italian.

"If you're asking 'how long,' I should tell you I don't speak Italian," the voice said in English, in an accent that was pure New York. "But I can tell you that it's about an hour. If you want a drink, there are some Pepsis in the bar back there."

"Thanks," Berringer said, leaning down to open the small refrigerated bar in the back of the limousine. "So tell me, who called the meeting?"

"Do me a favor, huh, Father? Just drink your drink and don't ask no questions. *Capiche?*"

With a shrug, Father Berringer popped the pull-tab on his Pepsi and took a long, thirsty swig. The driver checked him in the mirror, then raised the smoked glass partition that separated the front from the back of the car, returning his attention to his driving.

After another swallow, Father Berringer set the Pepsi aside and reached into his flight bag, pulling out a small map of Italy. He decided that if they stuck to the coast road, an hour would bring them somewhere near Orbetello; if they turned inland, they could be going almost anywhere. Not that it mattered. The summons was not to be questioned.

He stuffed the map back in his bag and finished off his Pepsi, then stretched out across the seat and closed his eyes. Might as well try to catch a nap, since his driver was not going to be helpful.

Despite the fourteen hours spent on the plane, Father Berringer found sleep impossible as the limousine rocked gently from side to side along the twisting coast road. He dozed, but he never really dropped off. The snippets of dreams he could recall were a trifle odd, as one might expect, but provided no insight into what might lie ahead.

Finally, he could feel the car slowing to a near halt, and he sat up and looked out. The limo was turning left, toward the sea. A sign by the side of the road read "Monte Argentario."

Sweeping across the causeway that linked the island to the coast of Italy, the limousine turned onto the narrow road that ran between the two villages at opposite ends of the island. After about a mile, the driver turned between the gateposts of a white-washed villa whose circular driveway was paved with crushed clamshells, blindingly white. They stopped at the far side of the drive in the shade of an olive tree. The driver's shoes made a crunching sound as he came around to the back door and opened it for Berringer, directly in front of the steps going up to the villa's entrance.

"Hop out, Father," he said. "You're here."

Berringer got out of the car and allowed himself the pleasure of a good stretch before heading up the steps. As he stepped onto the porch, two men in silk shirts and white linen pants emerged and stopped him.

"Hands up," one of them said in Italian, gesturing to Father Berringer to raise his hands as he spoke.

Berringer raised his hands, and the other man frisked him. Satisfied that Father Berringer was clean, the first man motioned for the priest to follow him into the villa. The second one followed.

There was a toilet just off the entry to the villa, and the two men indicated that Father Berringer should use it. It didn't matter that he didn't need to use the toilet; they made it clear from their gestures that he was expected to use the toilet before his meeting.

Father Berringer went in and washed his hands, splashed some water on his face, and dried off on an immaculate linen towel from a rack to one side. Before he left he flushed the toilet, then stepped back out into the entry.

One of the men motioned for him to follow, while the other one stayed at Father Berringer's elbow. The three of them walked through the front hall of the villa and out onto the terrace that overlooked the sparkling Mediterranean. It took Father Berringer several seconds to recognize the man in the pale blue polo shirt, white linen slacks, and pale straw Panama, standing at the railing of white wrought iron.

"Your Eminence," he said, bowing as the cardinal turned to smile at him.

"Hello, Thomas," the cardinal said, extending his hand. "No need to kiss the ring. A handshake will do as well."

A nod dismissed Berringer's keepers. The two men shook hands, and then the cardinal led Father Berringer over to some chairs pulled up around a white wrought iron table underneath a striped umbrella.

"Sit down. Take off your coat, if you want," he said, inviting Berringer to sit. "Myself, I can't abide clericals in this heat. Take off your collar, if you want."

Father Berringer did take off his coat, draping it over the back of one of the spare chairs, but he decided that removing his collar tab might be a bit too presumptuous, even though the cardinal had suggested it.

"Thomas, we may have a problem," the cardinal said, leaning back in his chair when his guest had sat. "What have you found out about Captain John Drummond?"

Father Berringer reached into an inside pocket of his jacket and brought out a small notebook.

"Drummond is a captain with the Los Angeles Police

Department, in charge of the Homicide Division at Police Headquarters." He turned the page. "He has an excellent service record, a bachelor's degree in Social Science, an MBA, and is working on a doctorate in criminology. He's on the fast track to the chief's office."

"What about his personal life?" the Cardinal asked.

"Married to an actress seven years ago. She was injured in an accident on the set and has been in a coma for the last five years. Drummond dates occasionally, but no real relationships." Father Berringer closed his notebook. "The guy's a real saint."

"So it would seem," the cardinal said. "Is he still married?"

"He is. Still wears his wedding ring. Like I said, a real saint."

Father Berringer put his notebook away just as a servant brought over a pitcher of iced tea and two frosty glasses on a tray. The cardinal himself poured, handing one to Berringer and then sipping silently at his own for several minutes, gazing out at the deep blue of the Mediterranean.

"What does our agent in the LAPD have to say about Drummond?" he finally asked.

"Not much," Father Berringer replied. "He was shot near Police Headquarters last week."

"Killed?" the cardinal interrupted.

"No, but he'll be out of commission for at least another month."

"Go on," the cardinal said.

"According to Morwood's last report, the Israeli Secret Service stopped by Drummond's office the day before the shooting. They accused him of being involved with a bunch of Austrian Nazis and of the death of some old Jew in Vienna. Drummond seemed to have cleared himself, but the next day, the same guys tried to hit him. They got Morwood by mistake. It was later determined that the men were Mossad."

Father Berringer topped up the cardinal's iced tea at his gesture and poured himself another glass.

"Are you convinced that the Morwood shooting was an accident?" the cardinal asked.

"It seems reasonable. Morwood was wearing Drummond's raincoat, and the hit man shot him in the back." Father Berringer sipped his iced tea. "Yes, I'd say the shooting was a mistake."

"I see." The cardinal stretched his legs, and a bit of red silk stocking flashed at his ankle. "Aside from the incident with the Mossad, did Morwood give you any other information about Drummond?"

"Only that he seemed very interested in any killings where the victims displayed an inordinate amount of blood loss," Father Berringer said. "Probably something to do with his doctoral thesis on the vampire murders in Los Angeles back in the seventies. That's what first brought him to my attention, as you know."

"And where do you think Drummond is now?" the cardinal asked.

Berringer considered. "A very good question. He's not at his home or his beach house, and he's not at his office. At first I thought he might be at one of the LAPD safe houses up at Big Bear Lake, but he isn't. I heard from one of our contacts in the FBI that he got on a flight to Sweden, but he didn't arrive at the other end. He did make it as far as London." Father Berringer set down his glass. "My guess is, he's on the run."

"I would say that's a fair guess," the cardinal said, leaning forward. "But where, Thomas? From the Mossad, or to the Nazis?"

Father Berringer gave him a blank look. "I don't think I understand," he began.

"Thomas," the cardinal interrupted, "I want you to go to Luxembourg. There's a doctor there that I want you to contact, and when you do, show him this." He handed Father Berringer a small black velvet bag. "Go ahead," he said. "Open it."

Father Berringer pulled open the mouth of the little bag and dumped a gold signet ring out into the palm of his hand.

"Am I supposed to wear this?" he asked.

"Not yet," the cardinal said. "The doctor will give you your instructions. If he tells you to wear the ring, then put it on. Otherwise," the cardinal's voice took on a hard edge, "it stays in the bag. Understood?"

"Yes, Your Eminence." Realizing the meeting was over, Father Berringer stood up, returning the ring to its bag and slipping it into his trouser pocket.

"Good," the cardinal said, extending his hand. "I'll have my driver see to the details."

Father Berringer genuflected in front of the cardinal, kissing the ring, then rose and collected his jacket.

"By the way, Thomas," the cardinal said, as Berringer turned to leave. "Do be careful."

Berringer nodded and left the terrace. When he had disappeared in the company of the two men who had escorted him in, the cardinal signaled to the servant who had brought out the iced tea.

"Adolfo, contact Dr. LeBlanc. I want to speak with him."

In the gray Audi, Anton von Liebenfalz was audibly willing Drummond's car to pull off at the next service plaza. Since swinging around Munich and heading out toward Stuttgart, the combination of a near-empty tank and a near-full bladder had added increasingly to his motoring discomfort.

"Gruss Gott!" von Liebenfalz exclaimed, when at last he saw Drummond put on his turn indicator and head towards the fast-approaching off ramp.

While Drummond drove directly to the petrol pumps, von Liebenfalz swung wide of the Esso station and pulled into the parking lot of an adjoining restaurant. As he climbed out of the Audi, he felt as if his bladder was about to burst. He made a dash for the restaurant's restrooms, emerging just in time to see Drummond heading into the shop to pay for his petrol. Starting the Audi, von Liebenfalz drove up to the far set of pumps and began filling his tank, keeping his back turned to the shop entrance.

The Audi's tank was only half-filled when Drummond came out, climbed into his car, and drove over to the separate building that housed the station's toilets.

Half a tank would have to do. Turning off the pump, von Liebenfalz dashed into the shop to pay his bill. A fat truck driver with vintage body odor was blocking the cash register. Oblivious to his lack of charms, the driver was doing his best to impress the homely woman behind the counter.

In a panic, von Liebenfalz watched as Drummond pulled up by the toilets, got out of his car, and headed inside.

The truck driver's heavy-handed compliments to the Esso station attendant continued unabated, and to von Liebenfalz growing horror, the woman seemed to be encouraging him.

Drummond left the toilets and sauntered back to his Range Rover, stretching and yawning before he climbed in and started his car. Watching Drummond drive away from the service plaza, von Liebenfalz broke out in a cold sweat. He felt like he was going to throw up.

The truck driver and the woman behind the counter exchanged a laugh, and the driver finally heaved his stinking bulk out of von Liebenfalz' way and wedged himself between an ice cream freezer and a rack of girlie magazines.

Muttering the number of his pump, von Liebenfalz threw a handful of deutsche marks on the counter and dashed back out to his car. As the Audi's engine roared to life, he raced off toward the autobahn in a squeal of rubber, in pursuit of Drummond.

At da Vinci Airport in Rome, a Mitsubishi corporate jet sat on the edge of the tarmac runway, a dark blue Cadillac limousine parked next to it. Inside the jet, Father Tom Berringer finished changing into a well-cut pin-stripe suit as the cardinal's driver brought an elegant leather suitcase out of the car and handed it to the copilot, who stowed it in the tail of the plane. Stuffing his clerical garb into a black plastic bag, Father Berringer tossed it down to the driver, then settled back in one of the jet's thick leather seats and buckled up his seat belt.

They were airborne within minutes, headed toward Luxembourg. Once they had leveled off over the sea, the copilot came back to where Father Berringer was sitting and handed him a padded manila envelope. Opening it, Father Berringer removed a German passport made out in another name, a wallet containing several credit cards to match, and a plain white envelope stuffed with five thousand dollars in hundred-dollar bills.

Father Berringer put several hundred dollars in the wallet, tucked it and the passport inside his jacket, then slipped the envelope with the rest of the money in another inside pocket.

It was early evening as Drummond unwittingly led von Liebenfalz through Luxembourg City and up the main highway toward that small country's northern border. He thought briefly about stopping for something to eat, but decided to push on to the castle, where he was certain that Father Freise would be able to find him some kind of a meal.

Following along in the gray Audi, von Liebenfalz reached down to a hamper on the floor of the passenger side of the car and lifted its wicker lid to rummage inside. After a moment he retrieved a crested silver case containing some caviar and cress sandwiches. Setting these on the dash of the car, he next produced a heavy leaded crystal tumbler and a small, still-cold bottle of sparkling wine from an insulated bag.

Steering with his knees, von Liebenfalz managed to open the bottle of wine, then deftly poured himself a good measure of the pale golden effervescence. He wedged the bottle between the two front seats, then settled down to an acceptable snack at sixty-five miles an hour, Drummond's taillights two red dots a quarter mile ahead of him.

Tom Berringer filled out the required forms at the Avis desk and waited patiently while the young man at the computer keyboard laboriously tapped in all of the pertinent information.

"Ah, here you are, sir," he said in French. "Baron Manfried von Holtzhauser, prepaid. I see you had requested a Mercedes." He smiled apologetically at Berringer. "I'm afraid all I have left is a Ford Granada Scorpio, if that's all right?"

Berringer tried to mask his annoyance. "Certainly," he said in excellent French. "That will be fine. Now, if you don't mind, I have to be in Clervaux in a few hours."

The young man tapped at the computer keys again.

"Your car is in parking bay forty-six, on the south side of the terminal." He handed Berringer the rental contract and a square plastic token. "The keys are in the car, and this token will open the automatic barrier and let you out."

"*Merci,*" Berringer said.

It took two tries before Berringer found himself on the main road headed north. He had just turned onto the road to Clervaux when he came up fast on a gray Audi with Austrian number plates. Putting his foot down in the powerful Granada Scorpio, he swung around to pass. As he glanced into the car, he noticed the elderly driver carefully juggling a crystal tumbler and a bottle of wine around the steering wheel.

"Jeez," he said to himself, as he got around and tucked back into the righthand lane. "What Crackerjack box did that putz get his driver's license out of?"

Ahead Berringer saw the glow of brake lights as a large black Range Rover slowed down and turned off the road into the woods. Relieved that another slow driver was out of his way, Berringer raced on toward Clervaux.

Von Liebenfalz eased the Audi to the side of the road, near where he had seen Drummond turn off into the woods. He had nearly missed the spot, thanks to the Granada that had passed him and then pulled in between his car and Drummond's.

"Typical," von Liebenfalz muttered. "About the only option you can't get with a new car is courtesy."

It annoyed von Liebenfalz that he felt as stiff as a day-old corpse as he climbed out of the Audi. Age, or rather the subtle infirmities of age, annoyed him. Unlike many of his contemporaries, he didn't wish he was young again; he merely missed being supple.

Opening the trunk of the car, he took out a can of industrial yellow spray paint. In the dim light of the courtesy lamp, he squinted to read the directions: "Shake can until ball rattles, then point in safe direction and depress nozzle."

Depress is right, von Liebenfalz thought as he began shaking the can.

Finally, after what seemed like hours of shaking, he heard the faint clatter of the ball somewhere inside the can. Crouching down next to the road, he sprayed a neat arrow on the pavement and next to it a small dot. To anyone looking at it, it would appear to be some indecipherable surveyor's mark, the type road workers spray on highways around the world.

To the man in chain mail, watching from the edge of the woods, it seemed damned strange.

Returning to his car, von Liebenfalz tossed the can back in the trunk. After carefully wiping his hands on a paper towel, he climbed back into the car and drove quietly on into Clervaux.

CHAPTER 17

Drummond steered the black Range Rover slowly past the rusting hulk of the jeep in which Father Freise had been traveling in 1944 when a German ambush had led to his first encounter with the knights of the Order of the Sword. The twilight deepened as he drove farther along the forest track, and he turned on his headlights, keeping a sharp lookout. After several miles, he came to the wide, grassy meadow that surrounded Schloss Marbourg, the fortress of the Order of the Sword.

It looked unchanged since his first visit, the walls washed faintly golden with the fading sunset, reflecting into the still, dark moat that surrounded it. As before, the drawbridge was down—he wondered whether it even worked anymore—but the gate beyond was open. That was strange.

Pulling up next to the barbican arch that guarded the drawbridge, Drummond set the brake and got out of the car. He was not about to trust the drawbridge to take the car inside. Cautiously he walked over the drawbridge, wondering why no one challenged him.

The courtyard of the castle appeared to be deserted. Nor was there any sign of activity in any of the outbuildings lining the inside of the wall. The great hall door was standing open, though, and looking through the thick glass lozenges of a narrow window, Drummond thought he could see the faint silhouette of someone standing in front of a flickering fire laid against the hearth.

Reassured, he headed for the great hall entrance and was about to enter when a crossbow bolt whistled within inches of his head and slammed into the oak jamb of the iron-studded door.

Drummond dropped to his knees and rolled for cover behind a nearby rain barrel.

"Don't shoot!" he shouted. "It's me, Drummond."

"John? Is that you?" Father Freise's voice called out of the shadows. "Stand up so I can see you."

Drummond slowly stood up, half expecting to be shot.

"Frank?" he called. "What's going on? Where is everybody?"

Father Freise came out of the shadows, crossbow at the ready and loaded with another steel-tipped bolt.

"Step out into the light," he said, apparently still not sure that it was Drummond.

Drummond slowly emerged from behind the barrel, keeping his hands in sight.

"I think you can put the crossbow down now, Frank," he said. "It really is me."

Father Freise lowered the weapon with an audible sigh of relief.

"Thank God, it is you! Boy, am I glad to see you," he said as he trotted across the courtyard.

"Well, I never would have guessed it by the reception you just gave me," Drummond replied. "Where are de Beq and his men? What's going on?"

Shaking his head, Father Freise clapped Drummond in a bear hug.

"By God, you don't know how good it is to see you again! Come on inside, and I'll try to explain."

As the two men headed into the great hall, Father Freise paused for a second to pull the crossbow bolt from the heavy oak timber surrounding the door. "Can't afford to leave these lying around. Leastwise, not right now."

Inside, the two sat down on a bench in the inglenook of the fireplace, Father Freise keeping his back to the wall and the crossbow within easy reach.

"Okay," Drummond said. "Now, what the hell's going on?"

"Big problems, John," Freise began, nervously twisting his fingers together. "It started just after you left. It seems my coming here was both a blessing and a curse to the brethren of the Order of the Sword."

"What do you mean?" Drummond asked, searching the priest's face for some clue as to what in the world he was talking about.

"Well, after you had gone, I continued holding daily Mass for the knights and started hearing their confessions. Incidentally, Holy Communion doesn't harm them, the way the old legends say. I can't remember whether I told you before you left."

"No, you didn't."

"Well, it doesn't." Freise sighed. "Anyway, after you'd gone, several of them decided that, since they were back in God's grace, they were going on a sort of hunger strike."

He looked beyond Drummond, his eyes scanning the dark recesses of the room for signs of movement.

"A hunger strike?" Drummond murmured, wondering whether Freise really was hinting what Drummond thought he was. "What sort of hunger strike?"

Freise sighed. "Well, the sort where they refused to take any food—or blood. They simply went to their rooms one day, after receiving Communion, and they laid down to die." The priest's hand moved to the reassuring comfort of the crossbow stock.

"At first they just seemed to grow weaker, but after about a week, two of them became—well, violent. We gave them food and blood, but that only seemed to increase their fury, and one of them tried to attack me." Freise stopped and cocked his ear toward the courtyard door.

"Fortunately de Beq was there, and he and a couple of other knights pulled the man off me. That night they held a chapter meeting of the Order of the Sword, and it was decided to put the dying knights in cells in the dungeon." Leaning forward, Father Freise rested his elbows on his knees, his eyes meeting Drummond's. "John, you can't imagine the agony those men suffered. It was truly the agony of the damned."

Drummond looked at the priest in the flickering light of the fire and for the first time saw a tired old man.

"What about the others?" he asked, afraid of what the answer might be.

"They prayed for the souls of the dying, and prayed that they would have the strength to live until called to God." Freise leaned back in the inglenook and pulled the crossbow closer. "I think they would have had that strength, except for the horrors of death in the dungeon."

"I don't understand," Drummond said.

"Neither did I, at first. Do you know how a vampire dies when he starves himself, John?"

Drummond shook his head. "No."

"I'll tell you. They don't turn to dust and crumble up and blow away, like in the movies. It's much slower than that. They die in a screaming, cursing, agony of putrefaction and decay. They literally rot to death. The body melts into a vile-smelling pool of corruption. Eventually the heart stops pumping and they die. At least I think they die, but I'm not sure. It may be that they live on, in their brain, in their mind, until that too finally turns to slime." Freise held the crossbow before him like a giant crucifix, his hands white-knuckled on the stock.

"Did they all . . ." Drummond's voice was a hoarse whisper.

"No," Freise replied. "But the mortification of flesh in the dungeon was too much for one of the knights still living. Three days ago he confided in one of the other knights that he had seen how God punished their brothers, and that he would rather leave and live forever as a vampire than face the torment of dying that death."

Again Father Freise cocked his head toward the door, as if trying to catch a faint sound in the distance, then went on more softly.

"At confession that evening, the second knight told me about the torment facing his friend, and the decision the friend had made, and for the first time in my life, I violated one of my vows as a priest. I broke the seal of the confessional. I went to de Beq and told him what I had learned."

Father Freise stared into the fire, and Drummond found himself barely able to breathe.

"De Beq confronted the first knight and asked him if it were true he wanted to leave," Freise said. "The knight denied it, but he gave his friend the most hateful look I have ever seen. The next morning he was gone, and his friend was dead. His throat slit. His blood drained."

An eerie sound seemed to drift up from the floor of the great hall. Half moan, half groan, Drummond could barely hear it, but Freise froze at the whisper of it.

"One of them is dying," he murmured. "I must go to him."

"Where?" Drummond asked.

"In the dungeon. The last of those starving themselves." Freise looked at Drummond. "Will you cover me?" he asked, holding out the crossbow as he rose. "I promised them I wouldn't let them die alone."

Drummond took the crossbow, not knowing what to say, and followed Freise across the great hall and down the stairs to the dungeon level. Freise pulled a narrow purple stole from his pocket as they went and touched it to his lips before draping it around his neck. They stopped just outside the door that led to the dungeon corridor, and Freise fiddled with a box of matches as he lit a camp lantern set just outside. In the hissing yellow glow of the lantern, Drummond warily followed Father Freise into the blackness beyond.

The smell of rotting flesh—and something even worse—almost overpowered Drummond as he and Father Freise made their way along the dungeon corridor. Crouching to avoid hitting his head on the low, stone-vaulted ceiling, Drummond wondered what the cloying smell was that tried to hide itself in the stench of death. Then he recognized it. It was the smell of evil. Abruptly Father Freise stopped in front of one of the cell doors.

"Don't look in, John," the priest said, lifting the latch. "It's—too horrible."

The morbid curiosity of humanity overcame Drummond's desire to follow the priest's advice. "I'm a cop, Frank. . . ."

A low, wet, keening sound came from inside the cell, and Father Freise lifted his lantern as he opened the door. The light fell across something lying on a low cot at the far side of the little room, and Drummond's words died in his throat as the full blast of the stench hit him full in the face.

What remained of the body looked like an overripe banana oozing an iridescent slime. The skin had blackened and split from the swelling within, thick mucous running out of the wounds and pooling on the floor beside the cot.

"Dear God . . ." Drummond whispered in a strangled voice.

Father Freise set down his lantern on a small table near the cot. *"In Nomine Patris, et Filii, et Spiritus Sancti,"* he began, bending down near the dying knight.

An arm shot out and grabbed the priest by the throat, great globs of liquefying flesh dropping from the bone and sinew that held Father Freise in a vicelike grip, pulling him close to the rotting skull-face of the vampire.

"Sangre . . ." it hissed through a lipless mouth, loose teeth falling from blackened gums.

The vampire tried to sit up, to drag Father Freise closer, and as it did, its rib cage broke through its own rotted flesh, exposing the suppurating lungs and still-beating heart to Drummond's horrified gaze.

"Sangre de Christo . . ." the vampire wheezed, its skeletal fingers digging into Freise's throat, blood trickling from the five wounds tearing into the priest's flesh.

Suddenly, Drummond came alive. In a flash, the crossbow was to his shoulder, the bolt loosed at the vampire's chest. Black blood sprayed the room as the oak shaft sundered the vampire's heart, its steel tip embedding itself in the vampire's spine. The vampire arched upward in agony, a bubbling, mewling sound escaping the skeletal mouth, then slowly sank back down into the mushlike remains of its body.

On his knees, Father Freise calmly pulled the hand of the vampire off his throat and continued to give it the last rites of the Church. When he had finished, he crossed himself and got unsteadily to his feet, pulling the stole from around his neck and touching it to his lips before carefully folding it up and returning it to his pocket. Looking down at the vampire, he reached over to the shaft of the crossbow bolt and grasped it, ready to pull it out.

"Don't," Drummond said in an even tone. "It might come back to life."

"I doubt that, John," Father Freise said. "Not without a heart."

"But what about the legends?" Drummond asked.

"Just that. Legends." Father Freise pulled the bolt out of the vampire's corpse. "As we've discovered, vampires do have reflections, they can go outside in the sun, and they aren't affected by garlic. They can't turn into bats and," he held the bolt up for Drummond to see it, "they can't live without a heart."

With a strangled scream, the vampire lurched upward again, throwing its skeletal arms around Father Freise, trying to drag him down onto its body. Drummond sprang into action, swinging the crossbow like a baseball bat with all of his might. The weapon impacted on the side of the vampire's head, and with a sickening, tearing sound, ripped the bloody skull from its shoulders.

The vampire's arms went limp around Father Freise's waist. Reaching down, the priest disengaged the still-twitching hands and let the headless skeleton fall back into the ruin of the cot. Stepping back, his foot brushed the vampire's skull. The jaw was still opening and closing, reminding Drummond of the last gasps of a fish out of water.

"That," Drummond said, kicking the head under the cot, "is why the legends say to cut off their heads."

Sagging against Drummond, Father Freise was about to say something when they heard a sound at the end of the passage outside the vampire's cell. Grabbing the crossbow from Drummond, Father Freise only just managed to draw it to full cock. As he signaled Drummond to remain silent, he fumbled on the floor for the bolt, which he placed on the groove of the stock.

"Move the lantern close to the door," he whispered.

Drummond picked up the lantern to do as he was told, and as he moved toward the door he heard the soft rasp of steel against stone.

"Who goes there?" he suddenly said.

"Henri de Beq," came the reply. "Where is the priest?"

"I'm here, Henri," Father Freise said, lowering his crossbow. "Did you find him?"

"No," de Beq said flatly. "The rogue is still on the loose."

CHAPTER 18

A quarter hour later, de Beq stood watching with his back to the fire, grim-faced and silent, while William of Etton and five of the remaining knights unloaded Drummond's car, bringing the boxes and packages and luggage across the drawbridge and into the great hall.

"Gosh, John," Father Freise said, "it looks like you bought out the store."

"Just a few things I thought I might need. I don't know how long I'll be staying," Drummond said.

"Pray God it will be for a long time," de Beq said, his deep voice rumbling up from within his chain mail shirt. "We will need your help if we are to catch this rogue knight."

"And to finish off Kluge," Father Freise added. "Tell us you won't be going back."

"Well, I can't make any promises," Drummond said uncertainly. "But this much I can tell you: having seen that 'thing' in the dungeon, I can't leave until all of our work is finished."

"That thing," de Beq said in a harsh whisper, "was Hano von Linka."

He turned away at that, staring into the fire. Drummond, after an awkward moment, walked over to where his belongings were neatly stacked and rummaged through one of the boxes until he came up with a stack of magazines and a wrapped package.

"Here, Frank," he said, trying to retrieve a lighter tone as he handed the magazines to Father Freise. "I brought you some copies of *Guns & Ammo,* just in case they don't forward your mail from New Hampshire."

"Well, thank you. I do have to admit that we're a little short of reading material here at the castle." Father Freise settled down close to the fire, not looking at de Beq, and began thumbing self-consciously through one of the magazines.

"And this," Drummond said, coming up beside de Beq, "is for you." He held out a package wrapped in dark mauve paper printed with tiny golden hunting horns. "Take it, please."

After a moment's hesitation, de Beq took the package from Drummond's outstretched hands. Turning, he slowly sat on the edge of the hearth and carefully examined the paper for several minutes. Finally, he slipped the dark green ribbon from the package and delicately tore open one end of the paper wrapping. A look of rapt attention came over the knight's face as he slid the red Moroccan leather case from the paper.

Drummond was puzzled at first by de Beq's reaction to the gift; then he realized that it probably had been more than seven hundred years since anyone had given him anything. He watched as de Beq sat, childlike, in front of the fire, balancing the leather case on his knees, hefting its weight. There was a sense of wonderful anticipation on de Beq's face as he stared at the case, working up the courage to see what lay within. Finally, unable to resist any longer, he opened the box.

The ivory-hilted dagger seemed to glow in the firelight, and it was several seconds before de Beq lifted it almost reverently off its pale blue watered silk cushion. He held the knife close to his face, studying the finely wrought scene backed by dark blue leather on the scabbard.

"I know this," he said with satisfaction. "This is Parzival!" He turned to Drummond, who nodded reassuringly.

Pulling the blade from the scabbard, de Beq let out a gasp of amazement as he saw the Damascus blade with the hammered gold inscription.

"This is from heaven," he whispered. Then, looking at the inscription, he turned again to Drummond. "I can read this, John Drummond! It is the writing of my youth."

For a moment de Beq's eyes misted over, then he regained his composure.

"A True Knight," he said, gazing off into the fire. "A True Knight."

"What?" Father Freise asked, looking up from his magazine. With a word, the spell was broken.

"Sir John has given me a great gift, Father. One I must repay." De Beq stood up and walked quickly from the room.

"What was that all about?" Father Freise asked.

"Nothing that I could explain," Drummond said, wishing to keep the moment private.

"Oh." Father Freise buried his nose back in the pages of *Guns & Ammo.*

De Beq returned a few minutes later carrying a small doeskin bag.

"There is a tradition that says a knight must pay for a dagger, lest it cut the bonds of friendship." De Beq sat beside Drummond and dug into the bag, pulling out a small gold coin about the size of his little fingernail. "Here," he said, pressing the coin into Drummond's palm. "This is for friendship."

Drummond nodded, reminded of another friendship sealed the same way in Vienna.

"Thank you, Sir Henri," he said with a slight bow.

De Beq looked at Drummond with a twinkle in his eye. "Did you return with my sword?" he asked.

"Certainly," Drummond replied. "I would not have come without it."

He stood up and went back over to the boxes and luggage that had been brought in from the Range Rover. Picking up the golf bag, he returned to where de Beq stood admiring his new dagger by the fire. He unzipped the bag's cover, then reached into the folds of the towels he had wrapped around the sword, searching for the hilt.

"Here you are, Sir Henri," he said, drawing the sword from its scabbard and the golf bag with a flourish. For just an instant, the image flashed in his mind of King Arthur drawing the sword from the stone. "Forgive me for not having returned it sooner." He laid the blade of the sword across his arm, hilt toward de Beq. "Your sword, sir."

De Beq took the sword and studied it carefully for a moment, as if reacquainting himself with the heft and balance of the weapon as Drummond pulled the empty scabbard out of the bag and laid it on the bench between them.

"This was my father's sword," de Beq said after another moment. "His father carried it on the first great crusade, and when my uncle sent me off to the Holy Land, this was all he gave me, besides a few hundred ducats, two horses and my armor." He laid the sword across his arm and presented it, hilt first, to Drummond. "I give it now to you—less, of course, the two horses and armor." He laughed. "Besides, I find the balance less suited since I have been using one of the swords captured from the Order of the Nazis."

Drummond was struck speechless. De Beq had just given him his most prized possession: his family sword. All of his honor was embodied in that one possession, and he had just passed it over to Drummond.

"I—I am honored, Henri," Drummond stammered, searching for something to say that would convey how much he understood this gift meant to de Beq.

Then he remembered the tradition of paying for the blade to prevent its cutting the friendship. Reaching into his pocket, he brought out a symbolic coin—an American half-dollar.

"Here," he said. "In honor of the tradition that binds all warriors together as brothers."

De Beq gave Drummond a sly grin. "A good tradition as far as it goes, John Drummond, but one that does not apply to brothers or sons." He upended the doeskin bag and shook out a gold signet ring set with a large carnelian.

"Give me your left hand," he commanded, and Drummond obeyed.

"Sir John Drummond, Knight of the Order of the Sword, I hereby name you as my successor to the lands and estates of the Barony of Beq, and as seigneur of the manor, castle, and lands of Marbourg." He shoved the ring on Drummond's index finger.

"The sword I have given you is yours by right of inheritance, and no edge, no matter how sharp, can ever sever those bonds." De Beq smiled at the bewildered look on Drummond's face. "Tomorrow," he said, "I will have the priest draw up papers and send them to Rome. In the meantime, show us what other treasures you have brought back with you. Only, please—no more knives. That coin I gave you was the last one we have."

De Beq and the other knights proved to have little or no interest in most of what Drummond had bought at

Kettner's, although there was universal acclaim for the crossbow. William of Etton shouldered the weapon and stared down the scope attached to the stock. Not, perhaps, the most technically minded of the lot, he nonetheless immediately grasped the value of a telescopic sight.

"By Saint Sebastian!" William declared. "You'd put a bolt in a mouse's ear hole at a hundred paces with this."

"Aye," one of the other knights said, taking the crossbow and sighting through the scope. "Or bury it in a Turk's nipple at four hundred paces, I wager."

They continued to pass it among themselves, admiring its workmanship, now turning their attention to inspection of the various bolts he had bought for it to fire—bolts that might even stop one of Kluge's vampires. Drummond was willing to let the knights examine the crossbow all night, if they wanted, but he was starting to feel the strain of the day, and especially the evening. As discussion continued, in a variety of languages, most of which he could not understand, he found that all he wanted was a place to sleep.

"Frank," he said, as the priest wandered over to look at the crossbow. "Where can I bunk?"

"The tower is the best place," Freise said after a few seconds' thought. "I've got a room ready for you."

"Where are you sleeping?" Drummond asked, not wanting to put Father Freise out of his room.

"Oh, my room is above the chapel. There's a little stair that leads up to it from behind the altar." He grinned at Drummond. "I've got a fireplace, bed, bookshelves—even got a bar and color TV."

Drummond shook his head. "I dunno, Frank. Sounds pretty wild to me."

"Come on. I'll show you," Father Freise said with a grin.

Drummond picked up his sleeping bag and a few of his

things, including de Beq's sword, and followed Father Freise across the hall and into the stairs that led to the tower. As he trudged up the stone spiral, he realized how quiet a castle could be. They had hardly climbed any distance at all, and yet the sound of the knights in the great hall was completely lost. Only the muted sound of their shoes on the stone treads broke the stillness.

The other thing that Drummond noticed was how dark the castle was, as if the stones drank in the light, swallowing it up. Both he and Father Freise had flashlights, but for some reason, perhaps a trick caused by the upward spiral of the stairs, it seemed as if the beams were unable to penetrate the blackness. It reminded him of when he was first a policeman, working the waterfront. There had been a report of a dead body under one of the piers, and Drummond had been detailed to retrieve it.

After climbing into his wet suit and scuba gear, he had rolled off the deck of the police boat and swum on the oily surface to the pier. It had been dusk. Turning on his lamp, he dove down ten or twelve feet and began swimming further under the docks. The wet darkness seemed to swallow him up, his lamp barely able to penetrate the inky water.

Under the docks, Drummond had found himself floating in total darkness. Suddenly he sensed panic rising up in him. He was disoriented, and for a wild moment thought he was upside down, drowning. He took a deep breath, trying to control his panic. That was when the body appeared, its face against his.

In the darkness, his lamp failing to penetrate the black water that surrounded him, Drummond hadn't seen the body of the drowned surfer until its bloated face bumped against his own. His scream was lost in the hiss of bubbles escaping from the regulator on his tanks, and in his terror he would have lost his light if it hadn't been secured to his wrist by a cord.

He had broken the surface of the water and ripped off his mask gasping for air as a column of vomit erupted from his throat. Only after a few minutes on the surface had he regained his composure enough to dive again, this time to recover the corpse.

Trudging upwards in the closing black silence, Drummond sensed the same panic beginning to rise up in him, surging higher as he suddenly realized that Father Freise was no longer ahead of him.

"Frank?" he called out.

"I'm here," a voice said almost next to him. "My flashlight died."

Drummond swung his light toward the sound of Freise's voice, illuminating the priest in front of a heavy door with ornate brass hinges.

"Come on, John," Freise said, gesturing into the darkness. "This one will be yours."

The room Freise opened for him was small, not more than nine by twelve feet, with a barrel-vaulted ceiling, all whitewashed. A narrow lancet window pierced one wall, and beneath it a round hole in the stone floor angled down toward the moat.

"All the latest conveniences," Drummond muttered, as he shone his flashlight around the room and then tossed his sleeping bag on the box bed shoved up against one wall.

"There are a couple of candles and some matches in the aumbry by the door," Father Freise said, nodding towards a cupboard built into the thick stone walls beside a little fireplace. "I disinfected the walls and floor and bed, and one of the knights helped whitewash the walls. I hope you like it."

"Where's the bar and color television?" Drummond asked with a deadpan voice.

"Sorry, John, I got here first," Father Freise replied with mock seriousness. "You'll just have to rough it."

"I guess I will at that," Drummond said, lighting one of the candles.

"In that case, I'll borrow your flashlight and turn in," Father Freise said. "Good-night, John."

" 'Night, Frank," Drummond said, as the priest left his room and headed toward the chapel.

By the flickering light of the candle, Drummond spread out his sleeping bag and undressed, folding his clothes into a neat pile on the foot of the bag. He decided that he'd have to get some furniture in the morning—a chair and perhaps a chest.

Straddling the hole in the floor, he felt slightly awkward about standing in front of the small window while he urinated. As he stood there, gazing out across the clearing from high up in the tower, he thought he saw movement at the edge of the woods.

Was it the rogue vampire, he wondered, or merely a breeze moving through the underbrush? Extinguishing his candle, Drummond crawled into his sleeping bag and closed his eyes. He had stood de Beq's sword in a corner, near the head of the bed, and as he tried to drift off to sleep, he realized he was still wearing the signet ring de Beq had given him. He found himself absently rubbing his thumb over the coat of arms cut into the surface of the ring's carnelian seal, and that was the last thing he remembered before he drifted off.

De Beq was in his dreams, he and his knights fighting Kluge and his men—a horrible baptism of gore as swords slashed and hacked into the bodies of adversaries. As they fought, the flesh began to slough off of de Beq and his knights, falling away from their faces and arms, leaving the white bones exposed. In their agony they screamed as they fought on, slowly pushed back by Kluge's disciplined Nazis.

Somehow, Drummond remained detached from the slaughter that raged around him. With his dream-self clad in a flowing white robe and holding de Beq's family sword, he stood unable to move, until suddenly a red shadow fell over him, and he found himself facing the cardinal he had met at Maria's party.

"Your blood," the cardinal kept repeating, as Drummond began striking at him over and over again with the sword. "It is your blood, John de Beq, that will stop the slaughter."

Drummond closed his eyes and swung the sword for all he was worth. He felt the sword send a shudder through his arms as the blade connected, and he opened his eyes.

He could not see the cardinal, but all around him the dead were rising up, their flesh melting away as they stood up and began moving toward Drummond. He tried to defend himself, but his sword was embedded in something—something red, something he could almost recognize. He tried desperately to pull his sword free as the vampires closed on him, touching him, pulling him toward greedy skeletal mouths. Somehow the vampires vanished, and Drummond found himself alone with Kluge, shrinking from the vampire's touch.

Kluge held Drummond the way a young man would hold the woman he loved, tenderly, caressing her body. Desperately Drummond tried to wrench his sword from the red mass that held it, but he couldn't get it free. Kluge bent down and softly bit Drummond's throat, lapping with an obscene black tongue the blood that welled up. The horror of it lent Drummond new strength. Suddenly his sword was free, and with a single swipe of his blade he decapitated Kluge, a fountain of blood spraying out of the severed neck.

The blood sprayed higher and higher until it changed and took on the shape of the cardinal in his scarlet robes. "I want your blood, John de Beq. I want your blood. . . ."

Drummond woke with a start. A thin sliver of light speared through the lancet window and reflected off the hilt of his sword leaning against the corner, illuminating the tiny room. There was no one else in the room, either Kluge or the cardinal.

Still breathing hard, Drummond looked at his watch: 7:15. Climbing out of his sleeping bag, he went over to the window and looked out to where he thought he had seen the movement the night before. In the clear morning light, it was impossible to tell what he had seen, or what he had dreamed. . . .

CHAPTER 19

Drummond dressed in some of the new clothes he had bought at Kettner's and then headed down to the great hall in the hope that there would be food of some sort for breakfast. Although it was seven-thirty in the morning, the knights appeared to have been up and active for some time, although Drummond had heard not a sound up in the tower.

Father Freise was sitting at a long trestle table sipping a cup of coffee when Drummond came in.

"Good morning, John," he called out, as Drummond emerged from the turnpike stair. "There's coffee on the griddle, and you'll find a mug on the shelf."

"Thanks," Drummond said, crossing over to the hearth of the fireplace in the great hall. On a ledge just above the griddle was a variety of mugs of various sizes and shapes. Drummond took a large one emblazoned with the bug-eyed face of Bart Simpson and filled it with coffee.

"Any milk or sugar?" he asked.

"Sugar is in the tin can," Father Freise replied. "We haven't got milk, but there's some nondairy creamer stuff up there in a jar someplace."

Drummond found the necessary additives and doctored his coffee. Stirring it with the blade of his pocket knife, he walked over to where Freise was sitting. A large loaf of solid-looking brown bread was on the table in front of him, with a dagger alongside it. As Drummond sat down beside the priest, he decided that was probably the extent of breakfast.

"I spoke to de Beq this morning," Father Freise began without preamble. "He told me about last night. I knew something was going on, but I didn't want to intrude."

"Yeah," Drummond said. "I didn't know what to say, or do, when he shoved this ring on my finger." He held up the index finger of his left hand. The soft light of the great hall gave the carnelian a special glowing radiance of its own. "I'm not even sure I thanked him."

"Well, thanked or not, Henri de Beq is quite happy to have you as his adopted heir." Father Freise took another sip of his coffee. "It means that he can die now."

"Die?" Drummond asked, the vision of the dying vampire in the dungeon springing to his mind. "My God, he's not going to . . ."

"Starve himself?" Father Freise shook his head. "No, he won't do that. What he is going to do is let the rogue vampire kill him—or almost kill him. He's going to stake himself out in the woods tonight, and when attacked, offer little resistance. He plans on gutting the vampire with that fancy knife you gave him, just before he dies."

Drummond's coffee seemed to have gone cold in his cup, and he set it down in distaste.

"Christ, Frank, you can't let him do that," he said. "Who'll hold this place together once he's gone? And what if some of the other knights decide they don't want to die? We've both seen what happens when they starve. Suppose some more of them become rogues? What then?"

Father Freise pushed his cup away from him. "Well, John, just what options have these men got? Do you think I haven't worried myself sick, wondering what's to become of them? Counting de Beq, there are twelve knights left, and that includes the rogue who is out there somewhere in the woods. Did I say 'knights'? Let me rephrase that. There are twelve vampires left. Oh, sure, they were good men once—pious, even. But now? Well, I just don't know. They've changed, John. They're not even the same as when we found them a few weeks ago."

Drummond ran his hand over his face, trying to clear his mind. "So what do you suggest? Kill them all before they go bad? Treat them like some sort of benign horror that has reached its 'sell by' date? And what about Kluge? Have you forgotten about him? How do we deal with Kluge, if we don't have de Beq and his men?"

Silence descended between the two men like an impenetrable wall, and Drummond realized that he was angry—not at Father Freise, but at his growing impotence in dealing with the situation. The Mossad had tried to kill him simply because he knew about Kluge—and because, thanks to them, he now knew about the virus that had made Kluge a vampire.

The virus. That was it, or at least part of it. It had to be. The virus had been some sort of top secret project with the Russian military. Now, the doctor who had headed that project was working with the Mossad to track down Kluge on the pretext that he was a war criminal. But why?

Suddenly Drummond understood why. Rubinsky had told him how the virus would turn ordinary soldiers into supermen. Supermen, Drummond realized, who could live off their enemies. Supermen like the thing in the dungeon of the castle that he had watched die last night.

The realization sent a chill through his body. Somewhere in Israel, a madman planned to create an army of vampires. An army that would decimate their neighbors, creating Lebensraum far beyond the Israeli-occupied territories.

That's why he had been kidnapped by the Mossad: to see if he would become their willing agent. And that's why they had tried to kill him: because they must have sensed he wouldn't. Now that Drummond knew what they were after, one thing was obvious. No matter what, as long as even one vampire remained alive, the Mossad would not rest until he was a dead man.

"Are you all right, John?"

Father Freise's voice made him jump. "Yes," he said distractedly. "I'm fine. I'm sorry I snapped at you like that."

The priest smiled at him. "That's all right. I suppose we're both a mite touchy, right about now."

The sound of a motorbike interrupted them, coming from the courtyard outside.

"Oh, no, not again," Father Freise said, jumping up from the table and dashing for the door.

Drummond followed Father Freise out into the courtyard, where several of the knights were clustered around the red motorbike he had bought for Freise. Armand du Gaz was straddling the machine, a half-crazed look in his eye.

"If I can ride a horse," he bellowed, "I can ride a priest's machine!"

Cracking the throttle wide open, he crunched the motorbike into gear and lurched crazily forward, weaving to avoid his companions. Gaining a degree of balance, he pointed the red machine toward the gates and shot out across the drawbridge.

Drummond and Friese ran along with the other knights, following du Gaz out into the meadow that surrounded the castle.

"*Du Gaz et Victoire!*" the short Lyonaisse knight

shouted, as he wobbled around in a circle, now headed back toward the castle.

The tempo of the engine increased, and the knight raced forward at an even greater speed. Bumping across the meadow, mounted on a mechanical charger, the look on du Gaz' face was one of wide-eyed confusion.

"Whoa!" he shouted, pulling back on the handle bars in an attempt to slow the machine, now headed for the castle moat. "Whoa!"

Du Gaz and the machine hit a bump that sent it airborne, flying over the water.

"*Merrrrrrrrde!*" he shouted as the machine plunged downward, splashing into the moat, spattering the hysterical onlookers with mud and bits of lily pad.

A large bubble broke the surface of the moat, followed a moment later by du Gaz, gasping and sputtering as he floundered his way to the edge of the moat. Several hands grabbed him and dragged him onto the grassy berm between the drawbridge and the moat, where they left him spitting out brackish water and chunks of mud.

"That's the second time this week," Father Freise said, shaking his head.

"The second time in a week?" Drummond asked incredulously, as they walked back into the castle.

"Yup. Now, let's see, where'd I leave the recovery gear?" He lifted the lid of a barrel and reached in, bringing out a rope with a crude grappling hook on it. "Yes, here we are.

"You see, John, right after the battle with Kluge, a kind of change started coming over the knights. At first I thought it had to do with—well, with me. That they were delighted to be back in communion with the Church.

"After a few days, though, some of the knights started grumbling about staying in the castle. They thought they should head out to their own lands. Of course, most of them realized that everyone they knew was long gone, and de Beq reminded them of their vow to the Order of the Sword. They didn't like it, but after seven centuries of discipline they grumbled a lot but stayed in line.

"Then, a couple of days after you left, half the garrison decided to go on a hunger strike. You saw the last of them yesterday. Other members of the order saw them, too, and one of them decided to head out on his own, as I told you, to live forever as a vampire rather than die as a monster in the dungeon."

"So, what do you think caused this change to come over them?" Drummond asked.

"Well, at first I thought it was the reaction of warriors who had been cooped up for too long, a desire for action on their part. But now I'm not so sure. They're acting childish, almost like inmates in an old people's home. If I didn't know better, I'd think they were showing signs of senility. I wouldn't have thought vampires could go senile."

"I'm no doctor, Frank, but I don't think they're going senile," Drummond said. "I'd say it's more like sensory overload. This happens to a lot of inmates when they get out of prison. Some of them are giddy for days, even weeks after." He glanced at his watch. "I've got to get out to the car and make a call. We're going to have a guest tonight, so I'm afraid we'll need another room with a bed."

"No problem," Father Friese said, handing Drummond the rope with the hook on the end of it. "Just see if you can rescue my motorbike, okay?"

As Drummond took the coiled rope and headed out the door, Father Freise said to himself, "Now then, where the hell am I going to find another bed?"

Outside, Drummond crossed over the drawbridge to his

car. Not quite sure about the cellular telephone, he started the engine of the Rover before dialing Eberle's home number.

The number in Vienna rang half a dozen times before Eberle answered.

"Hello, Markus, John Drummond here."

"Glad you caught me, John, I was just leaving for Graz," Eberle said.

"Graz?"

"Yes, police business," Eberle went on smoothly. "Not to worry, though. I'll still meet you for dinner at the Bristol this evening."

"Okay," Drummond said cautiously. "See you in the bar."

"Right you are. Cheers." Eberle hung up.

Drummond slowly replaced the receiver back on its cradle. Something was wrong. Eberle's mention of Graz, which was south of Vienna, didn't make any sense. He couldn't fathom the reference to Bristol, either.

Puzzled, he pulled out the Austrian Automobile Club touring guide. Looking at the listings for Luxembourg City, he found it: the Bristol Hotel, 11 Rue de Strassbourg. Flipping to Vienna, he found another listing for the Hotel Bristol on Karntner Ring. Clever. Eberle was taking no risks on the off chance that the line might be tapped.

Drummond looked at his watch. It was almost eight-thirty. In the ten hours before he needed to leave for his meeting with Eberle, he decided he would unpack his belongings and get organized, and then get in some practice with the crossbow—if he could get it away from the knights for long enough.

* * *

In Vienna, Eberle backed the red Corvette out of its garage, navigated the driveway and gate posts, and headed across the city toward the autobahn. Checking his rearview mirror every few minutes, he spotted a white Volkswagen GTi that seemed to be staying right with him through the city traffic. At the traffic signals that controlled the traffic headed onto the ring, Eberle was able to get the number of the car's license.

Once the lights changed, he drove to his office and phoned the border police at Salzburg.

"Hello, this is Inspector Markus Eberle, Vienna. May I speak with your supervisor, please?" He waited for a moment until the supervisor came to the phone.

"Kleinmann here," said a raspy voice.

"This is Inspector Eberle. I'm looking for a white VW GTi that may try to cross into Germany later today. The number is 2179 V 1104. If it comes through, detain it and call my office, would you?"

"Certainly, Herr Inspektor. Are they to be arrested?" Kleinmann asked.

"Only if they resist, Inspector Kleinmann." Eberle grinned to himself. "Thank you," he said, and then hung up.

Pulling out of the parking lot at police headquarters, he was almost pleased to see the white GTi pull away from the curb down the street and tuck into traffic behind him. He flashed a stainless steel smile at his rearview mirror as he pulled onto the autobahn.

"Okay, asshole," he said to the reflection of the white GTi, "let's see how fast your little wheels roll."

Putting his foot down on the accelerator, he took the 350-horsepower Corvette up to 130 miles an hour before leveling off to 120-miles-an-hour cruising speed. "Don't want to lose you, little buddy," he said. "Just wear you out."

Eberle held that speed for nearly an hour, all the way to Linz, the VW breathlessly chasing half a mile behind. As he changed smoothly onto the Salzburg autobahn and began climbing into the mountains, he slowed the Corvette slightly until the white car was once again in his rearview mirror. After another twenty minutes, as they approached Salzburg and the German frontier, he slowed to 75 miles per hour.

At the border, Eberle halted only long enough to show his ID and have the guard wave him on. Once in Germany, still within sight of the border crossing, he pulled into a rest area and got out of his car, walking over to a drinking fountain by the side of the road. Taking a slow drink, he watched the Austrian Border Police stop the white Volkswagen and direct it toward the impound yard. In the morning sun, he thought he saw the gleam of weapons being displayed.

Smiling, he walked back to his Corvette just as the dark blue Saab driven by the partner of the man in the white GTi crossed the Austrian border into Germany. Three kilometers down the road, Eberle passed the blue Saab at speed, not noticing how it tucked in behind him.

CHAPTER 20

After scrounging through the castle, Drummond managed to find a small three-legged chair and a carved chest, which he and one of the knights lugged up the stairs to his room. The extra furniture made the small room even more crowded. Drummond shoved the chest against the wall next to the fireplace and used it to stow the clothes he'd bought at Kettner's in Vienna. His clothes of the night before went back into his luggage, which he piled in one corner of the room. Suddenly things didn't look so crowded. There was a peg in the wall above the chest, and from this Drummond hung the sword that de Beq had given him the night before. Satisfied that the room was at least semi-habitable, he set off down the stairs toward the great hall, looking for de Beq.

The mood of earlier in the morning had changed as Drummond came back into the great hall. As he emerged from the turnpike stair, he saw de Beq with half a dozen of the other knights at the other end of the hall, struggling out the door with an oblong box. He headed toward them, thinking to offer his assistance, then realized that the box was a coffin, and whose it must be.

Hano von Linka, de Beq had said, the night before. Drummond remembered the name from his earlier visit to the castle and even remembered a face to attach to the name. He found it difficult to reconcile the vision of the "thing" he had seen the night before with the handsome blond knight who had tended him after the battle with Kluge. More chillingly, he found himself wondering just how much remained of a man no longer immortal, who should have died seven centuries ago.

He drifted after them as they maneuvered the coffin out the door and into the courtyard, drawn both by his curiosity and by an odd sense of camaraderie that he could not explain, even though he technically was one of their number. He might be a Knight of the Sword, but he had yet to manifest any of the signs of immortality.

Slowly they headed out across the courtyard, making for the drawbridge. Father Freise came out of the chapel to join them, clad in his vestments. Out of respect for de Beq and his knights, Drummond held back, not sure if he should join them, but Freise saw him standing in the doorway and motioned him to follow. Coming down the steps from the great hall, Drummond fell in next to the priest as de Beq led the procession out of the castle and into the woods.

They carried the casket in silence for nearly a mile, until the little cortege came upon the ruin of a tiny chapel, much overgrown with ivy and creepers. De Beq swung open the door and then moved aside as his men manhandled the coffin into the small building, setting it down where the altar once had stood. Stepping back then, the knights ranged along both walls of the chapel.

Slowly, his head bowed, Father Freise walked between the rows of knights to stand over the humble coffin of their departed comrade and brother, tracing the sign of the cross over it with his hand.

"Orate, fratres," he said quietly, clasping his hands at his

breast as he began the prayers for the dead. *"Kyrie eleison, Kyrie eleison, Christe eleison. . . ."*

Quietly, in Latin, he chanted the prayers, the knights joining brokenly in half a dozen accents. Most of the Latin went over Drummond's head, but he recognized the Lord's Prayer at the end, even though he did not know all the words in Latin.

When the simple ceremony was over, four of the knights came forward and carefully slid back the stone slab covering one of the graves near the center of the church. When Father Freise had come and sprinkled holy water over the open grave, the knights carried von Linka's coffin over and removed the lid so that Father Freise could also sprinkle what remained inside, with softly murmured words of a final prayer. The bundle the knights tipped into the grave then, wrapped in what Drummond realized was one of their white mantles, looked far too small to contain human remains. . . .

In silence the knights replaced the stone slab, heading back to the castle then, as quietly as they had come. Only the prayers of the priest had broken the silence of their mourning. Drummond fell in next to de Beq on the way back. He had been profoundly moved by what he had seen and wanted to say something to the knight that would convey his regrets over what had happened, but he didn't know how to express it. The two men walked quietly together, and it was de Beq who finally broke the silence.

"Hano was a valiant knight," he said. "It was a shame that he could not die quickly in battle." He looked sideways at Drummond. "That is how warriors should die, is it not?"

"Yes, it is," Drummond said, seizing his chance. "A knight should face death on both feet, fighting against a worthy enemy. Otherwise, it would be as well to stake him out in a field and let him die there, like a sheep used to draw a wolf."

De Beq seemed to recoil a little at that, though he tried not to show it, and continued walking for several minutes before he spoke again.

"When there are no worthy enemies, knights become as sheep." He stopped and turned to Drummond. "Hano was a great knight, but in the end he died like a sick sheep. I think I will choose a better death."

"The only really better death would be to fall having killed the last of the Nazis." Drummond's voice made it sound like a challenge.

"Perhaps," de Beq said. "If we knew they were coming, I would stay to fight them."

"Would you lead your men to fight them, if we knew where they were?" Drummond asked.

"They could be anywhere. How would we find them?" A look of impatience crossed de Beq's face. "Do you know how old I am, John Drummond?"

Drummond shook his head.

"Well, I will tell you," de Beq continued. "I am nearly seven hundred and sixty years old. And do you know what I've done for the last seven hundred of those years? I've waited—waited for God to call me up to heaven. And I will tell you something else. I grow tired of waiting."

"I can take you to Kluge," Drummond said.

"I am so tired of—what was that you said?" de Beq asked, looking at him sharply.

"I said I think I know where the Nazis are." Drummond looked de Beq straight in the eye. "If you can wait a few more days, I may be able to lead you to him."

After a short silence, de Beq nodded.

"We will have need of horses," he said. "I cannot ask my knights to set out on foot."

"I'll see what I can do."

As they crossed the drawbridge back into the castle, Drummond smiled to himself. De Beq would wait a little longer.

Dr. LeBlanc's battered blue Citroën Dyane growled its way up the mountainside to the small town of Clervaux. After parking under the shadow of the fortress that had guarded the villagers since the Middle Ages, the doctor crossed the street to the Ardennes Hotel. He had no idea what Baron von Holtzhauser looked like; only that his instructions had been to meet him on the terrace of the small hotel.

There was only one guest on the terrace: a man in a blue blazer, Panama hat, and mirrored sunglasses, sitting at a white wrought iron table under a red umbrella. Somewhat hesitantly, Dr. LeBlanc approached the man.

"Vous êtes Baron von Holtzhauser?" he asked.

The mirrored sunglasses reflected LeBlanc's image for several long seconds before the man answered.

"Oui, je m'appelle von Holtzhauser," Berringer replied. "But if you don't mind, I'd rather we spoke English." He took off his sunglasses and set them on the table beside him. "Please sit down," he said indicating an empty chair next to him. "May I order you a drink?"

"A vermouth Cassis, please," Dr. LeBlanc said as he sat down.

Berringer signaled to the waiter, who came and took their order.

"Now, what, if any, instructions do you have for me?" Berringer asked.

"None that I am aware of," Leblanc replied. "I was told to give you some maps. . . ." He stopped talking as the waiter arrived with their drinks. "Maps of the local area."

He reached into his pocket and produced several folded maps. "Here," he said, handing them to Berringer.

Berringer spread one of the maps open on the table. With his pen, he drew a circle around Clervaux.

"Show me where your surgery is," he said.

LeBlanc pointed to a small village, and Berringer drew another circle. Using the edge of one of the folded maps as a ruler, he drew a straight line between the village and Clervaux. Circling the other nearby villages, he connected them to Clervaux as well. Then, after studying the map for a few seconds, he drew a series of other circles at or near the center of each of the lines.

All, that is, except one. There was no circle on the line that connected Clervaux to LeBlanc's village.

"The priest is somewhere along here," Berringer said, moving his finger up and down along the line between the village and Clervaux.

"How do you know?" LeBlanc asked, wide-eyed.

"Because midway between each of these other villages and Clervaux is a ruined castle—a medieval fortress placed in such a way that it could come quickly to the defense of the villages, or rush to the aid of the town.

"But there isn't a castle on the line you've drawn," LeBlanc said.

"Precisely. Although there should be, and," he smiled at LeBlanc, "I'll bet there is. Call your contact and ask him if he wants me to visit Father Freise."

The gray Audi pulled to the side of the road beside some yellow surveyor's marks painted on the pavement, and von Liebenfalz gritted his teeth as the car jumped the curb and bounced along the rough path between the trees. Several hundred yards into the woods, von Liebenfalz pulled the Audi well off the track and proceeded on foot. He hadn't gone very far when he had the sensation that he was being watched, perhaps even followed.

He glanced around but saw no one. Putting his hand in his pocket, he touched the pearl handles of his .25-caliber Browning pistol for reassurance, then moved deeper into the woods.

The sun had just set as von Liebenfalz reached the edge of the meadow surrounding the castle of the Order of the Sword. In the fading light, he could see Drummond's black Range Rover parked near the edge of the moat, over by the drawbridge. He was about to go forward toward the castle when he saw Drummond come out across the drawbridge and climb into his car. A moment later, the car started and the headlamps came on, and Drummond drove across the clearing and back into the woods. Puzzled as to what he should do next, von Liebenfalz sat down next to a tree to wait for Drummond's return.

As soon as he was on the highway, Drummond pushed the big four-wheel drive vehicle up to eighty-five miles an hour and headed south toward Luxembourg City. An hour later, he was easing into the outskirts of the city itself. Pulling off to the side of the road, he picked up his cellular phone and made a call.

"Hotel Bristol," said the slightly hollow voice that answered.

"Concierge, please," Drummond said. A few moments went by, then an urbane and cultured voice came on the line.

"Concierge desk. May I help you?" it asked.

"Yes," said Drummond. "I was wondering if you could give me directions to the hotel?"

The concierge gave precise directions, and in five minutes

Drummond was parking the black Range Rover out in front of the Hotel Bristol. Inside the hotel, Drummond crossed the lobby and went straight to the concierge's desk.

"Oui, monsieur?" the concierge said as Drummond approached his desk.

"I wanted to thank you for the directions to the hotel," Drummond said, slipping the man two hundred Austrian schillings. "I'm meeting a friend for drinks—sort of a thick set man with stainless steel teeth. If he asks, I'm in the bar. If anyone else asks, you haven't seen us. Okay?" He put another two hundred schillings on the desk.

"Certainly, sir. And your name?" The concierge's hand covered the Austrian bank notes.

Drummond thought fast. "Eberle," he said. "Hieronymous Eberle." Smiling at the concierge, he turned and went into the bar.

Sitting with his back to the wall, Drummond was able to watch the door of the hotel and the car park outside. As he slowly sipped a scotch and water, he saw a familiar red Corvette nose into the parking lot and pull up in front of the glass-fronted lobby. Markus Eberle got out, casually scanning the lot, and pushed his way through the old-fashioned revolving door. As Drummond watched him tromp over to the concierge's desk and speak to the man, a dark blue Saab slowed to a stop behind Eberle's red Corvette, then reversed into an empty space at the edge of the lot.

Eberle walked into the bar and sat down opposite Drummond.

"Hello, Cousin Hieronymous," he said with a silver grin. "Hear anything from Count Dracula and his pals lately?"

"Only that they're waiting to meet you," Drummond replied.

"Does this mean we haven't got time for dinner?" Eberle asked in a mock serious voice.

Drummond looked at his watch. "If we're fast, we can grab a bite at the Italian restaurant next door."

The driver of the Saab crouched low behind the wheel of his car and watched as Eberle left the hotel with Drummond and walked over to the small Italian restaurant. He had hardly dared to hope that Eberle really was going to meet Drummond. Having them both in the same place made life much easier. Satisfied that the two police officers were going to be occupied over their dinners for some time, he left his car and went into the hotel to phone his superiors.

"Travelcare Exports," the recorded voice on the other end of the line announced. "Our offices are closed for the day. If you would like to leave a message, please do so after the tone."

Once he had heard the tone signal, the driver of the Saab punched 3-3-3-6 on the keypad of the pay phone in the hotel lobby. The toned signals traveled down the line, and a computer in Omaha, Nebraska, automatically transferred his call to a satellite up-link that connected him to a Mossad office in New York.

"Status, please," a man's voice asked in Hebrew.

"Thirty-three thirty-six. I've followed our man to Luxembourg, where he has met with another man. They are having dinner at present. Please advise." The agent's report was brief and to the point. At four hundred dollars a minute, they weren't encouraged to waste time on the telephone.

"Call back?" the voice asked.

Quickly the Saab driver read back the number on the phone he was calling from.

The line went dead.

The agent replaced the phone on the cradle and waited

patiently for his control to call back with further instructions. A few minutes passed; then the phone rang. He let it ring four times, then picked up the receiver and once again tapped in his personal code. There was a slight hiss on the line, then a woman's voice came through the receiver.

"Cancel both flights, then return home," was all she said before the line went dead.

Returning to his Saab, the Mossad agent settled back behind the wheel to wait for Drummond and Eberle to come out of the restaurant, considering his options. So far as he could determine, there were three. He could shoot them in the restaurant, shoot them in front of the hotel, or shoot them in their rooms. By far the least risky, he decided, was to shoot them in their rooms. He had settled on a plan by the time he saw the two men leave the restaurant and head back toward the hotel.

But they did not go inside. Stopping by the red Corvette, the stockier of the two men unlocked the car and took out a small suitcase from behind the seats. Locking the car, he followed the other man over to a black Range Rover, parked several cars away, and stashed the case inside. Before the Mossad agent could get out of his car, both men had climbed into the Range Rover.

"Shit!" the agent hissed between clenched teeth.

Pulling a 9mm automatic out from under the seat, he bailed out of the car and ran toward Drummond's Range Rover. If they got away, he might never get another chance at them. Leveling his pistol, he was about to fire as Drummond pulled out of the parking lot and turned onto Rue de Strasbourg, but a passing bus momentarily blocked his target. When the bus had passed, Drummond was gone.

Swearing in Hebrew, the Mossad agent ran back to his car and followed Drummond out into the night.

CHAPTER 21

Once clear of Luxembourg City, Drummond switched on his high beams and headed north at a fairly sedate pace. A half mile behind, the dark blue Saab followed along, its angry driver waiting for the first good opportunity to kill Drummond and Eberle.

"So," Eberle said, "now that we're out of earshot of the prying public, perhaps you'll tell me where we're headed?"

"Sure," Drummond said. "The castle of the Order of the Sword."

"Where the vampires live, right?" Eberle quipped.

"Yup. And when we get there, they're going to ask you where Kluge and his men are holed up." Drummond turned on his wipers as a light rain began to fall. "So I hope you know where he is."

"Kluge is a clever man," Eberle grinned, "but not clever enough by half." He took a small notebook from his pocket. "Could you switch on the map light?"

Drummond pressed a button on the dash and a small light came on over Eberle's shoulder.

"I pulled Kluge's records down at the Wiesenthal Center and noticed that he grew up in Ulm," Eberle said, consulting his notebook. "I then had my sister at the bank run a credit check on Euro Plasma Technik and came up with a list of assets, including several subsidiary companies and rather a lot of property." He flipped to another page. "I checked them out and discovered that, among the properties that one might expect of a company involved in the blood products industry—clinics and even a few hospitals—they own Marienkampf Castle near Ulm."

"Marienkampf," Drummond repeated, considering the name. "And you think Kluge is there?"

"I do."

"Why there, as opposed to anywhere else?"

"I was just coming to that. I did a record search on Marienkampf Castle, and found that in 1908 Jorg von Lanz bought the castle for some splinter group in the Thule Society." Eberle shot a grin at Drummond. "As you may or may not know, most of the early Nazis had ties to the Thule Society, including the Big Cheese himself. Anyhow, in 1936 a chicken farmer named Heinrich Himmler put a deposit on the property, but that same year it was purchased by Otto Emil Kluge, who just happens to have been our SS officer's father."

"Markus, you are one smart sonofabitch." Drummond gave Eberle a big smile as he slowed the car. "I think my vampire friends are going to like you just fine."

As the driver in the Saab watched Drummond's Range Rover slowing down ahead of him, he reached under his seat and pulled out a 7.65mm Uzi, which he rested in his lap. Pressing a button on the console between the seats, he lowered the window on the passenger side and then accelerated up to where Drummond appeared to be pulling to the side of the road.

Just as the Saab swung around the Range Rover, Drummond slowed to a near stop and abruptly turned the car into the woods. The driver of the Saab fired a short burst from the Uzi that streaked past the Range Rover, missing its flanks by scant inches.

"Did you hear something?" Eberle asked, as the muffled sound of the Uzi just barely penetrated inside the Range Rover.

"Probably ran over something," Drummond replied. "Did you see the jerk that just passed us? Had to be doing close to a hundred. I thought for a minute that he was going to hit us."

"Probably some junior industrialist headed to Liege," Eberle said, as they bounced along the narrow track that led to the castle.

A quarter mile further along the highway, the dark blue Saab skidded to a halt. Cursing, the driver slammed the car into reverse and spun the steering wheel around, swinging the car across the center line and pointing it back in the direction of Luxembourg City. Slapping a fresh magazine into the Uzi with one hand, he raced back to where Drummond and Eberle had turned into the heavy woods.

The car came to a complete stop in the middle of the road, the driver straining to see where the Range Rover had gone. Very near some odd surveyors' marks on the pavement, he could see tire tracks where the car flattened the roadside grasses and headed into a narrow woodland track. Straining to see through the dense trees beyond, he caught just a glimpse of headlights moving through the woods. Tight-lipped, he turned the Saab off the road and began easing along the forest track, driving on his parking lights, watching for further gleams of the headlights he was following.

Baron von Liebenfalz had waited for Drummond to return for nearly an hour before he felt the first drops of rain spatter on his face. Looking at the dark clouds roiling up in the darkening sky, he buttoned the collar of his jacket around his neck and trudged back to his car. There he opened the boot of the gray Audi and took out a loden hunting cape, which he threw around his shoulders. Rummaging in an old-fashioned leather case produced a sandwich tin and a small silver flask. He washed down the cold roast venison with a swig of armagnac to keep out the chill of the evening, then took a shooting stick out of the back of the car, closed the boot lid, and went back to his post on the edge of the woods.

It was very quiet. Planting the shooting stick in the soft ground in front of a tree, von Liebenfalz spread the handle into a small seat and settled down to wait for Drummond's return. Wrapped in his cape, with the brim of his hat turned down, he studied the outline of the castle as it slowly vanished into the shadows of night, occasionally raising a compact pair of field glasses to scan the line of the battlements. He had seen no sign of life as yet.

Growing somewhat impatient, von Liebenfalz glanced at his watch and tried to make out the time, silently cursing the elegant Vascheron timepiece for not having luminous hands. Sitting in the dark, in the intermittent light rain that had been falling since just before sunset, he soon lost all track of the time. He was just about to reach for his flask when he thought he saw something move in the shadow of the castle.

Straining to make out a shape, von Liebenfalz concentrated on a dark patch of ground midway between the castle and the woods. A large cloud scudded away from the moon, and he was certain that he saw something move. The clouds covered the moon again for just a few seconds, and when the pale light of the night returned, the shadowy figure of the man von Liebenfalz had seen was gone.

Instinctively von Liebenfalz knew that the shadow figure he had seen was dangerous—more dangerous, perhaps, than anything he had faced in his life. Far from being frightened, a calm came over him, and he quickly resolved to remain where he was until morning, rather than seek the comparative safety of his car in the darkness of the woods. His hand went into his pocket and closed around the grip of his pistol. Drawing it, he rested his hand on his knee, the gun concealed beneath his heavy cape.

At the edge of the wood, the vampire who once had been known as Alfredo de Cuneo paused to listen, straining to determine whether the alarm had yet been sounded at the castle. He had fed, and fed well, on one of his brother knights foolish enough to venture out of the castle alone, and now, gorged with the man's blood, he again felt the slightly giddy sensation he had experienced after he first had fed on human blood. Was it this that the order had eschewed for seven hundred years, by settling for animal blood, when such bliss attended the taking of more satisfying prey?

His whole body tingled as the potency of his victim's life force raced through his veins, revitalizing every cell and sinew. He felt a tensing in his muscles, as if his strength were increasing with each beat of his heart. Looking into the darkness of the forest, he found that his vision penetrated the blackest corners of the woods. An exhilaration washed over him in waves, goading him to seek out another victim, to somehow make up for the years lost.

Standing in the darker shadows of an ancient, gnarled

oak tree, gazing across a rough clearing toward the edge of the meadow that surrounded the castle, he could see the condensation of someone breathing in the damp evening darkness—an old man in a dark cape and an odd hat, oddly propped on a strange, one-legged stool. With a quiet smile, the vampire began to circle the clearing.

As he sat watching the castle, von Liebenfalz saw the darkened courtyard come alive with flickering points of light. Lifting up his binoculars, he could see white-mantled men with torches and drawn swords slowly advancing over the drawbridge, cautiously peering out at the darkness of the woods beyond the meadow. He was about to sweep the woods with his glasses, hoping to catch a glimpse of the shadow he knew they were hunting, when he heard the sound of a vehicle crawling its way toward the meadow.

"Looks like the reception committee from a Frankenstein movie," Eberle said to Drummond, as their black Range Rover bumped over the root of a tree and headed across the meadow in front of the castle. "Do they usually turn out to welcome guests like this?"

"No, they don't," Drummond replied. "Something must be wrong."

He drove the car over to the drawbridge, where de Beq and William of Etton were organizing their men into two armed bands. All of them were clad in the red surcoats and white mantles of the order, chain mail gleaming at wrists and throats, helmets on their heads, swords in their hands.

"Wait here," Drummond said to Eberle, and got out of the car.

"With all the doors locked," Eberle muttered to himself,

as he watched Drummond walk over to the cluster of knights at the foot of the drawbridge.

Back in the woods, the vampire had paused in shadow as Drummond and Eberle drove past him. Moving forward again, he had covered only a few yards when he stopped again, this time to watch as a dark blue Saab glided to a halt beneath a large oak tree. Standing quietly in the shadows, he was invisible to the driver of the car, who got out and trotted in the direction taken by Drummond's Range Rover, an Uzi held casually at his side.

Flitting along in the shadows, the vampire paced his new quarry, drawing almost even with the Mossad agent but staying just out of his peripheral vision. As they moved through the dense tangle of the woods, the vampire reached down and scooped up several small stones with one hand, then tossed them at his intended victim.

The Mossad agent let out a muffled cry and dropped to the ground as the rocks pattered against his back. Uzi up and at the ready, he scanned the darkness, unable to spot his unseen adversary. He inched his way backwards, belly down, until he came to a tree large enough to shield him. Then he wormed his way around the thick trunk and rose into a half-crouch position.

Sweat ran down the Mossad agent's face, and with a dirty hand he smeared it from his eyes, still looking around him warily. Another stone bounced painfully off the side of his head, cutting his ear and causing him to whirl about in a frantic attempt to see his tormentor. A thin, black trickle of blood glistened in the moonlight as it ran down the side of his face and dripped onto the cold steel receiver of the Uzi.

Watching from the shadows, the vampire smiled to himself as he imagined the fear gnawing at his victim's guts. The smell of the fear was almost as tantalizing as the smell of blood. Picking up a stick, he tossed it into the brush near his victim.

The crashing sound sent the Mossad agent diving for the cover of another tree. He rolled and came to a sitting position with his back against it. Panting, he spread his legs wide and, digging his heels into the ground, pushed himself up until he could get his feet under him. The Uzi held in the ready position next to his face, he strained to pierce the darkness that hid his tormentor.

The darkness hid nothing from what was stalking him. Smiling grimly, the vampire bent down and picked up a jagged rock the size of a head. Holding the heavy chunk of flint lightly in his hand, hefting it with no more effort than a mere human might expend to heft an apple, he thrilled for a moment at his superhuman strength, then took careful aim and threw it with all his might at the Mossad agent.

A white hot flash of pain exploded in the agent's groin and upward into his brain as the rough flint smashed into his crotch, crushing his testicles. In a convulsive reflex, he squeezed the trigger of the Uzi, drowning his own agonized scream in a burst of gunfire. Clutching himself, all other concerns obliterated by the pain, he curled into a ball, rocking back and forth in agony.

Seeing his quarry helpless on the floor of the forest, the vampire merely walked over and grabbed him by the hair, jerking him roughly to his feet. Pinning him against the tree trunk with one hand, easily overcoming his weak struggles, he pulled an ancient hunting dagger from his belt and drew it sharply across the Mossad agent's throat. The burning bite of the blade felt like an insect sting compared to the pain in the Mossad agent's crotch, and before he could comprehend what was happening to him, the vampire had his mouth over the wound, drinking in the hot, frothy blood.

Von Liebenfalz lowered his binoculars and slowly backed away from the scene he had just witnessed. Turning around, he picked up his shooting stick and began walking briskly toward the clearing and Drummond's Range Rover.

"Did you hear that?" Drummond asked, as he got back into the car.

"If you mean the shots, yes," Eberle replied. "What the hell's going on?"

"One of the knights has been murdered," Drummond said. "It happened about twenty minutes before we got here. The others were just going out to look for the killer when we heard the shots."

"So the killer is armed?" Eberle asked.

"Yes, but not with a gun," Drummond replied. "Which means that someone else fired those shots—not one of ours." Popping the car into reverse, he slewed it around and headed back toward the forest.

"What do you think you are doing?" Eberle asked, as the car bumped across the meadow toward the woods.

"Heading over to where those shots came from, that's what," Drummond said.

"What about those other guys?" Eberle jerked his thumb in the direction of the knights.

"They're going to fan out through the woods and see if they can't drive the killer towards us," Drummond said, peering ahead into the gloom of the trees.

"I suppose you've got a gun?" Eberle said.

"Yeah, back at the castle."

"I figured as much," Eberle muttered. He leaned behind the seat of the car and rummaged in his luggage for a few seconds, emerging with a 9mm Walther automatic, which he handed to Drummond.

"Here," he said, when he had sat back down. "Take this. I thought it might be a good idea to bring along a spare."

Drummond took the pistol and tucked it into the waistband of his trousers as he pointed the car between two large trees.

"It sounded like the shots came from somewhere near the trail we followed to the castle, so I'm going to swing wide and then come in from the side," he said.

As he spoke, Drummond sawed away at the wheel, slaloming the Range Rover between the trees. Suddenly, the headlights revealed the dark blue Saab parked in the woods ahead of them. As Drummond slowed down, the body of the Mossad agent slammed onto the hood of the car, his chalk-white face lolling against the windshield.

"Jesus!" Eberle shouted, as Drummond slammed on the brakes and the body shifted but did not fall off. "What the fuck was that?"

"I'd guess that's what the shooting was all about," Drummond said, noting the smear of blood on the windshield.

"You mean someone shot the vampire?" Eberle's voice was pitched with nerves.

"No," Drummond said, "that's not the vampire. But we're close." He put the car into reverse and eased it back between two trees. Cutting the wheel hard to the right, he edged forward toward the Saab.

"Markus, can you put down your window and pull this guy off the car, so I can see where we're going?" he asked.

"Yeah, sure," Eberle replied, as if scraping dead men off

the hood of a car was an everyday experience. "If you're sure that the wipers won't clean him off."

Drummond chuckled nervously. "No, I'm all out of washer fluid."

Eberle put down the window and reached out for the dead man. Catching him by the collar, he dragged him across the hood of the car and pushed him headfirst off to the side. Once the head and shoulders were clear of the vehicle, gravity took over and the body slid from sight. Settling back in his seat, Eberle put the window back up, still looking around nervously.

"Did you notice anything about the body, Markus?" Drummond asked.

"Only that its throat had been cut," Eberle said.

"Didn't bleed much, did he?" Drummond looked at Eberle.

"You weren't kidding about vampires, were you?" Eberle said.

"Nope. They're real. And fortunately, most of them are on our side." Drummond turned past the Saab. "All except for—holy shit!"

He slammed on the brakes, and the Range Rover's tires bit into the leafy forest floor. Standing in the glare of Drummond's headlights was Baron von Liebenfalz, cape draped across his shoulders, his arm extended in the classic pose of a marksman, a gold-rimmed monocle clamped in his right eye. Not twenty-five feet in front of him stood the vampire, sword held at the ready in a semi-crouch. The vampire was mouthing something that could not be heard, glaring malevolently at von Liebenfalz, who stood his ground as if cast from bronze.

Suddenly the vampire lunged forward. As he did, Drummond and Eberle heard the distinctive pop of a .25-caliber automatic. The vampire's left leg buckled under him and he sagged toward the ground, only catching his balance on the point of his sword.

The vampire struggled to stand up, and Drummond realized that he had been shot through the knee. As he regained his feet, von Liebenfalz retreated by one carefully measured step.

"Drop the sword, knight, and I'll show you mercy," he said in the carefully structured language of Renaissance German.

"I'll have your blood first!" the vampire shouted back, red-foamed saliva drooling from his lips.

"Then you'll die," von Liebenfalz retorted. "Drop the sword."

The vampire screamed, and for a moment von Liebenfalz flinched. In that moment, the vampire launched himself at the baron, attempting to run him through with his sword.

Von Liebenfalz' pistol fired again. The vampire was momentarily knocked off balance then recovered, but not before von Liebenfalz had retreated another step. To Drummond and Eberle, watching in fascinated horror from their car, it looked as if the vampire's left eye had been replaced by a hard-boiled egg oozing watery ketchup.

"Drop the sword!" von Liebenfalz commanded.

"Die!" the vampire screamed in defiance, as he rushed toward von Liebenfalz.

The pistol cracked again and the vampire's other eye exploded.

Totally blind, the vampire swung his sword madly at von Liebenfalz, who only barely managed to avoid the blade that flashed in the harsh light of the Range Rover's headlamps.

Stepping back, von Liebenfalz leveled his pistol again.

"Drop the sword and accept mercy, Sir Knight," he said in an even tone. "Drop the sword."

"Never!" the vampire screamed. "I am supposed to live forever! You can't kill me! Nothing can kill—"

Von Liebenfalz fired again.

For a moment the vampire stood still, a look of utter amazement trying to express itself on his eyeless face. Then, dropping the sword, both hands went to his forehead and began clawing at the neat little blue hole centered just above his eyebrows.

Von Liebenfalz slowly lowered his arm and dropped the gold-plated Browning automatic into his pocket. With measured steps, he walked forward and carefully bent down, picking up the vampire's sword. Then, throwing his loden cape back over his shoulder, he raised the sword and held it poised above his head.

The vampire screamed in blind rage as he staggered about, clawing at the bullet hole in his skull. As he passed by von Liebenfalz, he stumbled on the root of a tree and fell to his knees. Von Liebenfalz brought the blade scything down on the vampire's neck with all of the strength he possessed, severing the head in a torrential fountain of blood.

Eberle barely managed to open the car door before he was sick.

Stepping back from the twitching body of the vampire, von Liebenfalz rolled it over with his foot. Then, raising the sword above his head once again, he plunged it downward with both hands, driving it into the heart of the vampire. He started trembling as he stepped back from the now motionless form on the ground, and crossed himself shakily as he sagged against a tree.

Drummond jumped from his car and ran over to the baron, helping to prop him up.

"Are you all right?" he asked.

Von Liebenfalz nodded weakly, fumbling for one of his pockets.

"Yes, yes," he whispered. "Just help me with my flask."

Drummond took the silver flask from the baron's shaking hands and undid the stopper.

"Here," he said, passing the flask back to von Liebenfalz.

The baron took a long swig, then handed the flask back to Drummond.

"Do help yourself," he said after a moment, apparently refortified. "And when you've finished, I really wouldn't mind a lift back to the castle."

CHAPTER 22

"Where," Eberle asked von Liebenfalz, "did you learn to shoot like that?"

"In the basement of my apartment," the baron replied. "Every day since 1934, I have shot a minimum of ten rounds at a target in my coal bunker, exactly eight paces away."

"Is that why you kept backing up?" Drummond asked.

"No, it was to keep the headlights of your Range Rover out of my eyes." He nodded toward Drummond. "Frankly, if you hadn't arrived when you did, I'm not sure I could have survived."

"What do you mean by that?"

"Well, I shot him in the knee, just before you got there, but he didn't go down. That convinced me to try for a head shot—always a tricky thing in the dark. When your headlights hit us, I knew there was still a chance that he might just yield to me after all. Sadly, for him," he gave an eloquent shrug, "he chose otherwise."

The baron drew his cape around his shoulders and moved closer to the fire, just as Father Freise came up to the table carrying four steaming mugs of coffee.

"There you are, old-timer," he said, setting a mug in front of von Liebenfalz.

"I beg your pardon, young man," the baron replied, giving the priest a frosty look.

"Sorry," Freise said. "Nothing personal, just a figure of speech."

A little awkwardly, Freise distributed mugs of coffee to Drummond and Eberle, keeping one for himself. The slightly strained silence that descended among them lasted only a moment before de Beq and his men came in from recovering the bodies of the Mossad agent and Alfredo de Cuneo. Beyond them, through the open door that led to the castle's courtyard, Drummond could see the knights putting down two blanket-wrapped bundles, one of them considerably shorter than the other.

De Beq scanned the hall as he came in, looking for them, then left William of Etton standing by the door with a sack containing something about the size and shape of a large melon as he strode across the hall to the fire.

"So," he said, glancing at Drummond, "this is the man who will lead us to Kluge." He nodded toward Eberle. "And this old man—" He jerked a thumb toward von Liebenfalz. "Who is he?"

Von Liebenfalz shot to his feet. "I am Baron Anton von Liebenfalz, Knight of the Swan. And who, might I ask, are you?"

"Baron Henri de Beq, seigneur of Marbourg, Knight of the Order of the Sword." De Beq looked von Liebenfalz straight in the eye. "And this," he said with a sweeping gesture, "is my castle."

The two men glowered at each other across the table, each taking the measure of the other, until Drummond decided it was time to intervene.

"The Baron von Liebenfalz is the one who killed the rogue vampire," he said.

De Beq's steel-eyed gaze softened to iron but did not shift from the baron.

"Really?" he said. "By himself?"

"Yes, Sir Henri," Drummond replied. "By his own hand. Eberle and I can swear to it."

"Was there trickery in their combat?" de Beq asked, looking for some reason to continue disliking von Liebenfalz.

"No, sire. It was fair combat." Drummond wondered privately if matching a sword against a pistol really was fair combat, but then again, any man in his seventies facing a vampire needed a slight edge to balance the scales. "Also, the Knight of the Swan did offer quarter to his adversary three times before killing him."

"Humph," de Beq said. "Then you are welcome, Sire von Liebenfalz."

"I am most honored, Sire de Beq," von Liebenfalz said with a courtly bow.

"Now," de Beq said, turning to Eberle, "where is this Nazi, Kluge?"

A cold, dry wind blew through the woods surrounding Marienkampf Castle, making the sparks from the torches fly high into the ink-black sky like a thousand tiny red stars twinkling through the clouds. It stirred the sacred banners flanking Kluge—the black and silver labrium of the SS and the tattered scarlet of the *Blutfahne,* the most sacred relic of the old Third Reich.

Standing before Kluge in two perfectly aligned ranks were his six most senior knights save himself and Baumann, each standing next to a candidate ready to be received into full membership in the Order of the Knights of the Blood. The new knights' formal training was now complete, but recruiting would continue in order to draw in Germany's finest. Kluge could feel the pride welling up inside him at their accomplishments. Meanwhile, under the new moon, twelve immortal knights would share in the blood of their ancient enemy tonight.

A faint smile of satisfaction crossed Kluge's face as he thought of the young Russian soldiers that Baumann had swept off the streets in Berlin the week before. It had been so easy. The *Scharführer* had told him of it over a bottle of good Rhine wine, the night he returned with their quarry. He had begun the operation in a sleazy *Ratskeller* in one of the less salubrious quarters of Berlin.

"Do you want to earn a few dollars, Ivan?" the *Scharführer* had said to the two, fingering a thick wad of currency. "Come back to my studio with me. Let me take your picture."

In the shabby surroundings of the photo parlor, the Ivans had proven quite willing to strip naked and pose for the camera in exchange for the promise of a few American dollars. By promising more dollars, backed up with a liberal supply of Western whiskey, Baumann had cajoled them into performing increasingly intimate acts. Finally, when the last of the film had been exposed, he had reached behind an old-fashioned portrait camera and brought out a Luger.

The taller of the two Ivans didn't seem to comprehend what was happening, even when Baumann shot him in the forehead. He crumpled to the floor with a look of utter surprise on his face, like a marionette with its strings cut. His partner simply froze, unable to believe. Ignoring him, Baumann set down the Luger and went casually over to where the Russians had dumped their uniforms when they had undressed, pretending great interest as he bent to go through the pockets.

Seizing his chance, the smaller soldier darted past

Baumann and grabbed the Luger from the table near the cameras. Pointing the gun at Baumann, he pulled the trigger. The hollow metallic click of the firing pin striking an empty chamber filled the room. Smiling, Baumann had turned slowly around and pointed a Mauser HSc at the Ivan, gesturing for him to drop the Luger. The man offered no further resistance.

All according to plan, Baumann had ordered the naked Ivan to sit cross-legged facing into the corner of the room, his hands on top of his head and a strip of silver duct tape over his mouth. He took both men's wallets but left their uniforms in a heap on the floor, casually kicking the Luger closer to the body.

Looking around, he was satisfied that he had left enough clues to give the police all they needed to piece together what had happened: a camera with the sexually explicit photos, a dead Russian soldier, and a murder weapon with his comrade's fingerprints all over it. It was so obvious that even the Berlin police should have no trouble figuring it out for themselves.

Grabbing the Ivan's fingers and a handful of his hair, he had pulled him to his feet, jabbing the Mauser pistol into the small of his back to march him, still naked, down the back stairs of the photo studio, where he locked him in the trunk of the Mercedes-Benz. On the way back to the castle, Baumann stopped at a train station and tossed the dead Russian's wallet into a trash can in the men's room. By this time tomorrow, the police would be looking for a Soviet deserter who had murdered his gay comrade and then fled to the West—an open and shut case.

They had kept the Ivan in a cage for the last week. Tonight, he would serve a useful purpose at last: to feed the knights of Kluge's new order, his hand-picked successors to the inner order of the SS—the first of many who, in the years to come, would truly establish a race of Aryan supermen.

"*Achtung!*" Baumann's voice rang out, and twelve pairs of steel-shod heels clicked together.

"*Sieg Heil!*" he cried, and thirteen arms shot forward in a stiff-armed salute.

Slowly, imperiously, Kluge stepped up onto a stone heavily carved with runic inscriptions, his black cape billowing in the night wind with the banners. Later, the stone would serve as an altar for the holy communion that bound them in blood. Just now, it was Kluge's pulpit, and he the high priest of a new and glorious resurgence of their holy cause.

"*Heil!*" he returned, not loudly but in a voice that reached to every corner of the clearing where they stood before him. His pale eyes swept them as he set gloved hands on the polished black belt circling his waist. He wore the black full dress uniform of his rank as *Sturmbannführer*, replete with silver braid and *Sigrunen* and the high, peaked cap with the SS pattern eagle and swastika cap badge. Just visible through the parting of his cape, circling his left arm above the elbow, was the blood-red armband that echoed the motif of the *Blutfahne*, with its white roundel bearing the black swastika.

"Brothers of the new Reich," he said quietly. "Tonight, as you receive the final symbol of full membership in our immortal order, you will join again in the mystical bonding that brings all Aryans together: the bonding of our blood and our soil.

"For centuries we have struggled against the evils of the East and against those degenerate swine who would sell out our own race, our own heritage, to those who have always been our mortal enemy.

"Our fight against the enemy transcends the defeat of

our order by the hordes of Bolshevism in 1945, and goes back to the time of the crusades in the holy lands and the holy wars against the pagans in Eastern Europe. Our struggle reaches back through the eons to a time before the advent of the weakening influences of the Christian Church, back to the time when giants ruled the earth and the Aryan man was supreme.

"Now I call upon each of you to swear again the sacred oath of our order."

Proudly Kluge looked down at the twelve ardent faces gazing up at him from beneath the brims of a dozen gleaming black coal-scuttle helmets. Right hands raised, the young knights chanted the blood oath of their order, swearing loyalty and bravery unto the blood and soil of their race and vowing absolute obedience to their Führer. When they had completed the oath they were led by their sponsors, one at a time, to stand to attention before Kluge and again give him the stiff-armed salute.

"Im Namen von unser Orden," Kluge said to each one, when he had returned the salute, *"vorwärts, Ritter."* In the name of our order, advance as a knight. . . .

Then, clutching in his left hand the tattered edge of the *Blutfahne,* Kluge received a sheathed SS dagger from Baumann for each man, presenting each weapon with an admonition never to draw it without reason or to sheathe it without honor. On receiving his dagger, each newly professed knight exchanged salutes with Kluge again before returning to his place with his escort, to be replaced by the next pair.

When the last knights had returned to their places, two gigantic braziers erupted into flames behind Kluge. At that same moment, the senior knights extinguished all of the torches, leaving the entire scene bathed in an eerie red glow.

"Brothers in blood, as knights of our new order, I call you forth to join in the communion of our fallen brethren," Kluge said, still standing upon the low stone altar.

From out of the darkness Baumann came, dragging the naked Russian soldier between the two ranks of SS knights. When he reached the foot of the altar, he shoved the Ivan to the ground, planting a boot in the back of his neck. The soldier gabbled out something quickly in Russian, but Baumann ground his boot harder into his neck, silencing him.

As Kluge stepped down from the altar, Baumann reached down and grabbed the Ivan in a wrist-lock, forcing him up and onto the carved gray stone on his stomach, naked legs and his free arm splayed out across the surface in futile attempt to escape the pain that Baumann was inflicting. Planting one knee in the small of the Russian's back, Baumann used his free hand to grab a handful of the Ivan's hair and yank his head back, exposing the neck. Stepping up to the altar again, Kluge drew his SS dagger and reached across to slit the Russian's throat.

The Ivan managed a garbled scream at the explosion of pain searing across his neck and sobbed out a weaker cry at the realization that he was dying. Blood spurted from severed vessels, drenching the altar and running in rivulets between the runes carved into the cold gray stone. At Kluge's beckoning gesture, an expressionless Ritter von Tupilow came forward with a great, golden chalice carved with runes and eagles and swastikas and set with precious stones, holding it by its twin handles to catch the dying man's blood. When it was full to the brim, he gave it reverently to Kluge, who held it up in offering to the ancient gods he now served.

One by one, first the senior knights and then the ones

new-made, the knights came forward and drank from the golden cup in silent communion with the fallen heroes of another age.

The telephone in Berringer's room purred softly several times before he was sufficiently awake to fumble for it at the side of his bed.

"Baron von Holtzhauser?" the night porter asked.

"Hier," came the half-awake reply.

"Please hold for a call from Dr. LeBlanc." The line went dead for a second, then LeBlanc came on the line.

"Baron, I am sorry to wake you, but I have just received instructions from—"

"Never mind from where you received them," Berringer interrupted. "Just repeat them to me."

"Very well," LeBlanc said. "The instructions were in English, but I'm not sure I understood them."

Berringer was growing impatient. "You don't have to understand them, just repeat them, okay?"

"All right. The message was this: Tell him to stick to Drummond and the priest like shit on a blanket. If there is any trouble, send the priest home and take Drummond to heaven." LeBlanc paused just slightly. "That was all." He sounded vaguely irritated with Berringer's treatment of him over the phone.

"Thanks. I'll be in touch." Berringer dropped the phone on the hook and rolled over to look at the alarm clock on the table next to his bed: 2:45. Resetting the alarm for 5:30, he rolled over and went back to sleep.

LeBlanc gently replaced the handset on the cradle. Berringer had his orders—but so did he. Looking at his watch, he decided that he had time to make something to eat before heading into the woods to try and find the castle he had been instructed to keep under close surveillance. Switching on the light on his bedside table, LeBlanc heaved a deep sigh and climbed out of bed.

Brian Stillman adjusted the bobbypin that held the yarmulke on top of his thatch of wiry red hair. At six foot three inches and nearly three hundred pounds, the football-playing ex-Green Beret looked more like a friendly bear than a Mossad agent.

Tucking his shirttail into his trousers for the umpteenth time that day, he knocked on the door of the small firm of Antwerp diamond merchants, Solomon and Hayes.

"Who is it?" came a voice in Yiddish from the other side of the door.

"It's me, Uncle Chaim," Stillman replied.

"So, come in," the voice answered back.

There was a mechanical buzzing as the electric lock on the door released, and Brian Stillman pushed his way into his uncle's small office.

"Well, *meshuggina*, why are you in Antwerp?" his Uncle Chaim asked.

"Just passing through, that's all," Stillman said. "I promised Mom I'd look you up."

"That's nice," Uncle Chaim said. "I hope the family is fine?"

"All except Aunt Flo," Stillman replied. "She's still married to Uncle Harry."

Chaim Solomon pressed a button on the underside of his desk, and a door opened in the paneling behind him.

"Through there," he said, motioning to Stillman.

Crouching low, Stillman managed to squeeze through the door and into the headquarters of one of the command centers for the Mossad's Western European network. Inside, a bored guard with an Uzi ran a metal detector over his body before passing him on to his control.

"Brian," the owlish young man said with forced sincerity. "How very good to see you."

"Thanks, Captain Berman." Stillman resented the yuppie who acted as his control, as much for his slimy insincerity as for his preppy bow ties, tweed jackets, and saddle shoes.

"Please, pull up a chair and let's talk." Berman pointed to a chair in the corner of the room.

Stillman pulled it up to the desk and sat down, his shirttail sliding out of his trousers as he did so.

"Now," Berman continued, "one of our units is down in Luxembourg, and we want you to go out and see if you can rectify the situation."

Stillman hated the "jargon." "So, do I just clean up the mess, or do you want me to kill someone?"

Berman flushed slightly. "First I want you to find out what happened to our agent." He handed Stillman photos of Drummond and Eberle. "Then, if the opportunity presents itself, I want you to take care of these minor details."

Stillman looked at the photos, then at Berman. "Do I shoot these minor details, or can I use an axe?"

"That's hardly appropriate, Brian." Berman handed him a satellite map of Luxembourg with a fluorescent orange dot on it near the Belgian border. "This is where the Lorcan-C receiver has located the car. See what you can do, and then report back. Okay?"

Stillman examined the satellite photo for several seconds, then pulled a ballpoint pen out of his pocket.

"I'm going to need an enhancement of this area," he said, drawing a rough square around the orange dot that marked the car's location. "Otherwise, it could take a couple of days to find the car in those woods."

Berman smiled indulgently. "Fine, Brian. I'll have the lab send the picture right down." Leaning over his desk, Berman pressed a button on his intercom. "Button, would you ask the lab to send down an enlargement of the satellite photo they brought over this morning?"

He leaned back in his chair, not looking at Stillman, and an awkward silence descended as the two men waited for the photo to be brought down from the lab. The minutes dragged on, and Stillman decided that it would be Berman who would have to break the silence. After about half an hour, Berman's secretary arrived with the photo, setting it on the desk and leaving without saying a word.

"Cute girl," Stillman said as he picked up the photo, instantly annoyed with himself for speaking first.

"Who, Button?" Berman asked. "Yeah, she's not bad. Came to us from the Wiesenthal Center in Vienna." He gave Stillman another one of his patented insincere smiles. "Another American on our team, huh?"

Declining to answer, Stillman scooped up the photos and the map. It was back to business as usual—just a simple hit. No big deal.

"Yes, sir," he said, then headed out the door, his shirttail hanging over his belt.

Out on the street, Stillman climbed behind the wheel of his 1965 Buick Riviera and started its massive 360-horsepower V-8 engine. As the rumble of the twin exhausts bounced off the cobblestone street, he looked briefly at a road map of Europe before setting off on the motorway to Luxembourg.

CHAPTER 23

In the sun from a window of the great hall the next morning, von Liebenfalz unfolded a road map on the table and used a yellow highlighter to trace the fastest route to Ulm.

"I make it about three hundred and fifty kilometers," he said, when he had finished drawing his bright yellow line. "In my Bugatti, I could drive it in a little over two hours. With a convoy, it may take closer to three hours."

"And to Marienkampf Castle?" Drummond asked.

"It doesn't show on this map, but I would guess that it should be within half an hour of Ulm," von Liebenfalz replied.

Eberle checked his watch. "If we leave now, we should be there by one o'clock."

"Well, I think its going to take us a couple of hours to get organized before we leave," Drummond said. "I'm not exactly thrilled with the prospect of driving a carload of knights in armor across Germany."

"I suppose we could get them some clothes in Clervaux," Father Freise suggested.

"We can't spare the time," Drummond replied, shaking his head, "not to mention the explanations."

"Frankly, I'd rather we got some serious firepower," Eberle said. "After watching the baron shoot that vampire last night, I'm not certain that I can put much faith in less than a dozen ancient men wielding swords."

"Actually, swords and axes are probably the best weapons to use," Drummond said. "You've seen how little effect bullets have on vampires."

"Well, if you really want some firepower, I think I can help," Father Freise said to Eberle. "Come on up to my room, all of you. I've got something to show you."

Ignoring their puzzled looks, he led them out of the great hall. As they passed through the chapel, the priest and von Liebenfalz both genuflected toward the altar before heading up the stair behind that led to the priest's snug quarters.

Friese pushed open the door and crossed to a small table, where he lit a small gas lantern. It flooded the room with a pale yellow light, revealing a veritable arsenal of WW II German military hardware.

"How simply delightful," von Liebenfalz said, as he picked up a Walther P-38. "Where did all of this come from?"

"The dungeons," Freise replied. "After the Battle of the Bulge, the knights wandered all through the forest burying the dead and rounding up their weapons. Most of what they brought back has become just so much rusted junk, but I was able to salvage a few pieces."

"Well, an extra pistol or two won't hurt," Eberle said, picking up a somewhat rusted-looking Schmeisser, "and a few of these rifles look like they might still fire, but I really wish we had something more substantial."

Friese gave Eberle a smile that reminded him of a naughty choir boy.

"You want something more substantial?" he said. "How about this?"

Reaching under the table, he brought up a long wooden

case and laid it on the table. Flipping open the metal catches, he pulled back the hinged lid to reveal a brand new MP44 assault rifle. For a moment, Eberle was speechless.

"Good God, Father. Where did this come from?" he finally asked.

"Downstairs with the rest of the stuff," Father Freise said, running an appreciative hand along the weapon's stock. "John, this is one of the beauties I found after you'd gone back to California. My guess is that it fell off a truck during the German retreat, and de Beq's men found it and brought it here."

"Speaking of de Beq and his men, where are they?" Drummond asked.

"Out disposing of the bodies from last night," Friese replied. "As soon as they get back, we can load up and head out."

"I don't think it's going to be 'we,' Frank," Drummond said, a little uneasily. "Somebody's got to stay behind and hold the fort, and you're the only likely candidate."

"Like hell I am!" Freise grumped. "There are one or two others who could stay behind." He shot a glance in the direction of von Liebenfalz, and Drummond took the priest by the elbow and began steering him toward the door.

"Frank, let's talk this over in my room," he said under his breath. "You aren't making this any easier."

"All right," Freise said, shaking loose of Drummond's grip. "But I ain't staying."

Muttering unintelligibly under his breath, the priest stomped off in the direction of Drummond's room in the tower, with Drummond following right behind.

"Okay," Friese said, the moment Drummond's door was closed. "What's going on?"

"Just this. We can't risk leaving any of the Order of the

Sword behind. If we don't come back—and there's every reason to believe that none of us might make it—what do you suppose would happen to the one surviving vampire? How long do you suppose it would be before he went rogue like Cuneo?" Drummond let the priest think about it for a few seconds before he continued.

"I need Eberle with me for obvious reasons, Frank. And I can't leave von Liebenfalz behind," he said softly. "I don't trust him."

"What's to trust?" Freise asked. "There's nothing here worth stealing."

"What I can only trust you to do, Frank," Drummond said, "is to stay here and kill any of the knights who return without me. I know it sounds hard, but one way or another, the Order of the Sword has to end with this battle."

For a long moment Freise was silent; then he slowly nodded his agreement.

"You're right," he murmured. "But what about Kluge? What if you don't kill him and his men?"

"If that happens, then you are going to have to recruit a new crop of knights to hunt him down and kill him." Drummond walked over to the wall and took down the sword de Beq had given him a few days earlier. "If I don't make it back, Frank, it means that Kluge is still on the loose."

Freise gave an explosive sigh, shaking his head.

"Well, dammit, what you say makes sense, even if I don't like it." The priest stuffed his hands in his pockets like some little boy who had just given in to the authority of an adult. "Just promise me this: you will come back."

"Frank, I promise."

The priest reached over and gave Drummond a hug.

"All right, then, John. Go with God."

* * *

Thomas Berringer smiled to himself. He had stumbled across the castle of the Order of the Sword in barely more than two hours of hiking through the woods. In the three hours that he had kept the castle under surveillance, he had seen a party of men in white cloaks and what looked like chain mail beneath red surcoats take out two bodies, returning empty-handed half an hour later. Well concealed by the trees, he scanned the moat-ringed fortress with a heavy pair of field glasses for the hundredth time that morning.

From the information that he had been given on the flight from Rome to Luxembourg, he knew that the black Range Rover parked next to the drawbridge belonged to Drummond. He also had come across two cars in the forest—a dark blue Saab and a gray Audi—and it was his guess that the owners either were somewhere in the castle or had been dropped down a convenient hole by the knights he saw on burial detail earlier that morning.

Berringer had just about decided that the owners of the cars were dead when he saw Drummond, Eberle, and von Liebenfalz cross the drawbridge and climb into the Range Rover. With Drummond at the wheel, the big four-wheel drive vehicle roared into life and headed back across the meadow, into the woods, and returned a few minutes later followed by the Saab and the Audi. The Range Rover parked in its previous place by the drawbridge, and the other two pulled in beside it.

The three drivers got out. As Berringer watched through his binoculars, the knights came out of the castle and loaded a number of bundles into the vehicles, including a long wooden box that two of them hoisted up into the back of the Range Rover. They had put aside their white mantles now, and he could get a clear look at the red surcoats they were wearing over what definitely was chain mail showing at wrist and neck and knee. The device on the front of the surcoats seemed to be a blue cross, like the swastika of Nazi infamy but with curved arms, somehow protective and even reassuring where the swastika seemed defiant. He had been told to watch for the device, but studying an illustration from a text on ancient history and seeing the device worn as the symbol of a living order of chivalry were two different things. He wondered, not for the first time, why the cardinal was interested in these men.

No time for speculation now, though. Once all of the bundles were stowed in the various cars, the drivers divided the knights among the three cars and got them all in, then backed the cars out and formed up in a convoy, which slowly began making its way back toward the forest.

Without hesitation, Berringer raced back to his own car, which he had left parked on the main road. He reached the silver Ford Granada just as the Saab rounded a bend in the road and vanished from sight, headed north. Starting the engine of his Ford, Berringer pulled out onto the main highway and followed after the three-car convoy that was carrying the Order of the Sword on its last crusade.

Brian Stillman loved his Buick Riviera. The car was five years older than he was, and in places the chrome on the jukebox-styled interior had worn thin, but Stillman wouldn't have traded it for any new car in Europe or America. To begin with, there were few cars made anymore that would accommodate anyone with Stillman's sheer bulk. Japanese computers didn't design cars for people built like an underfed Sumo wrestler.

There was a sentimental reason for his attachment to the car, as well. It had belonged to the first man he killed.

Stillman swung the gold Riviera into the exit lane of the motorway and headed up the off ramp to a Fina service plaza. Pulling up to the pumps, he stood by idly while the car consumed 90 liters of petrol, nearly the entire capacity of its 25-gallon tank. After paying for the gasoline, Stillman moved his car to the parking lot of the roadside cafe and went inside to study the satellite photo that Berman had given him.

The coffee was mediocre but the intelligence was good. Spreading open a road map of the area, Stillman had no difficulty in correlating it with the photo. From where he was on the outskirts of Liege, he decided that it was only fifty or sixty miles to the orange dot that the Lorcan-C tracking device had pinpointed as the location of the Mossad agent's car.

Looking more closely at the photo, Stillman was impressed with the details of the area it revealed. The car could just be seen in a patch of woods, bounded on one side by the highway and on the other by a clearing. There appeared to be the corner of a building of some sort jutting into the clearing, but unfortunately it had been cropped out of the enlargement that Stillman was looking at. Returning his attention to the highway, he easily located a turnout next to the woods that was only a few hundred meters from where the car was parked. Now somewhat better focused, Stillman finished his coffee and went back out to his Buick, to roar off in the direction of the Luxembourg border.

An hour later, Stillman was standing by his car parked at the side of the road in the densely forested area near Clervaux. Looking at the satellite photo, he quickly found his bearings and headed into the woods. Within minutes he had located the tracks left by the Saab as it headed along a forest track the satellite had not shown. Following the track into the forest, he soon came to the clearing where the car had been photographed by the satellite.

The car was gone.

Stillman checked the photo. It was obvious that he was in the right place, but the car was gone. That meant that either the agent had returned to the car and moved it, or that someone else had driven it away.

Cautiously Stillman moved around the edge of the clearing, deciding what to do next. Then he heard the flies. And saw the blood.

The trees and bushes on the far side of the clearing were drenched in blood. Black, congealing blood that had become the consistency and color of warm tar covered the bushes and tree trunks. Iridescent blue flies, some as large as wasps, crawled over the leaves and bark in a seething, humming mass. On the ground, thousands more flies swarmed where someone, presumably the missing agent, had died rather messily, though no trace of the body remained to be seen.

Sobered, Stillman drew back from the fly-infested gore. For a moment he was undecided what to do. Then he remembered the corner of the building just visible in the satellite photograph Berman had given him. Reaching into his waistband, he pulled out a .45 automatic and headed toward the castle.

LeBlanc had watched the knights load the cars and drive off into the wood, and was about to return to his own car when he saw the big man with the yarmulke emerge from the forest and lumber across the clearing toward the castle. The man slowed as he approached the drawbridge, his right hand drawing up beside his shoulder. It was then that LeBlanc clearly saw the pistol.

For a moment LeBlanc hesitated, not sure of his next

move. Unarmed, he was no match for a man with a pistol—especially not one built like a human bear. Still, he had his instructions. As he watched, the man crossed the drawbridge and vanished through the gates. Resigned, LeBlanc gave a characteristic gallic shrug, then trotted across the clearing and followed the armed man into the castle.

Father Freise was sitting at the long table in the great hall thumbing through a copy of *Guns & Ammo,* muttering to himself.

"Hold the fort," he said out loud. "Well, I suppose somebody had to stay behind, and it sure as shootin' couldn't have been that Baron von what's-his-name."

An ad for Winchester rifles caught his attention. Two campers in plaid shirts found themselves confronted by an angry bear, snarling and standing on its hind legs. One of the campers looked surprised, while the other confidently shouldered his trusty lever-action rifle.

Father Freise looked up from the magazine and saw Stillman's bearlike silhouette blocking the door. A look of surprise crossed the priest's face for just an instant, just before Stillman shot him.

Father Friese was confused. The jeep had hit a mine, and he'd been thrown clear, but he couldn't move. His driver, Tommy Costanza, was leaning over him, saying something.

"It's the bear, Father Frank. It's the bear," he said, although his voice seemed to come from a long way off.

Everything was getting dark, and Freise struggled to see his driver in the failing light.

"Tommy?" he said.

Then his eyes glazed over and rolled back into his head.

* * *

LeBlanc had just reached the door of the great hall when Stillman's shot toppled Father Friese from his chair. Ducking quickly behind an arras, he watched the big Mossad agent give the man he had just shot a casual nudge with his foot before he turned and left the great hall. As Stillman crossed the castle courtyard, Friese let out a low moan. Fumbling in the pocket of his waxed jacket for a first aid kit, Dr. LeBlanc darted from his hiding place and dropped to his knees beside the wounded man.

Outside, Stillman made a cursory search of the castle, pausing only long enough in each room to make certain that there was no one else there. Satisfied that the priest had been alone, he left the tomblike silence of the ancient fortress and trotted back through the woods to his car. A quarter hour later, he was parking the Buick at the edge of the village square in Clervaux.

Crammed into a phone booth in front of the village post office, Stillman waited patiently while the recorded voice told him that Travelcare Exports was closed for the day. As soon as he heard the electronic beep at the end of the message, he tapped in his personal identification number.

There was a metallic click, and a man's voice came on the line.

"Status?"

Stillman rattled off his code number.

"Call back?" the voice asked.

Stillman gave him the number of the telephone booth in Clervaux, then hung up.

The minutes ticked by, and Stillman had to open the door of the phone booth, which had become unbearable in the afternoon sun.

The phone rang four times and Stillman answered it.

There was a slight hiss on the line and then Stillman heard Berman's voice.

"Brian, delighted you called. How'd everything go in New York?" Berman obviously reveled in his job as an agent control officer.

"The car is gone," Stillman said, with total disregard for the so-called subtleties of their conversation.

"And the players?" Berman asked.

"One batter out, two to go," Stillman replied. "But I think you should know that the first player was a last-minute substitution."

"I see," Berman said. "Call back in an hour."

The line went dead, and Stillman replaced the receiver. Unwedging himself from the phone booth, he took a deep breath of fresh air that was stirred by a gentle breeze coming out of the mountains. Crossing the village square, he went into a small hotel and booked a room, then settled down on the terrace with a cold glass of beer.

CHAPTER 24

"You know, of course," von Liebenfalz said, with a tone of smug superiority creeping into his voice, "that all of this is fake."

Drummond looked up from the new map that he had spread out on the table of the sidewalk cafe, on the outskirts of Ulm.

"What do you mean?" he asked. "What's fake?"

"Why, Ulm," von Liebenfalz replied. "The whole city was bombed flat in the war. There isn't a building here that dates before 1947."

"Oh," Drummond said, returning to his map. "Yeah, it does look like it could do with a fresh coat of paint, now that you mention it."

"God, what Philistines!" von Liebenfalz muttered, in something several decibels above a whisper.

"Ah, found it!" Drummond exclaimed, drawing a neat circle around Schloss Marienkampf on the topographical map. "Now all we have to do is hope they're there when we arrive." He folded the map and looked around the sidewalk cafe.

"Where's Eberle gone with de Beq and his men?" he asked.

"To the toilet. It seems that the beer goes through them

almost as fast as they drink it." Von Liebenfalz yawned. "It just makes me drowsy."

Just then a commotion erupted in the back of the restaurant, followed by a woman's shriek and the sound of breaking glasses. Gruff laughter came echoing out of the restaurant, followed a moment later by Eberle, de Beq, and his remaining nine men.

"What was that all about?" Drummond asked, afraid of what the answer might be.

"It seems that one of the knights was fascinated by the legs on the waitress," Eberle said with a droll grimace, as the knights surrounded the adjacent tables they had occupied before and sat down, some of them calling for more beer. "I guess they've never seen a mini-skirt before, and all of that flesh was a bit too much for them. Anyway, I paid for the damage, so I don't think there will be any trouble."

"Don't look now," von Liebenfalz said. "Trouble has just pulled up at the curb."

Across the street, Tom Berringer watched from behind the wheel of his silver Ford Granada Scorpio as two burly policemen got out of a green-and-white BMW and headed purposefully toward where the knights, clad in chain mail and red surcoats, lounged rather boisterously around two tables, drinking beer. As they approached, Eberle stepped adroitly between the knights and the police.

"Is there a problem, gentlemen?" he asked, blocking their way to de Beq's men.

"Are you with this circus?" the gray-haired policeman asked.

"Actually," Eberle said, "we're filming a commercial, not performing in a circus."

"Commercial, huh?" the policeman said. "I don't see any cameras."

"We're filming at Schloss Marienkampf," Eberle said. "We're on a break until six o'clock."

"I see." The policeman looked at Drummond and von Liebenfalz. "Are these other guys with you?"

"Yes, as a matter of fact, they are," Eberle replied.

The policeman turned to Drummond.

"Who are you?" he asked in German.

Drummond gave him a blank look and turned to Eberle.

"Markus, what's up?"

"I told the policeman that we're shooting a commercial at Marienkampf Castle, and he wants to know who you are," Eberle said in English.

"Well, tell him—"

"I speak English," the policeman interrupted. "You are an American?"

"That's right. We're doing a beer commercial out at Schloss Marienkampf," Drummond said.

"So I understand." He gave them both a hard look. "I suggest your break is over. Take your actors and get back to the castle."

The two policemen climbed back into their BMW and sat watching as Drummond, Eberle, and von Liebenfalz tried to convince de Beq and his men that it was time to move along.

"Look, Henri," Drummond said. "If we don't get into the cars and head out to the castle right now, there is a very good chance that the cops will arrest us."

"They can't," de Beq said. "We answer only to the Prince of Antioch. Besides, there are only two of them and we are thirteen. We would make short work of them if they tried."

"All they have to do is call for a backup, and there'd be thirty of them here in five minutes. Now, for God's sake, let's go." Drummond could see that the policemen were just about at the end of their patience.

"Do not take the Lord's name in vain, John Drummond de Beq," de Beq said. "If the police want us to leave, let them make us." He smiled. "If they can."

De Beq's men grunted approval and gave no sign of being willing to leave.

Drummond pulled Eberle aside. "What are we going to do, Markus? Can you stall the police for a few minutes?"

"Stall German police?" Eberle asked. "In case you haven't heard, all the policemen in Hell are Germans. I'll try, but don't count on it."

Drummond turned again to de Beq. "Henri," he said, "we have to go."

"I am not running from some town constable," de Beq replied. "We are the Prince of Antioch's men, and not beholden to this lot here in Ulm."

"If you are the prince's men," von Liebenfalz said, "then perhaps you recognize this." From inside his shirt he produced a small golden disk ensigned with a Jerusalem cross surmounted with a princely crown that was attached to a black silk cord looped around his neck.

"Where did you get that?" de Beq asked, as he stared at the badge of a lieutenant of the Prince of Antioch.

"From his Highness. As his lieutenant, I am charged to ask you to please return to our cars." Von Liebenfalz gave de Beq a polite but commanding smile. "Sir Henri, will you gather your troops, please?"

De Beq opened his mouth as if he was about to argue, but then shut it again and turned to his men.

"Brothers," he said, "it is time we left to face the enemy."

* * *

Brian Stillman set down his beer and went over to the pay phone in the lobby of the hotel in Clervaux. Dialing the number of Travelcare Exports, he was connected to Berman at Mossad headquarters in a matter of minutes.

"Okay, Brian, just listen. Uptown isn't happy with your extra hit, so you'd better get your act together on this one before you're called in." Berman's voice managed to sound both angry and concerned at the same time.

"So, where's the car?" Stillman asked rather peevishly.

"Attitude, Brian," Berman said. "Don't push. The car is in Ulm. It's a dark blue Saab, and—wait a second. Oh, shit!"

"What's up?" Stillman asked.

"The goddamn car is moving again. The Lorcan system is having a hard time tracking. Don't move, I'll call you back." Berman's line went dead.

Stillman replaced the receiver and went into the bar to get another beer, staying in the vicinity of the pay phone in the lobby until he heard it ring. Setting down his drink, he went into the phone booth and picked up the receiver on the fourth ring.

"Okay, Brian. The car is just outside of Ulm, near a place called Schloss Marienkampf. It's on your big Michelin map, so you should have no trouble finding it." Berman's voice took on a patronizing tone. "And Brian, please. No more extra hits." The line went dead.

Stillman looked at the receiver mouthing: *No more extra hits.* "Fuck you" he said, and then hung up the phone.

As Drummond pulled the Range Rover to the side of the road opposite the drive that led to Schloss Marienkampf, Berringer drove past at a steady 100 kilometers an hour. Getting out, Drummond walked back to where Eberle and von Liebenfalz had pulled in behind his car, not noticing that the silver Ford Granada had stopped a quarter mile farther on, or that the driver was training a pair of field glasses on him.

"Okay, guys, everybody out," Drummond said. "Time for a council of war."

De Beq's men gathered around the Range Rover while de Beq, Drummond, Eberle, and von Liebenfalz discussed their next move.

"I think we really only have one option," Drummond said. "That's a surprise attack on the castle. Does anybody have any other ideas?"

"Well, we could wait until nightfall," von Liebenfalz suggested.

"But what if they decide to leave before it gets dark?" Eberle asked.

Drummond turned to de Beq. "What do you think, Henri? You've fought them before. What do you suggest?"

"I agree with you, John Drummond de Beq." De Beq rested his hand on the hilt of his captured Nazi sword. "If we could create a diversion of some sort, that might make storming the gate easier."

"Well," Eberle said. "If all you want is a diversion, that's easy." He opened the wooden box containing the MP44 assault rifle and pulled it out. "I've got three hundred rounds of ammunition, and a grenade launcher and six grenades. I say we blow the door off its hinges and rush the place."

"Do you think that will cause enough confusion to let us get in?" von Liebenfalz asked.

"Well," Drummond replied, "if Kluge's current batch of recruits are anything like the punkers who attacked us at de Beq's castle, I'd say we'll have the element of surprise on our side the moment the door blows. Henri?" Drummond looked to the leader of the knights for agreement.

"I think it is a good plan," de Beq said. "Which is fortunate," he added after a moment's pause.

"Why fortunate?" von Liebenfalz asked.

"Because it is our only plan—that's why." De Beq
tapped the hilt of his sword impatiently. "Shall we be off,
then?"

Berringer watched as Drummond and his war party
crossed the road and moved off along the side of the drive
leading to Kluge's headquarters. The knights all seemed to
be armed with swords, though one of them had a rather
deadly looking crossbow over his shoulder. The other
three carried firearms of various sorts. Most strange.

Tossing his binoculars on the seat of his car, he reached
into the glove box and brought out a SIG P228 9mm pistol and trotted off after Drummond and his men.

Moving along the edge of the wooded drive, Drummond and his men came to a second set of closed gates,
this one with a sentry posted in a small box set on the top
of the wall. De Beq signaled for Miles Brabazon to come
forward with the crossbow Drummond had provided, a
reel of shark-line attached. The knight hurried forward
and dropped to the ground next to de Beq without making
a sound.

De Beq reached over and touched Brabazon lightly on
the throat. The knight nodded, then shouldered the crossbow. Standing up, de Beq coughed loudly. The sentry
turned and looked at de Beq, and for a brief moment
couldn't believe his eyes. In that brief instant, Brabazon
fired the crossbow.

The heavy, broad bolt slammed into the sentry's throat,
tearing through the vocal cords and severing the carotid
artery. Gasping, the man grabbed the shaft of the bolt and

tried to pull the short arrow out of his neck. The shaft slipped easily from the arrowhead, which had embedded itself in the roof of his mouth.

Grabbing the heavy nylon shark-line, Brabazon wrapped it quickly around the stock of the crossbow and pulled, dragging the sentry halfway out of the box on the wall. Realizing that he was caught like a fish, the Nazi vampire grabbed a handful of the line and tried to jerk it out of Brabazon's grasp.

Brabazon gave the man a little slack—just enough to wrap the line once around his hand. The moment he had done that, Brabazon pulled again. The line cut through the flesh and sank to the bones of the sentry's hand. Throwing his arm around Brabazon's waist, de Beq helped him to pull the sentry from the box, watching with grim satisfaction as he fell with a sickening thud onto the driveway of the castle. De Beq rushed forward as the vampire struggled to push himself up from the pavement and cut off his head with a powerful swipe of his sword.

After dragging the sentry off the drive, de Beq pushed the gates open and rushed through, closely followed by Drummond and the rest of the warriors. Inside Kluge's inner compound, the drive turned sharply to the right and headed for the castle, nearly two hundred meters away. Sliding to an abrupt halt, de Beq turned toward the stragglers and waved them forward with his sword.

Coming up to where de Beq was crouched at the edge of the bend in the drive, Eberle dropped down onto one knee and fitted a grenade into the launcher on the end of the barrel of his assault rifle. Taking careful aim at the door to the castle, he fired.

With a muffled bang the grenade was launched in a gentle arc towards the studded oak door. The grenade banged against the door and then clattered harmlessly against the cobbles in the courtyard.

Shaking his head, Eberle quickly reloaded and fired again. Another dud struck the door. He had just fitted the third grenade to the launcher when one of Kluge's knights opened the door to see what was the cause of the pounding they could hear inside.

Eberle fired, and the grenade streaked in through the open door and vanished into the great hall of the castle. A bright orange flash filled the doorway, followed an instant later by a deafening explosion. The knight who, a moment before, had opened the door seemed to dissolve into a mass of shredded rags as the shrapnel from the grenade tore through his body. Shrieking, he was blown clear of the door and landed in the courtyard, a tangle of intestines and shredded uniform.

"Dieu le veult!" de Beq thundered at the top of his lungs, as he sprinted down the drive and launched himself into the castle. Hot on his heels Drummond charged in, de Beq's crusader sword swinging wildly as he crossed the threshold of the castle door.

The speed with which de Beq and Drummond stormed the castle took the others by surprise, and for a brief moment the two were alone in their charge against the enemy. Then, as if they were one being, the knights of the Order of the Sword broke into a screaming yell and charged into the castle.

In the courtyard, Eberle jerked the grenade launcher from the muzzle of the MP44 and pushed the selector lever to full auto. Slapping von Liebenfalz on the shoulder, he gave him a smile.

"Come on, Tony," he shouted. "Let's kick ass!" And he was running toward the castle, von Liebenfalz trying hard to keep up.

Unsure of what was happening, Berringer slowly made his way to the edge of the drive, his SIG at the ready. He had almost reached the discarded grenade launcher when the sound of firing inside the castle made him drop to the ground and scurry for cover.

Inside the great hall, the fighting was intense as two dozen men armed with broadswords and daggers hacked and slashed at each other in grim determination to avoid the grave. In the corner, his back to the wall, the monocle in his right eye gleaming, von Liebenfalz stood at parade ground attention, a P-38 in each hand, as one of Kluge's men bore down on him with a titanium-bladed sword. The black-clad knight raised his sword to attack, and as he did so, von Liebenfalz fired. His bullet took off his adversary's thumb.

Unable to grasp the sword with his wounded hand, the black-clad knight tried to shift the weapon to his other, just as von Liebenfalz fired again. The bullet struck the sword just below the crossguard, spinning the weapon from the knight's hand. A look of confusion crossed the vampire's face as von Liebenfalz pumped two rounds into its chest. The pain slowed the vampire for a moment, but then he recovered and lunged for the baron.

Bringing his pistol instantly to bear, von Liebenfalz fired again, this time blowing off the top of the vampire's skull. Mortally wounded, it fell to the ground literally at von Liebenfalz' feet.

Drummond put all of his weight behind his sword as he swung it at the head of an attacking Nazi. Jumping back, the Nazi tried to avoid the blade, but it caught him on the side of the head, severing the top half of his left ear and embedding itself deep in the skull. Drummond wrenched at the sword but was unable to free it. Stumbling on something as he tried again to pull the sword free, Drummond glanced down and saw the Nazi's own weapon lying at his feet. Releasing his own sword, he grabbed that dropped by his opponent and, swinging it upward, slashed open the belly of the vampire.

Behind him Drummond heard a scream of anguish and turned just in time to see one of de Beq's men disemboweled by a black-clad vampire. Swinging his sword in a murderous arc, Drummond brought his blade cleaving down on the vampire's shoulder, nearly severing its arm.

Screaming, the vampire threw himself at Drummond, knocking him down as he landed. Drummond managed to retain his sword and with a back-handed swing cut through the calf muscles of the vampire's left leg. The vampire staggered back, and as he did a burst of fire from Eberle's MP44 turned his head into pulp.

Suddenly Drummond found himself alone in the great hall, surrounded by men who were fighting to the death. As he watched in horror, he saw two adversaries, slipping on their own entrails, repeatedly stabbing each other until finally one tripped and they both fell down. Against one wall, Etienne Lefroi was slumped peacefully, a sword through his body, and at his feet the headless torso of one of the Nazis.

Gradually the fighting subsided until only five men remained standing in the great hall—two red-surcoated ones and three in black. William of Etton, a gaping wound on his thigh, stood back-to-back with Henri de Beq as three SS vampires circled them, looking for an opening. Suddenly one of them rushed in, and as he did, William and de Beq stepped away from each other and then just as suddenly turned to meet their opponent with three feet of steel.

The move caught all three SS vampires off guard, and as William of Etton ran through the charging vampire, de

Beq turned on the SS man nearest him and brought his sword down on his head, slicing it in half. He then turned to help William of Etton, but he was too late.

If it hadn't been for the massive wound on his leg, William might have been able to turn and parry the blow that the last SS vampire aimed at his neck. The sword crashed down on William, slicing through his chain mail as if it were muslin. The titanium blade bit diagonally down through flesh and into bone. A fine mist of blood shot up from William's severed arteries, drawing a crimson veil across his final expression. Sinking slowly to his knees, William of Etton died.

De Beq turned just as William started to collapse, and swinging his sword like a baseball bat drove it deep into the side of the Nazi vampire who had killed him. Pushing back, de Beq withdrew his sword and swung again, this time cutting the vampire in two. It fell to the floor screaming, its fingers briefly scrabbling to drag its two body halves together.

Slowly Drummond looked around the room. In the corner, von Liebenfalz still stood rigidly to attention, a pistol in each hand and a cut across his forehead. Behind him Eberle stood with his assault rifle, a fresh magazine in the receiver. In front of him was Henri de Beq, Knight of the Sword.

De Beq looked at Drummond and smiled.

"So, this is what it comes down to: you and me. The last two knights of the Order of the Sword. This was a good battle, John Drummond—the finest, I think, that I have ever fought. When we set out today, I thought this would be my last battle. In fact, I even prayed that it would be. But it wasn't. And you know what? I'm glad— glad because this battle has given me a new desire to live, to live forever."

As de Beq spoke, Drummond saw a change come over him, a certain feral wildness that he couldn't quite identify until he remembered the rogue vampire that von Liebenfalz had killed the day before. De Beq had the same look to him as the vampire in the woods, when the baron had finally been forced to kill it.

Suddenly de Beq launched himself at Drummond, his sword gripped with both hands raised high above his head—a yell, almost a scream, rising up from his throat.

Instinctively Drummond brought his sword up, point forward to defend himself. He no more than got the point up when he felt de Beq impact against the sword, his own momentum driving it deep into his body.

For a moment de Beq was frozen in position, both hands clutching a sword held high above his head. Then, slowly, the hands came down and his sword fell clattering onto the floor of the great hall. De Beq's eyes were closed as if in great pain, although once he had dropped his sword, he opened them to look at Drummond.

"Thank you, John de Beq," he whispered with a slight smile. "It was a fine battle to die in."

Drummond felt the sword go heavy in his hands, and slowly lowered Henri de Beq to the floor.

"Come on, we have to go." It was Eberle, reaching down and prying Drummond's fingers loose of the hilt of the sword that was now sheathed in Henri de Beq, urging him toward the door. "Leave him, John. It's done.

Numbly Drummond moved toward the door with Eberle, stopping then as a grim thought occurred to him.

"Wait a minute, I want to see something," he said, turning back to the great hall.

Slowly Drummond went to each of the bodies of the SS vampires, turning them over, looking into their faces.

"He's not here," Drummond said. "The bastard's not here!"

"Who? Who isn't here?" von Liebenfalz asked.

"Kluge, that's who," Drummond said. "The bastard's not here. He's escaped!"

In the courtyard, Berringer had watched as three men in Nazi uniforms came out of the castle and climbed into a silver-blue Mercedes-Benz and raced off down the drive. It was his guess that, dressed as they were, they couldn't be going far.

Stillman was traveling over eighty miles per hour when he saw the dark blue Saab parked by the side of the road with two other vehicles. Slowing down, he drove past the Saab and then made a U-turn to come back and inspect it up close. Just as he pulled into the parking area, a silver blue Mercedes 500 pulled out of the gates at speed and turned up the road headed in the direction of Stuttgart.

CHAPTER 25

Starting to tremble in after-reaction, Drummond walked over to the body of the Nazi he had killed with de Beq's family sword and grabbed the hilt. He pulled as hard as he could, but the blade remained embedded in the vampire's skull. In the end, he had to brace one foot against the skull and wrench the sword free. While he did this, Eberle and von Liebenfalz began dragging all of the bodies of the Knights of the Sword into the center of the great hall.

"Check around and see if you can find some petrol, will you, John?" Eberle said, as he started dragging at another body. "We need to torch this place and get the hell out of here."

"First, I want to see if we can find Kluge's office," Drummond said. "We can't let him get away. That may give us a lead as to where he's going."

Eberle was beginning to look a little antsy.

"Look, John, it's getting late. People are bound to come by here eventually, even if it's only the milkman." His smile was a little strained. "I don't know about you, but I don't really want to take the rap for offing all of these guys. Okay?"

"Ten minutes. That's all. Just give me ten minutes, and

if I can't find Kluge's office, we'll leave. Fair enough?"
Drummond looked from Eberle to von Liebenfalz. "Well?"

Von Liebenfalz shrugged, and Eberle shook his head
unenthusiastically.

"Okay, but make it fast. In ten minutes, this whole
place goes up in flames."

Drummond raced up the stairs leading from the great
hall to the private apartments of the castle. Kicking in
door after door, he searched for Kluge's office. On the
next two floors, all of the doors were locked, leading
Drummond to the inescapable conclusion that Kluge's office, if indeed he had one, must be elsewhere in the castle, or perhaps in the adjoining stable complex.

He had seen the stable as they approached, about one
hundred yards from the castle. Dashing back
downstairs—Eberle was dousing the bodies with a jerry
can of petrol he had found somewhere—Drummond ran
across the castle yard and over to the stables, momentarily
daunted as he was faced with the vast expanse of the indoor riding school.

But the office had to be here, if Drummond had any
hope of finding it. Undoubtedly this was where Kluge had
trained his Nazi knights in the skills of chivalry. After ran-
sacking what proved to be the tack room and feed rooms,
he was about to toss in the towel when he noticed a small
stair leading up from what had been the coach house to
the loft space in the attic. Hardly daring to hope, he
dashed up the stairs and found it: Kluge's office.

He wished he had time to fully investigate, but even ri-
fling quickly through the top layer of papers on the desk,
Drummond quickly discovered three things: Kluge was
rich, he owned more companies that most people can
count, and one of those companies had its world head-

quarters in Stuttgart. Even the name was familiar: Euro Plasma Technik.

Smiling nastily, Drummond rushed back to the great hall brandishing a sheaf of documents.

"Okay, Markus, let 'er rip," he said, as he came into the hall. "The sonofabitch has an office in Stuttgart. My money says that's where he's heading."

Eberle already had a torch going and handed it to Drummond as he and von Liebenfalz drew back. They had gathered up the bodies of the dead Nazis as well, but had left these around the perimeter of the room, though also doused with petrol. Drummond had not thought that much about what they were going to do and found himself hesitating as he turned to the pile of bodies in the center of the room—the bodies of men he had come to know and respect in so short a time, especially one of them.

"So long, Henri," he whispered, not daring to look too closely at the petrol-soaked pile.

As he tossed the torch and the flames shot up, he found himself remembering his conversation with Father Freise about whether vampires ever actually died and hoped desperately that these men had found their peace after seven hundred years of waiting. His eyes were moist as he turned away from the growing conflagration, but he told himself it was from the smoke. The heft of Henri de Beq's family sword in his hand gave him a solid sort of comfort as he looked back at the flames for the last time.

The great hall was already well ablaze as he and his two companions silently made their way out across the courtyard, gathering up stray ordnance and heading down the drive to their waiting cars. Eberle started to stash his MP44 in Drummond's Range Rover, but Drummond caught his sleeve and shook his head.

"Take the Saab, Markus," he said. "I think this is the place where we all say good-bye."

"No way, John," Markus replied. "There is still one, and possibly more vampires on the street. You worked hard enough to convince me; I'm not pulling back until we have him. How about you, Baron?"

"Well, I am sorry to have to withdraw, after this remarkable little adventure we have just shared, but I must get back to Vienna." He bowed curtly. "So if you gentlemen will excuse me?"

As Drummond looked on in some astonishment, von Liebenfalz climbed into his car and started the engine.

"Do give my regards to Father Freise," he said through an open window, just before he drove off into the night.

"Well, it looks like it's down to just you and me, old buddy," Eberle said, as the baron's taillights receded. "Where to now?"

"Like I said, the offices of Euro Plasma Technik in Stuttgart," Drummond replied. "That's where Kluge has his worldwide headquarters, and that's where I think he'll go to ground." He knitted his brow for a moment. "We'll have more flexibility if we take two cars. Can you follow along in the Saab?"

"Indeed, why not?" Eberle quipped. "After mass murder and arson, what's a little grand theft auto?"

Brian Stillman watched both men from across the road with a pair of infrared binoculars. As soon as he saw them get into their cars and head back in the direction of Stuttgart, he climbed into his Buick and followed. A quarter mile further down the road, Tom Berringer also watched as von Liebenfalz left and then Drummond and Eberle drove off together in the remaining two cars. He was about to follow when another car pulled out of a small farm lane and tucked in behind them.

Never one to believe in coincidence, Berringer let the gold Buick pull ahead before switching on his headlights and joining the queue, following them into Stuttgart.

Driving into the city, Drummond had time to think and found himself wondering whether he was walking into an elaborate trap set by Kluge. He had no idea how many vampires Kluge had made in the half century since the Second World War. For all he knew, there could be dozens, even hundreds, of vampires lurking about Euro Plasma Technik. His only hope was that Kluge would not think he was being followed, or would not have time to mobilize another vampire battle unit.

As he and Eberle threaded their way toward the center of Stuttgart, Drummond checked the street plan of the city in his road atlas. If he had read the map correctly, Kluge's offices should be up ahead and to the left, in the vicinity of a place called the *Katharinenhospital*.

Drummond spotted a sign for the *Katharinenhospital* and made his turn. Two blocks on, he came upon the six-story office building that housed the world headquarters of Kluge's international blood bank operation. Looking at the massive structure, so solid and respectable looking, he decided that there could be no better cover in the world for a vampire than running one of the largest blood services companies in the world. Kluge would have at his disposal lawyers, accountants, scientists, and a worldwide network of blood banks to feed on.

Well, they say an army marches on its stomach, Drummond mused. *I wonder how big an army Kluge has? If he has two hundred blood banks around the world, and each blood bank feeds twenty-five vampires . . .* That was five thousand vampires, ready, willing, and eager to carry out Kluge's orders. . . .

Shivering, Drummond pulled into the parking lot next to the Euro Plasma Technik building, Eberle following right behind. Cruising slowly toward the back of the parking lot, he spotted an up-ramp marked "Executive Parking Only," and turning off his headlights, eased the Range Rover up the ramp. The lot above was well lit, and over by the far wall, next to a set of elevator doors, was a silver-blue Mercedes very like one they had seen back at Marienkampf Castle.

Drummond stopped the Range Rover about thirty feet back from the Mercedes and signaled Eberle to park similarly on the other side of the car, effectively turning it and the elevator door behind it into a lethal killing zone. Eberle waved to Drummond and pulled up as directed, then stepped out of his car and laid the barrel of his MP44 assault rifle over the hood of the Saab. Drummond then slid across to the passenger side of his car. As he did so, his foot struck something lying on the floor.

He reached for it, still keeping the Mercedes warily in view, and his fingers closed around the hilt of a dagger— the one he had bought for de Beq in Vienna. Pulling it from its sheath, he slipped the blade under his belt in the small of his back, glad for this small part of the presence of Henri de Beq. Then, easing himself out the passenger side of his car, he dropped down onto all fours and crawled over to the Mercedes.

It was an old survival tactic he had learned long ago. Pulling his pistol from his waistband and holding it at the ready, he placed his left hand next to the car, his fingers spread wide, the tips just resting on the door. If there was anyone inside the car, he would feel their slightest movement.

Sixty seconds ticked by and nothing moved. Cautiously Drummond raised his head above the level of the doors and peered into the car. It was empty, but there were bloodstains on the upholstery.

Crouching low, Drummond trotted back to the Rover. Just as he reached the midway point between the two cars, the elevator doors opened and a man in a white lab coat and silver-rimmed spectacles stepped out, a Schmeisser machine gun at the ready. Eberle immediately opened fire, distracting the man long enough for Drummond to sprint back to the cover of the Rover.

Eberle's first burst of gunfire went wide, smacking great craters in the concrete walls. The man in the lab coat dropped to the floor and rolled back into the elevator, coming up in a combat crouch. Pushing the gun around the corner of the door, he sprayed a long burst in the general direction of Eberle, then ducked back inside.

They exchanged several more ineffectual bursts of gunfire. From his position behind the Range Rover, Drummond could see that it was a Mexican standoff: neither man could get a clear shot at the other without exposing himself to the other man's fire. Drummond might have a clear shot when the vampire returned Eberle's fire, but to really hit him, they'd have to drag him out into the open.

Suddenly Drummond had a plan. It was obvious from the fire-fight between Eberle and the vampire that their quarry didn't know where Drummond was. If Drummond could keep his whereabouts uncertain for just a few minutes longer, he might be able to drag the man out of the elevator and kill him.

Moving around to the back of the Range Rover, Drummond dropped the tailgate and took Miles Brabazon's crossbow from the rear of the car. After rummaging in the back, he found one of the shark bolts with an expanding head and a reel of the shark-line.

Flat on his stomach, Drummond crawled under the Range Rover and worked himself to the front of the vehicle. After reeling off about sixty feet of the heavy monofilament, he fixed the spool to the cable on the winch located on the front bumper of his car. The other end he passed through the small eye on the head of the bolt.

Crouching in front of the Range Rover, Drummond cocked the crossbow and snapped the bolt into the channel along the stock, making sure to keep his line clear. When he was satisfied that everything was ready, he waited for Eberle to let off another burst, then stood up to get a clear shot as his quarry returned fire.

The vampire detected Drummond's movement in his peripheral vision and swung around to fire. Anticipating him by a fraction of a second, Drummond fired the crossbow and dove for cover in one simultaneous movement. The bolt drove deep into the man's chest, and the three razor-sharp barbs popped open as the bolt head passed between his ribs.

Scrambling under the Range Rover, Drummond reached forward and pressed the switch that activated the winch. It ground away, slowly reeling in the heavy monofilament until the line went taut, and Kluge's vampire found himself being slowly dragged out of the elevator.

Recovering from the initial shock of his wound, he grabbed the shaft of the crossbow bolt and tried to pull it from his body. The shaft slipped easily from the socket of the arrowhead, leaving the latter firmly planted in his chest. He spread his legs and braced himself on either side of the elevator door, pushing with all of his might to keep from being dragged out into the killing zone between the Mercedes and Eberle's Saab.

The winch slowed, its mechanical hum becoming a deep-throated, grinding sound. To Drummond's amazement, the vampire continued to strain against the winch and seemed to be holding his own.

With a loud crack, the vampire's left knee shattered and dislocated. Screaming, he twisted sideways in the elevator door, his rigid left leg acting as a brace to prevent him from being dragged out of the stainless steel cubicle. The tension on the line increased, and it began to hum as it vibrated between the slowly winding winch and the vampire's tightly wedged body.

Suddenly a wet, sucking sound backed by an agonized scream echoed off the concrete walls of the car park as the barbed arrow head was pulled from his body, its recurved barbs catching on the vampire's heart and lungs and ripping them out through a three-inch hole in his chest. The vampire fell back without a further sound, the silence of the car park now broken only by the whine of the winch and the wet, slopping sound of his lungs being dragged along the concrete.

Faintly sickened, Drummond grabbed his sword from the back of the Rover and dashed to the elevator.

"Stay here and cover me," he shouted to Eberle, and he shoved the vampire's hollow carcass out of the elevator.

The key to the executive penthouse was still in the control panel, and Drummond turned it to the up position. The doors closed, and Drummond began his ascent into hell.

In his penthouse suite, Kluge had watched the death of his vampire on closed circuit television in the same dispassionate way that the guards in the death camps had looked on as the inmates were herded into the gas chambers. It was unfortunate, he decided, that he hadn't been able to send Baumann to rescue his man, but at that moment the *Scharführer* was engaged in a more important mission. For an instant, Kluge felt isolated and alone in his immortality.

The knowledge that he and Baumann were the last of the *Alte Kameraden* brought Kluge's thoughts to focus on his most promising disciple, Anton von Tupilow. He turned to the younger man and regarded him silently for a moment, then made up his mind.

"Here," he said, handing von Tupilow a thick leather satchel from a desk drawer. "This is my escape kit. Take it and go down the back stairs to the basement parking lot. You will see a door marked 'Generator Room.' Use this key—" he tossed it to von Tupilow "—to open the door. The tunnel beyond leads to the underground parking lot at the *Katharinenhospital*. There's a black Porsche Speedster in the lot. The same key that opens the generator room works the ignition. If you see Baumann with the others loading the vans, tell him that I want to see him when he's finished."

At von Tupilow's nod, Kluge continued more confidently.

"Get out of Stuttgart and go to Vienna. I have a suite of rooms at the Bristol Hotel under the name of Count Metterdorf. Use that name when you sign in. I'll join you as soon as I can. If I haven't contacted you within a month, open that case and follow the instructions. Do you understand?"

Von Tupilow clicked his heels. "Yes, *Hochmeister*!"

"Good. *Sieg Heil!*"

Kluge saluted von Tupilow, then opened the door in the paneling that led down to his freedom.

"One word of advice, Anton," Kluge said, just before

the younger man stepped into the opening. "Never hunt alone."

When von Tupilow had gone, Kluge turned back to the security monitor on his desk. The black-and-white image showed a lifeless hulk crumpled beside Kluge's Mercedes and a man with an assault rifle covering the elevator and surrounding car park. The display above the elevator door indicated that the elevator was on its way up.

Kluge started to turn away, then looked again as an old American car entered the frame, pulling up behind the Mercedes. Despite the menacing motions of the man with the rifle, a big, bearlike man got out of the car, displaying empty hands to his challenger. Although there was no sound to accompany the picture, Kluge could imagine what was being said.

As the two men in the parking structure mouthed unheard imprecations, Kluge went to a glass-topped case on the far side of his office and removed a sword that had once belonged to the Grand Master of the Teutonic Knights. First things first. Far more immediate than the two men in the car park was the question of the man in the elevator—an opponent to be reckoned with. His handling of the vampire in the elevator showed that he was both brave and resourceful. It remained to be seen how adept he was with a sword.

Glancing again at the screen of his security monitor, Kluge noticed for the first time that the bearlike man was wearing a yarmulke.

A Jew, he thought. *Probably the Mossad.* The big man's shirttail hung out, nearly—but not quite—concealing the butt of an automatic pistol.

What was that old proverb about the Russians? Something about being nice until they tucked in their shirts?

He doubted the big Jew was a nice person. His experience in the Russian camps had been that no one was nice, whether or not their shirttail was tucked in.

No, the Jew almost certainly was after him. Kluge had expected it since the day he literally bumped into a former camp inmate in Vienna. The old man had gone straight to the authorities—the most dangerous thing that had happened to Kluge since his escape from Russia—but in the end, no one believed him.

Or had they? Kluge looked at the monitor again. Suddenly he was certain that the big man in the yarmulke was there for one of only two reasons: to kill Kluge in retribution for the death of the old Jew in Vienna a few weeks before, or to kidnap him, take him to Israel, and experiment on him just like the Russians had done.

In an instant, Kluge's mind was made up. He would never allow the Jews or anyone else to use him like some laboratory animal. This man on the elevator had better be damned good, because if he wasn't, the Jew would have to be better. Kluge had decided to die rather than risk falling into the hands of the Mossad—and better in battle against a worthy opponent than forced to take his own life.

A bell sounded out in the lobby, alerting Kluge that the elevator had arrived. Hefting his sword, Kluge opened the door of his office and stepped outside to meet his adversary.

The little lobby looked empty, but Kluge could sense the presence of someone else in the room.

"I saw you on the security monitor," Kluge said in German. "You were very impressive. I admire cleverness and courage. Also prowess. I hope I won't be disappointed."

"Ich spreche nicht Deutsch, Herr Kluge," Drummond said as he stepped cautiously from the elevator, de Beq's sword at the ready.

"Well," Kluge said, shifting to English, "you have the advantage of me. Do you mind telling me who you are?"

"John Drummond," Drummond replied.

"I see," Kluge said. "And now that our paths have crossed, Mr. Drummond, what can I do for you?" he asked, bringing his own sword up into a defensive position.

"You can die, that's what," Drummond said, circling to Kluge's right. "You can die and go to hell."

"Hardly a charitable wish," Kluge said, "but if that's the way you feel, I'll give you the opportunity here and now to do your best to kill me."

Kluge held his sword away from his body and at a downward angle, the point inches from the floor. Stepping forward and to his left, he halted Drummond's feint with a quick upward slash of his blade.

Drummond leaped back, swinging de Beq's sword like a golf club, and only managed to deflect Kluge's blade at the last instant. Bringing his weapon back like an edged pendulum, he swung wildly at Kluge, who deftly parried the attack and stepped back into a guard position.

"So," Kluge said, looking at Drummond and trying to decide whether to kill him or let him live, "who are you with? The Israelis?"

"No, the police," Drummond replied. "LAPD."

Kluge regarded Drummond quizzically. "You are a bit out of your jurisdiction," he finally said.

Drummond gave Kluge a cold smile. "Let's just call it 'hot pursuit.'"

"Yes, but on whose behalf?" Kluge replied. *"To protect and serve*—isn't that what it says on your police cars, Mr. Drummond? They do on all the TV shows, at least. Tell me, whom do you protect and serve today?" Kluge began slowly edging around behind the security desk in the lobby as he spoke.

"Do you protect *your* home? Do you serve *your* people? No. You are here to kill me, to protect Jews and to serve Jewish interests. It would be better, Mr. Drummond, to join with me in the Aryan struggle than to die for the Jews."

"One of us is going to die, Kluge, and it isn't going to be me." Drummond swung overhand at Kluge. The vampire deflected Drummond's blade easily with his own, then riposted with a blow that nearly knocked the sword from Drummond's hand. As Drummond recovered his weapon, Kluge glanced at the monitor on the desk.

"Do you really believe that, you insignificant fool?" he retorted. "There is a Jew—probably with the Mossad—dealing with your friend right now." A flicker of disbelief crossed Drummond's face. "You don't believe me? Well, see for yourself."

Reaching to the end of the desk, Kluge turned the security monitor toward Drummond. On the black-and-white screen, Drummond could see Eberle holding a big man at gunpoint, keeping him at a distance, hands over his head. Kluge pressed a button on the control panel on the desk, and the remote security camera zoomed in on the pair, unmistakably showing the yarmulke the big man was wearing.

"A Jew, Mr. Drummond," Kluge said. "A Jew who is here to kill us both. Only he doesn't know the bond we share."

"I don't share anything with you, Kluge," Drummond said, glaring at the vampire.

"We share the bond of our race, Drummond." Kluge smiled. "And the blood of the immortals."

"No, that's where you're wrong, Kluge." Drummond's

voice had the flat ring of authority. "I'm not like you. I'm not a Nazi and I'm not a vampire. I'm a cop. You asked who do I protect, who do I serve? Well, I'll tell you. I protect the innocent and I serve the good. And you, asshole, are neither."

Drummond brought his sword down on the security monitor, shattering it in a shower of exploding sparks, following through immediately with a slash at Kluge's arm which—quite unexpectedly—actually connected.

It was only a flesh wound, but Kluge screamed in outrage and slashed back at Drummond, who managed to parry Kluge's sword with his own and then vaulted over the desk and swung his sword overhead, bringing it down on Kluge's shoulder.

Kluge's parry was late. He managed to deflect Drummond's blade enough to prevent it cutting, but not to stop it from shattering bone. His collarbone snapped with a brittle crack, and his left arm dropped uselessly to his side.

Snarling, his sword still clutched in his right hand, Kluge scrambled awkwardly around the desk and made a dash for the elevator. Grimacing with pain and staggering as he ran, the vampire careened into the elevator and collapsed to his knees, scrambling to get his back to a corner. Drummond, thinking he had done the vampire serious injury, charged after him, his sword above his head, ready to smash on Kluge like an executioner's axe.

Kluge dropped his sword as he frantically tried to prop himself in a sitting position in the corner. Just in time, as Drummond arched his back to bring his sword down in a killing blow, Kluge snatched his sword from the floor of the elevator and, with a cunning smile on his face, brought it up with a powerful thrust into Drummond's side.

Drummond's first sensation was not pain but an icy blow to his side as the blade passed through his body. *Then* the pain hit, in a wave that crashed over him with such intensity that he staggered against the wall, paralyzed with agony, spitted on Kluge's blade. As Kluge pulled back his sword and Drummond felt the blade slip out of his body—a burning sensation, as if his very life were being pulled out with it—he felt himself sinking slowly to his knees, de Beq's sword slipping from fingers suddenly gone cold and numb.

In that instant, Drummond knew that Kluge had deceived him into believing he was seriously injured. He also knew that he was a dead man. His vision narrowed to a distant tunnel, and in his ears he could hear the last of his life rushing away from him. Sinking forward helplessly, into Kluge's very arms, he was dimly aware of the vampire's gloating laughter.

A part of him seemed to be floating near the ceiling of the elevator, looking down on himself as he slowly collapsed across Kluge's chest, dying. But suddenly anger began to replace the floating complacency that was carrying Drummond away. In the darkening, twilight world into which he was drifting, one final thought came to Drummond—that even if he died, Kluge must not survive.

Determination gave him strength for one final act. As he watched, he saw himself reach to the small of his back and grab the hilt of de Beq's dagger—the Damascus blade the knight had said came from heaven. That last movement brought the knife around to slash deeply into the side of Kluge's neck. It was the last thing of which Drummond was aware, before he slid into merciful blackness.

The shock of Drummond's dying attack burned into Kluge's consciousness. Using his good arm, he instinctively reached around Drummond's body and clamped his hand over the wound the broad-blade dagger had inflicted as Drummond fell forward, but he knew it was little use. He tried to shift from under Drummond's body, but its weight held him pinned against the floor of the elevator. Vampiric blood still might have saved him, but there was none. Drummond clearly had not been a vampire as Kluge had believed. Kluge could feel his strength ebbing, and knew that in only a matter of minutes, he would be so weak that the Mossad agent waiting below would have no difficulty in capturing him.

He shifted slightly, pressing his lips against Drummond's throat. Faintly, distantly, he felt Drummond's pulse slowly fading. A smile curved at Kluge's lips. The Mossad wouldn't have him after all. He would give them Drummond instead.

Letting go of his wound, Kluge used his right hand to grab Drummond by the hair and force his mouth over the wound on his throat. He heard Drummond cough weakly as the vampire's blood welled into his mouth and he swallowed—a survival instinct—and he pressed Drummond's face harder to the wound, willing him to swallow more, smiling. . . .

Slowly, as Kluge's blood infused him, Drummond found himself being dragged back from the darkness he wished to embrace and pushed into the painful light of life. Instinctively his hand groped to his side, closing his wound, staunching the flow of his own blood.

The movement told Kluge that Drummond would survive. At the same time, he could feel himself slipping away, and he fought for yet a few more seconds of consciousness. Grabbing his sword for the last time, he stretched up and, with the tip of the blade, tried to push the down button on the control panel. His vision blurred, the effort was too much, and Kluge felt his sword sink to the floor. . . .

Moments later, when Baumann found them, he lifted Kluge from under Drummond's body with an effortless heave and laid him carefully on a hospital trolley. Then, returning to the elevator car, he pulled a syringe from his white lab coat and jabbed it into Drummond's neck, slowly injecting him with a massive dose of adrenaline. Straightening then, he leaned over Drummond and pushed the button that would send the elevator down to the executive parking level.

Gradually Drummond became aware that he was not dead. He could feel a hot tingling spread through his body, and his wounds began to throb and itch as they closed up and the bleeding stopped. Despite his light-headedness, he found himself being propelled back into consciousness, almost as if some other being was willing him to wake from his dreamless black sleep.

Just as the elevator reached the executive parking level, Drummond became fully aware of what Kluge had done. Wiping the back of one hand across his blood-smeared mouth, Drummond pushed himself unsteadily to his feet, propping himself up with de Beq's sword, just as the door opened.

"Ah, Captain Drummond." It was Berringer who spoke, a pistol held to the head of a very compliant Brian Still-man, the fingers of his other hand locked in the tangle of Stillman's thick shock of curls. "Things are a bit tense here, so if you could just make it to my car under your own power, I'd appreciate it."

Drummond blinked, trying to make his eyes focus better and also comprehend what was happening.

"Where's my car?" he asked.

"Your friend has removed it from the crime scene. Whoever rented that blue Saab," he nodded toward the vehicle Eberle had driven into the parking lot, "will probably get the blame for the mess."

In a flash, Drummond understood what Berringer and Eberle were doing—though why and how Berringer was involved, Drummond had no idea. But whatever the motivation, he realized that any hope of escape lay in following Berringer's instructions. Dragging his sword behind him, he trudged wearily to the silver Granada and climbed in the passenger side, clutching the sword to his chest. Behind him, Berringer returned his full attention to his prisoner.

"I'd really like to kill you," he said conversationally. "I really would. But that would leave one too many bodies, so I won't." He raised his pistol and brought it down quick and hard against the side of Stillman's head. Stillman gasped as bone crunched, and he sagged to his knees.

"Good-bye," Berringer said, disentangling his fingers from Stillman's hair and letting him slump onto his hands and knees. "The police should be here in about fifteen minutes. I'd suggest that you be out of here by then, or you may have to answer some rather awkward questions."

With that, Berringer trotted back to his car and got in, driving off into the night with Drummond sitting silent and still a little dazed next to him. Finally, after they had been driving for more than an hour, Drummond spoke.

"Where are we going?" he asked.

"Rome."

"Why?" Drummond asked, for it made no sense.

"Because you'll be safe there," Berringer said. "As safe as in heaven."

EPILOGUE

The orderly in the starched white lab coat stood by impassively as the team of doctors worked frantically to revive the patient on the table before them. Finally, with the last of the IVs in place in the patient's neck, one of the doctors applied two paddles to the patient's motionless chest and called, "Clear." As everyone stepped back, a jolt of electricity shot through the body, causing it to arch several inches off the table. On the oscilliscope, where moments before only a flat line had appeared, the line spiked, indicating the first faint beat of the heart.

The orderly adjusted his eye-patch and stepped forward to get a better view of the spiking line on the scope. Satisfied that the heart was beating, he pulled up his sleeve and drew a scalpel across his wrist. As the blood welled up, he placed his wrist to the mouth of the unconscious man on the table.

"Drink, *Hochmeister*," Baumann said. And as he spoke, the electronic pulse on the oscilliscope grew stronger.